M

IS FOR MALICE

IS FOR MALICE

SUE GRAFTON

a marian wood book

henry holt and company • new york

Henry Holt and Company, Inc.
Publishers since 1866
115 West 18th Street
New York, New York 10011

Henry Holt® is a registered
trademark of Henry Holt and Company, Inc.

ISBN 0-8050-3637-7

Henry Holt books are available for special promotions and
premiums. For details contact: Director, Special Markets.

Printed in the United States of America

For my good friends . . .
Barbara Brightman Jones and Joe Jones
and
Joanna Barnes and Jack Warner

The author wishes to acknowledge the invaluable assistance of the following people: Steven Humphrey; John Mackall, attorney-at-law, Seed, Mackall & Cole; Sam Eaton, attorney-at-law; B. J. Seebol, J.D.; William Tanner, Tanner Investigations; Dan Deveraux, plant manager, Granite Construction; Marcia and David Karpeles, The Karpeles Manuscript Library; Captain Ed Aasted, Detective Sergeant Don F. Knapp, Detective Jill Johnson, Detective Roger Aceves, Detective Lieutenant Nicholas Katzenstein, and Lieutenant Richard Glaus, Santa Barbara Police Department; Dana Motley; Melinda Johnson, Santa Barbara Newspress; and Lucy Thomas, Reeves Medical Library, Cottage Hospital.

1

Robert Dietz came back into my life on Wednesday, January 8. I remember the date because it was Elvis Presley's birthday and one of the local radio stations had announced it would spend the next twenty-four hours playing every song he'd ever sung. At six A.M. my clock radio blared on, playing "Heartbreak Hotel" at top volume. I smacked the Off button with the flat of my hand and rolled out of bed as usual. I pulled on my sweats in preparation for my morning run. I brushed my teeth, splashed water on my face, and trotted down the spiral stairs. I locked my front door behind me, moved out to the street where I did an obligatory stretch, leaning against the gatepost in front of my apartment. The day was destined to be a strange one, involving as it did a dreaded lunch date with Tasha Howard, one of my recently discovered first cousins. Running was the only way I could think of to quell my uneasiness. I headed for the bike path that parallels the beach.

Ah, January. The holidays had left me feeling restless and the advent of the new year generated one of those lengthy internal discussions about the meaning of life. I usually don't pay much attention to the passing of time, but this year, for some reason, I was taking a good hard look at myself. Who was I, really, in the scheme of things, and what did it all add up to? For the record, I'm Kinsey Millhone, female, single, thirty-five years old, sole proprietor of Kinsey Millhone Investigations in the southern California town of Santa Teresa. I was trained as a police officer and served a two-year stint with the Santa Teresa Police Department before life intervened, which is another tale altogether and one I don't intend to tell (yet). For the last ten years, I've made a living as a private investigator. Some days I see myself (nobly, I'll admit) battling against evil in the struggle for law and order. Other days, I concede that the dark forces are gaining ground.

Not all of this was conscious. Much of the rumination was simmering at a level I could scarcely discern. It's not as if I spent every day in a state of unremitting angst, wringing my hands and rending my clothes. I suppose what I was experiencing was a mild form of depression, triggered (perhaps) by nothing more complicated than the fact it was winter and the California sunlight was in short supply.

I started my career investigating arson and wrongful-death claims for California Fidelity Insurance. A year ago, my relationship with CFI came to an abrupt and ignominious halt and I'm currently sharing space with the law firm of Kingman and Ives, taking on just about anything to make ends meet. I'm licensed, bonded, and fully insured. I have twenty-five thousand dollars in a savings account, which affords me the luxury of turning down any client who doesn't suit. I haven't refused a case yet, but I was strongly considering it.

Tasha Howard, the aforementioned first cousin, had called to offer me work, though the details of the job hadn't yet been specified. Tasha is an attorney who handles wills and estates, working for a law firm with offices in both San Francisco and Lompoc, which is an hour north of Santa Teresa. I gathered she divided her time just about equally between the two. I'm normally interested in employment, but Tasha and I aren't exactly close and I suspected she was using the lure of business to insinuate herself into my life.

As it happened, her first call came on the day after New Year's, which allowed me to sidestep by claiming I was still on vacation. When she called again on January 7, she caught me off guard. I was at the office in the middle of a serious round of solitaire when the telephone rang.

"Hi, Kinsey. This is Tasha. I thought I'd try you again. Did I catch you at a bad time?"

"This is fine," I said. I crossed my eyes and pretended I was gagging myself with a finger pointed down my throat. Of course, she couldn't see that. I put a red eight on a black nine and turned up the last three cards. No play that I could see. "How are you?" I asked, perhaps a millisecond late.

"Doing well, thanks. How about you?"

"I'm good," I said. "Gee, your timing's uncanny. I was just picking up the phone. I've been making calls all morning and you were next on my list." I often use the word *gee* when I'm lying through my teeth.

"I'm glad to hear that," she said. "I thought you were avoiding me."

I laughed. Ha.Ha.Ha. "Not at all," said I. I was about to elaborate on the denial, but she plowed right on. Having run out of moves, I pushed the cards aside and began to tag my blotter with a little desktop graffiti. I block-printed the word *BARF* and gave each of the letters a three-dimensional cast.

She said, "What's your schedule like tomorrow? Can we get together for an hour? I have to be in Santa Teresa anyway and we could meet for lunch."

"I can probably do that," I said with caution. In this world, lies can only take you so far before the truth catches up. "What sort of work are we talking about?"

"I'd rather discuss it in person. Is twelve o'clock good for you?"

"That sounds fine," I said.

"Perfect. I'll make reservations. Emile's-at-the-Beach. I'll see you there," she said, and with a click she was gone.

I put the phone down, set the ballpoint pen aside, and laid my little head down on my desk. What an idiot I was. Tasha *must* have known I didn't want to see her, but I hadn't had the nerve to say so. She'd come to my rescue a couple of months before and though I'd repaid the money, I still felt I owed her. Maybe I'd listen to her politely before I turned her down. I did have another quick job in the works. I'd been hired to serve two deposition subpoenas in a civil case for an attorney on the second floor of our building.

I went out in the afternoon and spent thirty-five bucks (plus tip) on a legitimate salon haircut. I tend to take a pair of nail scissors to my own unruly mop about every six weeks, my technique being to snip off any tuft of hair that sticks out. I guess I must have been feeling insecure because it wouldn't ordinarily occur to me to pay real bucks for something I can do so handily myself. Of course, I've been told my hairstyle looks exactly like a puppy dog's backside, but what's wrong with that?

The morning of January 8 inevitably arrived and I pounded along the bike path as if pursued by wild dogs. Typically, I use my jog as a way to check in with myself, noting the day and the ongoing nature of life at the water's edge. That morning, I had been all business, nearly punitive in the energy I threw into the exercise. Having finished my run and my morning routine, I skipped the office altogether and hung around my place. I paid some bills, tidied up my desk, did a load of laundry, and chatted briefly with my landlord, Henry Pitts, while I ate three of his freshly baked sticky buns. Not that I was nervous.

As usual, when you're waiting for something unpleasant, the clock seems to leap forward in ten-minute increments. Next thing I knew I was standing at my bathroom mirror applying cut-rate cosmetics, for God's sake, while I emoted along with Elvis, who was singing "It's Now Or Never." The sing-along was taking me back to my high school days, not a terrific association, but amusing nonetheless. I hadn't known any more about makeup in those days than I do now.

I debated about a new outfit, but that's where I drew the line, pulling on my usual blue jeans, turtleneck, tweed blazer, and boots. I own one dress and I didn't want to waste it on an occasion like this. I glanced at the clock. It was 11:55. Emile's wasn't far, all of five minutes on foot. With luck, I'd be hit by a truck as I was crossing the street.

Almost all of the tables at Emile's were occupied by the time I arrived. In Santa Teresa, the beach restaurants do the bulk of their business during the summer tourist season when the motels and bed-and-breakfast establishments near the ocean are fully booked. After Labor Day, the crowds diminish until the town belongs to the residents again. But Emile's-at-the-Beach is a local favorite and doesn't seem to suffer the waxing and waning of the out-of-town trade.

Tasha must have driven down from Lompoc because a sassy red Trans Am bearing a vanity license plate that read TASHA H was parked at the curb. In the detective trade, this is what is known as a clue. Besides, flying down from Lompoc is more trouble than it's worth. I moved into the restaurant and scanned the tables. I had little appetite for the encounter, but I was trying to stay open to the possibilities. Of what, I couldn't say.

I spotted Tasha through one of the interior archways before she spotted me. She was seated in a small area off the main dining room. Emile had placed her by the front window at a table for two. She was staring out at the children's play equipment in the little beach park across the street. The wading pool was closed, emptied for the winter, a circle of blue-painted plaster that looked now like a landing pad for a UFO. Two preschool-age children were clambering backward up a nearby sliding board anchored in the sand. Their mother sat on the low concrete retaining wall with a cigarette in hand. Beyond her were the bare masts of boats slipped in the harbor. The day was sunny and cool, the blue sky scudding with clouds left behind by a storm that was passing to the south of us.

A waiter approached Tasha and they conferred briefly. She took a menu from him. I could see her indicate that she was waiting for someone else. He withdrew and she began to peruse the lunch choices. I'd never actually laid eyes on Tasha until now, but I'd met her sister Liza the summer before last. I'd been startled because Liza and I looked so much alike. Tasha was cut from the same genetic cloth, though she was three years older and more substantial in her presentation. She wore a gray wool suit with a white silk shell showing in the deep V of the jacket. Her dark hair was streaked with blond, pulled back with a sophisticated black chiffon bow sitting at the nape of her neck. The only jewelry she wore was a pair of oversized gold earrings that glinted when she moved. Since she did estate planning, she probably didn't have much occasion for impassioned courtroom speeches, but she'd look properly intimidating in a skirmish nonetheless. Already I'd decided to get my affairs in order.

She caught sight of me and I saw her expression quicken as she registered the similarities between us. Maybe all the Kinsey girl cousins shared the same features. I raised a hand in greeting and moved through the lunch crowd to her table. I took the seat across from hers, tucking my bag on the floor beneath my chair. "Hello, Tasha."

For a moment, we did a mutual assessment. In high school biology, I'd studied Mendel's purple and white flowering peas; the crossbreeding of colors and the resultant pattern of "offspring." This was the very principle at work. Up close, I could see that her eyes were dark where mine were hazel, and her nose looked like mine had before it was broken twice. Seeing her was like catching a glimpse of myself unexpectedly in a mirror, the image both strange and familiar. Me and not me.

Tasha broke the silence. "This is creepy. Liza told me we looked alike, but I had no idea."

"I guess there's no doubt we're related. What about the other cousins? Do they look like us?"

"Variations on a theme. When Pam and I were growing up, we were often mistaken for each other." Pam was the sister between Tasha and Liza.

"Did Pam have her baby?"

"Months ago. A girl. Big surprise," she said dryly. Her tone was ironic, but I didn't get the joke. She sensed the unspoken question and smiled fleetingly in reply. "All the Kinsey women have girl babies. I thought you knew."

I shook my head.

"Pam named her Cornelia as a way of sucking up to Grand. I'm afraid most of us are guilty of trying to score points with her from time to time."

Cornelia LaGrand was my grandmother Burton Kinsey's maiden name. "Grand" had been her nickname since babyhood. From what I'd been told, she ruled the family like a despot. She was generous with money, but only if you danced to her tune—the reason the family had so pointedly ignored me and my aunt Gin for twenty-nine years. My upbringing had been blue collar, strictly lower middle-class. Aunt Gin, who raised me from the age of five, had worked as a clerk/typist for California Fidelity Insurance, the company that eventually hired (and fired) me. She'd managed on a modest salary, and we'd never had much. We'd always lived in mobile homes—trailers, as they were known then—bastions of tiny space, which I still tend to prefer. At the same time, I recognized even then that other people thought trailers were tacky. Why, I can't say.

Aunt Gin had taught me never to suck up to anyone. What she'd neglected to tell me was there were relatives worth sucking up to.

Tasha, likely aware of the thicket her remarks were leading to, shifted over to the task at hand. "Let's get lunch out of the way and then I can fill you in on the situation."

We dealt with the niceties of ordering and eating lunch, chatting about only the most inconsequential subjects. Once our plates had been removed, she got down to business with an efficient change of tone. "We have some clients here in Santa Teresa caught up in a circumstance I thought might interest you. Do you know the Maleks? They own Malek Construction."

"I don't know them personally, but the name's familiar." I'd seen the company logo on job sites around town, a white octagon, like a stop sign, with the outline of a red cement mixer planted in the middle. All of the company trucks and job-site Porta Potti's were fire engine red and the effect was eye-catching.

Tasha went on. "It's a sand and gravel company. Mr. Malek just died and our firm is representing the estate." The waiter approached and filled our coffee cups. Tasha picked up a sugar pack, pressing in the edges of the paper rim on all sides before she tore the corner off. "Bader Malek bought a gravel pit in 1943. I'm not sure what he paid at the time, but it's worth a fortune today. Do you know much about gravel?"

"Not a thing," I said.

"I didn't either until this came up. A gravel pit doesn't tend to produce much income from year to year, but it turns out that over the last thirty years environmental regulations and land-use regulations make it very hard to start up a new gravel pit. In this part of California, there simply aren't that many. If you own the gravel pit for your region and construction is booming—which it is at the moment—it goes from being a dog in the forties to a real treasure in the 1980s, depending, of course, on how deep the gravel reserves are and the quality of those reserves. It turns out this one is on a perfect gravel zone, probably good for another hundred and fifty years. Since nobody else is now able to get approvals . . . well, you get the point I'm sure."

"Who'd have thunk?"

"Exactly," she said and then went on. "With gravel, you want to be close to communities where construction is going on because the prime cost is transportation. It's one of those backwater areas of wealth that you don't really know about even if it's yours. Anyway, Bader Malek was a dynamo and managed to maximize his profits by branching out in other directions, all building-related. Malek Construction is now the third-largest construction company in the state. And it's still family owned; one of the few, I might add."

"So what's the problem?"

"I'll get to that in a moment, but I need to back up a bit first. Bader and his wife, Rona, had four boys—like a series of stepping-stones, all of them two years apart. Donovan, Guy, Bennet, and Jack. Donovan's currently in his mid-forties and Jack's probably thirty-nine. Donovan's the best of the lot; typical first child, steady, responsible, the big achiever in the bunch. His wife, Christie, and I were college roommates, which is how I got involved in the first place. The second son, Guy, turned out to be the clunker among the boys. The other two are okay. Nothing to write home about, at least from what Christie's said."

"Do they work for the company?"

"No, but Donovan pays all of their bills nonetheless. Bennet fancies himself an 'entrepreneur,' which is to say he loses great whacks of money annually in bad business deals. He's currently venturing into the restaurant business. He and a couple of partners are opening a place down on Granita. Talk about a way to lose money. The man has to be nuts. Jack's busy playing golf. I gather he's got sufficient talent to hit the pro circuit, but probably not enough to earn a living at it.

"At any rate, back in the sixties, Guy was the one who smoked dope and raised hell. He thought his father was a materialistic, capitalistic son of a bitch and told him so every chance he could. I guess Guy got caught in some pretty bad scrapes—we're talking criminal behavior—and Bader finally cut him off. According to Donovan, his father gave Guy a lump sum, ten grand in cash, his portion of the then-modest family fortune. Bader told the kid to hit the road and not come back. Guy Malek disappeared and he hasn't been seen since. This was March 1968. He was twenty-six then, which would make him forty-three now. I guess no one really cared much when he left. It was probably a relief after what he'd put the family through. Rona had died two months before, in January that same year, and Bader went to his attorney with the intention of rewriting his will. You know how that goes: 'The reason I have made no provision for my son Guy in this will is not due to any lack of love or affection on my part, but simply because I have provided for him during my lifetime and feel that those provisions are more than adequate—blah, blah, blah.' The truth was, Guy had cost him plenty and he was sick of it.

"So. Fade out, fade in. In 1981, Bader's attorney died of a heart attack and all of his legal files were returned to him."

I interrupted. "Excuse me. Is that common practice? I'd assume all the files would be kept by the attorney's estate."

"Depends on the attorney. Maybe Bader insisted. I'm not really sure. I gather he was a force to be reckoned with. He was already ill by then with the cancer that finally claimed him. He'd also suffered a debilitating stroke brought on by all the chemo. Sick as he was, he probably didn't want to go through the hassle of finding a new attorney. Apparently, from his perspective, his affairs were in order and what he did with his money was nobody else's business."

I said, "Oh, boy." I didn't know what was coming, but it didn't sound good.

" 'Oh, boy' is right. When Bader died two weeks ago, Donovan went through his papers. The only will he found was the one Bader and Rona signed back in 1965."

"What happened to the later will?"

"Nobody knows. Maybe the attorney drew it up and Bader took it home for review. He might have changed his mind. Or maybe he signed the will as written and decided to destroy it later. The fact is, it's gone."

"So he died intestate?"

"No, no. We still have the earlier will—the one drawn up in 1965, before Guy was flung into the Outer Darkness. It's properly signed and fully executed, which means that, barring an objection, Guy Malek is a devisee, entitled to a quarter of his father's estate."

"Will Donovan object?"

"He's not the one I'm concerned about. The 1965 will gives him voting control of the family business so he winds up sitting in the catbird seat regardless. Bennet's the one making noises about filing an objection, but he really has no proof the later will exists. This could all be for naught in any case. If Guy Malek was hit by a truck or died of an overdose years ago, then there's no problem—as long as he doesn't have any kids of his own."

"Gets complicated," I said. "How much money are we talking about?"

"We're still working on that. The estate is currently assessed at about forty million bucks. The government's entitled to a big chunk, of course. The estate tax rate is fifty to fifty-five percent. Fortunately, thanks to Bader, the company has very little debt, so Donovan will have some ability to borrow. Also, the estate can defer payment of estate taxes under Internal Revenue Service code section 6166, since Malek Construction, as a closely held company, represents more than thirty-five percent of the adjusted gross estate. We'll probably look for appraisers who'll come up with a low value and then hope the IRS doesn't argue too hard for a higher value on audit. To answer your question, the boys will probably take home five million bucks apiece. Guy's a very lucky fellow."

"Only nobody knows where he is," I said.

Tasha pointed at me. "That's correct."

I thought about it briefly. "It must have come as a shock to the brothers to find out Guy stands to inherit an equal share of the estate."

Tasha shrugged. "I've only had occasion to chat with Donovan and he seems sanguine at this point. He'll be acting as administrator. On Friday, I'm submitting the will to the probate court. In essence, all that does is place the will on record. Donovan's asked me not to file the petition for another week or so in deference to Bennet, who's still convinced the later will will surface. In the meantime, it makes sense to see if we can determine Guy Malek's whereabouts. I thought we'd hire you to do the search, if you're interested."

"Sure," I said promptly. So much for playing hard to get. The truth is, I love missing-persons' cases, and the circumstances were intriguing. Often when I'm on the trail of a skip, I hold out the prospect of sudden riches from some recently deceased relative. Given the greediness of human nature, it often produces results. In this case, the reality of five million dollars should make my job easier. "What information do you have about Guy?" I asked.

"You'll have to talk to the Maleks. They'll fill you in." She scribbled something on the back of a business card, which she held out to me. "This is Donovan's number at work. I wrote the home address and home phone number on the back. Except for Guy, of course, the 'boys' are all still living together on the Malek estate."

I studied the back of the card, not recognizing the address. "Is this city or county? I never heard of this."

"It's in the city limits. In the foothills above town."

"I'll call them this afternoon."

2

I walked home along Cabana Boulevard. The skies had cleared and the air temperature hovered in the mid-fifties. This was technically the dead of winter and the brazen California sunshine was not as warm as it seemed. Sunbathers littered the sand like the flotsam left behind by the high tide. Their striped umbrellas spoke of summer, yet the new year was just a week old. The sun was brittle along the water's edge, fragmenting where the swells broke against the pilings under the wharf. The surf must have been dead cold, the salt water eye-stinging where children splashed through the waves and submerged themselves in the churning depths. I could hear their thin screams rising above the thunder of the surf, like thrill seekers on a roller-coaster, plunging into icy terror. On the beach, a wet dog barked at them and shook the water from his coat. Even from a distance I could see where his rough hair had separated into layers.

I turned left onto Bay Street. Against the backdrop of evergreens, the profusion of bright pink and orange geraniums clashed with the magenta bougainvillea that tumbled across the fences in my neighborhood. Idly, I wondered where to begin the search for Guy Malek. He'd been gone for eighteen years and the prospects of running him to ground didn't seem that rosy. A job of this kind requires ingenuity, patience, and systematic routine, but success sometimes hinges on pure luck and a touch of magic. Try billing a client on the basis of *that*.

As soon as I got home, I washed off my makeup, I changed into Reeboks, and traded my blazer for a red sweatshirt. Downstairs in the kitchenette, I turned on the radio and tuned the station to the Elvis marathon, which was moving right along. I lip-synched the lyrics to "Jailhouse Rock," doing a bump and grind around the living room. I pulled out a city map and spread it on my kitchen counter. I leaned on my elbows, backside still dancing while I located the street where the Maleks lived. Verdugo was a narrow lane tucked between two parallel roads descending from the mountains. This was not an area I knew well. I laid Donovan's business card on the counter beside the map, reached for the wall phone, and dialed the number printed on the front.

I was routed through the company receptionist to a secretary who told me Malek was out in the field but due back at the office momentarily. I gave my name and phone number, along with a brief explanation of my business with him. She said she'd have him return the call. I'd just hung up when I heard a knock at the door. I opened the porthole and found myself face-to-face with Robert Dietz.

I opened the front door. "Well, look who's here," I said. "It's only been two years, four months, and ten days."

"Has it really been that long?" he asked mildly. "I just drove up from Los Angeles. Mind if I come in?"

I stepped back and he moved past me. Elvis had launched into "Always On My Mind," which, frankly, I didn't need to hear just then. I reached over and turned off the radio. Dietz wore the same blue jeans, same cowboy boots, the same tweed sportscoat. I'd first seen him in this outfit, leaning against the wall in a hospital room where I was under observation after a hit man ran me off the road. He was two years older now, which probably put him at an even fifty, not a bad age for a man. His birthday was in November, a triple Scorpio for those who set any store by these things. We'd spent the last three months of our relationship in bed together when we weren't up at the firing range doing Mozambique pistol drills. Romance between private eyes is a strange and wondrous thing. He looked slightly heavier, but that was because he'd quit smoking—assuming he was still off cigarettes.

"You want some coffee?" I asked.

"I'd love some. How are you? You look good. I like the haircut."

"Forty bucks. What a waste. I should have done it myself." I put a pot of coffee together, using the homey activity to assess my emotional state. By and large, I didn't feel much. I was happy to see him in the same way I'd be happy to see any friend of long standing, but aside from mild curiosity, there was no great rush of sexual chemistry. I felt no strong joy at his arrival or rage that he'd shown up unannounced. He was a man of impulse: impatient, restless, abrupt, reticent. He looked tired and his hair seemed much grayer, nearly ashen along his ears. He perched on one of my kitchen stools and leaned his forearms on the counter.

I flipped on the coffeepot and put the bag of ground coffee back in the freezer. "How was Germany?"

Dietz was a private eye from Carson City, Nevada, who'd developed an expertise in personal security. He left to go to Germany to run antiterrorist training exercises for overseas military bases. He said, "Good while it lasted. Then the funding dried up. These days, Uncle Sam doesn't want to spend the bucks that way. I was bored with it anyway; middle-aged man crawling through the underbrush. I didn't have to get out there with 'em, but I couldn't resist."

"So what brings you back? Are you working a case?"

"I'm on my way up the coast to see the boys in Santa Cruz." Dietz had two sons with a common-law wife, a woman named Naomi who had steadfastly refused to marry him. His older son, Nick, was probably twenty by now. I wasn't sure how old the younger boy was.

"Ah. And how are they?"

"Terrific. They've got papers due this week so I said I'd hold off until Saturday and then drive up. If they can get a few days off, I thought we'd take a little trip somewhere."

"I notice you're limping. What's that about?"

He gave a pat to his left thigh. "Got a bum knee," he said. "Tore the meniscus during night maneuvers, stumbling on a pothole. That's the second time I've injured it and the docs say I need to have a knee replacement. I'm not interested in surgery, but I agreed to give the knee a rest. Besides, I'm in burnout. I need a change of scene."

"You were burned out before you left."

"Not burnout. I was bored. I guess neither one is cured by doing more of the same." Dietz's gray eyes were clear. He was a good-looking man in a very nonstandard way. "I thought I might stay on your couch for four days if you don't object. I'm supposed to stay off my feet and put ice on my knee."

"Oh, really. That's nice. You drop out of my life for two years and then you show up because you need a nurse? Forget that."

"I'm not asking you to make a fuss," he said. "I figure you're busy so you'll be off at work all day. I'll sit here and read or watch TV, minding my own business. I even brought my own ice bags to stick in the freezer. I don't want anyone hovering. You won't have to lift a finger."

"Don't you think this is a tiny bit *manipulative,* springing it on me like this?"

"It's not manipulative as long as you have the option of saying no."

"Oh, right. And feel guilty? I don't think so," I said.

"Why would you feel guilty? Turn me down if it doesn't suit. What's the matter with you? If we can't tell the truth then what's the point in a relationship? Do as you please. I can find a motel or I can drive on up the coast tonight. I thought it'd be nice to spend a little time together, but it's not compulsory."

I regarded him warily. "I'll think about it." There was no point in telling him—since I was barely willing to admit it to myself—how flat the light had seemed in the days after he left, how anxiety had stirred every time I came home to the empty apartment, how music had seemed to whisper secret messages to me. Dance or decline. It didn't seem to make any difference. I'd imagined his return a hundred times, but never this way. Now the flatness of it was inside and all of my past feelings for him had shifted from passionate involvement to mild interest, if that.

Dietz had been watching me and his squint showed he was perplexed. "Are you *mad* about something?"

"Not at all," I said.

"Yes, you are."

"No, I'm not."

"What are you so mad about?"

"Would you *stop* that? I'm not mad."

He studied me for a moment and then his expression cleared. He said, "Ohhh, I get it. You're mad because I left."

I could feel my cheeks brighten and I broke off eye contact. I lined up the salt and pepper shakers so their bases just touched. "I'm not mad because you *left.* I'm mad because you came back. I finally got used to being by myself and here you are again. So where does that put me?"

"You said you *liked* to be alone."

"That's right. What I don't like is being taken up and then abandoned. I'm not a pet you can put in a kennel and retrieve at your convenience."

His smile faded. " 'Abandoned'? You weren't *abandoned.* What's that supposed to mean?"

Just then the telephone rang, saving us from any further debate.

Donovan Malek's secretary said, "Miss Millhone? I have Mr. Malek on the line for you. Can you hold?"

I said, "Sure."

Dietz mouthed *Did not.*

I stuck my tongue out at him. I'm very mature that way.

Donovan Malek came on the line and introduced himself. "Good afternoon, Miss Millhone . . ."

"Call me Kinsey if you would."

"Thanks. It's Donovan Malek here. I just spoke to Tasha Howard and she said she talked to you at lunch. I take it she filled you in on the situation."

"For the most part," I said. "Is there some way we can get together? Tasha wants to get moving as soon as possible."

"My attitude exactly. Listen, I've got about an hour before I have to be somewhere else. I can give you some basic information—Guy's date of birth, his Social Security number, and a photograph if that would help," he said. "You want to pop on out here?"

"Sure, I can do that," I said. "What about your brothers? Is there some way I can talk to them, too?"

"Of course. Bennet said he'd be home around four this afternoon. I'll call Myrna—she's the housekeeper—and leave word you want to talk to him. I'm not sure about Jack. He's a little harder to catch, but we can work something out. What you don't get from me, you can pick up from them. You know where I am? On Dolores out in Colgate. You take the Peterson off-ramp and turn back across the freeway. Second street on the right."

"Sounds good. I'll see you shortly."

When I hung up the phone, Dietz was checking his watch. "You're off and running. I've got to touch base with an old friend so I'll be out for a while. Are you free later on?"

"Not until six or so. Depends on my appointment. I'm trying to track down a guy who's been gone eighteen years and I'm hoping to pick up some background from his family."

"I'll buy you dinner if you haven't eaten, or we can go out and have a drink. I really don't want to be a burden."

"We can talk about it later. In the meantime, you'll need a key."

"That'd be great. I can grab a shower before I take off and lock up when I leave."

I opened the kitchen junk drawer and found the extra house key on a ring of its own. I passed it across the counter.

"Are you okay with this? I know you don't like to feel crowded. I can find a little place on Cabana if you'd prefer peace and quiet."

"This is fine for now. If it's too much, I'll say so. Let's just play it by ear," I said. "I hope you like your coffee black. There's no milk and no sugar. Cups are up there."

He put the key in his pocket. "I know where the cups are. I'll see you later."

Malek Construction consisted of a series of linked trailers, arranged like dominoes, located in the cul-de-sac of an industrial park. Behind the offices, a vast asphalt yard was filled with red trucks: pickups, concrete mixers, skip loaders, and pavers, all bearing the white-and-red company logo. A two-story corrugated metal garage stretched across the backside of the property, apparently filled with maintenance and service equipment for the countless company vehicles. Gas pumps stood at the ready. To one side, against a tangle of shrubs, I could see six bright yellow Caterpillars and a couple of John Deere crawler dozers. Men in hard hats and red coveralls went about their business. The quiet was undercut by the rumble of approaching trucks, an occasional shrill whistle, and the steady *peep-peep-peep* signal as a vehicle backed up.

I parked in the side lot in a space marked VISITOR beside a line of Jeeps, Cherokee Rangers, and battered pickups. On the short walk to the entrance, I could hear the nearby freeway traffic and the high hum of a small plane heading for the airport to the west. The interior of the office suggested a sensible combination of good taste and practicality: glossy walnut paneling, steel blue wall-to-wall carpet, dark blue file cabinets, and a lot of matching dark red tweed furniture. Among the male employees, the standard attire seemed to be ties, dress shirts, and slacks without suit coats or sports jackets. Shoes looked suitable for hiking across sand and gravel. The dress code for the women seemed less codified. The atmosphere was one of genial productivity. Police stations have the same air about them; everyone committed to the work at hand.

In the reception area where I waited, all the magazines were work-related, copies of *Pit & Quarry, Rock Products, Concrete Journal,* and the *Asphalt Contractor.* A quick glance was sufficient to convince me that there were issues at stake here I never dreamed about. I read briefly about oval-hole void forms and multiproperty admixtures, powered telescopic concrete chutes, and portable concrete recycling systems. My, my, my. Sometimes I marveled at the depths of my ignorance.

"Kinsey? Donovan Malek," he said.

I looked up, setting the magazine aside as I rose to shake hands with him. "Is it Don or Donovan?"

"I prefer Donovan, if you don't mind. My wife shortens it to Don sometimes, but I make a rare exception for her. Thanks for being so prompt. Come on back to my office and we can chat." Malek was fair-haired and clean shaven, with a square, creased face and chocolate brown eyes behind tortoiseshell glasses. I judged him to be six feet tall, maybe two hundred twenty pounds. He wore chinos and his short-sleeved dress shirt was the color of café au lait. He had loosened his tie and opened his collar button in the manner of a man who disliked restrictions and was subject to chronic overheating. I followed him out a rear door and across a wooden deck that connected a grid of double-wide trailers. The air conditioner in his office was humming steadily when we walked in.

The trailer he occupied had been subdivided into three offices of equal size, extending shotgun style from the front of the structure to the back. Long fluorescent bulbs cast a cold light across the white Formica surfaces of desks and drafting tables. Wide counters were littered with technical manuals, project reports, specs, and blueprints. Sturdy metal bookshelves lined the walls in most places, crammed with binders. Donovan didn't seem to have a private secretary within range of him and I had to guess that one of several women up front fielded his calls and helped him out with paperwork.

He motioned me into a seat and then settled into the high-back leather chair behind his desk. He leaned sideways toward a bookshelf and removed a Santa Teresa high school annual, which he opened at a page marked by a paper clip. He held out the annual, passing it across the desk. "Guy, age sixteen. Who knows what he looks like these days." He leaned back and watched for my reaction.

The kid looking out of the photograph could have been one of my high school classmates, though he preceded me by some years. The two-by-two-inch black-and-white head shot showed light curly hair worn long. Braces on his teeth gleaming through partly opened lips. He had a bumpy complexion, unruly eyebrows, and long, fair side-burns. His shirt fabric was a wild floral pattern. I would have bet money on bell-bottom trousers and a wide leather belt, though neither were visible in the photograph. In my opinion, all high school annuals should be taken out and burned. No wonder we all suffered from insecurity and low self-esteem. What a bunch of weirdos we were. I said, "He looks about like I did at his age. What year did he gradu-ate?"

"He didn't. He got suspended six times and finally dropped out. As far as I know, he never even picked up his GED. He spent more time in Juvie than he did at home."

"Tasha mentioned criminal behavior. Can you tell me about that?"

"Sure, if I can think where to start. Remember the rumor that you could get high off aspirin and Coca-Cola? He went straight out and tried it. Kid was disappointed when it had no effect. He was in the eighth grade at that point. Discounting all the so-called 'harmless pranks' he pulled back then, I'd say his first serious transgressions dated back to high school when he was busted twice for possession of marijuana. He was into dope big time—grass, speed, uppers, downers. What did they call 'em back then? Reds and yellow jackets and something called soapers. LSD and hallucinogens came in about the same time. Teenagers didn't do heroin or cocaine in those days, and nobody'd ever heard of crack. I guess that's been a more recent development. For a while he sniffed glue, but said he didn't like the effect. Kid's a connoisseur of good highs," he said derisively. "To pay for the stuff, he'd rip off anything that wasn't nailed down. He stole cars. He stole heavy equipment from Dad's construction sites. You get the picture, I'm sure."

"This may sound like an odd question, but was he popular?"

"Actually, he was. You can't tell much from the photograph, but he was a good-looking kid. He was incorrigible, but he had a sort of goofy sweetness that people seemed to find appealing, especially the girls."

"Why? Because he was dangerous?"

"I really can't explain. He was this shy, tragic figure, like he couldn't help himself. He only had one buddy, fellow named Paul Trasatti."

"Is he still around somewhere?"

"Sure. He and Jack are golfing buddies. Bennet pals around with him, too. You can ask when you talk to him. I don't remember any other friends offhand."

"You didn't hang out with Guy yourself?"

"Not if I could help it," he said. "I was busy keeping as much distance between us as possible. It got so I had to lock the door to my room so he wouldn't walk off with everything. You name it, he'd boost it. Stereos and jewelry. Some stuff he did for profit and some was just plain raising hell. After he turned eighteen, he got kind of crafty because the stakes went up. Dad finally flat told him he'd hang him out to dry if he fucked up again. Excuse my bad language, but I still get hot when I think about this stuff."

"Is that when he took off?"

"That was when he shifted gears. On the surface, he cleaned up and got a job out here, working in the maintenance shed. He was clever, I must say. Good with his hands and he had a good head on his shoulders. He must have seen this place as the answer to his prayers. He forged checks on Dad's accounts. He used the company credit card to charge stuff and then sold the goods. Dad, God bless him, was still covering. I begged him to blow the whistle, but he just couldn't bring himself to do it. Guy strung him along, telling lie after lie.

"What can I tell you? Dad wanted to believe him. He'd talk tough. I mean, he'd act like he was really cracking down this time, but when it came right down to it, he always gave in and offered him 'one more chance.' Jesus, I got sick of his saying that. I did what I could to close the loopholes, but I could only do so much." Donovan tapped his temple. "Kid had a screw loose. He was really missing some essential sprocket in the morals department. Anyway, the last stunt he pulled— and this didn't come out until he'd been gone a couple months—was a scam where he cheated some 'poor old widder woman' of her nest egg. That was the last straw. Dad had already kicked his ass out, but we were still stuck with the mess."

"Where were you at that time? I take it you were working for your father."

"Oh, yeah. I'd graduated by then. I'd been in and out of Vietnam, and I was working here as a mining engineer. I got my degree at Colorado School of Mines. My dad's degree was civil engineering. He started Malek Construction back in 1940, the year I was born, and bought his first gravel pit in forty-three. We were a construction outfit first and ended up owning all our aggregate sources. In fact, we built the business around that because it gives us a competitive edge. There's a lot of companies around here that do construction that don't own their aggregate sources and they end up buying from us. I'm the only one of the kids who went into the family business. I didn't get married till I was thirty-five."

"I understand your mother died the year Guy left," I said.

"That's right. She'd been diagnosed with lung cancer maybe ten years before. Fought like an alley cat, but she finally went under. I'm sure the uproar didn't help. Dad never remarried. He didn't seem to have the heart for it. All he cared about was the company, which is why I was so surprised about the will. Even in 1965, I can't believe he wanted Guy getting so much as a nickel from his estate."

"Maybe someone will come across the second will."

"I'd like to think so, but so far I've turned the house upside down. There was nothing like it in the safe deposit box. I hate to consider what's going to happen if Guy shows up again."

"Meaning what?"

"He'll cause trouble of some kind. I can guarantee it."

I shrugged. "He might have changed. People sometimes straighten out."

Donovan gestured impatiently. "Sure, and sometimes you win the lottery, but the odds are against. That's how it is and I guess we'll have to live with it."

"You have any idea where he might be?"

"No. And I don't lie awake at night trying to figure it out either. Frankly, it makes me crazy to think of him coming home to roost. I understand that by law he's entitled to his fair share of the estate, but I think he ought to be a brick about it and keep his hands to himself." He picked up a piece of paper and slid it in my direction. "Date of birth and his Social Security number. His middle name is David. What else can I tell you?"

"What about your mother's maiden name?"

"Patton. Is that for ID purposes?"

"Right. If I find him, I'd like to have a way to confirm it's really Guy we're dealing with."

"You're picturing an impostor? That's hard to imagine," he said. "Who'd want to be a stand-in for a loser like him?"

I smiled. "It's not that far-fetched. The chances are remote, but it's been done before. You don't want to end up turning money over to a stranger."

"You got that right. I'm not all that thrilled to give the money to *him*. Unfortunately, it's not up to me. The law's the law," he said. "At any rate, I leave this to you. He was a hard-livin', hard-drinkin' kid before the age of twenty-one. As to his current whereabouts, your guess is as good as mine. You need anything else?"

"This should do for the time being. I'll talk to your brothers and then we'll see where we stand." I got to my feet and we shook hands across the desk. "I appreciate your time."

Donovan came around the desk, walking me to the door.

I said, "I'm sure Tasha will have the proper notices published in the local paper. Guy may get wind of it, if he hasn't already."

"How so?"

"He might still be in touch with someone living here."

"Well. That is possible, I suppose. I don't know how much more we're obliged to do. If he never turns up, I guess his share of the estate gets placed in an escrow account for some period of time. After that, who knows? The point is, Tasha insists we get it settled and you don't want to mess with *her.*"

"I should think not," I said. "Besides, closure is always nice."

"Depends on what kind you're discussing."

3

I stopped by the office and opened a file on the case, recording the data Donovan had given me. It didn't look like much, the merest scrap of information, but the date of birth and Social Security number would be invaluable as personal identifiers. If pressed, I could always check with Guy Malek's former high school classmates to see if anybody'd heard from him in the years since he left. Given his history of bad behavior, he didn't seem like a kid others would have known well or perhaps cared to have known at all, but he might have had confederates. I made a note of the name Donovan had given me. Paul Trasatti might provide a lead. It was possible Guy had turned respectable in the last decade and a half and might well have come back to his reunions from time to time. Often the biggest "losers" in high school are the most eager to flaunt their later successes.

If I had to make an educated guess about his original destination on the road to exile, I'd have to say San Francisco, which was only six hours north by car, or an hour by plane. Guy left Santa Teresa when the Haight-Ashbury was at its peak. Any flower child who wasn't already brain-dead from drugs had gravitated to the Haight in those days. It was the party to end all parties, and with ten grand in his pocket his invitation would have been engraved.

At three-thirty, I locked up my office and went down to the second floor to pick up instructions for service on the two deposition subpoenas. I retrieved my car and headed to the Maleks' place. The house was at the end of a narrow lane, the fifteen-acre property surrounded by an eight-foot wall intersected by an occasional wooden gate. I'd grown up in this town and I thought I knew every corner of it, but this was new to me, prime Santa Teresa real estate dating back to the thirties. The Maleks must lay claim to the last section of flat land for miles. The rear portions of the property must have tilted straight uphill because the face of the Santa Ynez Mountains loomed above me, looking close enough to touch. From the road, I could pick out individual patches of purple sage and coyote brush.

The iron gates at the entrance to the property stood open. I followed the long, curved driveway past a cracked and neglected tennis court into a cobblestone turnaround tucked into the L of the main residence. Both the house and the wall that encompassed the grounds were faced with dusky terra-cotta stucco, an odd shade of red halfway between brick and dusty rose. Massive evergreens towered above the grounds and a forest of live oaks stretched out to the right of the house as far as the eye could see. Sunlight scarcely penetrated the canopy of branches. Near the front of the house, the pine trees had dropped a blanket of needles that must have turned the soil to acid. There was little if any grass and the damp smell of bare earth was pervasive. Here and there, a shaggy palm tree asserted its spare presence. I could see several outbuildings to the right—a bungalow, a gardener's shed, a greenhouse—and on the left, a long line of garages. The driveway apparently continued on around the rear of the house. A Harley-Davidson was parked on a gravel pad to one side. There were flowerbeds, but even the occasional suggestion of color failed to soften the somber gloom of the mansion and the deep shade surrounding it.

The architectural style of the house was Mediterranean. All of the windows were flanked with shutters. A series of balustrades punctuated the stark lines of the facade and a lovers' stairway curved up along the left to a second-story veranda. All the trim was done in dark green, the paint color chalky with age. The roof was composed of old red tile, mottled with soft green algae. The poured concrete urns on either side of the front door were planted with perennials that had died back to sticks. The door itself looked like something that had been lifted from one of the early California missions. When I pressed the bell, I could hear a single resonating note strike within, tolling my presence to the occupants.

In due course, the door was opened by a white woman of indeterminant age in a gray cotton uniform. She was of medium height, thick through the middle, her shoulders and breasts slumping toward a waist that had expanded to accommodate the gradual accumulation of weight. I pegged her in her early forties, but I couldn't be sure.

"Yes?" Her eyebrows needed plucking and her blond hair showed dark roots mixed with gray. This was a woman who apparently whacked at her own hair with some kind of dull instrument, a not-unfamiliar concept. Her bangs had been cut slightly too short, curling across her forehead unbecomingly. Maybe forty dollars for a haircut wasn't too much to pay.

I handed her my business card. "Are you Myrna?"

"That's right."

"I'm Kinsey Millhone," I said. "I believe Donovan called to say I'd be stopping by this afternoon. Is Bennet at home?"

Her expression didn't change, but she seemed to know what I was talking about. She was plain, her nose maybe half a size too big for her face. Her lips were antiqued with the remnants of dark lipstick, probably eaten off at lunch or imprinted on the edge of her coffee cup. Now that I'd become an aficionada of drugstore cosmetics, I was acting like an expert. What a laugh, I thought.

"He just got in. He said to put you in the library if you arrived before he came down. Would you like to follow me?"

I said, "Sure." I loved the idea of being "put" in the library, like a potted plant.

I followed her across the foyer, toward a room on the right. I took in my surroundings surreptitiously, trying not to look like a mouth breather in the process. In the homes of the rich, it doesn't do to gape. The floor was dark parquet, a complicated herringbone pattern with the polished wooden chevrons blending together seamlessly. The entrance hall was two stories high, but little if any light filtered down from above. Tapestries were hung along the walls at intervals, faded depictions of women with high waists and faces shaped like hard-boiled eggs. Gents in cloaks rode on horseback, trailed by hunting dogs on chains. Behind them, a merry band of woodcutters toted a dead stag that had spears sticking out of its torso like Saint Sebastian. I could tell right away that theirs was a world devoid of animal-rights activists.

The library had the look of a private men's club, or what I imagine such a place would look like if women were allowed in. Several large red Oriental carpets had been laid side by side to form a continuous floor covering. One wall was paneled in dark walnut and there were floor-to-ceiling bookshelves on the other three. The windows were tall and narrow, diamonds of leaded glass admitting more chill air than afternoon light. There were three groupings of ripped red-leather club chairs and an enormous gray stone fireplace with a gas starter, its inner hearth blackened by countless fires. The room smelled of charred oak and book mold and suggested the kind of dampness associated with poorly laid foundations. For a family that had amassed a fortune in the construction business, they really ought to think about pumping money into the place. Failing major home improvements, a quick trip to Pier I would have done wonders.

For once, left to my own devices, I didn't bother to snoop. Guy Malek had been gone for eighteen years. I wasn't going to find a copy of his outbound bus schedule or a drawer filled with personal diaries he'd kept as a lad. I heard someone walking on the second floor, the ceiling creaking as the steps passed from one side to the other of the room above. I circled the library, glancing out of every window I passed. The room was a good thirty feet long. At the far end, a solarium looked out on the rear lawn, a large expanse of dormant grass with a murky-looking koi pond in the center. The surface of the water was choked with lily pads.

I moved back toward the door and heard someone come down the stairs and traverse the hall. The door opened and Bennet Malek came in. He was four years younger than Donovan with the same fair hair. Where Donovan's was glossy, Bennet's was coarse, and he kept it cut short to discourage a visible tendency to curl. He'd apparently given up his battle to stay clean shaven and a blond beard and mustache now defined the lower portion of his face. He was heavyset, looking beefy across the shoulders and thick through the chest. He wore jeans and a navy sweatshirt with the sleeves pushed up along forearms densely matted with hair. Tasha had tagged him as a man who invested and lost sums of money on various faulty commercial ventures. I wondered how I might have responded to him if I hadn't been told in advance of his poor business sense. As it was, I found myself disregarding the hearty confidence he was at pains to project. Belatedly, I noticed that he carried the last half inch of a drink in his right hand, gin or vodka over ice with a twist. He set the drink on the end table closest to him.

He held out his hand and shook mine with unnecessary strength. We weren't about to arm wrestle so what was the point? His fingertips were icy and faintly moist to the touch. "Bennet Malek, Miss Millhone. Nice to meet you. Don said you'd be coming. Can I offer you a drink?" He had a big booming voice and made solid eye contact. Very manly, I thought.

"Thanks, but I'm fine. I don't want to take any more time than I have to. I know you're busy."

"Fair enough. Why don't you have a seat?" he said. His attentiveness seemed feigned, a salesman's maneuver for putting the customer at ease. I'd been in this man's company thirty seconds or less and I'd already developed an aversion to him.

I perched on the edge of a club chair with a wide, sunken seat. The leather surface was slippery and I had to fight a tendency to skid backward into the depths. As a child, I used to polish the trailer park sliding board to lightning-fast speeds by vigorous rubbings with sheets of Cut-Rite waxed paper. The glossy leather cushion had the same slick feel to it. To avoid losing traction, I had to keep my weight pitched forward, feet together and flat on the floor.

Bennet settled into the chair to my left with a series of creakings. "I understand you're a private investigator," he said.

"That's right. I've been licensed for ten years. I was a police officer before that. What about you? What sort of work do you do?"

"I'm into venture capital. I look for promising little companies with cash-flow problems."

And drain them dry, no doubt. "Sounds like fun," I remarked.

"It's gratifying. Let's put it that way." His voice had dropped into a confidential tone. "I take it you met with Don?"

"That's right. I talked to him earlier this afternoon."

He shook his head almost imperceptibly. "Did he mention the missing will?"

"Tasha told me about that when she was briefing me at lunch," I said. Vaguely, I wondered why he was raising the subject. The existence of a second will was really not my concern. "I guess your brother lucked out," I said.

He snorted. "I'll tell you what bugs me. I remember when Dad signed the second will. I can picture the day just as clear as I'm sitting here. Dad's attorney and two witnesses came out to the house."

"Well, that's interesting. Do you remember who they were?"

"The witnesses? Two women. I remember that much. I assumed they worked for the attorney, but I may have made that up. They weren't personal friends of Dad's as far as I know. The four of them came in here and emerged maybe half an hour later."

"Have you told Tasha about this?"

"I mentioned I was here the day the second will was signed. I can't remember now if I mentioned witnesses or not."

"I'd tell her, if I were you. She may find a way to determine who they were. From what I've heard, no one disputes the fact that a second will was drawn up, but was it signed in your presence? Were you apprised of the provisions?"

"Well, I wasn't in the room with him if that's what you're getting at. Dad referred to it later, but he never spelled it out. The question is, what happened to it?"

I shrugged. "Your father could have changed his mind. He could have torn it up and tossed it out."

Bennet stirred restlessly. "So everyone says, though I'm not convinced. It's an interesting issue, if you think about it. I mean, look at the facts. The will comes up missing and the black sheep of the family makes out like a bandit. Dad signed it in March and Guy left within days."

"You're saying your brother stole it?"

"I'm saying, why not? I wouldn't put it past him. He stole everything else."

"But what good would that do? Even if he snitched a copy, the attorney probably kept the original. Once Guy was gone, he had no way of knowing your father wasn't going to turn around and make another will just like it. Or write a third will altogether. From what Donovan's told me, your father was good at talking tough and not so good when it came to follow-through."

He shook his head and his expression was patronizing. "True enough. That's why I'm going back through all of Dad's personal papers. It's not that we want to deny Guy any monies he may be entitled to, but this is bullshit in my opinion. He collected his share once. Dad had the second will drawn up with every intention of eliminating Guy's claim. That's why he gave him the cash to begin with—to pay him off in full. I heard him allude to it many times over the years. As far as he was concerned, the ten grand he gave my brother was the end of it."

"Well, I wish I could help, but this is really not my turf. Tasha's the expert. I suggest you sit down and talk to her."

"What about my father's deal with Guy?" he went on argumentatively. "It was a verbal agreement, but doesn't that count for anything?"

"Hey, you're asking the wrong person. I have no idea. No one knows where Guy is, let alone what kind of bargain he made the day he left."

His smile flickered and I could see him curb a desire to continue arguing the point. "You're right, of course," he said. "So what can I tell you about Guy?"

"Let's start with the obvious. Did he say anything to you about his plans before he left?"

"I'm afraid Guy wasn't in the habit of discussing anything with me."

I shifted the subject slightly. "Could he have headed up to San Francisco? Donovan says he was into drugs in those days and the Haight might have been a draw."

"It's always possible. If that's where he went, he never said a word to me. I should probably warn you, the two of us weren't close. I don't mean to seem uncooperative, but I don't have much to offer in the way of information."

"Did you ever hear him mention a possible career? Did he have any personal passions?"

Bennet's smile was thin. "He made a career out of doing as little as possible. His passion was getting into trouble, making life miserable for everyone else."

"What about his employment? What kind of jobs did he have?"

"None significant. When he was still in his teens, he worked in a pizza place until he got caught skimming cash. He also got a job doing telephone sales. That lasted two days. I don't remember his ever doing much else until he started working for Dad. He pumped gas for a while so I suppose he might have become a career gas station attendant."

"What kind of car did he drive?"

"He drove the family Chevy until he was involved in a hit-and-run accident and his license was suspended. After that, Dad refused to let him use any of the family vehicles."

"Do you know if his license was ever reinstated?"

"If it wasn't, he probably drove without. He never cared much about life's petty little rules and regulations."

"Did he have any hobbies?"

"Not unless you count smoking dope and getting laid."

"What about his personal interests? Did he hunt, or fish? Did he skydive?" I was floundering, casting about in an attempt to develop a sense of direction.

Bennet shook his head. "He was a vegetarian. He said nothing should ever have to die so that he could eat. He was petrified of heights so I doubt he ever jumped out of airplanes or climbed mountains or bungee-jumped."

"Well, at least we can eliminate that," I said. "Did he have medical problems?"

"Medical problems? Like what?"

"I don't know. I'm just trying to find ways to get a bead on him. Was he diabetic? Did he have allergies or any chronic illnesses?"

"Oh. I see what you're getting at. No. As far as I know, his health was good—for someone so heavily into drink and drugs."

"Donovan says he had one good friend. Somebody named Paul?"

"You're talking about Paul Trasatti. I can give you his telephone number. He hasn't gone anywhere."

"I'd appreciate that."

He recited the number off the top of his head and I made a quick note in the little spiral-bound notebook I carry.

I tried to think about the areas I hadn't covered yet. "Was he a draft dodger? Did he protest the war in Vietnam?"

"He didn't have to. The army wouldn't take him. He had bad feet. Lucky him. He never gave a shit about politics. He never even voted as far as I know."

"What about religion? Did he do Yoga? Meditate? Chant? Walk on hot coals?" This was like pulling teeth.

He shook his head again. "None of the above."

"What about bank accounts?"

"Nope. At least he didn't have any back then."

"Did he own any stocks or bonds?"

Bennet shook his head again. He was beginning to seem amused at my persistence, which I found irritating.

"He must have cared about something," I said.

"He was a fuckup, pure and simple. He never lifted a finger for anyone except himself. Typical narcissist. The girls couldn't get enough of him. You figure it out."

"Look, Bennet. I understand your hostility, but I can do without the editorializing. You must have cared about him once."

"Of course," he said blandly, averting his gaze. "But that was before he became such a pain in the ass to all of us. Besides, he's been gone for years. I suppose at some level I have some kind of family feeling, but it's hard to sustain given his long absence."

"Once he left, none of you ever heard from him?"

His eyes came back to mine. "I can only speak for myself. He never called me or wrote. If he was in touch with anyone else, I wasn't told about it. Maybe Paul knows something."

"What sort of work does he do?"

"He's a rare-book dealer. He buys and sells autographs, letters, manuscripts. Things like that." He closed his mouth and smiled faintly, volunteering nothing unless I asked point-blank.

I wasn't getting anywhere and it was probably time to move on. "What about Jack? Could Guy have confided in him?"

"You can ask him yourself. He's right out there," Bennet said. He gestured toward the windows and I followed his gaze. I caught a glimpse of Jack as he crossed the back lawn, heading away from the house toward a slope to the left. The rear of the property picked up just enough sun to foster a mix of coarse, patchy grasses, some of which were dormant at this time of year. He had a couple of golf clubs tucked carelessly under one arm and he carried a bucket and a net in a blue plastic frame.

By the time we caught up with him and Bennet had introduced us, Jack was using a sand wedge to smack golf balls at the net he'd set up twenty yards away. Bennet withdrew and left me to watch Jack practice his chipping shots. He'd swing and I could hear the thin whistle as the club cut through the air. There'd be a whack and the ball would arc toward the net, with an unerring accuracy. Occasionally, a shot would hit the grass nearby, landing with a short bounce, but most of the time he nailed the target he was aiming for.

He wore a visor with PEBBLE BEACH imprinted on the rim. His hair was light brown, a shock of it protruding from the Velcro-secured opening at the back. He wore chinos and a golf shirt with the emblem for St. Andrew's stitched on the front like a badge. He was leaner than his two brothers and his face and arms were tanned. I could see him measure the trajectory of the ball as it sailed through the air. He said, "I hope this doesn't seem rude, but I've got a tournament coming up."

I murmured politely, not wanting to break his concentration.

Whistle. Whack. "You've been hired to find Guy," he said when the ball landed. He frowned to himself and adjusted his stance. "How's it coming?"

I smiled briefly. "So far all I have are his date of birth and his Social Security number."

"Why did Donovan tell you to talk to me?"

"Why wouldn't I talk to you?"

He ignored me for the moment. I watched as he walked out to the net and leaned down, gathering the countless balls, which he tossed in his plastic bucket. He came back to the spot where I was standing and started all over again. His swing looked exactly the same—time after time, without variation. Swing, whack, in the net. He'd put the next ball down. Swing, whack, in the net. He shook his head at one shot, responding to my comment belatedly. "Donovan doesn't have much use for me. He's a Puritan at heart. It's all work, work, work with him. You have to be productive—get the job done. All that rah-rah-rah stuff. As far as he's concerned, golf isn't worthy of serious consideration unless it nets you an annual income of half a million bucks." He paused to look at me, leaning lightly on his golf club, as if it were a cane. "I don't have any idea where Guy went, if that's what you're here to ask. I was finishing my senior year at Wake Forest, so I heard about it by phone. Dad called and said he'd told Guy to hit the road. They'd had a quarrel about something and off he went."

"When was the last time you saw him?"

"When I was home for Mother's funeral in January. When I came home again for spring break, he'd been gone maybe three days. I figured the whole thing would blow over, but it never did. By the time I graduated and came home in June, the subject was never mentioned. It's not like we were forbidden to refer to him. We just didn't, I guess out of consideration for Dad."

"You never heard from Guy at all? Not a call or a postcard in all these years?"

Jack shook his head.

"Didn't that bother you?"

"Of course. I adored him. I saw him as a rebel, a true individual. I hated school and I was miserable. I did poorly in most classes. All I wanted was to play golf and I didn't see why I had to have a college education. I would have gone off with Guy in a heartbeat if he'd told me what was going on. What can I tell you? He never called. He never wrote. He never gave any indication he gave a shit about me. Such is life."

"And nobody outside the family ever reported running into him?"

"Like at a convention or something? You're really scraping the bottom of the barrel on that one."

"You think you'd have heard *something*."

"Why? I mean, what's the big deal? People probably pull this shit all the time. Go off, and nobody ever hears from them again. There's no law says you have to stay in touch with people just because you're related."

"Well, true," I said, thinking of my own avoidance of relatives. "Do you know of anyone else who might help? Did he have a girlfriend?"

Jack smiled mockingly. "Guy was the kind of fellow mothers warn their little girls about."

"Donovan told me women found him attractive, but I don't get it. What was the appeal?"

"They weren't women. They were girls. Melodrama is seductive when you're seventeen."

I thought about it briefly, but this seemed like another dead end.

"Well. If you have any ideas, could you get in touch?" I took a card from my handbag and passed it over to him.

Jack glanced at my name. "How's the last name pronounced?"

"*Mill*-hone," I said. "Accent on the first syllable. The last rhymes with bone."

He nodded. "Fair enough. You won't hear from me, of course, but at least you can say you tried." He smiled. "I'm sure Don was way too cool to mention this," he said mildly, "but we're all hoping you won't find him. That way we can file a petition asking the court to declare him dead and his share can be divided among the three of us."

"That's what 'diligent search' is all about, isn't it? Tell Donovan I'll call him in a day or two," I said.

I walked back across the grass toward the house. What a bunch, I thought. Behind me, I could hear the whistle of Jack's swing and the sound of the clubhead on impact. I could have knocked at the front door again and asked the housekeeper if Donovan's wife, Christie, was at home. As an old college chum of Tasha's, she might at least be gracious. On the other hand, she wasn't married to Donovan at the point when Guy departed, and I couldn't believe she'd have anything of substance to contribute. So where did that leave me?

I got in my car and started the engine, shifting into first. I eased down the long drive toward the street beyond. At the front gate, I paused, shifting into neutral and letting the car idle while I considered the possibilities. As nearly as I could tell, Guy Malek hadn't been a property owner in Santa Teresa County, so there wasn't any point in checking the tax rolls or real property records. From what his brothers had indicated, he'd never even rented his own apartment, which meant I couldn't consult with a past landlord, or query the water, gas, electric, or phone companies for a forwarding address. Most of those records aren't kept for eighteen years anyway. What else? At the time he'd left Santa Teresa, he had no job and no significant employment history, so there wasn't any point in checking with the local labor unions or with Social Security. He didn't vote, own a car or a gun, didn't hunt or fish, which probably meant he didn't have any permits or licenses on record. He'd probably acquired a driver's license and a vehicle by now. Also, using past behavior as a future indicator, he probably had a criminal history in the system somewhere, certainly with the National Crime Information Center. Unfortunately, I didn't have access to that information and, offhand, I couldn't think of anyone who'd be willing to run a computer check. A law enforcement officer with proper authorization has all sorts of databases available that I couldn't tap into as a licensed private eye.

I put the VW in first gear, hung a left, and drove over to the Department of Motor Vehicles. It was just shy of closing time and the place was clearing out. I filled out a form, asking for a records' search. Often, DMV records will be out of date. People move, but the change of address won't show up in the DMV computers until a driver's license or a vehicle registration is renewed. In this case, if Guy Malek had left the state, all the data might well be years out of date, if it showed up at all. At the moment, however, it seemed like the quickest way to get a preliminary fix on the situation. Since I didn't have his driver's license number, I picked up an ANI Multiple Record Request Form, filling in his full name and date of birth. The Automated Name Index file would either show no record for the criteria given, or would show a match for last name, first name, middle initial, and birthdate. As soon as I got back to the office, I'd put the form in the mail and ship it off to Sacramento. With luck, I could at least pick up his mailing address.

In the meantime, since the office was nearly empty, I asked one of the DMV clerks to check the name through her computer.

She turned and gave me her full attention. "Are you nuts? I could get fired for doing that," she said. She turned the monitor on its swivel so I couldn't peek at the screen.

"I'm a PI," I said.

"You could be the Pope for all I care. You'll have to wait to hear from Sacramento. You get nothing from me."

"It was worth a try," I said. I tried a winsome smile, but it didn't get me far.

"You got a nerve," she said. She turned away with a reproving shake of her head and began to pack away her desk.

So much for my powers of persuasion.

4

I returned to the office, typed up the envelope, wrote a check to the state, attached it to the form, affixed a stamp, and stuck the packet in the box for outgoing mail. Then I picked up the phone and called Darcy Pascoe, the secretary/receptionist at California Fidelity Insurance. We chatted briefly about the old days and I caught up on minor matters before making the same request to her that I'd made to the DMV clerk. Insurance companies are always running DMV checks. Darcy wasn't actually authorized to inquire, but she knew how to bend the rules with the best of them. I said, "All I need is a mailing address."

"What's your time frame?"

"I don't know. How about first thing tomorrow?"

"I can probably do that, but it'll cost you. What's this kid's name again?"

When I got home, lights were on in the apartment, but Dietz was still out someplace. He'd brought in a soft-sided suitcase that he'd placed beside the couch. A quick check in the closet showed a hanging garment bag. In the downstairs bathroom, his Dopp kit was sitting on the lid to the toilet tank. The room smelled of soap and there was a damp

towel hung across the shower rod. I went back to the kitchen and
turned on the radio. Elvis was singing the final chorus of "Can't Help
Falling In Love."

"Spare me," I said crossly and turned the thing off. I went up the
spiral stairs to the loft where I kicked off my Reeboks and stretched
out on the bed. I stared up at the skylight. It was well after five o'clock
and the dark had fallen on us like a wool blanket, a dense, leaden
gray. Through the Plexiglas dome, I couldn't even see the night sky
because of the overcast. I was tired and hungry and strangely out of
sorts. Being single can be confusing. On the one hand, you sometimes
yearn for the simple comfort of companionship; someone to discuss
your day with, someone with whom you can celebrate a raise or tax
refund, someone who'll commiserate when you're down with a cold.
On the other hand, once you get used to being alone (in other words,
having everything your way), you have to wonder why you'd ever take
on the aggravation of a relationship. Other human beings have all
these hotly held *opinions,* habits, and mannerisms, bad art and peculiar taste in music, not to mention mood disorders, food preferences,
passions, hobbies, allergies, emotional fixations, and attitudes that in
no way coincide with the correct ones, namely yours. Not that I was
thinking seriously of Robert Dietz in this way, but I'd noticed, walking
into the apartment, an unnerving awareness of the "otherness" of
him. It's not that he was intrusive, obnoxious, or untidy. He was just
there, and his presence acted on me like an irritant. I mean, where was
this going? Nowhere that I could tell. I'd no more than get used to
him than he'd hit the road again. So why bother to adjust when his
company wasn't permanent? Personally, I don't consider flexibility
that desirable a trait.

I heard a key turn in the lock and I realized, with a start, I'd drifted
off to sleep. I sat up, blinking fuzzily. Below me, Dietz was turning on
additional lights. I could hear the crackle of paper. I got up and
moved over to the railing, looking down at him. He turned on the
radio. I put my fingers in my ears so I wouldn't have to listen to Elvis
sing soulfully about love. Who needs that shit? Dietz was a big country
music fan and I was hoping he'd flip the station to find something
more twangy and a lot less to the point. He sensed my presence and
tilted his face in my direction. "Good. You're home. I didn't see your
car outside," he said. "I picked up some groceries. You want to help
me unload?"

"I'll be there in a minute." I made a quick detour to the bathroom,
where I ran a comb through my hair, brushed my teeth, and availed
myself of the facilities. I'd forgotten how domesticated Dietz could be.

When I thought about the man, it was his personal-security expertise that came foremost to mind. I padded down the stairs in my sock feet. "How'd you know what we needed?"

"I checked. Surprise, surprise. The cupboards were bare." He had the refrigerator open, placing eggs, bacon, butter, lunch meats, and various other high-fat, high-cholesterol items in the bins. On the counter was a six-pack of beer, two bottles of Chardonnay, extra-crunchy peanut butter, canned goods and assorted condiments, along with a loaf of bread. He'd even remembered paper napkins, paper towels, toilet paper, and liquid detergent. I put the canned goods in the cabinet and turned off the radio. If Dietz noticed, he said nothing.

Over his shoulder, he said, "How'd the interview go?"

I said, "Fine. I haven't made a lick of progress, but you have to start someplace."

"What's the next move?"

"I'm having Darcy run a DMV check through the insurance company I used to work for. She hopes to have something early tomorrow morning. Then we'll see what's what. I have other lines of pursuit, but she's my best bet so far."

"You're not working for California Fidelity these days?"

"Actually, I'm not. I got my ass fired because I wouldn't kiss someone else's. I rent an office in a law firm. It works out better that way."

I could see him toy with other questions, but he must have decided that the less said the better.

He changed the subject. "Can I talk you into eating out?"

"What'd you have in mind?"

"Something in walking distance where we don't have to dress."

I looked at him for a moment, feeling strangely unwilling to cooperate. "How's the old friend?"

Dietz surpressed a smile. "He's fine. Is that what's bothering you?"

"No. I don't know. I think I've been depressed for weeks and just now got in touch with it. I'm also nervous about the job. I'm working for my cousin Tasha, which I probably shouldn't be doing."

"A cousin? That's a new one. Where did she come from?"

"God, you *are* out of date."

"Grab a jacket and let's go. You can talk about it over dinner and bring me up to speed."

We walked from my apartment to a restaurant on the breakwater, three long blocks during which little was said. The night was very chilly and the lights strung out along the harbor were like leftover Christmas decorations. Over the softly tumbling surf, I could hear the tinkle of a buoy, the tinny sound mixing with the gentle lapping of water against the boats in the marina. Many vessels were alight and the occasional glimpses of the live-aboards reminded me of a trailer park, a community of small spaces, looking cozy from outside. Dietz's pace was rapid. He had his head bent, his hands in his pockets, heels clicking on the pavement. I kept up with him, my mind running back over what I knew of him.

His upbringing had been a strange one. He'd told me he was born in a van on the road outside Detroit. His mother was in labor and his father was too impatient to find an emergency room. His father was a brawler and a bully who worked the oil rigs, moving his family from one town to the next as the mood struck. Dietz's granny, his mother's mother, traveled with them in the vehicle of the moment—a truck, a van, or a station wagon, all secondhand and subject to breakdown or quick sale if the money ran low. Dietz had been educated out of an assortment of old textbooks while his mother and granny drank beers and threw the cans out the window onto the highway. His dislike of formal schooling was an attribute we shared. Because he'd had so little experience with institutions, he was fiercely insubordinate. He didn't so much go against regulations as ignore them, operating on the assumption that the rules simply didn't apply to him. I liked his rebelliousness. At the same time, I was wary. I was into caution and control. He was into anarchy.

We reached the restaurant, the Tramp Steamer, a cramped and overheated gray-frame establishment located up a narrow flight of wooden stairs. A modest effort had been made to give the place a nautical feel, but its real attraction was the fare: raw oysters, fried shrimp, peppery chowder, and homemade bread. There was a full bar near the entrance, but most of the clientele preferred beer. The air was saturated with the smell of hops and cigarette smoke. Between the honky-tonk jukebox, the raucous laughter, and conversations, the noise was palpable. Dietz scanned the room for seating, then pushed through a side door and found us a table on the deck, overlooking the marina. Outside, it was quieter and the chill air was offset by the red glow of wall-mounted propane heaters. The briny scent of the ocean seemed stronger up here than it had down below. I took a deep breath, sucking it into my lungs like ether. It had the same sedative effect and I could feel myself unwind.

"You want Chardonnay?" he asked.

"I'd love it."

I sat at the table while he moved back inside to the bar. I watched him through the window in conversation with the bartender. As he waited for the order, his gaze moved restlessly across the crowd. He

crossed to the jukebox and studied the selections. Dietz was the sort
of man who paced and tapped his fingers, subterranean energy constantly bubbling to the surface. I seldom saw him read a book because
he couldn't sit still that long. When he did read, he was out of commission, utterly absorbed until he was finished. He liked competition. He
liked guns. He liked machines. He liked tools. He liked climbing
rocks. His basic attitude was "What are you saving yourself for?" My
basic attitude was "Let's not jump right into things."

Dietz wandered back to the bar and stood there jiggling the change
in his pocket. The bartender set a mug of beer and a glass of wine on
the counter. Dietz peeled off some bills and returned to the deck,
trailing the smell of cigarette smoke like a strange aftershave. He said,
"Service is slow. I hope the food's good." We touched glasses before
we drank, though I wasn't sure what we were drinking to.

I opened a menu and let my eyes trace the choices. I wasn't really
that hungry. Maybe a salad or soup. I usually don't eat much at night.

"I called the boys," he remarked.

"And how are they?" I asked. I'd never met his two sons, but he
spoke of them with affection.

"They're fine. The boys are great," he said. "Nick turns twenty-one
on the fourteenth. He's a senior at Santa Cruz, but he just changed his
major so he'll probably be there another year. Graham's nineteen and
a sophomore. They're sharing an apartment with a bunch of guys this
year. They're smart kids. They like school and seem to be motivated.
More than I ever was. Naomi's done a good job, without a lot of help
from me. I support 'em, but I can't say I ever spent much time on the
scene. I feel bad about that, but you know how I am. I'm a rolling
stone. I can't help it. I could never settle down and buy a house and
work nine to five. I can't behave myself in a situation like that."

"Where's Naomi?"

"San Francisco. She got a law degree. I paid her tuition—I'm good
about that end—but all the hard work was hers. The boys say she's
getting married to some attorney up there."

"Good for her."

"How about you? What have you been up to?"

"Not a lot. Mostly work. I don't take vacations so I haven't been
anywhere that didn't somehow involve a stakeout or a background
check. I'm a bundle of laughs."

"You should learn how to play."

"I should learn how to do a lot of things."

The waitress approached, moving toward us from a table in the
angle of the deck. "You two ready to order?" She was probably in her

late twenties, a honey blond with her hair in a boy-cut and braces on her teeth. She wore matching black shorts and tank top as if it were August instead of January 8.

"Give us a minute," Dietz said.

We ended up splitting a big bowl of steamed mussels, nestled in a spicy tomato broth. For entrées, Dietz had a rare steak and I had a Caesar salad. We both ate as though we were racing against the clock. We used to make love the same way, like some contest to see who could get there first.

"Tell me about the depression," he said when he had pushed his plate aside.

I gestured dismissively. "Forget it. I don't like to sit around feeling sorry for myself."

"Go ahead. You're allowed."

"I know I'm allowed, but what's the point?" I said. "I can't even tell you what it's about. Maybe my serotonin levels are off."

"No doubt, but what's the rest of it?"

"The usual, I guess. I mean, some days I don't get it, what we're doing on the planet. I read the paper and it's hopeless. Poverty and disease, all the bullshit from politicians who'd tell you anything to get elected. Then you have the hole in the ozone and the destruction of the rain forests. What am I supposed to do with this stuff? I know it's not up to me to solve the world's problems, but I'd like to believe there's a hidden order somewhere."

"Good luck."

"Yeah, good luck. Anyway, I'm struggling for answers. Most of the time, I take life for granted. I do what I do and it seems to make sense. Once in a while I lose track of where I fit. I know it sounds lame, but it's the truth."

"What makes you think there are any answers?" he said. "You do the best you can."

"Whatever that consists of," I remarked.

"Therein lies the rub." He smiled. "What about the job? What scares you about that?"

"I always get amped on the eve of a big one. One of these days I'm going to fail and I don't like the thought. It's stage fright."

"Where'd the cousin come from? I thought you didn't have any family."

"Don't I wish," I said. "Turns out I have a bunch of cousins up in Lompoc, all girls. I'd prefer not to have anything to do with them, but they keep popping up. I'm too old to cope with 'togetherness.' "

"Such a liar," he said fondly, but he let it pass.

The waitress came by. We declined dessert and coffee. Dietz asked for the check, which she produced from a sheaf tucked in the small of her back, taking a few seconds to total it out. Her yellow socks and black high-tops really gave the outfit some class. She placed the bill facedown on the table slightly closer to Dietz's side than to mine. This was probably her tactic for playing it safe in case we were a twosome whose roles were reversed.

She said, "I can take that anytime you want." She moved off to deliver ketchup to another table. She must have the metabolism of a bird. The cold wasn't even producing goose bumps.

Dietz glanced at the check briefly, recalculating the total in the blink of an eye. He leaned sideways to extract his wallet and pulled out a pair of bills that he slid under his plate. "Ready?"

"Whenever you are."

We took the long way home. It seemed easier talking in the dark without looking at each other. The conversation was superficial. I'm an expert at using words to keep other people at bay. When we got home, I made sure Dietz had everything he needed—sheets, two pillows, an extra blanket, a small alarm clock, and a fresh towel—all of life's little amenities, except me.

I left him below and headed up the spiral stairs. When I got to the top, I leaned over the rail. "With your bum knee, I take it you won't be jogging with me in the morning."

"Afraid not. I'm sorry. It's something I miss."

"I'll try not to wake you. Thanks for dinner."

"You're welcome. Sleep well."

"Use your ice pack."

"Yes ma'am."

As it turned out, I slept a lot sooner than he did. Dietz was a night owl. I'm not sure how he occupied himself. Maybe he polished his boots or cleaned his handgun. He might have watched late-night television with the sound turned down. I sure never heard him. Once in a while, in turning over, I realized the light was still on in the living room. There was something so parental about his being on the premises. One thing about being single, you don't often feel protected. You tend to sleep with your mental shoes on, ready to leap up and arm yourself at the least little noise. With Dietz on guard duty, I got to cruise through a couple of rounds of REM, dreaming right up to the split second before the alarm went off. I opened my eyes, reached out, and caught it just before it blared.

I did my morning ablutions behind closed doors so the sound of running water wouldn't carry. Shoes in hand, I crept down the stairs in my stocking feet and tiptoed out the front door without waking him. I laced up, did a quick stretch, and set off at a fast walk to get warmed up. The night had shifted from pitch black to charcoal gray and by the time I reached Cabana, the darkness was beginning to lift. Dawn painted the early-morning sky in pale watercolor hues. The ocean was silver blue, the sky washing up from a smoky mauve to soft peach. The oil derricks dotted the horizon like clusters of iridescent sequins. I love the sound of the surf at that hour, the squawk of seagulls, the soft cooing of the pigeons already strutting along the path. A platinum blond and a black standard poodle were heading in my direction, a pair I saw most of the mornings I was out.

The run was good. Often three miles just feels like a pain in the ass, something I do because I know I must. For once, here I was feeling grateful to be physically fit. I wouldn't do well with an injury like Dietz's that prevented exercise. I'll never be any kind of champ, but for lifting a depression there's really nothing better. I did the turn at East Beach and started back, picking up my pace a bit. The sun was coming up behind me, sloshing rivulets of yellow light across the sky. Walking home again, winded and sweating, my mood was light and I was feeling good.

Dietz was in the shower when I got in. He'd brought in the paper and set it on the kitchen counter. He'd tidied the bedcovers and folded up the sofa bed, tucking the pillows out of sight somewhere. I put on a pot of coffee and then went upstairs, waiting until I heard him turn off his shower before I started mine. By 8:35, I was dressed, I'd finished breakfast, and I was gathering up my jacket and my car keys. Dietz was still sitting at the kitchen counter with his second cup of coffee and the morning paper spread out before him.

"See you later," I said.

"Have a good one," he replied.

On the way downtown, I stopped off at a nearby condominium with the two subpoenas in hand. I served both without incident, though the fellow and his girlfriend were hardly happy with me. Occasionally, I'll have someone who goes to absurd lengths to avoid service, but for the most part people seem resigned to their fates. If someone protests or turns ugly, my response is usually the same: "Sorry, pal, but I'm like a waitress. I don't cook up the trouble, I just serve it. Have a nice day," I say.

For a change, I parked in the public lot across from the courthouse and walked the two blocks to work. My current office is the former conference room for the law firm of Kingman and Ives, located in downtown Santa Teresa. From my apartment, the drive takes about ten minutes, given the usual traffic conditions. The Kingman building appears to be a three-story stucco structure, but the ground floor is an illusion. Behind a fieldstone facade, complete with barred and shuttered windows, there's actually a small parking lot, with twelve assigned spaces. Most of the office staff and the lesser tenants in the building are forced to scrounge parking elsewhere. The surrounding blocks aren't metered, but parking is restricted to ninety minutes max and most of us receive at least one ticket a month. Some mornings, it's comical watching us pass and repass, trying to beat one another to the available spaces.

I climbed the two flights of stairs, forgoing the pleasures of the elevator, which is small and takes forever, often giving the impression it's on the verge of getting stuck. Once in the office, I exchanged pleasantries with the receptionist, Alison, and Lonnie Kingman's secretary, Ida Ruth. I seldom see Lonnie, who's either in court or working doggedly behind closed doors. I let myself into my office, where I paused to make a note of the date, time, and a brief physical description of the couple to whom I'd served the subpoenas. I typed up a quick invoice, then picked up the telephone, leaning back in my swivel chair as I tossed the paperwork in my out box. California Fidelity didn't open until nine, but Darcy usually came in early.

"Hey, Darcy. It's me," I said when she answered on her end.

"Oh hi, Kinsey. Hang on a minute. I'm not at my desk." She put me on hold and I listened to leftover Christmas carols while I waited, feeling mildy optimistic. I figured if she hadn't found anything she'd have said so.

Half a minute passed and then she clicked back in. "Okay. Guy David Malek doesn't have a current driver's license in the state of California. His was surrendered in 1968 and apparently it's never been reissued."

"Well, shit," I said.

Darcy laughed. "Would you just *wait?* You're always jumping to conclusions. All I said was he doesn't drive. He has a California identification card, which is where I picked up the information. His mailing address is Route 1, Box 600, Marcella, California, 93456. That's probably the same as his residence. Sounds like a ranch or a farm. You want to see the picture?"

"You have a current *picture* of him? This is great. I don't believe it. You're a wizard."

"Hey, you're dealing with a pro," she said. "What's your fax number?"

I gave her Lonnie's fax number while I reached for the telephone book. "Are you sure he's in Marcella? That's less than a hundred miles away."

"According to DMV records. That should make your job easy."

"Ain't that the truth. What do I owe you?"

"Don't worry about it. I had to fake out some forms to make the request look legitimate, but nobody's going to check. Took less than a minute."

"You're a doll. Thanks so much. I'll be in touch and we'll have lunch. I'll pay."

Darcy laughed. "I'll take you up on that."

I put the phone down and paged through the telephone book, looking up the area code for Marcella, California. It was actually in the 805 area, the same as Santa Teresa. I tried directory assistance, giving the operator Guy Malek's name. There was no telephone listed at the address I'd been given. "You have any other listing for Guy Malek in the area? G. Malek? Any kind of Malek?"

"No ma'am."

"All right. Thanks."

I trotted down the hall to the fax machine just in time to see a copy of Guy Malek's photo ID slide out. The black-and-white reproduction had a splotchy quality, but it did establish Guy David Malek's SEX: M; HAIR: BLND; EYES: GRN; HT: 5-08; WT: 155; DOB: 03-02-42. He looked ever so much better than he had in his high school annual. Three cheers for him. I confess I felt smug as I sat down at my desk, the little show-off in my nature patting herself on the back.

I called Tasha's office and identified myself to her secretary when she picked up. She said, "Tasha's in a meeting, but let me tell her it's you. She can probably take a quick call if it's important."

"Trust me, it is."

"Can you hold?"

"Sure." While I waited, I laid out a hand of solitaire. One card up and six cards down. In some ways, I was sorry everything had come together so fast. I didn't want Donovan to think he was paying for something he could have done himself—though in truth, he was. There's a lot of information available as a matter of public record. Most people simply don't have the time or the interest in doing the grunt work. They're all too happy to have a PI do it for them, so in the end everybody benefits. Still, this one was almost too easy, especially since I wasn't sure the family would believe their real interests had been served by my discovery. I turned the next card up on the second pile and placed another five cards down.

Tasha clicked on, sounding terse and distracted. "Hi, Kinsey.

What's up? I hope this is important because I'm up to my ass in work."

"I have an address for Guy Malek. I thought I'd better let you know first thing."

There was half a second's silence while she processed the information. "That was fast. How'd you manage?"

I smiled at her tone, which was the perfect blend of surprise and respect. "I have my little ways," I said. Ah, how seductive the satisfaction when we think we've impressed others with our cleverness. It's one of the perversities of human nature that we're more interested in the admiration of our enemies than the approbation of our friends. "You have a pencil?"

"Of course. Where's he living?"

"Not far." I gave her the address. "There's no telephone listed. Either he doesn't have phone service or it's in someone else's name."

"Amazing," she said. "Let me pass this along to Donovan and see what he wants to do next. He'll be delighted, I'm sure."

"I doubt that. I got the impression they'd all be happier if Guy turned up dead."

"Nonsense. This is family. I'm sure things will work out. I'll have him give you a call."

Within fifteen minutes, my phone rang. Donovan Malek was on the line. "Nice work," he said. "I'm surprised how quick it was. I thought the search would take weeks."

"It's not always this easy. We got lucky," I said. "You need anything else?"

"Tasha and I just had a chat about that. I suggested we have you go up there in person. She could contact him by letter, but people sometimes react oddly getting mail from an attorney. You feel threatened before you even open the envelope. We don't want to set the wrong tone."

"Sure, I can talk to him," I said, feeling puzzled what the right tone would be.

"I'd like a firsthand report about Guy's current circumstances. Are you free sometime in the next two days?"

I checked my calendar. "I can go this afternoon if you like."

"The sooner the better. I want this handled with kid gloves. I have no idea if he's heard about Dad's death, but even with the estrangement, he could be upset. Besides, the money's a touchy issue. Who knows how he'll react."

"You want me to tell him about the will?"

"I don't see why not. He's bound to find out eventually."

5

I glanced at my watch. Since there was nothing on my schedule, I thought I might as well hit the road. It was just now nine-thirty. A round-trip to Marcella would take a little more than an hour each way. If I allowed myself an hour to track down Guy Malek, I'd still have plenty of time left to grab a quick lunch and be back midafternoon. I opened my bottom desk drawer and took out my map of California. According to the legend, Marcella was maybe eighty miles north, with a population of less than fifteen hundred souls. I didn't think it would take even an hour to locate him once I hit town, assuming he was still there. The conversation itself probably wouldn't take more than thirty minutes, which meant I might get this whole job wrapped up by the end of the day.

I put a call through to Dietz and let him know what was going on. I could hear the television in the background, one of those perpetual news broadcasts riddled with commercials. At the end of the hour, you know more about dog food than you do about world events. Dietz indicated he had no particular plans. I wasn't sure if he was angling for an invitation to accompany me, but since he didn't ask the question, I didn't answer it. I didn't want to feel responsible for his entertainment anyway. I told him I expected to be back by three and would bypass the office and come straight home. We could figure out what to do about dinner when I finally rolled in.

I gassed up my VW and headed north on 101. The sunshine was short-lived. Where the highway hugged the coastline, the fog had rolled in and the sky was now milky white with clouds turning thick at the edge. Along the road, the evergreens stood out against the horizon in a variety of dark shapes. Traffic moved steadily, mostly single-passenger cars with an occasional horse van, probably heading to the Santa Ynez valley just north of us. We hadn't had much rain and the hills looked like dull hay-colored mounds with an occasional oil rig genuflecting in a series of obsequious bows toward the earth.

The road turned inland and within the hour, the clouds had burned off again, fading back into a sky of pale blue, streaked with a residual haze as wispy as goose down. Just outside Santa Maria, I took 166 east and drove for ten miles on the two-lane road that paralleled the Cuyama River. The heat from the January sun was thin up here. Through the valleys and canyons, the earth smelled dry and a string of bald brown hills rose up in front of me. Rain had been promised, but the weather seemed to flirt, teasing us with high clouds and a hint of a breeze.

The town of Marcella was situated in the shadow of the Los Coches Mountain. Driving, I was aware of the unseen presence of the great San Andreas Fault, the 750-mile fracture that snakes up the California coastline from the Mexican border to the triple junction near Mendocino, the Pacific and North American plates grinding against each other since time began. Under the thin layers of granite and marine sediment, the crust of the earth was as cracked as a skull. In this area, the San Andreas Fault was intersected by the Santa Ynez Fault with the White Wolf and the Garlock not far away. It's speculated that the mountains in this part of the state once ran north-south like other mountains along the coast. According to theory, the southern tip of this chain was snagged by the Pacific plate many millions of years ago and dragged sideways as it passed, thus shifting the range to its current east-west orientation. I'd been driving my car once during a minor quake and it felt like the VW had suddenly been passed by a fast-moving eighteen-wheeler. There was a lurch to the right, as if the car had been sucked into a sudden vacuum. In California, where the weather seems to change so little, we look to earthquakes for the drama that tornadoes and hurricanes provide elsewhere.

At the junction of two roads, I caught sight of a discreet sign and turned southward into the town of Marcella. The streets were six lanes wide and sparsely traveled. An occasional palm or juniper had been planted near the curb. There were no buildings over two stories high and the structures I saw consisted of a general store with iron bars across the front windows, a hotel, three motels, a real estate office, and a large Victorian house surrounded by scaffolding. The only bar was located in a building that looked like it might have been a post office once, stripped now of any official function. A Budweiser sign was hanging in a window. What did the citizens of Marcella do for a living, and why settle here? There wasn't another town for miles and the businesses in this one seemed weighted toward drinking beer and going to bed soon afterward. If you wanted fast food or auto parts, if you needed a prescription filled, a movie, a fitness center, or a wedding gown, you'd have to drive into Santa Maria or farther north on 101 to Atascadero and Paso Robles. The land surrounding the town seemed barren. I hadn't seen anything that even halfway resembled a citrus orchard or a plowed field. Maybe the countryside was devoted to ranches or mines or stock-car races. Maybe people lived here to escape the hurly-burly of San Luis Obispo.

I found a gas station on a side street and stopped for directions. The youth who emerged was about seventeen. He was skinny, had pale eyes, hair shaved very close up to his ears, and a tangle of teeth, all reminiscent of someone in an early episode of *The Twilight Zone.* I said, "Hi. I'm looking for a friend of mine named Guy Malek. I think he lives on Route 1 somewhere, but he didn't give me directions." Well, okay. I was fudging, but I didn't outright *lie.* I *would* be Guy's friend when he heard the news about the five million bucks.

The youth said nothing, but he pointed a trembling finger like the Ghost of Christmas Past.

I glanced over my shoulder. "Back that way?"

"That's the house."

I turned to stare with astonishment. The property was enclosed by chain-link fencing. Beyond a rolling chicken wire gate, I could see a small house, a shed, a large barn with corrugated metal siding curling away from the seams, an old yellow school bus, a single gas pump, and a sign too faded to read at any distance. The gate was open. "Oh. Well, thanks. Do you know if he's home?"

"No."

"He's not?"

"No, I don't know. I didn't see him today."

"Ah. Well, I guess I'll go knock."

"You could do that," he said.

I pulled out of the station and drove across the road. I nosed the VW through the open gate and parked on a length of raw dirt that I took for a driveway. I got out. The surface of the yard was white sand with a rim of brown grass around the edge. The house was frame, painted once-upon-a-time white, one story with a wooden porch built across the front. A trellis that shielded the windows on the left sported only one bare vine, which twisted through the latticework like a boa constrictor. A matching trellis on the right had collapsed under its burden of dry, brown vegetation. Various wires extended from the roofline, connecting the occupants to telephone, cable, and electricity.

I climbed the wooden stairs and knocked on the dilapidated screen. The front door was shut and there were no signs of life. There was a fine dusting of soot everywhere, as if the structure were downwind of a smelting plant. The porch floor began to tremble in a way that suggested that someone was traversing the wooden floor inside of the house. The door was opened and I found myself face-to-face with the man I took to be Guy Malek. Aside from a three-day growth of beard, he didn't look anywhere near his age. His hair looked darker and straighter than it had in his high school yearbook, but his features were still boyish: khaki green eyes fringed with dark lashes; a small, straight nose; and a generous mouth. His complexion was clear and his color was good. Age had sketched in fine lines around his eyes and the flesh along his jaw was beginning to sag, but I'd have pegged him in his mid-thirties. At fifty and sixty, he'd no doubt look just the same, the years making only moderate adjustments to his good looks. He wore denim overalls on top of what looked like a union suit. He was in the process of putting on a blue jeans jacket when he answered the door, and he paused to straighten the collar in the back before he said, "Hey."

As an adolescent, Guy Malek had been as dorky looking as the rest of us. He was the bad kid, lawless and self-destructive, one of life's lost souls. He must have been appealing because he was so in need of rescue. Women can't resist a man who needs saving. Now his good angel had apparently taken up residence, bestowing on his countenance the look of serenity. It seemed odd that his brothers had matured so differently. Already, I liked this man better than his siblings. Aside from the scruffiness, he didn't look like he was snorting, sniffing, or mainlining illegal substances.

"Are you Guy Malek?"

His smile was hesitant, as though I might be someone he had met before whose name he wished he remembered. "Yes."

"My name is Kinsey Millhone. I'm a private investigator from Santa Teresa." I gave him a business card. He studied the card, but didn't offer to shake hands. His were as soiled as an auto mechanic's. I could see a muscle work in his jaw.

His eyes came up to mine and his entire body became still. The smile faded. "My family hired you?"

"Well, yes," I said. I was about to launch into a diplomatic account of his father's death when I saw tears rise in his eyes, blurring the clear green of his gaze. He looked upward, blinking, and took a deep breath before he brought his attention back to mine. He dashed at his cheeks, laughing with embarrassment.

He said, "Whoa," pinching at his eyes with the fingers of one hand. He shook his head, trying to compose himself. "Sorry. You caught me by surprise. I never thought it would matter, but I guess it does. I always wished they'd send someone, but I'd about given up hope. How'd you find me?"

"It wasn't that hard. I ran a DMV check and came up with your California identification card. I tried directory assistance, but they didn't have you listed. I take it you don't have a phone."

"Can't afford one," he said. "You want to come in?" His manner was awkward and he seemed unsure of himself. His gaze fell away from mine and then came back again.

"I'd like that," I said.

He stepped back to allow me entrance and I passed into a room that was about what you'd expect. The interior construction was crude and featured wide, unfinished floorboards and windows that didn't quite shut. Various pieces of old furniture had been moved into the space, probably cadged from the city dump . . . if there was one in this town. Every surface was piled high with soiled clothes and books and magazines and utensils, pots and pans and canned goods and tools. There were also what looked like farm implements whose functions were unclear. There was a tower of used tires in one corner of the room and a toilet that didn't seem connected to much of anything. Guy caught my puzzlement. "I'm holding that for a fellow. I have a real bathroom in there," he said, smiling shyly.

"Glad to hear that," I said and smiled back at him.

"You want a cup of coffee? It's instant, but it's not bad."

"No, thanks. Were you on your way out?"

"What? Oh, yeah, but don't worry about that. I have to be some-place shortly. Have a seat." He pulled out a handkerchief and paused to blow his nose. I could feel anxiety stir in my chest. There was something touching about his openness. He gestured toward a frayed, lumpy couch with a spring sticking through the cushion. I perched on the edge, hoping not to do serious damage to my private parts. My discomfort was related to the fact that Guy Malek apparently thought his family had hired me to conduct the search out of sentiment. I knew their real attitude, which was actually hostile if the truth be known. I did a quick debate with myself and decided I'd better level with him. Whatever the outcome of our conversation, it would be too humiliating for him if I let him harbor the wrong impression.

He pulled up a wooden chair and sat facing me directly, occasionally mopping at his eyes. He didn't apologize for the tears that continued to spill down his cheeks. "You don't know how hard I prayed for this," he said, mouth trembling. He looked down at his hands and began to fold the handkerchief in on itself. "The pastor of my church . . . he swore up and down it would come to pass if it was meant to be. No point in praying if it isn't God's will, he said. And I kept saying, 'Man, it seems like they'd have found me by now if they cared enough, you know?' "

I was struck by the fact that his circumstances were oddly reminiscent of mine, both of us trying to assimilate fractured family connections. At least he welcomed his, though he'd misunderstood the purpose of my visit. I felt like a dog having to set him straight. "Guy, as a matter of fact, it's more complicated. I have some bad news," I said.

"My father died?"

"Two weeks ago. I'm not sure of the date. I gather he'd had a stroke and he was also struggling with cancer. He'd been through a lot and I guess his body just gave up on him."

He was silent for a moment, staring off into space. "Well. I guess I'm not surprised," he said. "Did he . . . do you know if he was the one who asked for me?"

"I have no idea. I wasn't hired until yesterday. The probate attorney is getting the process underway. By law, you're required to be notified since you're one of the beneficiaries."

He turned to me, suddenly getting it. "Ah. You're here on official business and that's all it is, right?"

"More or less."

I watched as the color rose slowly in his cheeks. "Silly me," he said. "And here I thought you were sent by someone who actually gave a shit."

"I'm sorry."

"Not your fault," he said. "What else?"

"What else?"

"I'm wondering if you have any other news to impart."

"Not really." If he'd picked up on the fact that he was due to inherit money, he gave no indication.

"I don't suppose there's any chance my father asked for me."

"I wish I could help, but I wasn't given any details. It's possible, I'm sure, but you may never know. You can ask the attorney when you talk to her. She knows a lot more than I do about the circumstances of his death."

He smiled fleetingly. "Dad hired a woman? That doesn't sound like him."

"Donovan hired her. She went to school with his wife."

"What about Bennet and Jack? Are they married?" He said the names as if the sounds hadn't been uttered for years.

"No. Just Donovan. I don't think he and Christie have any kids as yet. He runs the company, which I understand is now the third-largest construction firm in the state."

"Good for him. Donnie was always obsessed with the business," he said. "Did you talk to the other two?"

"Briefly."

The character of his expression had completely changed as we spoke. What had started out as happiness had shifted to painful enlightenment. "Correct me if I'm wrong, but I get the impression they're not really interested in me. The attorney said they had to do this so they're doing it. Is that it? I mean, the three of them aren't burdened by a lot of warm, gooey feelings where I'm concerned."

"That's true, but it probably stems from the situation when you left. I was told you were in a lot of trouble, so their memories of you aren't that flattering."

"I suppose not. Nor mine of them if it comes right down to it."

"Besides, nobody really believed I'd find you. It's been what, eighteen years?"

"About that. Not long enough, apparently, from their perspective."

"Where'd you go when you left? Do you mind if I ask?"

"Why would I mind? It doesn't amount to much. I went out to the highway to hitch a ride. I was heading for San Francisco, zonked out of my head on acid. The fellow who picked me up was a preacher, who'd been hired by a church about a mile from here. He took me in. I was tripped out so bad I didn't even know where I was at."

"And you've been here all this time?"

"Not quite," he said. "It wasn't like I cleaned up and got straight, just like that. I screwed up more than once. I'd backslide . . . you know, get drunk and take off . . . but Pete and his wife always found me and brought me back. Finally, I realized I wasn't going to shake 'em off. Didn't matter what I did. They were sticking to me like glue.

That's when I took a stand and found Jesus in my heart. It really turned my life around."

"And you never got in touch with your family?" I said.

He shook his head, his smile bitter. "They haven't exactly been clamoring for me, either."

"Maybe that will change when I talk to them. What else can I tell them? Do you work?"

"Sure, I work. I do maintenance at the church and, you know, general handyman jobs around town. Painting and repairs, plumbing, electrical. About anything you need. Mostly minimum wage, but I'm the only one does it, so I stay busy."

"Sounds like you've done all right for yourself."

He looked around him. "Well, I don't have much, but I don't need much either. Place isn't mine," he said. "The church provides my housing, but I make enough to take care of the basics. Food and utilities, that sort of thing. I don't drive, but I have a bike and that gets me most places in a town this size."

"You've changed quite a lot."

"I'd be dead otherwise." He glanced at his watch. "Listen, I don't mean to rush you, but I probably ought to get myself on over to the church."

"I won't keep you then. I appreciate your time. Can I give you a lift?"

"Sure. We can talk on the way."

Once in the car, he directed me back to the highway. We turned right onto 166, heading east again. We drove for a while in companionable silence. He slid a look in my direction. "So what's your assignment? Find me and report back?"

"That's about it," I said. "Now that we have a current address, Tasha Howard, the attorney, will be sending you notice of the probate."

"Oh, that's right. I forgot. I'm a beneficiary, you said." His tone had turned light and nearly mocking.

"That doesn't interest you?"

"Not particularly. I thought I needed something from those people, but as it turns out, I don't." He pointed at an upcoming junction and I took a right-hand turn onto a small side road. The roadbed had been downgraded from blacktop to loose gravel, and I could see the plumes of white dust swirling up in my rear window as we drove. The church was situated at the edge of a pasture about a half mile down. The sign said: JUBILEE EVANGELICAL CHURCH.

"You can pull up right here," he said. "You want to come in and see the place? If you're paid by the hour, you might as well have the full tour. I'm sure Donnie can afford it."

I hesitated slightly. "All right."

He cocked his head. "You don't have to worry. I won't try to convert you."

I parked and the two of us got out. He didn't issue a proclamation, but I could tell from his manner that he was proud of the place. He took out a ring of keys and let us in.

The church was small, a frame building, little more than one room. There was something about its plain appearance that spoke of goodness. The stained glass windows were not elaborate. Each was divided into six simple panels of pale gold with a scripture written across the bottom. There was an unadorned wood pulpit at the front, positioned to the left of a raised and carpeted platform. On the right, there was an organ and three rows of folding chairs for the choir. Last Sunday's flowers consisted of a spray of white gladiola. "Place was destroyed by fire about ten years back. Congregation rebuilt everything from the ground right on up."

I said, "How'd you get on track? That must have been hard."

He sat down in one of the front pews and I could see him look around, perhaps seeing the place as I saw it. "I give credit to the Lord, though Pete always says I did the work myself," he said. "I grew up without much guidance, without values of any kind. I'm not blaming anybody. That's just how it was. My parents were good people. They didn't drink or beat me or anything like that, but they never talked about God or faith or their religious beliefs, assuming they had any, which I don't guess they did. My brothers and I . . . even when we were little kids . . . never went to Sunday school or church.

"My parents disliked 'organized religion.' I don't know what that phrase meant to them or what their perception was, but they took pride in making sure none of us were ever exposed to it. Like a disease of some kind. I remember they had a book by this guy named Philip Wylie. *Generation of Vipers.* He equated the church teachings with intellectual corruption, the stunting of young minds."

"Some people feel that way," I said.

"Yeah, I know. I don't get it, but it's something I run into out there in the world. It's like people think just because you go to church you're not all that bright. I mean, just because I'm born-again doesn't mean I lost IQ points."

"I'm sure you didn't."

"Thing is, I was raised without a moral compass. I couldn't get a sense of what the rules were so I just kept pushing. I kept crossing the line, waiting for somebody to tell me where the boundaries were."

"But you were getting into trouble with the law from what I heard. You must have known the rules because every time you broke one, you ended up in court. Donovan says you spent more time in Juvenile Hall than you did at home."

His smile was sheepish. "That's true, but here's what's weird. I didn't mind Juvie all that much. At least I could be with kids as screwed up as I was. Man, I was out of control. I ran wild. I was a maniac, freaked out about everything. It's hard to think about that now. I have trouble relating to myself and who I was back then. I know what happened. I mean, I know what I did, but I can't imagine doing it. I wanted to feel good. I've thought about this a lot and that's the best explanation I've been able to come up with. I felt bad and I wanted to feel better. Seemed to me dope was the quickest way to get there. I haven't touched drugs or hard liquor for more than fifteen years. I might have a beer now and then, but I don't smoke, don't play cards, don't ballroom dance. Don't take the Lord's name in vain and don't cuss . . . all that much. Stub my toe and I can turn the air blue, but most of the time, I avoid swear words."

"Well, that's good."

"For me, it is. Back then, I was always teetering on the brink. I think I was hoping my parents would finally draw the line and mean it. That they'd say, 'Here, this is it. You've finally gone and done it this time.' But you know what? My dad was too soft. He waffled on everything. Even when he kicked my ass from here to next Tuesday, even when he threw me out of the house, he was saying, 'Give this some thought, son. You can come back when you've figured it out.' But like what? Figured what out? I didn't have a clue. I was rudderless. I was like a boat going full throttle but without any real direction, roaring around in big circles. Know what I mean?"

"Sure I do. In high school, I was a screwup myself. I ended up as a cop before I did this."

He smiled. "No kidding? You drank and smoked dope?"

"Among other things," I said, modestly.

"Come on. Like what?"

"I don't know. Kids in my class were all clean-cut, but not me. I was a wild thing. I ditched school. I hung out with some low-life dudes and I liked that. I liked *them,*" I said. "I was the odd one out and so were they, I guess."

"Where'd you go to high school?"

"Santa Teresa High."

He laughed. "You were a low-waller?"

"Absolutely," I said. Low-wallers were the kids who quite literally perched on a low wall that ran along the back of the school property. Much smoking of cigarettes, funky clothes, and peroxided hair.

Guy laughed. "Well, that's great."

"I don't know how great it was, but it's what I did."

"How'd *you* get on track?"

"Who says I am?"

He got to his feet as if he'd come to a decision. "Come on out to the parsonage and meet Peter and Winnie," he said. "They'll be in the kitchen at this hour setting up supper for the Thursday night Bible study."

I followed him up the center aisle and through a door at the rear. I could feel the first stirrings of resistance. I didn't want anyone pushing me to convert. Too much virtue is just as worrisome as wickedness in my book.

6

The parsonage was situated on the property adjacent to the church and consisted of a rambling white frame farmhouse, two stories tall, with green shutters and a shabby green shingled roof broken up with dormers. Across one end was a wide screened-in porch distinctly tilted, as though an earthquake had pulled the concrete foundation loose. Behind the house, I could see a big red barn with a dilapidated one-car garage attached. Both the house and the barn were in need of a fresh coat of paint, and I noticed sunlight slanting through the barn roof where it was pierced with holes. Metal lawn chairs were arranged in a semicircle in the yard under a massive live oak tree. A weathered picnic table flanked with benches was set up close by where I pictured Sunday school classes and church suppers during the summer months.

I followed Guy across the yard. We went up the back steps and into the kitchen. The air was scented with sautéed onions and celery. Peter was a man in his sixties, balding, with a wreath of white hair that grew down into sideburns and wrapped around his jaw in a closely trimmed beard linked to a matching mustache. Pale sunlight coming through the window illuminated a feathery white fuzz across his pate. He wore a red turtleneck with a ribbed green sweater over it. He was just in the process of rolling out biscuit dough. The baking sheets to his right were lined with rows of perfect disks of dough ready for the oven. He looked up with pleasure as the two of us came in. "Oh, Guy. Good, it's you. I was just wondering if you were here yet. The furnace over at the church has been acting up again. First it clicks on, then it clicks off. On then off."

"Probably the electronic ignition. I'll take a look." Guy's posture was self-conscious. He rubbed his nose and then stuck his hands in his overall pockets as if to warm them. "This is Kinsey Millhone. She's a private detective from Santa Teresa." He turned and looked at me, tilting his head at the minister and his wife as he made the introductions. "This is Peter Antle and his wife, Winnie."

Peter's complexion was ruddy. His blue eyes smiled out at me from under ragged white brows. "Nice to meet you. I'd offer to shake hands, but I don't think you'd like it. How are you at homemade biscuits? Can I put you to work?"

"Better not," I said. "My domestic skills leave something to be desired."

He was on the verge of pursuing the point when his wife said, "Now, Pete . . ." and gave him a look. Winnie Antle appeared to be in her late forties with short brown hair combed away from her face. She was brown-eyed, slightly heavy, with a wide smile and very white teeth. She wore a man's shirt over jeans with a long knit vest that covered her wide hips and ample derriere. She was chopping vegetables for soup, a mountain of carrot coins piled up on the counter next to her. I could see two bunches of celery and assorted bell peppers awaiting her flashing knife. She was simultaneously tending a stockpot filled with vegetable cuttings boiling merrily. "Hello, Kinsey. Don't mind him. He's always trying to pass the work off onto the unsuspecting," she said, sending me a quick smile. "What brings you up this way?"

Peter looked at Guy. "You're not in trouble, I hope. You have to watch this man." His smile was teasing and it was clear he had no real expectation of trouble where Guy was concerned.

Guy murmured the explanation, apparently embarrassed to be the recipient of such bad news. "My father died. Probate attorney asked her to track me down."

Peter and Winnie both turned their full attention on Guy, whose earlier emotions were well under control. Peter said, "Is that the truth. Well, I'm sorry to hear that." He glanced over at me. "We've often talked about his trying for a reconciliation. It's been years since he had any contact with his dad."

Guy shifted his weight, leaning against the counter with his arms crossed in front of him. He seemed to be directing his comments at me, his tone wistful. "I don't know how many letters I wrote, but none of them got sent. Every time I tried to explain, it just came out sounding . . . you know, wrong, or dumb. I finally let it be till I could work out what it was I wanted to say. I kept thinking I had time. Mean, he wasn't old, by any stretch."

"It must have been his time. You can't argue with that," Peter said.

Winnie spoke up. "If you don't feel like work today, you go ahead and take off. We can manage just fine."

"I'm all right," Guy responded, again with discomfort at being the center of attention.

We spent a few minutes going through an exchange of information; how I'd managed to locate Guy and what I knew of his family, which wasn't much.

Peter was shaking his head, clearly regretful at the news I was bringing. "We think of Guy as one of our own. First time I ever saw this boy, he's a sorry sight. His eyeballs were bright red, sort of rolling around in his head like hot marbles. Winnie and me, we'd been called to this church and we'd driven all the way out to California from Fort Scott, Kansas. We'd heard all sorts of things about hippies and potheads and acid freaks, I think they called 'em. Kids with their eyes burned out from staring at the sun completely stoned. And there stood Guy by the side of the road with a sign that said 'San Francisco.' He was trying to be 'cool,' but he just looked pitiful to me. Winnie didn't want me to stop. We had the two kids in the backseat and she thought sure we'd be turned into homicide statistics."

"It's been a lot of years since then," Winnie said.

Pete looked over at Guy. "What are you thinking to do now, Guy, go back to Santa Teresa? This might be time to sit down with your brothers and talk about the past, maybe clean up some old business."

"I don't know. I suppose. If they're willing to sit down with me," Guy said. "I guess I'm not quite ready to make a decision about that." He glanced at me. "I know they didn't send you up here begging me to come back, but it seems like I might have *some* say in the matter. Would it be all right if I called you in a day or two?"

"No problem. In the meantime, I need to head home," I said. "You've got my card. If I'm not in the office, try that second number and the call will be forwarded automatically." I took out a second business card and jotted down Tasha Howard's name. "This is the attorney. I don't remember her phone number offhand. She has an office in Lompoc. You can call directory assistance and get the information from them. She's not that far away. If nothing else, you might make an appointment to have a chat with her. You'll need advice from an attorney of your own. I hope everything works out."

"I do, too. I appreciate the fact you made the trip," Guy said. "It's a lot more personal."

I shook hands with him, uttered polite noises in the direction of Peter and Winnie Antle, and made my getaway. I cruised down the main street of Marcella again, trying to get a feel for the place. Small and quiet. Unpretentious. I circled the block, driving along the few residential streets. The houses were small, built from identical plans, one-story stucco structures with flat rooflines. The exteriors were painted in pastel shades, pale Easter egg colors nestled in winter grass as dry as paper shreds. Most of the houses seemed shabby and dispirited. I saw only an occasional occupant.

As I swung past the general store, heading out to the main road, I spotted a sign in the window advertising fresh sandwiches. On an impulse, I parked the car and went in and ordered a tuna salad on rye from the woman at the deli counter in the rear. We chatted idly while she busied herself with the sandwich preparations, wrapping my dill pickle in a square of waxed paper so it wouldn't make the bread all mushy, she said. Behind me, two or three other customers went about their business, guiding small grocery carts up and down the aisles. No one turned to stare at me or paid me the slightest attention.

I let her know I'd just been over at the church. She exhibited little curiosity about who I was or why I was visiting the pastor and his wife. Mention of Guy Malek produced no uneasy silences nor any unsolicited confidences about his past history or his character.

"This seems like a nice town," I said as she passed my lunch across the counter. I handed her a ten, which she rang into the cash register.

"If you like this kind of place," she remarked. "Too quiet for my taste, but my husband was born here and insisted we come back. I like to kick up my heels, but about the best we can manage is a rummage sale now and then. Whooee." She fanned herself comically as if the excitement of used clothing was almost more than she could bear. "You want a receipt?" she said, counting out seven ones and change.

"I'd appreciate it."

She tore off the register receipt and handed it to me. "You take care of yourself."

"Thanks. You, too," I said.

I ate while I drove, steering with one hand as I alternated bites of dill pickle and tuna sandwich. The price had included a bag of potato chips, and I munched on those, too, figuring I'd cover all the necessary food groups. I'd forgotten to ask Guy his mother's maiden name, but the truth was, I had no doubt he was who he said he was. He reminded me of Jack, whose coloring and features were quite similar. Donovan and Bennet must have favored one parent while Guy and Jack looked more like the other. As cynical as I was, I found myself taking at face value both the reformation of Guy Malek and his current association with Jubilee Evangelical. It was always possible, I supposed, that he and the minister were singularly crafty frauds, who'd cooked up a cover story for any stranger who came calling, but for the life of me I didn't see it and I didn't believe anything sinister was afoot. If bucolic Marcella was the headquarters for some cult of neo-Nazis, Satanists, or motorcycle outlaws, it had sure escaped my notice.

It was not until I had passed Santa Maria, heading south on 101, that I realized Guy Malek had never asked how much his share of the estate would be. I probably should have volunteered the information. I could have at least given him a ballpark figure, but the question had never come up and I'd been too busy trying to evaluate his status for my report to Donovan. His emotional focus was on his father's death and the loss of his opportunity to make amends. Any profit was apparently beside the point as far as he was concerned. Oh, well. I figured Tasha would be in touch with him and she could give him the particulars.

I arrived in Santa Teresa without incident at two P.M. Since I was home earlier than I'd thought, I went into the office, typed up my notes, and stuck them in the file. I left two phone messages, one for Tasha at her office and one on the Maleks' home machine. I calculated my hours, the mileage, and miscellaneous expenses, and typed an invoice for my services to which I affixed the receipt for the tuna sandwich. Tomorrow, I'd include it with the typed report of my findings, send a copy to Tasha and one to Donovan. End of story, I thought.

I retrieved my car, unticketed, from an illegal space and drove home, feeling generally satisfied with life. Dietz fixed supper that night, a skilletful of fried onions, fried potatoes, and fried sausages with liberal doses of garlic and red pepper flakes, all served with a side of drab, grainy mustard that set your tongue aflame. Only two confirmed single people could eat a meal like that and imagine it was somehow nutritious. I handled the cleanup process, washing plates, flatware, and glasses, scrubbing out the frying pan while Dietz read the evening paper. Is this what couples did any given night of the week? In my twice-married life, it was the drama and grief I remembered most clearly, not the day-to-day stuff. This was entirely too domestic . . . not unpleasant, but certainly unsettling to someone unaccustomed to company.

At eight, we walked up to Rosie's and settled into a back booth together. Rosie's restaurant is poorly lighted, a tacky neighborhood establishment that's been there for twenty-five years, sandwiched between a Laundromat and an appliance repair shop. The chrome-and-Formica tables are of thrift-shop vintage and the booths lining the walls are made of construction-grade plywood, stained dark, complete with crude hand-gouged messages and splinters. It's an act of reckless abandon to slide across the seats unless your tetanus shots are current. Over the years, the number of California smokers has steadily diminished, so the air quality has improved while the clientele has not. Rosie's used to be a refuge for local drinkers who liked to start early in the day and stay until closing time. Now the tavern has become popular with assorted amateur sports teams, who descend en masse after every big game, filling the air with loud talk, raucous laughter, and much stomping about. The regulars, all four bleary-eyed imbibers, have been driven to other places. I rather missed their slurred conversation, which was never intrusive.

Rosie was apparently gone for the night and the bartender was someone I'd never seen before. Dietz drank a couple of beers while I had a couple of glasses of Rosie's best screw-top Chardonnay, a puckering rendition of a California varietal she probably bought by the keg.

I freely confess it was the alcohol that got me into trouble that night. I was feeling mellow and relaxed, somewhat less inhibited than usual, which is to say, ready to flap my mouth. Robert Dietz was beginning to look good to me, and I wasn't really sure how I felt about that. His face was chiseled in shadow and his gaze crossed the room in restless assessment while we chatted about nothing in particular. Idly, I told him about William and Rosie's wedding and my adventures on the road, and he filled in details about his stay in Germany. Along with the attraction, I experienced a low-grade sorrow, so like a fever that I wondered if I were coming down with the flu. At one point, I shivered and he looked over at me. "You okay?" he asked.

I stretched my hand out on the table and he covered it with his, lacing his fingers through mine. "What are we doing?" I asked.

"Good question. Why don't we talk about that? You go first."

I laughed, but the issue wasn't really funny and we both knew it. "Why'd you have to come back and stir things up? I was doing fine."

"What have I stirred up? We haven't done anything. We eat dinner. We have drinks. I sleep down. You sleep up. My knee's so bad, you're in no danger of unwanted advances. I couldn't make it up those stairs if my life depended on it."

"Is that the good news or the bad?"

"I don't know. You tell me," he said.

"I don't want to get used to you."

"A lot of women can't get used to me. You're one of the few who seems remotely interested," he said, smiling slightly.

Here's a word to the wise: In the midst of a tender discussion with one woman, don't mention another one—especially in the plural. It's bad policy. The minute he said it, I had this sudden vision of a long line of females with me standing not even close to the front of the pack. I could feel my smile fade and I retreated into silence like a turtle encountering a dog.

His look became cautious. "What's wrong?"

"Nothing. I'm fine. What makes you think there's anything wrong?"

"Let's don't talk at cross-purposes," he said. "You obviously have something to say, so why don't you say it?"

"I don't want to. It doesn't matter."

"Kinsey."

"What."

"Come on. Just say it. There's no penalty for being honest."

"I don't know how to say it. You're here for four days and what am I supposed to do with that? I'm not good at being left. It's the story of my life. Why get enmeshed when all it means is I get to have my heart ripped out?"

He lifted his eyebrows, shrugging with his face. "I don't know what to tell you. I can't promise to stay. I've never stayed in one place for more than six months max. Why can't we live in the present? Why does everything have to have a guarantee attached?"

"I'm not talking about guarantees."

"I think you are," he said. "You want a lien against the future, when the fact is you don't know any more than I do about what's coming next."

"Well, that's true and I'm not arguing that. All I'm saying is I don't want to get involved in an on-again-off-again relationship, which is what this is."

Dietz's expression was pained. "I won't lie. I can't pretend I'll stay when I know I won't. What good would that do?"

I could feel my frustration rise. "I don't want you to pretend and I'm not asking you to promise. I'm just trying to be honest."

"About what?"

"About everything. People have rejected me all my life. Sometimes it's death or desertion. Infidelity, betrayal. You name it. I've experienced every form of emotional treachery there is. Well, big deal. Everybody's suffered something in life and so what? I'm not sitting around feeling sorry for myself, but I'd have to be a fool to lay myself open to that shit again."

"I understand that. I hear you and believe me, I don't want to be the one to cause you pain. This is not about you. It's about me. I'm restless by nature. I hate to feel trapped. That's how I am. Pen me in and I'll tear the place apart trying to get out," he said. "My people were nomads. We were always on the move. Always on the road. We lived out of suitcases. To me, being in one spot is oppressive. You want to talk about death. It's the worst. When I was growing up, if we stayed in one town for long, my old man would get busted. He'd end up in county jail or in the hospital or the local drunk tank. Any school I attended, I was always the new kid and I'd have to fight my way across the school yard just to stay alive. The happiest day of my life was the day we hit the road again."

"Free at last," I interjected.

"That's right. It's not that I might not want to stay. It's that I'm incapable of it."

"Oh, right. 'Incapable.' Well, that explains it. You're excused," I said.

"Don't be so touchy. You know what I mean. God almighty, I'm not proud of myself. I don't relish the fact that I'm a rolling stone. I just don't want to kid myself and I don't want to kid you."

"Thank you. That's great. In the meantime, I'm sure you have ways of amusing yourself."

He squinted. "Where did that come from?"

"This is hopeless," I said. "I don't know why we even bother with this. You're addicted to wandering and I'm rooted in place. You can't stay and I can't leave because I love where I am. This is your biennial interlude and I'm here for the duration, which means I'm probably doomed to a lifetime of guys like you."

" 'Guys like *me?*' That's nice. What does that mean?"

"Just what it says. Emotionally claustrophobic. You're a basket case. So as long as I'm attracted to guys like you, I can bypass my own—" I stopped short, feeling like one of those cartoon dogs, skidding on a cartoon floor.

"Your own what?"

"None of your business," I said. "Let's drop the conversation. I should have kept my mouth shut. I end up sounding like a whiner, which is not what I intend."

"You're always so worried about sounding like a whiner," he said. "Who cares if you whine? Be my guest."

"Oh, *now* you say that."

"Say what?" he said, exasperated.

I assumed an attitude of patience that I scarcely felt. "One of the first things you ever said to me was that you wanted—how did you phrase it—'obedience without whining.' You said very few women ever mastered that."

"*I* said that?"

"Yes, you did. I've tried very hard ever since not to whine in your presence."

"Don't be ridiculous. I didn't mean it that way," he said. "I don't even remember saying it, but I was probably talking about something else. Anyway, don't change the subject. I don't want to leave it on this note. As long as the issue's on the table, let's get it settled."

"What's to settle? We can't settle anything. There's no way to resolve it, so let's drop the whole business. I'm sorry I brought it up. I've already got this ongoing family nonsense. Maybe I'm upset about that."

"What nonsense? You're related to these people, so what's the problem?"

"I don't want to get into it. Aside from whining, I hate to feel like I'm repeating myself."

"How can you repeat yourself when you never told me to begin with?"

I ran a hand through my hair and stared down at the tabletop. I'd been hoping to avoid the subject, but the topic did seem safer than discussing our relationship, whatever that consisted of. I couldn't come up with any rational defense of my reluctance to engage with this newfound family of mine. I just didn't want to do it. Finally, I said, "I guess I don't like to be pressured. They're so busy trying to make up for lost time. Why can't they just mind their own business? I'm not comfortable with all this buddy-buddy stuff. You know how stubborn I get when I'm pushed."

"Why did you agree to work for that attorney then? Isn't she your cousin?"

"Well, yes, but I didn't *intend* to agree. I intended to turn her down, but then greed and curiosity got the better of me. I have a living to earn and I didn't want to refuse out of perversity. I know I'll regret it, but I'm into it now so there's no sense beating myself up."

"Sounds harmless enough on the face of it."

"It's not harmless. It's annoying. And besides, that isn't the point. The point is, I'd like for them to respect my boundaries."

"What boundaries? She hired you to do a job. As long as you get paid, that's the end of it."

"Let's hope. Besides, it's not her so much as the other two. Liza and Pam. If I give an inch, they'll invade my space."

"Oh, bullshit. That's California psychobabble. You can't live your life like a radio talk show."

"What do you know? I don't notice you all cozied up to your family."

I could see him flinch. His expression shifted abruptly to one of injury and irritation. "Low blow. What I say about my kids, I don't want you throwing back in my face."

"You're right. I'm sorry. I withdraw the remark."

"Withdraw the knife and the wound's still there," he snapped. "What's the matter with you? You're so bristly these days. You're doing everything you can to keep me at arm's length."

"I am not," I said, and then I stared at him, squinting. "Is that true?"

"Well, look at your behavior. I haven't even been here two days and we're already fighting. What's that about? I didn't travel all this way to pick a fight with you. I wanted to see you. I was excited we'd have time together. Hell. If I'd wanted to fight, I could have stayed with Naomi."

"Why didn't you? I don't mean the question in a mean-hearted way, but I'm curious. What happened?"

"Oh, who knows? I have my version, she has hers. Sometimes I think relationships have a natural lifespan. Ours ran out. That's all it was. The explanations come afterwards when you try to make sense of it. Let's get back to you. What's going on in your head?"

"I'd rather fight than feel nothing."

"Those are your only two options?"

"That's what it feels like, but I couldn't say for sure."

He reached out and gave my hair a tug. "What am I going to do with you?"

"What am I going to do with *you?*" I replied.

7

When we returned to the apartment at ten-fifteen, Henry's kitchen light was on. Dietz said his knee was killing him, so he let himself into the apartment where he intended to take a couple of pain pills, prop his feet up, and put his ice pack to work. I said I'd be along momentarily. Our conversation at Rosie's hadn't really gone anywhere. I couldn't bear to continue and I couldn't bear behaving as though the subject hadn't been broached. I didn't know what I wanted from him and I wasn't sure how to say it anyway, so I just ended up sounding needy. My general policy is this: If your mind isn't open, keep your mouth shut, too.

I knocked on Henry's backdoor, waving at him through the window when he looked up at me. He was sitting in his rocking chair with the evening paper and his glass of Jack Daniel's. He smiled and waved back, setting the paper aside so he could let me in. He had the heat turned up and the inside air was not only warm, but deliciously scented with yesterday's cinnamon rolls.

"This feels great. It's really cold out there," I said. The kitchen table was covered with old black-and-white photographs sorted into piles. I glanced at them briefly as I pulled out a kitchen chair and turned my attention to him. From my point of view, Henry Pitts is perfection—smart, good-natured, and responsible—with the cutest legs I've ever seen. He's been my landlord for five years, since the day I spotted the ad for the apartment in a Laundromat. Henry was looking for a long-term tenant who was clean and quiet; no children, loud parties, or small, yapping dogs. As a lifelong mobile-home inhabitant, I was addicted to compact spaces, but ready to limit contact with a lot of close, unruly neighbors. Trailer-park life, for all its virtues, entails an intimate acquaintance with other people's private business. Since I make a living as a snoop, I'd just as soon keep my personal affairs to myself. The converted single-car garage Henry was offering was better than my fantasies and affordable as well. Since then, the place had been bombed and rebuilt, the interior fitted out in teak and as cleverly designed as a ship's.

From the outset, Henry and I established just enough of a relationship to suit us both. Over the years, he's managed to civilize me to some extent and I'm certainly more agreeable now than I was back then. Little by little, we forged the bond between us until now I consider him the exemplary mix of friend and generic family member.

"You want a cup of tea?" he asked.

"No, thanks. I just stopped to say hi before I hit the sack. Are these family pictures?" I asked, picking one at random.

"That's the claim," he said. "Nell sent me those. She came across two boxes of old family photographs, but none are labeled. No names, no dates. She hasn't any idea who these people are and neither do the other sibs. What a mess. Take my word for it. You should mark all your photographs, even if it's just a quick note on the back. You might know who's who, but nobody else will."

"Do they look familiar to you?"

"A few." He took the print I was looking at and squinted as he held it to the light. I peered over his shoulder. The woman in the picture must have been in her twenties, with a broad, bland face and hair drawn back in a bun. She wore a white middy blouse, with a calf-length skirt, dark stockings, and flat, dark shoes with a bow across the instep. Standing beside her was a glum-faced girl of eight with a drop-waist sailor dress and ankle-high lace-up shoes. "I believe this is a picture of my mother's younger sister, Augusta, taken in Topeka, Kansas, back in 1915. The child's name was Rebecca Rose, if memory serves. She and her mother both died in the big influenza epidemic of 1918." He picked up another one. "This is my mother with my grandfather Tilmann. I'm surprised Nell didn't recognize them except her eyesight's fading. Now that I think of it, I'm not sure why it matters.

None of us have children, so once we're gone, it won't make any difference who these people are."

"Well, that seems sad. Why don't you put 'em in an album and pass them on to me? I'll pretend they're mine. What was his first name?"

"Klaus. My mother's name was Gudrun." The man staring fixedly at the camera must have been in his late seventies, the daughter beside him in her fifties by the look of her. I said, "What's the name Tilmann. Is that German? I somehow imagined you were all Swedes or Finns."

"Oh no, we're not Scandinavian. They're gloomy sorts, in my opinion. The Tilmanns were good German stock. Headstrong, autocratic, vigorous, and exacting. Some would say impossible, but that's a matter of interpretation. Longevity is genetic and don't ever let anybody tell you otherwise. I read those articles about folks who live to be a hundred. They all try to take credit, claim it's because they smoke or don't smoke, eat yogurt, take vitamins, or a tablespoon of vinegar a day. What nonsense. War and accidents excepted, you live a long time because you come from other people who live a long time. You have to take responsibility. You can't subject yourself to any kind of gross mistreatment. My mother lived to be a hundred and three and I imagine the remaining five of us will live that long as well."

"You certainly seem to be in good shape. Nell's what, ninety-six? And you have your eighty-sixth birthday coming up on Valentine's Day."

Henry nodded, making a motion as if to knock on wood. "We're healthy, in the main, though we're all shrinking down to some extent. We've talked about this and it's our contention that the shrinkage is nature's way of assuring you don't take up so much space in your coffin. You lighten up, too. Feels like taking air into your bones. Makes it easy on the pallbearers. And, of course, your faculties shut down. You get blind as a bat and your hearing fades. Charlie says it sounds like he's got a pillow on his head all the time these days. Get old, you might as well not worry about your dignity. Anybody talks about dignity for old folks has never been around one as far as I can tell. You can keep your spunk, but you have to give up your vanity early on. We're all in diapers. Well, I'm not, but then I'm the baby in the family. The rest of them leak any time they cough or laugh too hard.

"Nell says one reason she misses William so much now he's moved out here is because they can't play bridge like they used to. Have to play three-handed, which isn't as much fun. Lewis was thinking about asking a cousin to move in, but Nell won't tolerate another woman in the house. She says she's had her brothers to herself now for sixty years and she's not about to change. Nell says once she 'goes' they can do anything they want, depending on whose left."

"I can't believe they're still willing to endure the winters in Michigan. Why don't they all move out here? You could play all the bridge you want."

"There's talk of that. We'll just have to see. Nell has her ladies' luncheon group and she hates to leave them." Henry put the photo down and took his seat again. "Now then, how are you? I had a nice chat with your friend Dietz. He says you picked up some work."

"Actually, I finished it. One of those quickies you remember fondly when the tough ones come along," I said. I took a few minutes to fill him in on the search for Guy Malek.

Henry shook his head. "What's going to happen? Do you think he'll get his share of the estate?"

"Who knows? I don't always hear the end of it, but Tasha thinks they'll be able to work something out."

"How long will Dietz be here? I thought I'd have the two of you over for supper one night."

"Probably not long. He's on his way up to Santa Cruz to see his sons," I said.

"Well, let me know if he's still going to be here Saturday and I'll cook something special. We'll invite William and Rosie and Moza Lowenstein, if she's free."

By the time I let myself into my place, Dietz had fallen asleep in his underwear, slouched down in his chair, snoring lightly. The television set was on, the volume low, the channel tuned to a nature show about underwater shark attacks. Dietz had his leg propped up on the edge of the sofa bed, a blanket pulled up across his chest and shoulders. The partially melted ice pack had toppled to the floor. I put that ice pack in the freezer and took out a second one, laying it carefully across his knee without waking him. His kneecap was swollen, the bare flesh looking pale and vulnerable. I left him as he was, knowing he'd wake long before morning. He sleeps in fits and starts like an animal in the wild, and I knew from past experience he seldom manages to make it through the night without getting up at least twice.

I eased off my shoes and made my way up the spiral stairs. From above, I stared down at him. His lined face looked alien in sleep, as if sculptured in clay. I seldom saw him at ease. He was restless by nature, perpetually in motion, his features animated by the sheer force of his nervous energy. Even as I watched, he stirred himself awake, jerking upright with a look of disorientation. I could see him wince, reaching for the ice pack balanced on his distended joint. I stepped away from the loft rail and went into the bathroom, where I washed my face and brushed my teeth. It was no doubt the proximity to all that testosterone, but I could feel the murmur of sexuality at the base of my spine. I grabbed an oversized T-shirt from a hook on the bathroom door. I usually sleep in the nude, but it seemed like a bad idea.

Once ready for bed, I turned out the light and slipped under the quilt. I reached out and set my alarm, watching the digital clock flip from 11:04 to 11:05. Below, I could hear Dietz get up and move into the kitchen. The refrigerator door opened and closed. He took down a glass and poured himself a drink—wine, orange juice, or milk—something liquid at any rate. I heard him pull out a kitchen stool, followed by the rustle of newspaper. I wondered what he was thinking, wondered what would happen if I heard him climbing the stairs. Maybe I should have pulled on a robe and gone down to join him, thrown caution to the wind and to hell with the consequences, but it was not in my nature. Being single for so long had made me cautious about men. I stared up at the Plexiglas skylight above my bed, thinking about the risks involved in reaching out to him. Passion never lasts, but then what does? If you could have it all, but only briefly, would the rush of love be worth the price in pain? I could feel myself sinking into sleep as though weighted down with stones. I didn't rise again until 5:59 A.M.

I pulled on my sweats, preparing for my run as usual. Dietz was in the shower when I left the house, but I noticed with a pang he was in the process of packing. He'd laid the soft-sided suitcase open on the floor near the sofa bed, which he'd folded away. The blanket had been refolded and placed across one end. He'd piled the sheets he'd used near the washer. Maybe he felt his exodus would address my issues with him, minimizing the chances of my forming an attachment. What I noticed, perversely, was that, having felt nothing on his arrival, I was now afflicted with a stinging sense of loss at his departure. He'd been with me for two days and I was already suffering, so maybe I'd been smart not to take things any further. I'd been celibate for so long, what was another year without sex? I made an involuntary sound that might have been a whimper if I allowed myself such things.

I closed the door quietly behind me, breathing deeply as though the damp morning air might ease the fire in my chest. Having passed through the front gate, I paused while I stretched, keeping my mind a blank. In the last several years as a private investigator, I've developed a neat trick for shutting off my feelings. Like others who work in the "helping" professions—doctors and nurses, police officers, social workers, paramedics—emotional disconnection is sometimes the only way to function in the face of death with all its tacky variations. Originally, my detachment took several minutes of concentrated effort, but now I make the shift in the blink of an eye. Mental-health enthusiasts are quick to assure us that our psychological well-being is best served by staying in touch with our feelings, but *surely* they're not referring to the icky, unpleasant ones.

The run itself was unsatisfactory. The dawn was overcast, the sky a brooding gray unrelieved by any visible sunrise. Gradually, daylight overtook the lowering dark, but the whole of it had the bleached look of an old black-and-white photograph. My gait felt choppy and I never really hit my stride. The air was so chilly I couldn't even generate a decent sweat. I dutifully counted off the miles, feeling gratified to be doing it in spite of myself. Some days the discipline is an end in itself, a way of asserting the will in the face of life's little setbacks. I walked the half block home, carefully brushing aside any slovenly sentiment.

Dietz was sitting at the counter when I got in. He'd put on a pot of coffee and set out my cereal bowl. His bowl was already washed, rinsed, and drying in the dish rack. His suitcase, fully zipped, was waiting by the door along with his garment bag. Through the open bathroom door, I could see he'd tidied the basin of all his personal possessions. The scent of soap mingled with his aftershave, a damp male perfume permeating everything.

"I thought it might be easier if I took off," he said.

"Sure, no problem. I hope you're not doing it on my account."

"No, no. You know me. I'm not that good at staying put," he said. "Anyway, you probably have a lot of work to do."

"Oh, tons," I said. "You're heading up to Santa Cruz?"

"Eventually, yes. I'll drive on up the coast, maybe spend a day in Cambria. With this knee, I have to break up the trip, anyway. You know, get out and stretch every hour or so. Keep it warm and loose. Otherwise, it locks up."

"What time are you taking off?"

"Whenever you leave for work."

"Well, great. I'll just grab a shower then and you can hit the road."

"Take your time. I'm in no hurry," he said.

"I can see that," I remarked, as I headed up to the loft. This time he didn't ask if I was mad. This was good because, in truth, I was furious. Under the fury was the old familiar pain. Why does everyone end up leaving me? What did I ever do to them? I went through my morning routine as efficiently as possible, flung on my clothes, and ate my cereal without pausing to read the paper. To demonstrate my indifference to his abrupt departure, I took out fresh sheets and asked him to help me remake the sofa bed. I hoped the implication was that some other guy was lined up for bed space as soon as he left. Neither of us said much and what we said was transactional. "Where's the other pillowcase?" About like that.

Once the sofa was redone, he took his suitcase to the car and came back for the garment bag. I walked him out to the curb and we exchanged one of those insincere kisses with the sound effects attached. *Mmch!* He fired up his Porsche and I dutifully waved as he roared off down the street. You little shit, I thought.

I went into the office, ignoring a faint tendency to tear up for no reason. The day yawned in front of me like a sinkhole in the street. This was just what it felt like when he left before. Now how does this happen to someone of my rare spunk and independence? I played a few rounds of solitaire, paid some bills, and balanced my checkbook. Anxiety whispered in my gut like a stomachache. When the phone finally rang just before lunch, I snatched up the receiver, absurdly grateful at the interruption.

"Kinsey. This is Donovan. How are you?"

"Gee, I'm just fine. How are you?"

"Well enough. Uh, listen, we got your message and we'd like to compliment you on a job well done. Tasha had to fly back to San Francisco this morning, but she said she didn't think you'd mind giving us the information firsthand. Could you stop by the house for a drink late this afternoon?"

"Well, sure. I could do that. I was going to type up my report and put it in the mail, but I can give you a rundown in person if you'd prefer."

"I'd appreciate that. I expect Jack and Bennet will want to be there as well. That way, if they have questions, you can fill us all in at the same time and save yourself the repetition. Would five-thirty be convenient?"

"Fine with me," I said.

"Good. We'll look forward to seeing you."

After I hung up, I could feel myself shrug. I had nothing against an informal report as long as I didn't somehow get sucked into the family drama. Aside from Guy, I wasn't crazy about the Malek brothers. I happened to believe Guy had changed his wicked ways, so maybe I could do him a service and convince the others. Not that it was any of my business how the monies were distributed, but if there were any lingering questions about his "worthiness," I certainly had an opinion. Besides, with Dietz now gone, I didn't have anything better to do.

I skipped lunch and spent the afternoon cleaning my office. Lonnie

Kingman had a maintenance crew that serviced the premises weekly on Friday afternoons, but it felt therapeutic to get in there and scrub. I even spent twenty minutes dusting the artificial ficus plant someone had once mistaken for real. The space I occupied had originally been a conference room with a full "executive" bathroom attached. I found a plastic bucket, sponges, cleansers, a toilet brush, and mop and entertained myself mightily killing imaginary germs. My method of coping with depression is to take on chores so obnoxious and disgusting that reality seems pleasant by comparison. By three o'clock, I smelled of sweat and household bleach and I'd forgotten what I was so unhappy about. Well, actually, I remembered, but I didn't give a shit.

Having sanitized the suite, I locked the door, stripped off my clothes, hopped in the executive shower, and scrubbed myself. I dressed again in the same jeans, pulling on a fresh turtleneck from the ready supply I keep handy for sudden travel. What's life without a toothbrush and clean underpants? I typed up the official version of my encounter with Guy Malek, tucking one copy in my office files, another in my handbag. The third I addressed to Tasha Howard at her San Francisco office. The end. Finito. Done, done, done. This was the last job I'd ever take from her.

By 5:25, dressed in my best (and only) wool tweed blazer, I drove through the entrance to the Malek estate. It was close to dark by then, the winter-shortened days still characterized by early twilights. My headlights swept in a forlorn arc across the stucco wall surrounding the fifteen-acre property. Along the rim of the wall, three strands of rusted barbed wire had been strung years ago, broken now in places and looking singularly ineffective. Who knows what intruders were anticipated back then? A chilly wind had picked up and the darkened treetops swayed and shivered, whispering together about things unseen. There were lights on in the house, two upstairs windows illuminated in pale yellow where much of the first floor was dark.

The housekeeper had neglected to turn on the outside lights. I parked in the turnaround and picked my way across the cobblestone courtyard to the shadowy portico that sheltered the entranceway in front. I rang the bell and waited, crossing my arms for warmth. The porch light was finally flipped on and Myrna opened the door a crack.

"Hi, Myrna. Kinsey Millhone. I was here the other day. Donovan invited me for drinks."

Myrna didn't exactly break into song at the news. Apparently, advanced classes in Housekeeper's Training School cautioned the students not to give expression to sudden bursts of joy. In the two days since I'd seen her last, she'd renewed the dye job in her hair and the whole of it was now a white blond that looked like it would be cold to the touch. Her uniform consisted of a gray top worn over matching gray pants. I would have bet money the waistband was unbuttoned underneath the tunic. "This way," she said. Her crepe-soled shoes squeaked slightly on the polished parquet floor.

A woman called down from somewhere above our heads. "Myrna? Was that the front door? We're expecting someone for drinks." I glanced up, following the sound of her voice. A brunette in her late thirties was leaning on the stair rail above our heads. She caught sight of me and brightened. "Oh, hi. You must be Kinsey. You want to come on up?"

Myrna veered off without another word, disappearing into the rear of the house as I climbed the stairs.

Christie held out her hand when I reached the upper landing. "I'm Christie Malek. Nice to meet you," she said as we shook hands. "I take it you've met Myrna."

"More or less," I said. I took her in at a glance, like an instant Polaroid. She was a fine-featured brunette with shiny dark hair, worn shoulder length. She was very slender, wearing jeans and a bulky black-ribbed sweater that came down almost to her knees. She had the sleeves rolled back and her wrists were thin, her fingers long and cool. Her eyes were small, a dark penetrating blue, beneath a lightly feathered brow. Her teeth were as perfect as a mouthwash ad's. The absence of eye makeup gave her a recessive, slightly anxious air, though her manner was friendly and her smile was warm enough. "Donovan called to say he'd be a few minutes late. Jack's on his way home and Bennet's around some place. I'm just going through Bader's papers and I'd love some company."

Still talking to me, she turned and moved toward the master bedroom, which I could see through an open doorway. "We're still looking for the missing will, among other things. Ever hopeful," she added wryly.

"I thought Bennet was going to do that."

"This is how Bennet does things. He loves to delegate."

I hoped there was a touch of irony in her tone. I couldn't be sure so I kept my mouth shut.

The suite we entered was enormous; two substantial rooms separated by a pair of doors that had been pushed into their respective wall pockets. We passed through the outer room, which had been furnished as a bedroom. The walls were padded fabric, covered in rose-colored silk with a watered sheen to the finish. The carpet was off-white, a dense, cut pile. Pale, heavy drapes had been pulled back to reveal the leaded glass windows that looked out onto the cobblestone entrance at the front of the house. There was a marble fireplace on the wall to the left. Two matching sofas were arranged on either side of it, plump, upholstered pieces covered in a subdued floral chintz. The four-poster bed had been flawlessly made, not a ripple or a wrinkle in the snowy-white silk coverlet. The surface of the bed table seemed unnaturally bare, as if once-personal items had now been hidden from sight. It might have been my imagination, but the room seemed to harbor the lingering scent of sickness. I could see that closets were being emptied, the contents—suits and dress shirts—packed into large cardboard boxes supplied by the local Thrift Store Industries downtown.

"This is gorgeous," I said.

"Isn't it?"

Beyond the sliding doors, a home office had been set up, with a large walnut desk and antique wooden file cabinets. The ceilings in both rooms were twelve feet high, but this was by far the cozier of the two. A fire had been laid in a second marble fireplace and Christie paused to add a log to an already snapping blaze. The walls here were paneled in walnut as dark and glossy as fudge. I could see a copier, a fax machine, computer, and a printer arranged on the built-in shelves on either side of the fireplace. A paper shredder stood on one side of the desk, its green On button lighted. I could see printed acknowledgments stacked up waiting to be addressed to those who'd sent flowers to the funeral.

Christie returned to the desk where she'd emptied the contents of two drawers into banker's boxes that she'd labeled with a black marker. There were two big plastic garbage bags bulging with discarded papers. Thick files were stacked on the desktop and a number of empty file folders were strewn across the carpet. This was the kind of task I knew well, classifying the odds and ends left behind by the dead. Below, in the courtyard, we could hear a motorcycle cruise in, the engine being revved once more before it was silenced.

Christie cocked her head. "I hear the Harley. Sounds like Jack's home."

"How's it going so far?"

Her expression was a wry mix of skepticism and despair. "Bader was supremely organized for the most part, but he must have lost his enthusiasm for jobs like this. Look at all this stuff. I swear, if I'm ever diagnosed as terminal, I'm going to clean out my files before I get too sick to care. What if you kept pornographic pictures or something like that? I'd hate to think of someone sorting through my private affairs."

"Nothing in my life is that interesting," I said. "You want help?"

"Not really, but I could use the moral support," she said. "I've been in here for hours. I have to look at every single piece of paper and figure out if it's worth saving, though most aren't as far as I can tell. I mean, what do I know? Anything I'm not sure about, I put in one pile. The really junky stuff, I go ahead and shove in a garbage bag. I don't dare shred a thing and I'm afraid to toss much. I know Bennet. As sure as I pitch something, he tears in here and wants to know where it is. He's done that to me twice and it was just dumb luck the trash hadn't been picked up. I'm out there in the dark, like a bag lady, pulling crumpled papers out of the garbage can. This third pile is everything that looks important. For instance, here's something you might like." She picked up a file from the stack on top of the desk and handed it to me. "Bader must have put this together back in the early sixties."

A quick glance inside revealed a collection of newspaper clippings related to Guy's past misbehavior. I read one at random, an article dating back to 1956 detailing the arrest of two juveniles, boys ages fourteen and thirteen, who were believed to be responsible for a spree of graffiti vandalism. One of the teens was booked into Juvenile Hall, the other released to his parents. There must have been twenty-five such snippets. In some cases, the authorities withheld the names because the boy or boys arrested were still minors. In other articles, Guy Malek was identified by name.

"I wonder why Bader kept clippings. It seems odd," I said.

"Maybe to remind himself why he disinherited the kid. I figure Bennet will want 'em for ammunition if it comes down to that. It's exhausting just trying to make these decisions."

"Quite a job," I said and then shifted the subject matter. "You know, it occurred to me that since the two wills were drawn up only three years apart, the two witnesses for the first might have been witnesses for the second will, too. Especially if they were paralegals or law clerks working in the attorney's office."

She looked at me with interest. "Good point. You'll have to mention that to Donovan. None of us are anxious to see five million bucks flying out the window."

There was a tap at the door and we both turned to see that Myrna had reappeared. "Donovan's home. He asked me to serve the hors d'oeuvres in the living room."

"Tell him we'll be down in a second, as soon as I wash my hands. Oh, and see if you can round up the other two."

Myrna took in the request, murmured something inaudible, and withdrew from the room.

Christie shook her head, lowering her voice a notch. "She may be on the glum side, but she's the only person in the house who doesn't argue with everyone."

8

Lights were on and Donovan was in the living room when Christie and I came downstairs. He'd changed out of his work clothes, pulling on a heavy cream-colored knit sweater over casual pants. He'd exchanged his dress shoes for a pair of sheepskin slippers that made his feet look huge. A fire had been laid and he was poking at the logs, turning a bulky wedge of oak so that its uppermost side would catch. Donovan picked up another piece of wood and thunked it on top. A shower of sparks flew up the chimney. He replaced the fire screen and wiped his hands on his handkerchief, glancing over at me. "I see you've met Christie. We appreciate your coming over. Keeps it simpler all around. Can I make you a drink? We've got just about anything you'd want."

"A glass of Chardonnay would be fine."

"I'll get it," Christie said promptly. She moved over to a sideboard crowded with liquor bottles. A bottle of Chardonnay had been chilling in a cooler beside a clear Lucite ice bucket and an assortment of glasses. She began to peel the foil from the neck of the wine bottle, with a look at Donovan. "You having wine?"

"Probably with dinner. I think I'll have a martini first. Gin is Bennet's winter drink," he added as an aside to me.

Ah, the seasonal alcoholic. What a nice idea. Gin in the winter, maybe vodka in spring. Summer would be tequila and he could round out the autumn with a little bourbon or scotch. While she opened the wine, I took a momentary survey.

Like the bedroom above, this room was immense. The twelve-foot ceiling was rimmed with ten-inch crown molding, the walls papered in a narrow blue-and-cream stripe that had faded with the years. The pale Oriental carpet had to be seventeen feet wide and probably twenty-five feet long. The furniture had been arranged in two groupings. At the far end of the room, four wing chairs faced one another near the front windows. Closer to the center of the room, three large sofas formed a U in front of the fireplace. All of the side pieces—an armoire, an escritoire, and two carved and inlaid wooden tables— were the sort I'd seen in antique stores, heavy, faintly fussy, with price tags that made you squint because you thought you'd read them wrong.

Christie returned with two glasses of wine and handed one to me. She took a seat on one of the sofas and I sat down across from her with a murmured "thanks." The blue floral pattern was faded to a soft white, the fabric threadbare along the arms and the cushion fronts. There was a large brass bowl filled with fresh flowers and several copies of *Architectural Digest* lined up on the square glass coffee table in the crook of the U. There was also an untidy stack of what looked like condolence cards. While I was thinking about it, I took out my typed report and placed it on the table in front of me. I'd leave it for Donovan so he'd have a copy for his files.

I heard footsteps in the hall and the sound of voices. Jack and Bennet came into the living room together. Whatever they'd been discussing, their expressions were now neutral, conveying nothing but benign interest at the sight of me. Bennet wore a running suit of some silky material that rustled when he walked. Jack looked as if he'd just come in off the golf course, his hair still disheveled from the imprint of his visor. He wore a bright orange sweater vest over a pink short-sleeved golf shirt and his gait tended to a lilt as if he were still wearing cleats. Jack poured himself a scotch and water as dark as iced tea while Bennet made a pitcher of martinis that he stirred with a long glass wand. I made note of his vermouth-to-gin ratio—roughly two parts per million. He poured one for himself and one for Donovan, adding olives to both. He brought the martini pitcher over to the coffee table and set it down within range.

While drinks were being poured, various pleasantries were exchanged, none of them heartfelt. As with tobacco, the rituals of alcohol seemed to be a stalling technique until those assembled could get themselves psychologically situated. I had an odd sensation in my chest, the same itch of anxiety I'd felt before a third-grade dance recital in which I played a bunny, not a specialty of mine. My aunt Gin was ill and unable to attend, so I'd been forced to do my hippy-hopping in front of countless alien adults, who didn't seem to find me winsome. My legs were too skinny and my fake ears wouldn't stand up. The brothers Malek watched me with about the same enthusiasm. Donovan took a seat next to Christie on the couch across from me while Jack sat facing the fireplace with Bennet on his left.

It was interesting to see the three brothers in the same room together. Despite the similarities in their coloring, their faces were very different, Bennet's the more so because of his beard and mustache. Donovan and Jack were built along finer lines though neither was as appealing as their errant brother, Guy. Jack leaned forward and began to sift idly through the sympathy cards.

I thought Donovan was on the verge of asking for my report when Myrna came into the room with assorted edibles on a serving tray. The tray itself was the size of a manhole cover, very plain, probably sterling silver, and distinctly tarnished along the edges. The hors d'oeuvres, in addition to what looked like Cheez Whiz on saltines, consisted of a bowl of peanuts and a bowl of unpitted green olives in brine. No one said a word until she'd departed, closing the door behind her.

Jack leaned forward. "What the fuck is this?"

Bennet laughed at the very moment he was swallowing a mouthful of martini. He made a snorting sound as he choked and I saw gin dribble out his nose. He coughed into his handkerchief while Jack shot a smile in his direction. I bet as children they'd paused in the midst of dinner, opening their mouths to one another to exhibit masticated food.

Christie flashed them a look of disapproval. "It's Enid's night off. Would you quit with the criticism? Myrna's a nurse. She was hired to look after Dad, not to wait on the two of you. We're lucky she stayed on and you bloody well know it. Nobody else lifts a finger around here except me."

"Thanks for setting the record straight, Christie. You're a fuckin' peach," Jack said.

"Knock it off," Donovan said. "Could we hold off on this until we hear from her?" He grabbed a handful of peanuts, eating one at a time as his focus returned to me. "You want to fill us in?"

I took a few minutes to detail the means by which I'd managed to locate Guy Malek. Without mentioning Darcy Pascoe or California Fidelity Insurance, I played out the steps that led to the information on his identification card. I'll admit I stretched it out, making it sound more problematic than it had actually been. "As nearly as I can tell, your brother's cleaned up his act. He's working as the custodian for the Jubilee Evangelical Church. I gather he doubles as a handyman for various people in Marcella. He says he's the only one in town doing home maintenance, so he earns decent money, by his standards. His lifestyle is simple, but he's doing okay."

Donovan said, "Is he married?"

"I didn't ask if he was married, but he didn't seem to be. He never mentioned a wife. His housing's provided by the church in exchange for his services. The place is pretty funky, but he seems to manage all right. I grant you these are superficial judgments, but I didn't really stop to investigate."

Bennet shaved an olive with his teeth and placed the pit on a paper napkin. "Why Marcella? That's a dirt bucket of a place."

"The pastor of this fundamentalist church picked him up hitchhiking out on 101 the day he left home. Essentially, he's been in Marcella ever since. The church he joined seems pretty strict. No dancing, card playing, things like that. He did say he had a beer now and then, but no drugs. That's been for the better part of fifteen years."

"If you can believe him," Bennet said. "I don't know how much you could tell from the brief time you spent. You were there for what, an hour?"

"About that," I said. "I'm not exactly an amateur. I've dealt with addicts in the past and believe me, he didn't look like one. I can spot a liar, too."

"No offense," he said. "I'm skeptical by nature when it comes to him. He always put on a good show." He finished his martini, holding the glass by the stem. The last vestiges of the gin formed a distinct scallop along the rim. He reached for the pitcher and poured himself another drink.

"Who else did you talk to?" Donovan asked, reasserting his presence. He was clearly running the show and wanted to make sure Bennet remained aware of it. For his part, Bennet seemed more interested in his martini than the conversation. I could see the lines of tension in his face smooth out. His questions were meant to demonstrate his control of himself.

I shrugged. "I made one stop in town and mentioned Guy in passing to the woman who runs the general store. There couldn't be more than five or six hundred residents and I figure everyone there knows everybody else's business. She didn't bat an eye and had no comment about him one way or the other. The pastor and his wife seemed genuinely fond of him and spoke with some pride of the distance he's come. They could have been lying, putting on a show, but I doubt it. Most people aren't that good at improvising."

Jack picked up a cracker and lifted the dollop of Cheez Whiz off the surface like he was licking the filling from an Oreo. "So what's the deal? Is he born-again? Has he been baptized? Do you think he's accepted our Lord Jesus in his heart?" His sarcasm was offensive.

I turned to stare at him. "You have a problem with that?"

"Why would I have a problem? It's his life," Jack said.

Donovan shifted in his seat. "Anybody else have a question?"

Jack popped the cracker in his mouth and wiped his fingers on a napkin while he munched. "I think it's great. I mean, maybe he won't want the money. If he's such a good Christian, maybe he'll opt for the spiritual over the materialistic."

Bennet snorted with annoyance. "His being a Christian has nothing to do with it. He's penniless. You heard her. He's got nothing. He's flat broke."

"I don't know that he's broke. I never said that," I interjected.

Now it was Bennet's turn to stare. "You seriously think he's going to turn down a great big whack of dough?"

Donovan looked at me. "Good question," he said. "What's your feeling on the subject?"

"He never asked about the money. At the time I think he was more interested in the idea that you'd hired someone to find him. He seemed touched at first and then embarrassed when he realized he'd misunderstood."

"Misunderstood what?" Christie said.

"He thought I'd been asked to locate him because of family interest or concern. It became obvious pretty quickly that the point of the visit was to notify him of his father's death and advise him he was a possible beneficiary under the terms of Bader's will."

"Maybe if he thinks we're all kissy-kissy, he'll give up the money and opt for love instead," Jack suggested.

Donovan ignored him. "Did he say anything about talking to an attorney?"

"Not really. I told him to get in touch with Tasha, but she's the attorney for the estate and she's not going to advise him about that aspect of the situation. If he calls her, she'll refer him to a lawyer unless he already has one."

Donovan said, "In other words, what you're saying is we don't have any idea what he'll do."

Bennet spoke up. "Of course we do. There's no mystery. He wants the *money*. He's not a fool."

"How do you know what Guy wants?" Christie responded with a flash of irritation.

Bennet went right on. "Kinsey should have asked for his signature on a quitclaim. Get him signed off. Make a settlement before he has a chance to think too much."

Donovan said, "I asked Tasha about that. I suggested we draw up a disclaimer, thinking Kinsey could take it with her. Tasha nixed that. She said a disclaimer would be meaningless because he could always maintain later he wasn't properly represented or he was unduly influenced, overcome by the emotions of the moment, shit like that, which would make it useless. I thought her point was well taken. Tell the man his father's dead and then whip out a quitclaim? It's like waving a red flag in front of a bull."

Christie spoke up again, saying, "Kinsey had a good idea. She pointed out that since the two wills were drawn up just three years apart that the witnesses for the second will might have been the same as the ones for the first. If we can track down the witnesses, it's always possible one of them was aware of the provisions."

"Like a secretary or a paralegal?" Donovan asked.

"It's possible. Or maybe the clerk/typist acted as a witness. *Somebody* had to be involved in the preparation of that document," I said.

"If there was one," Jack said.

Donovan's mouth pulled down as he considered the point. "Worth a try."

"To what end?" Jack asked. "I'm not saying we shouldn't make the effort, but it probably won't do any good. You can be a witness to a will without being aware of what's in it. Besides, what if the second will left everything to Guy? Then we'd really be screwed."

Bennet was impatient. "Oh come on, Jack. Whose side are you on? At least the witnesses could testify the second will was signed. I heard Dad say half a dozen times Guy wasn't getting a thing—we all heard him say that—so wouldn't that make a difference?"

"Why should it? Dad had the will. He kept it in a file right upstairs. How do you know he didn't revoke it in the end? Suppose he tore it up before he died? He had notice enough. He knew his days were numbered."

"He would have told us," Bennet said.

"Not necessarily."

"Jesus, Jack. I'm telling you, he said Guy would get nothing. We've been over this a hundred times and he was adamant."

"It doesn't matter what he said. You know how he was when it came to Guy. He never stuck to his guns. *We* might have been forced to toe the mark, but not him."

Donovan cleared his throat and set his glass down with a sharp tap. "All right. Knock it off, you two. This is getting us nowhere. We've been through enough of this. Let's just see what Guy does. We might not have a problem. We don't know at this point. Tasha said she'd contact him if he doesn't get in touch with her first. I might drop him a note myself and we'll take it from there."

Bennet sat up straight. "Wait a minute. Who put you in charge? Why can't we discuss this? It concerns all of us."

"You want to discuss this? Fine. Go ahead," Donovan said. "We all know your opinion. You think Guy's a slimeball. You're completely antagonistic and with *that* attitude, you'll be pushing him right to the wall."

"You don't know any more about him than I do," Bennet said.

"I'm not talking about him. I'm talking about you. What makes you so sure he wants the money?"

"Because he hated us. That's why he left in the first place, isn't it? He'd do anything to get back at us and what better way than this?"

"You don't know that," Donovan said. "You don't know what went on back then. He may not harbor any ill will towards us at all. You go in there punching and he's going to go on the offensive."

"I never did anything to Guy. Why would he hate me?" Jack said blithely. He seemed amused at the fireworks between his two brothers and I wondered if he didn't habitually goad them.

Bennet snorted again and he and Jack locked eyes. Something flashed between them but I wasn't sure what.

Donovan intervened again with a warning look at both. "Could we stick to the subject? Anybody have something new to contribute?"

"Donovan runs the family. He's the king," Bennet said. He looked at me with the slightly liquid eyes of someone who's had too much to drink. I'd seen him suck down two martinis in less than fifteen minutes and who knew what he'd consumed before he entered the room? "The man thinks I'm a dick. He may pretend to be supportive, but he doesn't mean a word of it. He and my father never actually gave me enough money to succeed at anything. And then when I failed—when a business went under—they were quick to point out how I'd misman-aged it. Dad always undercut me and the notion that Guy can come along now and insist on his share is just more of the same as far as I'm concerned. Who's looking out for our interests? It ain't *him*," he said, jerking a thumb at Donovan.

"Wait a minute. Hold it! Where's that coming from?"

"I've never really stood up and asked for what's mine," Bennet said. "I should have insisted a long time ago, but I bought into the program, the story you and Dad cooked up. 'Here, Bennet, you can have this pittance. Do the best you can with this pathetic sum of money. Make something of yourself and there'll be more where that came from. You can't expect us to underwrite the whole venture.' Blah blah blah. That's all I ever heard."

Donovan squinted at him, shaking his head. "I don't believe this. Dad gave you hundreds of thousands of dollars and you pissed it all away. How many chances do you think you get? There isn't a bank in this town that would have given you the first *dime*—"

"Bullshit! That's bullshit. I've worked like a dog and you know it. Hell, Dad had a lot of business failures and so have you. Now suddenly I have to sit here and fuckin' justify every move I make—just to get a little seed money."

Donovan looked at him with disbelief. "Where's all the money your partners put in? You blew that, too. You're so busy playing big shot, you're not tending to business. Half of what you do is outright fraudulent and you know it. Or if you don't, more's the pity because you'll end up in jail."

Bennet pointed a finger, poking the air repeatedly as if it were an elevator button. "Hey, I'm the one taking risks. I'm the one with my ass on the line. You never put yourself out there on the firing line. You played it safe. You were Daddy's little boy, the little piggy who stayed home and did exactly what Daddy said. And now you want credit for being such an all-fired success. Well, fuck that. To hell with you."

"Watch the *f* word. Ladies present," Jack said in a singsong tone.

"Shut up, you little piss. No one's talking to you!"

Christie cast a look in my direction and then raised a hand, saying, "Hey, fellas. Couldn't we postpone this until later? Kinsey doesn't want to sit here and listen to this. We asked her to have a drink, not a ringside seat."

I took my cue from her and used the opportunity to get to my feet. "I think I should leave you alone to discuss this, but I really don't think you need to worry about Guy. He seems like a nice man. That's the bottom line from my perspective. I hope everything works out."

A paragraph of awkward verbiage ensued: apologies for the outburst, hasty explanations of the strain everyone was under in the wake of Bader's death. Personally, I thought they were a bunch of ill-mannered louts and if my bill had been paid I might have told them as much. As it was, they assured me no offense was intended and I assured them, in turn, that none had been taken. I can fib with the best of them when there's money at stake. We shook hands all around. I was thanked for my time. I thanked them for the drink and took my leave of them.

"I'll walk out with you," Christie said.

There was a moment of quiet as we left the living room. I hadn't realized I was holding my breath until the door closed behind us and I could suck in some fresh air.

"Let me grab a jacket," Christie said as we crossed the foyer. She made a detour to the closet, pulling on a dark wool car coat as we passed into the night air.

The temperature had dropped and a dampness seemed to rise up from the cobblestones. The exterior lights were now on, but the illumination was poor. I could see the dim shape of my car, parked on the far side of the courtyard, and we headed in that direction. The lighted front windows threw truncated panels of yellow on the driveway in front of us. In the living room, the three Malek brothers were more than likely engaged in fisticuffs by now.

"Thanks for getting me out of there."

"I'm sorry you had to see that. What a zoo," she said. She shoved her hands in her pockets. "That goes on all the time and it drives me insane. It's like living in the middle of a giant preschool free-for-all. They're all three years old. They're still slugging it out over the same toy truck. The tension in this house is unreal half the time."

"Bennet's drinking doesn't help."

"It's not just that. I came into the marriage thinking I was going to be part of a loving family. I never had any brothers and I thought the idea was keen. They seemed close at first. I mean, they sure fooled me. I guess I should have figured out that three grown men still living together under Daddy's roof didn't exactly speak of mental health, but what did I know? My family's so screwed up, I wouldn't know a healthy one if it leapt up and bit me. I wanted kids. Looks like I got 'em," she remarked in a wry aside. "I hate sitting around watching these 'boys' bicker and connive. You ought to see them operate. They fight over absolutely everything. Anything that comes up, they all instantly take the most disparate positions possible. Then they all take sides and form these temporary coalitions. It'll be Donovan and Jack against Bennet one day. The next day, Bennet and Jack form a team against Donovan. The allegiances vary according to the subject matter, but there's never accord. There's never any sense of all for one and one for all. Everybody wants to be right—morally superior—and at the same time, everybody feels completely misunderstood."

"Makes me glad to be an orphan."

"I'm with you on *that* one." She paused with a smile. "Or maybe I'm just annoyed because none of them are ever on my side. I live with a perpetual stomachache."

"You don't have any kids?"

"Not yet. I keep trying, but of course I can't seem to get pregnant in this atmosphere. I'm coming up on forty so if something doesn't happen soon, it's going to be too late."

"I thought women were having babies into their fifties these days."

"Not me. Forget it. Life's hard enough as it is. I mean, what kid would volunteer to come into a house like *this?* It's disgusting."

"Why do you stay?"

"Who says I'll stay? I told Donovan last fall, I said, 'One more round, buddy, and I'm outta here.' So what happens next? Bader up and dies. I don't feel I can walk out when things are such a mess. Also, I suppose I still harbor the dim hope that things'll work out somehow."

"I'm sure my finding Guy couldn't be a help," I said.

"I don't know about that. At least now maybe the three of them will gang up against *him.* In the end, that might be the only issue they agree on."

I glanced toward the lighted windows of the living room. "You call *that* 'agreement'?"

"Oh, they'll get around to it. There's nothing like the common enemy to unify the troops. The truth is, Guy's the one I feel sorry for. They'll take him to the cleaners if they have half a chance and from what you say, he's the best of the lot."

"Donovan seems okay," I said.

"Ha. That's what I thought, too. He puts up a good front, but that's all that is. He's learned how to function in the business world so he's got a little more polish. I'm sure nobody said so, but I know they were impressed with the job you did."

"Well, I appreciate that, but at this point, these people don't need a PI—."

"They need a referee," she laughed. "Tasha didn't do you any favors when she got you involved in this. I'm sorry you had to see 'em at their worst. Then again, at least you can appreciate what I have to live with."

"Don't worry about it. It's finished business," I said.

We said our good-nights and I slid in behind the wheel, taking a few minutes to get my car warmed up. The residual tension had left me feeling icy cold and I drove home with the VW heater level pulled to maximum effect. This consisted of a thin tongue of warm air licking at the bottoms of my shoes. The rest of me was freezing, a cotton turtle-neck and wool blazer providing little in the way of insulation. As I turned onto my street, I gave brief consideration to having dinner up at Rosie's. I hadn't managed to eat so much as an unpitted olive at the Maleks' during the cocktail hour. I'd pictured sumptuous canapés that I could chow down instead of dinner, but the uproar had made even the Cheez Whiz seem less than appetizing. At the back of my mind, I knew I was avoiding the idea of going home to an empty apartment. Better now than later. It was only going to get worse.

I parked my car close to the corner and hoofed my way back to Henry's driveway. A dense fog had begun to blow in from the beach and I was heartened by the fact that I'd left a light on in my living room. At least letting myself in wouldn't feel so much like breaking and entering. I passed through the squeaky gate with my house key at the ready, unlocked my door, and tossed my handbag on the kitchen counter. I heard the downstair's toilet flush and a thrill of fear washed over me. Then the bathroom door opened and Robert Dietz walked out, looking as startled as I was. "I didn't hear you come in," he said. "I forgot to give back your key."

"What are you doing here? I thought you left."

"I got as far as Santa Maria and had to come back. I was halfway down the street and I missed you like crazy. I don't want us leaving each other on a bad note."

I felt a pain in my chest, something fragile and sharp that made me take a deep breath. "I don't see a way to resolve our basic differences."

"We can be friends without resolution. I mean, can't we?"

"How do I know?" I tried to shut down, but I couldn't quite manage it. I had an inexplicable urge to weep about something. Usually good-byes do that, tender partings in movies accompanied by music guaranteed to rip your heart out. The silence between us was just as painful to me.

"Have you had dinner?"

"I hadn't decided about that yet. I just had drinks with the Maleks," I said faintly. The words sounded odd and I wanted to pat myself on the chest as a way of consoling myself. I could have handled the situation if only he hadn't come back. The day had been hard, but I'd survived it.

"You want to talk?"

I shook my head, not trusting my voice.

"Then what? You decide. I'll do anything you want."

I looked away from him, thinking about the fearful risks of intimacy, the potential for loss, the tender pain implicit in any bond between two creatures—human or beast, what difference did it make? In me, the instinct for survival and the need for love had been at war for years. My caution was like a wall I'd built to keep me safe. But safety is an illusion and the danger of feeling too much is no worse than the danger of being numb. I looked back at him and saw my pain mirrored in his eyes.

He said, "Come here." He made a gesture with his hand, coaxing me to move closer.

I crossed the room. Dietz leaned into me like a ladder left behind by a thief.

9

Dietz's knee was so swollen and painful he couldn't make it up the stairs, so we unfolded the sofa bed. I brought the duvet down from the loft. We turned off the lamp and crawled naked beneath the comforter's downy weight like polar bears in a cave. We made love in the puffy igloo of the quilt while around us streetlights streamed through the porthole window like moonlight on snow. For a long time, I simply drank in the musky scent of him, hair and skin, feeling my way blindly across all his textured surfaces. The heat from his body thawed my cold limbs. I felt like a snake curling up in a patch of sunlight, warmed to the depths after a long unforgiving winter. I remembered his ways from our three months together—the look on his face, the hapless sounds he made. What I'd forgotten was the smoldering response he awakened in me.

There was a brief time in my youth when my behavior was both reckless and promiscuous. Those were the days when there seemed to be no consequence to sex that wasn't easily cured. In the current marketplace, you'd have to be a fool—or suicidal—to risk the casual encounter without a lot of straight talk and doctors' certificates changing hands. For my purposes, celibacy is my habitual state. I suppose it's a lot like living in times of famine. Without hope of satiation, hunger diminishes and the appetite fades. With Dietz, I could feel all my physical senses quicken, the yearning for contact overcoming my natural reticence. Dietz's injury required patience and ingenuity, but somehow we managed. The process entailed considerable laughter at our contortions and quiet concentration during the moments between.

Finally, at ten, I flung the covers aside, exposing our sweaty bodies to the arctic temperatures surrounding us. "I don't know about you, but I'm starving," I said. "If we don't stop and eat soon, I'll be dead before morning."

Thirty minutes later, showered and dressed, we found ourselves sitting up at Rosie's in my favorite booth. She and William were both working, he behind the bar and Rosie out waiting tables. Ordinarily, the kitchen closed down at ten, and I could see she was just on the verge of saying as much when she noticed the whisker burn that had set my cheeks aflame. I put my chin in my palm, but not before she caught sight of my sex rash. The woman may be close to seventy, but she's not unperceptive. She seemed to take in at a glance both the source of our satisfaction and our avid interest in food. I thought the application of my makeup had successfully disguised my chafed flesh, but she was visibly smirking as she recited the meal she intended to prepare for us. With Rosie, there's no point in even pretending to order. You eat what she decides will be perfect for the occasion. In honor of Dietz's return, I noticed her English was marginally improved.

She parked herself sideways to the table, wiggling slightly in place, refusing to look directly at either of us after that first sly glance. "Now. Here's what you gonna get and don't make with the usual face—like this—while I'm telling you." She pulled her mouth down, eyes rolling, to show Dietz my usual enthusiasm for her choices. "I'm fixing Korhelyleves, is also called Souse's Soup. Is taking couple pounds of sauerkraut, paprika, smoked sausage, and some sour cream. Is guaranteed to perk up tired senses of which you look like you got a lot. Then, I'm roasting you little cheeken that I'm serve with mushroom pudding—is very good—and for efter, is hazelnut torte, but no coffee. You need sleep. I'm bringing wine in a minute. Don't go way."

We didn't leave until midnight. We didn't sleep until one, wound together on the narrow width of the sofa bed. I'm not accustomed to sleeping with someone else and I can't say it netted me any restful results. Because of his knee, Dietz was forced to lie on his back with a pillow supporting his left leg. This gave me two choices: I could lie pressed against him with my head resting on his chest, or flat on my back with our bodies touching along their lengths.

I tried one and then the other, tossing relentlessly as the hours ticked away. Half the time, I could feel the sofa's metal mechanism cut across my back, but if I switched to the other position with my head on his chest, I suffered from heatstroke, a dead arm, and a canned left ear. Sometimes I could feel the exhalation of his breath on my cheek and the effect drove me mad. I found myself counting as he breathed, in and out, in and out. In moments, the rhythm changed and there'd be a long pause in which I wondered if he were in the process of dropping dead. Dietz slept like a soldier under combat conditions. His snores were gentle snuffles, just loud enough to keep me on sentry duty, but not quite loud enough to draw enemy fire.

I slept finally—amazingly—and woke at seven energized. Dietz had made coffee and he was reading the paper, dressed, his hair damp, a pair of half-glasses sitting low on his nose. I watched him for a few minutes until his gaze came up to mine.

"I didn't know you wore glasses."

"I was too vain before this. The minute you were out the door, I put 'em on," he said with that crooked smile of his.

I turned on my side, folding my right arm under my cheek. "What time will the boys be expecting you?"

"Early afternoon. I have motel reservations at a place close by. If they want to spend the night, I'll have room."

"I'll bet you look forward to seeing them."

"Yes, but I'm nervous about it, too. I haven't seen them for two years—since I left for Germany. I'm never quite sure what to talk about with them."

"What do you talk to anyone about? Mostly bullshit."

"Even bullshit requires a context. It gets awkward for them, too. Sometimes we end up going to the movies just to have something to talk about later. I'm not exactly a fount of paternal advice. Once I quiz them about girlfriends and classes, I'm about out of conversation."

"You'll do fine."

"I hope. What about you? What's your day looking like?"

"I don't know. This is Saturday, so I don't have to work. I'll probably nap. Starting soon."

"You want company?"

"Dietz," I said, outraged, "if you get in this bed again, I won't be able to walk."

"You're an amateur."

"I am. I'm not used to this stuff."

"How about some coffee?"

"Let me brush my teeth first."

After breakfast, we went down to the beach. The day was cloudy, the marine layer holding in the heat like foam insulation. The temperature was close to seventy and the air soft and fruity, with a tropical scent. Santa Teresa winters are filled with such contradictions. One day will feel icy while the next day feels mild. The ocean had a slick sheen, reflecting the uniform white of the sky. We took off our shoes and carried them, scuffling along the water's edge with the frothy play of waves rolling across our bare feet. Seagulls hovered overhead, screeching, while two dogs leaped in unison, snapping at the birds as if they were low-flying Frisbees.

Dietz took off at nine, holding me crushed against him before he got in the car. I leaned on the hood and we kissed for a while. Finally, he pulled back and studied my face. "If I come back in a couple of weeks, will you be here?"

"Where else would I go?"

"I'll see you then," he said.

"Don't worry about me. Any old day will do," I remarked, waving, as his car receded down the block. Dietz hated to be specific about dates because it made him feel trapped. Of course, the effect of his vagueness was to keep me feeling hooked. I shook my head to myself as I returned to my place. How did I end up with a man like him?

I spent the rest of the morning getting my apartment tidied up. It didn't really take much work, but it was satisfying nonetheless. This time I wasn't really feeling depressed. I knew Dietz would be coming back, so my virtuous activity had more to do with reestablishing my boundaries than warding off the blues. Since he'd done the grocery shopping, my cupboard was full and my refrigerator stocked, a state that always contributes to my sense of security. As long as you have sufficient toilet paper, how far wrong can life go?

At lunchtime I spotted Henry sitting in the backyard at a little round picnic table he'd picked up in a garage sale the previous fall. He'd spread out some graph paper, his reference books, and a cross-word key. As a pastime, Henry constructs and sells crossword puzzles for those wee yellow books sold near grocery store checkout lanes. I made a peanut-butter-and-pickle sandwich and joined him in the sunshine.

"You want one?" I asked, holding out my plate.

"Thanks, but I just had lunch," he said. "Where'd Dietz disappear to? I thought he intended to stick around."

I filled him in on the "romance" and we chatted idly while I ate my sandwich. The texture of the peanut butter was a sublime contrast to the crunch of the bread-and-butter pickles. The diagonal cut exposed

more filling than a vertical cut would and I savored the ratio of salti-
ness to tart. This ranked right up there with sex without taking off any
clothes. I made a sort of low moan, nearly swooning with pleasure,
and Henry glanced up at me. "Give me a bite of that."

I let him have the plump center portion, keeping my fingers positioned so he couldn't take too much.

He chewed for a moment, clearly relishing the intense blend of
flavors. "Very weird, but not bad." This is what he always says when he
samples this culinary marvel.

I tried another bite myself, pointing to the puzzle he was working
on. "How's this one coming? You've never really told me how you go
about your business." Henry was a crossword fanatic, subscribing to
the *New York Times* so he could do the daily puzzle, which he completed in ink. Sometimes, to amuse himself, he left every other letter
blank, or filled in the outer borders first in a spiral moving toward the
center. The puzzles he wrote himself seemed very difficult to me,
though he claimed they were easy. I'd watched him construct dozens
without understanding the strategy.

"I've actually upgraded my technique. My approach used to be
haphazard. I'm better organized these days. This is a small one, only
fifteen by fifteen. This is the pattern I'm using," he said, indicating a
template with the gridwork of black squares already laid in.

"You don't devise the format as well?"

"Usually not. I've used this one several times and it suits my purposes. They're all symmetrical and if you'll notice, no area is closed
off. The rules say the black squares can't exceed more than one sixth
of the total number. There are a few other rules tossed in. For example, you can't use any words of fewer than three letters, stuff like that.
The good ones have a theme around which the answers are organized."

I picked up one of his reference books and turned it over in my
hand. "What's this?"

"That book lists words in alphabetical order from three through
fifteen letters. And that one's a crossword finisher that lists words in a
complicated alphabetical order up through seven letters."

I smiled at the enthusiasm that had crept into his voice. "How'd
you get into this?"

He waved dismissively. "Do enough of 'em and you can't help it.
You have to have a go at it yourself, just to see what it's like. They
even have crossword championships, which started in 1980. You ought
to see those puppies go. The puzzles are projected on an overhead

screen. A real whiz can answer sixty-four questions in under eight minutes."

"Are you ever tempted to enter?"

He shook his head, penciling in a clue. "I'm too slow and much too easily rattled. Besides, it's a serious business, like bridge tournaments." His head came up. "That's your phone," he said.

"It is? Your hearing must be better than mine." I hopped up from the table and made a beeline for my place, picking up the receiver just as my answering machine did. I reached for the Off button as my voice completed its request for messages. "Hello, hello. It's me. I'm really home," I sang.

"Hey," a man's voice said mildly. "This is Guy. Hope you don't mind my calling on a weekend."

"Not at all. What's up?"

"Nothing much," he said. "Donovan called me at the church. I guess last night the three of them—him and Bennet and Jack—had a meeting. He says they want me to come down for a few days so we can talk about the will."

I felt my whole body go quiet. "Really. That's interesting. You going to do it?"

"I think so. I might, but I'm not really sure. I had a long talk with Peter and Winnie. Peter thinks it's time to open up a dialogue. He's got a prayer meeting in Santa Teresa tomorrow, so it works out pretty good. They can bring me down after church, but he thought it'd be smart to talk to you about it first."

I was silent for a moment. "You want the truth?"

"Well, yeah. That's why I called."

"I wouldn't do it if I were you. I was over there last night and it all seems very tense. It's nothing you'd want to be exposed to."

"How so?"

"Feelings are running high and your showing up at this point is only going to make things worse."

"That was my first reaction, but then I got to thinking. I mean, Donovan called me. I didn't call him," he said. "Seems to me if the three of them are offering a truce, I should at least be willing to meet 'em halfway. It can't hurt."

I suppressed an urge to start shrieking at him. Shrieking, I've discovered, is really not a sound method for persuading other people to your point of view. I'd seen his brothers in action and Guy was no match. I wouldn't trust those three under any circumstances. Given Guy's emotional state, I could see why he'd be tempted, but he'd be a fool to go into that house without counsel. "Maybe it's a truce and maybe not. Bader's death has brought up all kinds of issues," I said. "You go in unprepared and you'll end up taking on a whole raft of shit. You'd be walking into a nightmare."

"I understand."

"I don't think so," I said. "Not to criticize your brothers, but these are not nice fellows, at least where you're concerned. There's a lot of friction between them and your appearance is only going to add fuel to the fire. I mean, honestly. You can't imagine the dynamic." I noticed the pitch and volume of my voice going up.

"I have to try," he said.

"Maybe so, but not *that* way."

"Meaning what?"

"You're going to find yourself in exactly the same position you were in when you left. You'll be the fall guy, the scapegoat for all their hostility."

I could hear him shrug. He said, "Maybe we need to talk about that then. Get it out in the open and deal with it."

"It's out in the open. Those three aren't shy about anything. The conflicts are all right out there in front of God and everyone and believe me, you don't want their venom directed at you."

"Donovan doesn't seem to bear me any ill will and from what he says, Bennet and Jack don't either. The truth is, I've changed and they need to see that. How else can I persuade 'em if it isn't face-to-face?"

I could feel my eyes cross while I tried controlling my impatience. I knew I'd be smarter to keep my mouth shut, but I've never been good at keeping my opinions to myself. "Look, Guy, I don't want to stand here and try to tell you your business, but this isn't about you. This is about their relationship to each other. It's about your father and whatever's been going on in the years since you left. You'll end up being the target for all the anger they've stored up. And why put yourself through that."

"Because I want to be connected again. I screwed up. I admit that and I want to make it up to them. Peter says there can't be any healing unless we sit down together."

"That's all well and good, but there's a lot more at stake. What if the subject of the money comes up?"

"I don't care about the money."

"Bullshit. That's bull. Do you have any idea how much money we're talking about?"

"Doesn't make any difference. The money doesn't matter to me. I don't need money. I'm happy as I am."

"That's what you say now, but how do you know that won't change?

Why create problems for yourself later on? Have you talked to Tasha? What's she say about this?"

"I never talked to her. I called the office in Lompoc, but she'd already left for San Francisco and after that, the secretary said she was taking off for Utah on a ten-day ski trip."

"So call her in Utah. They have phones up there."

"I tried that. They wouldn't give me her number. They said if she called in, they'd give her my name and number and she'd call if she could."

"Then try someone else. Call another attorney. I don't want you talking to your brothers without legal advice."

"It's not about legalities. It's about mending the breach."

"Which is exactly what's going to make you a sitting duck. Your agenda has nothing to do with theirs. They don't give a shit about forgiveness, if you'll pardon my French."

"I don't see it that way."

"I know you don't. That's why we're having this argument," I shrieked. "Suppose they try to pressure you into making a decision?"

"About what?"

"About anything! You don't even know what's in your best interest. If your sole aim is to make peace, you're only going to get screwed."

"How can I get screwed if I don't want anything? They can keep the money if that's the only thing standing between us."

"Well, if *you* don't want the money, why not give it to the church?" The minute I said it, I wanted to bite my tongue. His motives were clean. Why introduce the complication?

He was silent for a moment. "I hadn't thought about that. That's a good point."

"Forget it. Just skip that. All I'm saying is don't go in there alone. Get help so you don't do something you'll regret."

"Why don't you go?"

I groaned and he laughed in response. Going with him was the last thing I wanted to do. He needed protection, but I didn't think it was appropriate for me to step in. What did I have to offer in the way of assistance? "Because it's not my place. I'm not objective. I don't know the law and I don't have any idea what your legal position is. You'd be foolish to come down here and have a conversation with them. Just wait for ten days until Tasha gets back. Don't do anything yet. There's no reason you have to hop-to the minute Donovan whistles. You should be doing this on your terms, not his."

I could hear his reluctance to accept what I was saying. Like most of us, he'd made up his mind before he asked. "You know something?

This is the truth," he said. "I prayed about this. I asked God for guidance and this was the answer I got."

"Well, try Him again. Maybe you misunderstood the message."

He laughed. "I did that in a way. I opened my Bible and put my finger on the page. Know what the passage was?"

"I can't imagine," I said dryly.

" 'Be it known unto you therefore, men *and* brethren, that through this man is preached unto you the forgiveness of sins: And by him all that believe are justified from all things, from which ye could not be justified by the law of Moses.' " Like many of the faithful, he could recite Bible verses like song lyrics.

This time the silence was mine. "I can't argue that. I don't even know what it means. Look, if you're determined to do this, you'll do it, I'm sure. I'm just urging you to take someone with you."

"I just did. I asked you."

"I'm not talking about me! What about Peter and Winnie? I'm sure they'd be willing to help if you asked and they'd do a much better job. I don't know the first thing about counseling or mediation or anything else. Aside from that, all this family-related stuff gives me the willies."

I could hear Guy smile and his tone was affectionate. "Strange you should say that because somehow it feels like you're part of this. I don't know how, but it sure seems like that to me. Don't you have some kind of issue around family yourself?"

I held the phone away from me and squinted at the handset. "Who, me? Absolutely not. Why would you say that?"

Guy laughed. "I don't know. It just came to me in a flash. Maybe I'm wrong, but it feels like you're connected."

"My only connection is professional. I was hired to do a job. That's the only link I see." I kept my tone casual to demonstrate my nonchalance, but I was forced to put a hand against the small of my back, where an inexplicable drop of sweat was trickling down into my underpants. "Why don't you have a talk with Peter again. I know you're eager to make amends, but I don't want you walking into the lion's den. We all know how the lions and the Christians came out."

He was silent for a moment and then seemed to change the subject. "Where's your apartment?"

"What makes you ask?" I was unwilling to be specific until I knew where he was headed.

"How about this? Maybe we can do this another way. Donovan says everyone's gone tomorrow until five o'clock. Peter'll give me a lift into town, but his schedule's too tight to do much more than that. If he drops me off at your place, could you give me a ride the rest of the

way? You don't have to stay. I understand you don't want to be involved and that's fine with me."

"I don't really see how that addresses the point."

"It doesn't. I'm just asking for a ride. I can handle everything else if
you can get me over there."

"You're not going to listen to me, are you," I said.

"I did listen. The problem is I disagree."

I hesitated, but really couldn't see any reason to refuse. I was already feeling churlish because I'd put up such resistance. "That
sounds all right. Sure. I can do that," I said. "What time would you get
here?"

"Three? Somewhere around then. I don't mean to be a bother.
Peter's meeting is downtown, at that church on the corner of State and
Michaelson. Is that anywhere close? Because I could walk over to your
place and we could go from there."

"Close enough," I said, feeling crabby and resigned. "Look, why
don't you give me a call when you get in. I'll swing by the church and
pick you up."

"That'd be good. That's great. Are you sure this is okay?"

"No, but don't press your luck. I'm willing to do this much, but
don't go asking for reassurance on top of it."

He laughed. "I'm sorry. You're right. I'll see you then," he said. He
disconnected on his end.

As I hung up the phone, I was already having doubts. Amazing how
quickly someone else's problems become yours. Trouble creates a vacuum into which the rest of us get sucked.

I found myself pacing the living room, inwardly refuting his ridiculous claim about the relevance of his situation to mine. His conflict
about family had *nothing* to do with me. I sat down at my desk and
made some notes to myself. In case Tasha asked, I thought it might be
wise to keep a record of the discussion we'd just had. I hoped he
wasn't going to get a bug up his butt about giving all his money to the
church. That was really going to cause a problem if he got greedy on
behalf of Jubilee Evangelical. I omitted any reference to a charitable
donation, thinking if I didn't write it down, the subject wouldn't exist.

I picked up the phone again and put a call through to the Maleks.
Myrna picked up and I asked to speak to Christie. I waited, listening
as Myrna crossed the foyer and bellowed up the stairs to Christie.
When Christie finally picked up the phone on her end, I filled her in
briefly on my conversation with Guy. "Will you keep me informed
about what's going on?" I asked. "I'll drop him off, but after that he's
on his own. I think he needs protection, but I don't want to get into

my rescue costume. He's a big boy and this is really none of my business. I'd feel better if I knew there was someone in your camp keeping an eye on him."

"Oh, right. And leave the rescue to me," she said, her tone of voice wry.

I laughed. "Not to get trivial, but he *is* cute," I said.

"Really? Well, that's good. I'm a big fan of cute. In fact, that's how I vote for a presidential candidate," she said. "Personally, I don't think you have anything to worry about. After you left last night, the three of them talked long and hard. Once they got done ripping each other apart, they settled down into some meaningful conversation."

"I'm glad to hear that. I was actually a bit puzzled why Donovan had called him. What's their inclination? Do you mind if I ask?"

"I guess it depends on what he says to them. Ultimately, of course, this is probably something for the lawyers to discuss. I think they want to be honorable. On the other hand, five million dollars might distort anyone's notion of what's fair."

"Ain't that the truth."

10

I pulled over to the curb in front of the Faith Evangelical Church the next afternoon at three. Guy had called me at 2:45 and I'd left the apartment shortly thereafter, taking a few minutes to put gas in my car. The sun was out again and the day felt like summer. I wore the usual jeans and a T-shirt, but I'd traded my Reeboks and sweat socks for a pair of openwork sandals in honor of the sudden heat. The grass on the church lawn had been recently cut and the sidewalk was littered with fine green at the edge. The turf itself featured a pale dun-colored haze where the cut blades had browned in the sun. A number of gullible daffodils had taken these balmy temperatures as an invitation to pop their green shafts into view.

There was no sign of Peter, but Guy was standing on the corner with a backpack at his feet. He spotted my car and pretended to hitchhike, holding his thumb out with a smile on his face. I confess when I saw him I could feel my heart break. He'd had his hair cut and his face was so freshly shaved he still sported a dot of toilet paper where he'd nicked himself. He wore a navy blue suit that didn't fit well. The pants were baggy in the butt and slightly too long, the backs of his trouser cuffs brushing the sidewalk. The jacket was wide across the chest, which made the shoulder pads look as exaggerated as a

1940's zoot suit. The garment had probably been donated to a church rummage sale or maybe he'd bought it from someone weighing forty pounds more. Whatever the explanation, he wore his finery with a self-conscious air, clearly unaccustomed to the dress shirt and tie. I wondered if my own vulnerability had been as apparent during my lunch with Tasha. I'd approached my personal grooming with the same insecurity, perhaps netting myself the same sorry results.

Guy reached for his canvas backpack, clearly happy to see me. He seemed as innocent as a pup. There was a softness about him, something guileless and unformed, as if his association with Jubilee Evangelical had isolated him from worldly influences all these years. The reckless element in his nature was now tamed to a gentleness I'd rarely seen in a man.

He slid into the front seat. "Hey, Kinsey. How are you?" He held his backpack on his lap like a kid on his way to day camp.

I smiled in his direction. "You're all spiffed up."

"I didn't want my brothers to think I'd forgotten how to dress. What do you think of the suit?"

"The color's good on you."

"Thanks," he said, smiling with pleasure. "Oh. By the way, Winnie says hi."

"Hi to her," I said. "What's the deal on your return? When are you planning to go back to Marcella?"

Guy looked away from me out the car window on his side, the casualness of his tone belying its content. "Depends on what happens at the house. Donovan invited me to stay for a couple of days and I wouldn't mind that if everything works out all right. I guess if it doesn't work, it won't make any difference. I got money in my pocket. When I'm ready to leave, someone can give me a ride to the bus."

I was on the verge of volunteering my services and then thought better of it. I glanced over at him, making a covert study of his face in profile. In some lights, he looked every one of his forty-three years. In other moments his boyishness seemed a permanent part of his character. It was as if his development had been arrested at the age of sixteen, maybe twenty at the outside. He was scanning the streets, taking in the sights as if he were in a foreign country.

"I take it you don't get down here that often," I said.

He shook his head. "I don't have much occasion. When you live in Marcella, Santa Teresa seems too big and too far away. We go to Santa Maria or San Luis if we need anything." He looked over at me. "Can we do a quick tour? I'd like to see what's going on."

"I can do that. Why not? We have time."

I circled the block, coming back out onto State Street. I turned left, heading downtown, a short three blocks away. The business district wasn't much more than twenty blocks long and three or four blocks wide, terminating at Cabana Boulevard, which parallels the beach. For many years, the stores along upper State attracted the bulk of the downtown shoppers. Lower State was considered the less-desirable end of town, the street lined with thrift stores, third-rate eateries, a movie theater that smelled of urine, and half a dozen noisy bars and run-down transient hotels. Lately, the area had undergone a resurrection, and the classy businesses had begun to migrate southward along the thoroughfare. Now it was upper State that featured deserted storefronts while lower State had captured all the tourist trade. In warm weather, pedestrians drifted up from the beach, a ragtag parade of sight-seers in shorts, licking ice-cream cones.

"It's grown," he remarked.

With a population of eighty-five thousand, Santa Teresa wasn't big, but the town had been flourishing. I tried to see it as he did, cataloging in my mind all the changes that had taken place in the last twenty years. Time-lapse photography would have shown tree trunks elongating, branches stretching out like rubber, some buildings erected while others vanished in a puff of smoke. Storefronts would flicker through a hundred variations: awnings, signs, and window displays, the liquidation sales of one business flashing across the plate glass before the next enterprise took its place. New structures would appear like apparitions, filling in the empty spaces until no gaps remained. I could remember when the downtown sidewalks were made wider, State Street narrowing to accommodate the planting of trees imported from Bolivia. Spanish-style benches and telephone booths had been added. Decorative fountains had appeared, looking like they'd been there for years. A fire had taken out two commercial establishments while an earthquake had rendered others unfit for use. Santa Teresa was one of the few towns that looked more elegant as time passed. The strict regulations of the Architectural Board of Review imposed an air of refinement that in other towns was wiped out by gaudy neon, oversized signage, and a hodgepodge of building styles and materials. As much as the local residents complained about the lengthy approval process, the result was a mix of simplicity and grace.

At Cabana, I drove out along the wharf, wheels thumping along the length. I turned at the end until we were headed back toward town. I motored north on State, seeing the same sights again from the reverse perspective. At Olive Grove, I turned right, driving past the Santa Teresa Mission and from there into the foothills where the Malek estate was tucked. I could sense Guy's interest quicken as the road angled upward. Much of the terrain in this area was undeveloped, the landscape littered with enormous sandstone boulders and prickly cactus with leaves as large as fleshy Ping-Pong paddles.

The Malek estate sat close to the borders of the backcountry, an oasis of dark green in a region dense with pale chaparral. At irregular intervals, fires had swept across the foothills in spectacular conflagrations, the blaze advancing from peak to peak, sucking up houses and trees, consuming every shred of vegetation. In the wake of these burns, species of native plants known as fire followers appeared, dainty beauties emerging from the ashes of the charred and the dead. I could still see the occasional black, twisted branches of the manzanitas, though it had been five or six years since the last big fire.

Once again, the iron gates at the entrance stood open, the long driveway disappearing around a shaded curve ahead. Somehow the Maleks' evergreens and palms looked alien set against the backdrop of raw mountains. Entering the estate, I sensed how the years of careful cultivation and the introduction of exotic plants had altered the very air that permeated the grounds.

"You nervous?" I asked.

"Scared to death."

"You can still back out."

"It's too late for that. Feels like a wedding where the invitations have gone out—you know, it's still possible to cancel, but it's easier to go through with it than make a fuss for everyone else."

"Don't turn all noble on me."

"It's not about 'noble.' I guess I'm curious."

I pulled into the courtyard and eased the VW around to the left. The garages at the end of the drive were all closed. The house itself looked deserted. All the windows were dark and most of the draperies were drawn. The visage was scarcely welcoming. The silence was broken only by the idling of my engine. "Well. This is it, I guess. Call if you need me. I wish you luck."

Guy glanced at me uneasily. "You have to leave already?"

"I really should," I said, though the truth was I had nothing else to do that afternoon.

"Don't you want to see the place? Why don't you stay a few minutes and let me show you around."

"I was just here for drinks. It hasn't changed since Friday night."

"I don't want to go inside. I have to work up my nerve. Why don't I show you the place. We could walk around outside. It's really beautiful," he said. He reached out impulsively and touched my bare arm. "Please?"

His fingers were cold and his apprehension was contagious. I didn't have the heart to leave him. "All right," I said reluctantly, "but I can't stay long."

"Great. That's great. I really appreciate this."

I turned off the engine. Guy left his backpack on the front seat and the two of us got out. We slammed the car doors in two quick, overlapping reports, like guns going off. At the last moment, I opened my door again and tossed my handbag in the back before I locked the car. As we crossed the courtyard, Myrna opened the front door and came out on the porch. She was wearing a semblance of uniform; a shapeless white polyester skirt with a matching overblouse, some vague cross between nursiness and household help.

I said, "Hi, Myrna. How are you? I didn't think anyone was here. This is Guy. I'm sorry. I don't remember anyone ever mentioning your last name."

"Sweetzer," she said.

Guy extended his hand, which flustered her to some extent. She allowed him one of those handshakes without cartilage or bone. His good looks probably had the same effect on her that they had on me. "Nice to meet you," he said.

"Nice to meet you, too," she replied by rote. "The family's back around five. You're to have the run of the house. I imagine you remember where your room is if you want to take your things on up."

"Thanks. I'll do that in a bit. I thought I'd show her the grounds first if that's okay with you."

"Suit yourself," she said. "The front door will be open if you want to come in that way. Dinner's at seven." She turned to me. "Will you be staying on as well?"

"I appreciate the invitation, but I don't think I should. The family needs time to get reacquainted. Maybe another time," I said. "I do have a question. Guy was asking about his father and it just occurred to me that you might know as much as anyone else. Weren't you his nurse?"

"One of them," she said. "I was his primary caregiver the last eight months. I stayed on as housekeeper at your brothers' request," she said, looking at Guy. Her delivery was staunch, as if we'd challenged her right to remain on the premises. From what I'd seen of her, she tended to be humorless, but with Guy she'd now added a grace note of resentment, reflecting the family's general attitude.

Guy's smile was sweet. "I'd like to talk to you about my dad some-time."

"Yes sir. He was a good man and I was fond of him."

There was an awkward moment, none of us knowing how to termi-nate the conversation. Myrna was the one who finally managed, say-ing, "Well, now. I'll let you go on about your business. I'll be in the kitchen if you should need anything. The cook's name is Enid, if you can't find me."

"I remember Enid," he said. "Thanks."

As soon as the door closed behind her, Guy touched my elbow and steered me off to the right. We crossed the courtyard together, heat drifting up from the sunbaked cobblestones. "Thanks for staying," he said.

"You're full of thanks," I remarked.

"I am. I feel blessed. I never expected to see the house again. Come on. We'll go this way."

We cut around the south side of the house, moving from hot, patchy sunlight into shade. To me, it felt like another sudden shift in seasons. In the space of fifty feet, we'd left summer behind. In the gloom of heavy shadow, the drop in air temperature was distinct and unwelcome, as if the months were rolling backward into winter again. Vestiges of the hot dry winds blew down the mountainside behind us, tossing restlessly across the treetops above our heads. We rambled beneath a canopy of shaggy-smelling juniper and pine. A carpet of fallen needles dampened our footsteps to a silence.

Near the house, I could see evidence of the gardeners—raked paths, the trimmed shape of bushes, a profusion of ferns ringed with small perfect stones—but the larger portion of the property was close to wilderness. Many of the plants had been allowed to grow un-checked. A violet-colored lantana tumbled along the terrace wall. A salmon pink bougainvillea climbed across a tangled stretch of brush. To our right, a solid wash of nasturtiums blanketed the banks of an empty creek bed. In the areas of bright sun, where the dry breezes riffled across the blossoms, several scents arose and mingled in an earthy cologne.

Guy seemed to scrutinize every square foot we traversed. "Every-thing looks so much bigger. I remember when some of these trees were just planted. Saplings were this tall and now look at them."

"Your memories sound happy. That surprises me somehow."

"This was a great spot to grow up. Mom and Dad bought the place when I was three years old. Donovan was five and the two of us thought we'd died and gone to heaven. It was like one great big playground. We could go anywhere we wanted and no one ever had to worry. We made forts and tree houses. We had sword fights with sticks. We played cowboys and Indians and went on jungle expeditions in the wilds of the sticker bushes. When Bennet was a little guy, we used to tie him to a stake and he'd wail like a banshee. We'd tell him we were going to burn him if he didn't shut up. He was younger than us and he was fair game."

"Nice."

"Boy-type fun," he said. "I guess girls don't do that."

"How could your parents afford a place like this? I thought your father made his money later, in the years since you left."

"Mom had some money from a trust fund. The down payment was hers. Actually, it wasn't that much money even for the time. The house was a white elephant. It was on the market for nearly ten years and it was empty all that time. The story we heard was that the previous owner had been murdered. It's not like the house was haunted, but it did seem tainted. Nobody could make a deal work. We were told it fell out of escrow five or six times before my parents came along and bought it. It was big and neglected. The wiring was bad and the plumbing was shot. Daylight was showing through big holes in the roof. Tree rats ran everywhere and there was a family of raccoons living in the attic. It took 'em years to pull it all together. In the meantime, Dad's plan was to buy adjacent properties if they came up for sale."

"What is it now, fifteen acres?"

"Is that right? The original parcel was six. There probably isn't a lot more land available in this area."

"Is this city land or county?"

"We're right at the upper edges of the city limits. Lot of what you're looking at up there is part of the Los Padres National Forest." The term *forest* was a misnomer. The arching mountain range above us was overgrown with nettle, ceanothus, pyracantha, and coastal sage scrub, the soil too poor to support many trees. In the higher elevations, a few pines might remain if the wildfires hadn't reached them.

We passed the tennis court, its surface cracked and weedy along the edges. A tennis racket had been tossed to one side, exposed to the elements long enough to warp, its nylon strings sprung. Beyond the tennis court, there was a glass-enclosed structure I hadn't seen from the drive. The lines of the building were low and straight, with a red-tile roof that had altered with time until its color was the burnt brown of old bricks.

"What's that?"

"The pool house. We have an indoor pool. Want to see it?"

"Might as well," I said. I trailed after him as he approached a covered flagstone patio. He crossed to the building's darkened windows and peered in. He moved to the door and tried the knob. The door was unlocked, but the frame was jammed and required a substantial push before it opened with the kind of scrape that set my teeth on edge.

"You really want to do this?" I asked.

"Hey, it's part of the tour."

To me, it felt like breaking and entering, a sport I prefer to get paid for. The sense of trespass was unmistakable, nearly sexual in tone, despite the fact that we'd been given permission to roam. We entered an anteroom that was used to store an assortment of play equipment: badminton rackets, golf clubs, baseball bats, a rack lined with a full set of croquet mallets and balls, Styrofoam kickboards for the pool, and a line of fiberglass surfboards that looked as if they'd been propped against the wall for years. The gardener was currently keeping his leaf blower and a riding mower in the space to one side. While I didn't see any spiders, the place had a spidery atmosphere. I wanted to brush my clothes hurriedly in case something had dropped down and landed on me unseen.

The pool was half-filled and something about the water looked really nasty. The decking around the pool was paved with a gritty-looking gray slate, not the sort of surface you'd want to feel under your bare feet. At one end of the room was an alcove furnished in rattan, though the cushions were missing from the sofa and matching chairs. The air was gloomy and I could hear the sound of dripping water. Any hint of chlorine had evaporated long ago and several unclassified life-forms had begun to ferment in the depths.

"Looks like it's time to fire the pool guy," I remarked.

"The gardener probably does the pool when he remembers," Guy said. "When we were kids this was great."

"What'd you and Donovan do to Bennet down here? Drown him? Hang him off the diving board? I can just imagine the fun you must have had."

Guy smiled, his thoughts somewhere else. "I broke up with a girl once down here. That's what sticks in my mind. Place was like a country club. Swimming, tennis, softball, croquet. We'd invite dates over for a swim and then we'd end up making out like crazy. Girl in a bathing suit isn't that hard to seduce. Jack was the all-time champ. He was randy as a rabbit and he'd go after anyone."

"Why'd you break up with her?"

"I don't remember exactly. Some rare moment of virtue and self-sacrifice. I liked her too much. I was a bad boy back then and she was too special to screw around with like the other ones. Or maybe odd's the better word. A little nutsy, too needy. I knew she was fragile and I didn't want to take the chance. I preferred the wild ones. No responsibility, no regrets, no holds barred."

"Were your parents aware of what was going on down here?"

"Who knows. I'm not sure. They were proponents of the 'boys will be boys' school of moral instruction. Any girl who gave in to us deserved what she got. They never said so explicitly, but that's the attitude. My mother was more interested in being everybody's pal. Set limits on a kid and you might have to take a stand at some point. She was into unconditional love, which to her meant the absence of prohibitions of any kind. It was easier to be permissive, you know what I mean? This was all part of the sixties' feel-good bullshit. Looking back, I can see how much she must have been affected by her illness. She didn't want to be the stern, disapproving parent. She must have known her days were numbered, even though she survived a lot longer than most. In those days, they did chemo and radiation, but it was all so crudely calibrated they probably killed more people than they cured. They just didn't have the technology or the sophisticated choice of treatments. It's different today where you got a real shot at survival. For her, the last couple of years were pure hell."

"It must have been hard on you."

"Pure agony," he said. "I was the child most identified with her. Don't ask me why, but Donovan and Bennet and Jack were linked to Dad while I was my mother's favorite. It drove me wild to see her fail. She was faltering and in pain, going downhill on what I knew would be her final journey."

"Were you with her when she died?"

"Yes. I was. The rest of 'em were gone. I forget now where they were. I sat in her room with her for hours that day. Most of the time she slept. She was so doped up on morphine, she could hardly stay awake. I was exhausted myself and laid my head on the bed. At one point, she reached out and put her hand on my neck. I touched her fingers and she was gone, just like that. So quiet. I didn't move for an hour.

"I just sat by the bed, leaning forward, with my head turned away from her and my face buried in the sheets. I thought maybe if I didn't look, she might come back again, like she was hovering someplace close and might return to her body as long as no one noticed she'd left. I didn't want to break faith."

"What happened to the girl you broke up with?"

"Patty? I have no idea. I wrote to her once, but never heard back. I've thought of her often, but who knows where she is now or what's happened to her. It might be the best thing I ever did, especially back then. What a bastard I was. I have a hard time connecting. It's like somebody else was doing it."

"But you're a good person now."

He shook his head. "I don't think of myself as good, but sometimes I think I come close to being real."

We left the pool house behind, moving temporarily onto the sunny stretch of lawn where I'd watched Jack hit golf balls. We were on the terrace below the house, shadows slanting toward us as we crossed the grass.

"How do you feel? You seem relaxed," I said.

"I'll be fine once they get here. You know how it is. Your fantasies are always stranger than reality."

"What do you picture?"

He smiled briefly. "I have no idea."

"Well, whatever it is, I hope you get what you need."

"Me, too, but in the long run, what difference does it make? You can't hide from God and that's the point," he said. "For a long time, I was walkin' down the wrong road, but now I've turned myself around and I'm goin' back the other way. At some point, I'll meet up with my past and make peace."

We had, by then, reached the front of the house again. "I better scoot," I said. "Let me know how it goes."

"I'll be fine."

"No doubt, but I'll be curious."

As I got into my car and turned the key in the ignition, I watched him head toward the front door with his backpack. I waved as I passed and then watched him in my rearview mirror as I eased down the drive. I rounded the curve and he was gone from view. It's painful to think of this in retrospect. Guy Malek was doomed and I delivered him into the hands of the enemy. As I pulled through the gates, I could see a car approach. Bennet was driving. My smile was polite and I waved at him. He stared at me briefly and then glanced away.

11

At ten o'clock Monday morning I received a call that should have served as a warning. Looking back, I can see that from that moment on, troubles began to accumulate at an unsettling rate. I'd gotten a late start and I was just closing the front gate behind me when I heard the muffled tone of the telephone ringing in my apartment. I did a quick reverse, trotting down the walkway and around the corner. I unlocked the front door and flung it open in haste, tossing my jacket and bag aside. I snatched up the receiver on the fourth ring, half expecting a wrong number or a market survey now that I'd made the effort. "Hello?"

"Kinsey. This is Donovan."

"Well, hi. How are you? Whew! Excuse the heavy breathing. I was already out the door and had to run for the phone."

Apparently, he wasn't in the mood for cheery chitchat. He got straight to the point. "Did you contact the press?"

It was not a subject I expected the man to broach at this hour or any other. I could feel a fuzzy question mark forming over my head while I pondered what he could possibly be talking about. "Of course not. About what?"

"We got a call from the *Dispatch* about an hour ago. Somebody tipped off a reporter about Guy's return."

"Really? That's odd. What's the point?" I knew the *Santa Teresa Dispatch* occasionally struggled to find noteworthy items for the Local section, but Guy's homecoming hardly seemed like a big-time news event. Aside from the family, who'd give a shit?

"They're playing it for human interest. Rags to riches. You know the tack, I'm sure. A lowly maintenance worker in Marcella, California, suddenly finds out he's a millionaire and comes home to collect. It's better than the lottery given Guy's personal history, as you well know."

"What do you mean, as *I* well know? I never said a word to the press. I wouldn't do that."

"Who else knew about it? No one in the family would leak a story like that. This is a sensitive issue. The last thing we need is *publicity.* Here we are trying to hammer out some kind of understanding between us and the phone hasn't stopped ringing since the first call came through."

"I don't follow. Who's been calling?"

"Who hasn't?" he said, exasperated. "The local paper for starters and then the L.A. *Times.* I guess one of the radio stations got wind of it. It'll go out on the wire services next thing you know and we'll have six friggin' camera crews camped in the driveway."

"Donovan, I swear. If there was a leak, it didn't come from me."

"Well, someone spilled the beans and you're the only one who stands to benefit."

"Me? That makes no sense. How would I benefit from a story about Guy?"

"The reporter who called mentioned you by name. He knew you'd been hired and he was interested in how you'd gone about finding Guy after all these years. He as good as told me he intended to play that angle: 'Local PI locates heir missing eighteen years.' It's better than an advertisement for all the work you'll get."

"Donovan, stop it. That's ridiculous. I'd never blab client business under any circumstance. I don't need more work. I have plenty." This was not entirely true, but he didn't need to know that. The bottom line was, I'd never give client information to the media. I had a reputation to protect. Aside from ethical considerations, this was not a profession where you wanted to be recognized. Most working investigators keep a very low profile. Anonymity is always preferable, especially when you're inclined, as I am, to use the occasional ruse. If you're posing as a meter reader or a florist delivery person, you don't want the public to be aware of your true identity. "I mean, think about it, Donovan. If I'd actually given him the story, why would he be quizzing you about my methods? He'd know that already so why would he ask you?"

"Well, you might have a point there, unless he was looking for confirmation."

"Oh, knock it off. You're really stretching for that one."

"I just think it's damn suspicious that you got a plug."

"Who's the reporter? Did you ask where he got his information?"

"He never gave me the chance."

"Well, let me put in a call to him. Why don't we just ask him? It might be something simple or obvious once you hear. You remember his name?"

"Katzensomething, but I don't think it's smart for you to talk to him."

"Katzenbach. I know Jeffrey. He's a nice man."

Donovan plowed on, not wanting to yield his ground. "I'm telling you, lay off. I don't want you talking to him about anything. Enough is enough. If I find out you're behind this, I'll sue your ass from here to next Tuesday," he said and banged down the receiver on his end.

The "screw *you*" I offered snappishly came half a second too late, which was just as well.

The minute he'd broken the connection my adrenaline shot up. My mouth was dry and I could feel my heart begin to pound in my ears. I wanted to protest, but I could see how it looked from his perspective. He was right about the fact that I was the only one outside the family who knew what was going on. More or less, I thought, pausing to correct myself. Myrna could have tipped the paper, but it was hard to see why she'd do such a thing. And of course, Peter and Winnie knew what was going on, but again why would either one of them want to make the matter known? I had a strong impulse to pick up the phone and call Katzenbach, but Donovan's admonition was still ringing in my ears. Once in touch, I was worried the reporter would start pumping me for information. Any comment I made might be quoted in a follow-up and then my credibility would be shot for sure.

Dimly, I wondered if Guy could have tipped off the paper himself. It seemed unlikely, but not impossible and I could see a certain canny logic if the move was his. If the issue of his inheritance became public knowledge, his brothers would have a hell of a time trying to screw him out of it. The problem with that notion was that Guy had never demonstrated much interest in the money and he certainly hadn't seemed concerned about protecting his share. Could he be as devious and manipulative as his family claimed?

I snagged my jacket and my handbag and headed out again. I tried to shake off my anxiety as I walked the short distance to my car, which was parked half a block down. There was no way to convince the Maleks of my innocence. Accused of the breach, I found myself feeling apologetic, as if I'd actually been guilty of violating the family's trust. Poor Guy. In the wake of my denial, they'd probably turn on *him*.

By the time I reached the downtown area, I'd managed to distract myself, wondering if I'd find a parking space within a reasonable radius of Lonnie Kingman's building. I tried the spiral approach, like a crime scene investigation, starting at the inner point and working outward. If nothing opened up, I could always use the public parking lot, which was three blocks away.

The second time I circled, I saw a van pull into the stretch of red-painted curb in front of the building. The door on the passenger side slid back and a fellow with a camcorder swung himself out on the walk. The slim blond who anchored the six o'clock news hopped down from the front seat and scanned the numbers on the building, verifying the address from a note on her pad. Coming up from behind, I couldn't see the logo on the side of the van, but it had an aerial on top that looked fierce enough to receive messages from outer space. Oh, shit. As I passed the van, I could see KEST-TV painted on the side. I resisted the urge to speed away as the woman threw a glance in my direction. I peered to my left, turning toward the building across the street. I waved merrily at someone emerging from the Dean Witter office. Maybe the press would mistake me for a cruising mogul with some money to invest. I kept driving, eyes pinned on my rearview mirror as the cameraman and his companion went into the entrance-way.

Now what? I didn't like the idea of skulking in the bushes like a renegade. Maybe I was being paranoid and the crew was on its way to cover something else. I drove several blocks before I spotted a pay phone on the corner. I left my car at the curb, dropped a quarter in the slot, and dialed Lonnie's private line. He must have been in court because Ida Ruth picked up, thinking it was him. "Yessir?"

"Ida Ruth, this is Kinsey. Did a TV crew show up looking for me?"

"I don't think so, but I'm back here at my desk. Let me check with Alison up front." She put me on hold for a moment and then clicked back in. "I stand corrected. They're waiting for you in reception. What's going on?"

"It's too complicated to explain. Can you get rid of them?"

"Well, we can get 'em out of here, but there's no way we can keep them from hanging around on the street outside. What did you do, if I may be so bold?"

"Nothing, I swear. I'm completely innocent."

"Right, dear. Good for you. Stick to that," she said.

"Ida Ruth, I'm serious. Here's the deal," I said. I filled her in briefly and heard her cluck in response. "My, oh my. If I were you, I'd lay low. They can't stay long. If you tell me how to reach you, I'll call you when they're gone."

"I'm not sure where I'll be. I'll check back in a bit." I put the receiver down and scanned the street corner opposite. There was a bar on the corner that appeared to be opening. I could see a neon light in the window blink on. As I watched, a fellow in an apron opened the front door and kicked the doorstop into place. I could always hang out in there, drinking beer and sniffing secondhand smoke while I figured out what to do next. On the other hand, come to think of it, I hadn't *done* anything so why was I behaving like a fugitive. I fished around in the bottom of my bag and came up with a second coin. I put a call through to the *Dispatch* and asked for Jeffrey Katzenbach. I didn't know him well, but I'd dealt with him on a couple of occasions in the past. He was a man in his fifties, whose career had been stalled by his appetite for cocaine and Percocet. He'd always been sharp if you caught him early in the day, but as the afternoon progressed, he became harder to deal with. By nightfall, he could still function, but his judgment was sometimes faulty and he didn't always remember the promises he'd made. Two years ago, his wife had left him and the last I'd heard, he'd finally straightened up his act with the help of Narcotics Anonymous. Guy Malek wasn't the only one who'd undergone personal transformation.

When I got through to Katzenbach, I identified myself and we exchanged the usual pleasantries before getting down to business. "Jeffrey, this is strictly off the record. The Maleks are my clients and I can't afford to be quoted."

"Why? What's the problem?"

"There isn't any problem. Donovan's pissed off because he thinks I called you and spoiled the family reunion."

"Sorry to hear that."

"How'd you get wind of it? Or is this a 'confidential source'?"

"Nothing confidential about it. There was a letter on my desk when I got in last night. We've always encouraged our subscribers to get in touch if they think there's a story we might not've heard about. Sometimes it's just trivia or crank stuff, but this one grabbed my attention."

"Who sent the letter?"

"Some fellow named Max Outhwaite with an address on Connecticut out in Colgate. He thought it was an item worth bringing to our attention."

"How'd he hear about it?"

"Beats me. He talked like he'd known 'em all for years. Basically, the letter says a search was conducted and Bader Malek's son Guy was located after an absence of eighteen years. That's correct, isn't it? I mean, tell me I'm wrong and I'll eat my Jockey shorts."

"You're correct, but so what?"

"So nothing. Like he says, here's this fellow working as a janitor in some backwater town, finds out he's inheriting five million bucks. How often does that happen? He thought the community would be interested. I thought it sounded like a winner so I put a call in to the Maleks. The number's in the book, it didn't require any red-hot detective work. I talked to Mrs. Malek—what's her name, Christie—who confirmed the story before I even got to Donovan. Sure enough, that's the deal unless there's something I missed."

"And I was mentioned by name?"

"You bet. It's one of the reasons I figured it was on the up-and-up. I tried to reach you last night, but all I got was your answering machine. I didn't bother to leave a message. I figured you were on your way over there to help 'em celebrate. How'd you find the guy? Outhwaite's letter says you got a lead on him through the DMV."

"I don't believe this. Who is this man and where's he getting his information?"

"How do I know? He acted like he was maybe a friend of the family. You never talked to him yourself?"

"Jeffrey, knock it off. I didn't call so you could pump me. I'm trying to persuade the Maleks I didn't leak this thing."

"Too bad you didn't. You could have filled in the details. I went back to check with Outhwaite and the guy doesn't exist. There's no Outhwaite in the phone book and no such house number anywhere on Connecticut Avenue. I tried a couple of other possibilities and I came up with blanks. Not that it matters as long as the story's legitimate. I got confirmation from the family."

"What about the L.A. *Times*? How did they get wind of it?"

"Same way we did. Outhwaite dropped 'em a note—almost like a press release. It's been a slow week for news and we're always on the lookout for human-interest stuff. This was better than a little lost kitty-cat trapped in a well. I thought it was worth pursuing, especially when I saw you were involved."

"I wished you'd done some fact checking with me along the way."

"Why? What's the problem?"

"There isn't any *problem*," I said, irritably. "I just think the family might appreciate a little privacy before the whole world rushes in. By the way, Jeffrey, I've heard you tippy-tapping on your keyboard ever since we started this conversation. I told you this is off the record."

"What for? It's a nice story. It's a great fantasy. What's the deal with the Maleks? Why're they so pissed with the coverage? We did front page, second section when Bader Malek died. He was an important figure in the community and they were happy to have the tribute. What's so hush-hush about Guy? Are they trying to cut him out of his inheritance or something?"

I rolled my eyes skyward. The man couldn't help but press for information. "Listen, buddy, I'm as clueless as you. What about the letter? What happened to it?"

"It's sitting right here."

"You mind if I have a copy? It would go a long way toward restoring my credibility. I feel like a fool having to defend myself, but I have a reputation to maintain."

"Sure. I can do that. I don't see why not. We're interested in Guy's perspective if you can talk him into it."

"I'm not trading—but I'll do what I can."

"Terrific. What's your fax number?"

I gave him the number of Lonnie Kingman's machine and he said he'd fax the letter over. If I located Max Outhwaite, Jeffrey wanted to talk to him. Fair enough. I said I'd do what I could. It didn't cost me anything to profess my conditional cooperation. I tried not to be too profuse in my thanks. It's not like I planned to take the letter straight to Donovan, but I was curious about the contents and thought it made sense to have a copy for my files. At some point, Katzenbach would extract something from me in return, but for now, I was fine. I didn't believe Guy would agree to an interview, but maybe he'd surprise me.

I got back in my car and drove over to the public parking lot. From there, I hoofed it to the office on foot. There was no sign of the KEST-TV van out front. I took the stairs two at a time and entered Kingman and Ives through an unmarked door around the corner from the main entrance. In the back of my mind, I was mulling over the possibility that maybe Bennet or Jack had taken the letter to the *Dispatch*. I couldn't see what it would net either of them, but *someone* had an interest in seeing Guy's homecoming splashed across the news and it was someone who knew more than I was comfortable with. Again, I could feel the faint nudge of uneasiness. Darcy Pascoe's computer search had been a bit of a fudge. I hoped she wasn't going to find herself in trouble as a result of my request. I checked the fax machine in Lonnie's office and found the copy of Max Outhwaite's letter sitting in the slot as promised. I went to my office, reading as I went.

Dear Mr. Katzenbach,

    Thought you'd be interested in a Modern-Day
''Cinderfella'' story taking place right here in
Santa Teresa! As I recall, your the reporter,
who wrote about Bader Malek's death last month.
Now, word around town has it that his Probate
Attorney hired a Private Investigater (a
''Female'' no less) to locate his missing son,
Guy. If you've been around town as long as me,
you'll remember that as a youngster, Guy Malek
was caught in a number of scrapes, and finally
disappeared from the local scene, nearly twenty
years ago. You'd think finding someone like that
after all this time would prove daunting, but
Milhone (the aforementioned ''Female''
Detective) ran a DMV check, and turned him up in
less than two days!! Seems he's been up in
Marcella ever since he left, and he's working as
a janiter in a church up there! He's one of those
''Born-Agains,'' who probably didn't have two
nickles to rub together, but his father's death
has turned him into an instant millionnaire!! I
think people would be heartened to hear how he's
managed to turn his life around, threw his
Christian Faith. Folks might also enjoy hearing
what he's planning to do with his new-found
riches. With all the bad news that besieges us
from day to day, wouldn't this story give
everyone a nice lift? I think it would be a

wonderfull inspiration to the Community! Let's
hope Guy Malek is willing to share the story of
his ''good fortune'' with us. I look forward to
reading such an article and know you'd do a fine
job of writing it! Best of luck and God Bless!

                    Sincerely yours,
                    Max Outhwaite
                    2905 Connecticut Ave.
                    Colgate, CA

I noticed I held the letter by the corners, as if to avoid smudging
prints, a ridiculous precaution given the fact that it wasn't even the
original. The note was neatly typed, with no visible corrections and no
words XXX'd out. Granted, there were spelling errors (including my
name), an excessive use of commas, a tendency toward the emphatic,
and a bit of Unnecessary Capitalization! but otherwise the intentions
of the sender seemed benign. Aside from alerting the press to something that was nobody else's business, I couldn't see any particular
attempt to meddle in Guy Malek's life. Maximilian (or perhaps Maxine) Outhwaite apparently thought subscribers to the *Santa Teresa
Dispatch* would be warmed by this story of a Bad Boy Turned Good
and the Resultant Rewards! Outhwaite didn't seem to have an ax to
grind and there was no hint of malice to undercut his (or her) enthusiasm for the tale. So what was going on?

I set the letter aside, swiveling in my swivel chair while I studied it
covertly out of the corner of my eye. As a "Female" Detective, I found
myself vaguely bothered by the damn thing. I didn't like the intimate
acquaintance with the details and I couldn't help but wonder at the
motivation. The tone was ingenuous, but the maneuver had been effective. Suddenly, Guy Malek's private business had been given a public audience.

I placed the letter in the Malek file, turning it over to my psyche for
further consideration.

I spent the rest of the morning at the courthouse, taking care of
other business. As a rule, I'm working fifteen to twenty cases concur-
rently. Not all of them are pressing and not all demand my attention
at the same time. I do a number of background checks for a research
and development firm out in Colgate. I also do preemployment investigations, as well as skip traces for a couple of small businesses in the
area. Periodically, I'm involved in some fairly routine snooping for a
divorce attorney down the street. Even in a no-fault state, a spouse

might hide assets or conceal the whereabouts of communal items, like cars, boats, planes, and minor children. There's something restful about a morning spent cruising through the marriage licenses and death records in pursuit of genealogical connections, or an afternoon picking through probated wills, property transfers, and tax and mechanics' liens at the county offices. Sometimes I can't believe my good fortune, working in a business where I'm paid to uncover matters people would prefer to keep under wraps. Paper stalking doesn't require a PI to slip into a Kevlar vest, but the results can be just as dangerous as a gun battle or a high-speed chase.

My assignment that Monday morning was to probe the financial claims detailed in a company prospectus. A local businessman had been approached to invest fifty thousand dollars in what looked like a promising merchandising plan. Within an hour, I'd found out that one of the two partners had filed for personal bankruptcy and the other had a total of six lawsuits pending against him. While I was about it, I did a preliminary search for Max Outhwaite, starting with voter registration and working my way through local tax rolls. I crossed the street to the public library and tried the reference department. Under that spelling, there were no Outhwaites listed in the local phone books and none in the city directories going back six years. This meant nothing in particular as far as I could see. It did suggest that "Max Outhwaite" was a nom de plume, but under certain circumstances, I could relate to the maneuver. If I wanted to call an issue to the attention of the local paper, I might conceivably use a fake name and a phony address. I might be a prominent person, reluctant to have myself associated with the subject in question. I might be a family member, eager to get Guy in trouble, but unwilling to take responsibility. Writing such a letter was hardly a crime, but I might feel guilty nonetheless and not want the consequences blowing back on me.

For lunch I bought a sandwich and a soft drink from a vending machine and sat on a stretch of lawn out behind the courthouse. The day was hot, the treetops buffeted by dry winds coming off the desert. The branches of the big evergreens planted close to the street seemed to shimmer in the breeze, giving off the scent of pitch. I leaned back on my elbows and turned my face up to the sun. I can't say I slept, but I gave a good impression of it. At one o'clock, I roused myself and went back to the office where I began to type up my findings for the cases I'd worked. Such is the life of a PI these days. I spend more time practicing my skills with a Smith-Corona than a Smith & Wesson.

12

My run that morning had been unsatisfactory. I'd done what needed doing, dutifully jogging a mile and a half down the bike path and a mile and a half back, but I'd never developed any rhythm and the much-sought-after endorphin rush had failed to materialize. I've noticed on days when the run isn't good, I'm left with an emotional itch that feels like anxiety, in this case compounded by mild depression. Short of drink and drugs, sometimes the only remedy is to exercise again. I swear this is not a compulsion on my part so much as a craving for relief. I drove over to Harley's Beach and found a parking spot in the shelter of the hill. The lot was nearly empty, which surprised me somehow. Usually, there's an assortment of tourists and beachcombers, joggers, lovers, barking dogs, and parents with small children. Today, all I spotted was a family of feral cats sunning themselves on the hillside above the beach.

I staggered across an expanse of loose, dry sand until I reached the hard pack at the water's edge. I would have pulled off my shoes and socks, rolling up my pant legs so I could jog in the surf, however someone had recently given me a small book about tide pools. I'd leafed through with interest, imagining myself in the role of inquisitive naturalist, poking among the rocks for tiny crabs and starfish (though their undersides are completely disgusting and gross). Until I read this colorful, informative pamphlet, I'd had no idea what strange, ugly beasties existed close to shore. I'm not the kind of person who sentimentalizes nature. The outdoors, as far as I can see, is made up almost entirely of copulating creatures who eat one another afterward. To this end, almost every known animal has developed a strategy for luring others within range. Among life-forms in the sea—some quite minuscule—the tactic involves thorny parts or pincers or tiny three-jawed mouths or trailing stingers or vicious suckers with which they latch on to one another, causing painful death and dismemberment, all in the name of nourishment. Sometimes the juice is slurped out of the victim long before death occurs. The starfish actually takes out its own stomach, enfolds its live prey, and digests it outside its body. How would you like to put your bare foot down on that?

I ran in my shoes, splashing through the surf when the waves came close. Soon my wet jeans clung to my legs, the heavy fabric cold against my shins. My feet were weighted as though with stones and I could feel the sweat begin to soak through my shirt from the labor of the run. Despite the damp breeze coming off the ocean, the air felt oppressive. For the third day in a row, Santa Ana winds were blasting in from the desert, blowing down the local canyons, pulling moisture from the atmosphere. The mounting heat collected, degree by degree, like a wall of bricks going up. My progress felt slow and I forced myself to focus on the sand shimmering ahead of me. Since I had no way to measure distance, I ran for time, jogging thirty minutes north before I turned and jogged back. By the time I reached Harley's Beach again, my breathing was ragged and the muscles in my thighs were on fire. I slowed to a trot and then geared down to a walk as I returned to my car. For a moment, I leaned panting against the hood. Better. That was better. Pain was better than anxiety any day of the week and sweat was better than depression.

Home again, I left my soggy running shoes on the front steps. I padded upstairs, peeling out of my damp clothes as I ascended. I took a hot shower and then slipped into a pair of sandals, a T-shirt, and a short cotton skirt. It was now close to four and there was no point returning to the office. I brought in the mail and checked for phone messages. There were five: two hang-ups; two reporters who left numbers, asking me to get back to them; and a call from Peter Antle, the pastor of Guy's church. I dialed the number he'd left and he picked up so fast I had to guess he'd been waiting by the phone.

"Peter. I got your message. This is Kinsey in Santa Teresa."

"Kinsey. Thanks for being so prompt. Winnie's been trying to call

Guy, but she can't seem to get through. The Maleks have the answering machine on and nobody's picking up. I don't know what Guy's plans are, but we thought we'd better warn him. There are reporters camped out at the gas station across from his place. We have people knocking on the church door and a pile of messages for him."

"Already?"

"That was my reaction. Frankly, I don't understand how this got out in the first place."

"Long story. I'm still in the process of looking into it. I know the family was contacted by the local newspaper first thing this morning. The reporter here had had a letter delivered to him at the paper. I guess something similar was sent to the L.A. *Times*. I haven't seen the news yet, but I have a feeling it's going to get bigger before it goes away."

"It's even worse up here. The town's so small, none of us can manage to avoid the press. Do you have a way to get in touch with Guy? We're here for him if he needs us. We don't want him to lose his footing in the stress of the situation."

"Let me see if I can find a way to get through. I guess this is his fifteen minutes of fame, though frankly, I can't understand why the story's generating so much attention. Why should anyone give a fat rat's . . . aa . . . ah . . . ear? He doesn't even have the money yet and who knows if he'll ever see one red cent."

I could almost see Peter's grin. "Everyone wants to believe in something. For most people, a big windfall would literally be the answer to all their prayers."

"I suppose so," I said. "At any rate, if I reach him, I'll have him give you a call."

"I'd appreciate that."

After we hung up, I flipped on the TV set and tuned in to KEST. The evening news wouldn't air for an hour, but the station often ran quick promos for the show coming up. I suffered through six commercials and caught the clip I'd suspected would be there. The blond anchorwoman smiled at the camera, saying, "Not all news is bad news. Sometimes even the darkest cloud has a silver lining. After nearly twenty years of poverty, a Marcella maintenance man has just learned he'll be inheriting five million dollars. We'll have that story for you at five." Behind her, the camera showed a glimpse of a haggard-looking Guy Malek, staring impassively from the car window as Donovan's BMW swung through the gates of the Malek estate. I felt a pang of guilt, wishing I'd talked him out of coming down. Given his bleak expression, the homecoming wasn't a success. I picked up the phone again and tried the Maleks' number. The line was busy.

I called the number every ten minutes for an hour. The Maleks had probably taken the phone off the hook, or maybe their message tape was full. In either event, who knew when I'd get through to him.

I debated with myself briefly and then drove over to the house. The gate was now closed and there were six vehicles parked along the berm. Reporters loitered, some leaning against their car fenders, two chatting together in the middle of the road. Both men were smoking and held big Styrofoam coffee cups. Three camera units had been set up on tripods and it looked as if the troops were prepared to stay. The late-afternoon sun slanted between the eucalyptus trees across from the Malek property, dividing the pavement into alternating sections of light and shadow.

I parked behind the last car and went on foot as far as the call box near the front gate. All activity behind me ceased and I could feel the attention focus on my back. No one answered my ring. Like the others, I was going to have to hang around out here, hoping to catch sight of one of the Maleks exiting or entering the grounds. I tried one more time, but my ringing was greeted with dead silence from inside the house.

I returned to my car and turned the key in the ignition. Already, a dark-haired woman reporter was ambling in my direction. She was probably in her forties, with oversized sunglasses and bright red lips. As I watched, she fumbled in her shoulder bag and pulled out a cigarette. She was tall and slender, decked out in slacks and a short-cropped cotton sweater. I marveled she could bear it with the heat sitting where it was. Gold earrings. Gold bracelets. A daunting pair of four-inch heels. For my taste, walking in high heels is like trying to learn to ice-skate. The human ankle does not take readily to such requirements. I admired her balance, though I realized when she reached me that in bare feet she'd probably be shorter than I. She made a circling motion, asking me to roll down my car window.

"Hi. How are you?" she said. She held up the cigarette. "You have a light for this?"

"Sorry. I don't smoke. Why don't you ask one of them?"

She turned, her gaze sliding back to the two men standing in the road. Her voice was husky and her tone was dismissive. "Oh, them. That's the boys' club," she remarked. "Those two won't even give you the time of day unless you have something to trade." Her eyes flicked back to me. "What about you? You don't look like a reporter. What are you, family friend? An old sweetheart?"

I had to admire the placid way she eased right into it, casual, un-
concerned. She was probably wetting her pants, hoping I'd provide a
little tidbit so she could scoop her competition. I started rolling up my
window. Quickly, she raised her handbag and turned it sideways, in-
serting it into the space so the window wouldn't close all the way.
There was now a seven-inch gap where her leather bag was wedged.

"No offense," she said, "but I'm curious. Aren't you that private
investigator we've heard so much about?"

I turned the key in the ignition. "Please remove your bag." I
cranked the window down about an inch, hoping she'd pull the bag
free so I could be on my way.

"Don't be in such a hurry. What's the rush? The public has a right
to know these things. I'm going to get the information anyway so why
not make sure it's accurate? I heard the kid spent a lot of time in jail.
Was that here or up north?"

I cranked the window up a notch and put the car in gear. I pushed
my foot down lightly on the gas pedal and eased away from the berm.
She held on to the bag by its strap, walking beside the car, continuing
the conversation. I guess she was accustomed to having the driver at
her mercy once she used the old handbag trick. I increased my speed
sufficiently to force her into a trot. She yanked the strap, yelling
"Hey!" as I began to accelerate. I couldn't have been driving more
than two miles an hour, but that's a tough pace to maintain when
you're wearing heels that high. I inched my foot down on the gas. She
released the bag and stopped where she was, watching with consterna-
tion as I pulled away. I passed the two guys in the road who seemed to
enjoy the rude comment she was yelling after me. I couldn't hear the
words, but I got the drift. In the rearview mirror, I saw her flip me the
bird.

She removed a high heel and flung it at my rear window. I heard a
mild thump on impact and saw the shoe bounce off behind me as I
picked up speed. The long strap of the handbag dangled and flapped
against the car door. About a hundred yards down the road, I paused
long enough to roll down my window and give the bag a shove. I left it
there in the road, curled like a possum, and drove to my apartment.

There were two newspapers on the sidewalk when I got home. I
picked up both and left one on Henry's back doorstep before I let
myself in. I turned on some lights and poured myself a glass of wine,
then sat at the kitchen counter and spread the paper out in front of
me. The story was in the second section and the tone was odd. I'd
expected a fairy-tale version of Guy's life to date, his estrangement
from the family and his subsequent spiritual transformation. Instead,

Jeff Katzenbach had patched together, in excruciating detail, an inventory of all the sins from Guy's youth: countless episodes of reckless driving, vandalism, drunk and disorderly conduct, assault and battery. Some charges dated back to his juvenile record and should have been purged or remained sealed by the courts. Where had Katzenbach gotten his information? Some of it, of course, was a matter of public record, but I wondered how he'd known to look. He'd obviously been tipped off by Max Outhwaite's reference to Guy's earlier scrapes. I thought back uneasily to the file of news clippings Bader Malek had kept. Was there any way he could have seen that? This would have been a second leak of sorts. The first was the fact of Guy's return; the second, this detailed criminal history. I noticed Katzenbach had couched his revelations in typical journalistic fudgings. The word *alleged* appeared about six times, along with *confidential sources, informants close to the family, former associates,* and *friends of the Maleks who asked to remain anonymous.* Far from celebrating Guy's good fortune, the public was going to end up resenting his sudden wealth. Reading between the lines, you could tell Katzenbach considered Guy Malek an undeserving scoundrel. Somehow his current church affiliation looked self-serving and insincere, the convenient refuge of a culprit hoping to make himself look good in the eyes of the parole board.

For supper, I made myself a hot hard-boiled egg sandwich with lots of mayonnaise and salt and perched at the counter eating while I scanned the rest of the paper. I must have been more absorbed than I thought because when the telephone shrilled, I flung my sandwich sideways in response. I snatched up the receiver, heart thumping as though a gun had just been fired in my ear. If this turned out to be a reporter, I was going to hang up. "Yes."

"Hey."

"Oh shit. Guy, is that you? You scared the hell out of me." I leaned down and gathered up the remains of my sandwich, popping the crust in my mouth while I licked at my fingers. There was mayonnaise on the floor, but I could tend to that later.

"Yeah, it's me. How are you?" he said. "I tried calling a while ago, but you were out, I guess."

"Thank God you called. I was just over at the house, but I couldn't get anyone to answer my ring. What's happening?"

"We just finished dinner. Have you seen the news?"

"I have the paper in front of me."

"Not so good, huh."

"It's not that bad," I said, hoping to cheer him up. "It does look like somebody's really got it in for you."

"That's my assumption," he said lightly.

"Are you all right? Peter called earlier. He's been trying to get in touch, but all he's managed so far is the answering machine. Did you get his message?"

"No, but why would I? Everybody here is pissed at me. They think I notified the paper, trying to get attention. There's a powwow on for later, after Donovan gets home. He's got a meeting until nine. The delay's making me sick. Reminds me of that old business, 'You wait until your father gets home and he'll give you the what for.'"

I found myself smiling. "You want me to come get you? I can be there in fifteen minutes."

"Yes—no—I don't know what I want. I'd like to get out of here, but I don't dare take off with things as they are."

"Why not? The damage is done. Whoever spilled the beans, made it look as bad as they could. If *you'd* leaked the news, you'd have put a different spin on it."

"How would I manage that? You can't put a different spin on the truth."

"Of course you can. It's called politics."

"Yeah, but I did all those things. This is just payback time. I told you I was bad. At least, now you know the worst."

"Oh stop that. I don't care about that stuff. All I care about is getting you out of there."

"You want to come for a visit? I could sneak out for a few minutes. Jack and Bennet are downstairs and Christie's in the office, going through some of Dad's old papers."

"Sure. I can pop back over there. What do you want me to do? Shall I ring from the gate?"

"No, don't do that. I'll meet you out on Wolf Run Road," he said. "If the side gate's locked, I can scale the wall. I'm an expert at getting out. When I was a kid I used to do it all the time. That's how I managed to get in so much trouble back then."

"Why don't you bring your backpack and let me spirit you away," I said. "I'll drive you to Marcella and you can hire an attorney to handle your interests from here on."

"Don't tempt me. Right now, all I need is civilized conversation. Park in that little grove of trees just across from the gate. I'll be out there in fifteen minutes."

I took a few minutes to tidy up the kitchen and then I changed into jeans, a dark shirt, and my Reeboks. The evening air felt uncharacteristically warm, but I wanted to be prepared for night maneuvers if need be. Once at the Maleks', I took a quick swing by the front gate.

There were now two more news crews and the gathering had taken on the feel of a vigil outside a prison. Portable lights had been turned on and a man with a microphone spoke directly to a camera, making gestures toward the house. I saw the dark-haired reporter, but she didn't see me. She seemed to be bumming a light for her cigarette from a poor unsuspecting "source."

I followed the wall, circling the property as I turned left on Wolf Run. I spotted the gate, a dark blot in an otherwise unbroken expanse of wall. I pulled off onto the berm across the road, gravel crackling under my wheels. I shut down the engine and sat there, listening to the tick of hot metal and the murmur of the wind. There weren't any street lamps along this section of the road. The high night sky was clear, but the moon had been reduced to the merest sliver, a frail curve of silver in a sky pale with stars. The dust in the air was as fine as mist. In the ambient light, the pavement was a dull, luminous gray. The stucco wall enclosing the Malek property had been robbed of its pink luster and stretched now like a ghostly band of drab white. June and July were traditionally dry and I associated the Santa Ana winds with the end of summer—late August, early September, when the fire danger was extreme. For years, January had been the rainy season, two weeks of rain that we hoped would fill our annual quota. Yet here we were with the dry wind tossing in the treetops. The bend and sway of tree boughs set up a hushed night music, accompanied by the rustling percussion of dry palm fronds, the occasional snap of tree limbs. By morning, the streets would be littered with dead leaves and the small withered skeletons of broken branches.

The gate opened without a sound and Guy emerged, head down. He wore a dark-colored jacket, his fists shoved into his pockets as though he were cold. I leaned over and unlocked the door on the passenger side. He slid into the seat and then pulled the door shut without slamming it. He said, "Hey. Thanks for coming. I thought I'd go crazy without a friendly face. I'd have called you before, but they were watching me like a hawk."

"No problem. I don't know why you don't break and run while you can."

"I will. Tomorrow. Or maybe the day after that. I told you we're supposed to have another meeting tonight just to talk about some things."

"I thought you already talked."

"Well, we did. We do. Every time I turn around, we have another chat."

"That's because you haven't knuckled under yet," I interjected.

"I guess that's it." He smiled in spite of himself. His tension was contagious and I could have sworn I smelled alcohol on his breath. I found myself with my arms crossed, one leg wound around the other as if to protect myself.

"I feel like we're having an affair," I said.

"Me, too. I used to meet girls out here in the old days when I was grounded. I'd slip over the wall and we'd screw in the backseat of a car. There was something about the danger set me on fire, and them, too. Made most of 'em seem more interesting than they were."

"I know this is none of my business, but have you been drinking?" I asked.

He turned and looked out the passenger window, shrugging. "I had a couple of drinks last night before all this shit came down. I don't know what got into me. Don't get me wrong—they were being nice at that point, but you could tell they were nervous and so was I. I'm ashamed to say this, but the alcohol did help. It mellowed us out and smoothed the conversation. Tonight was pretty much the same except everybody's mood was different. Cocktail hour comes along and those guys really hit it."

"Bennet and his martinis."

"You bet. I figure that's the only way I'll get through. Peter wouldn't be too happy with me, but I can't help it. I can feel myself sliding back to my old ways."

"What'd you think of Christie?"

"She was nice. I liked her. I was surprised at Bennet—at the weight he'd put on, but Jack seemed the same, still nuts about golf. And Donovan hasn't changed."

"What've they said to you so far?"

"Well, we talked some about the money, what else? I mean, the subject does come up. It's like Donovan says, we can't just ignore the issue. It's like this big dark cloud hanging over us. I think we were all uncomfortable at first."

"Have you resolved anything?"

"Well, no. Nothing much. At first, I think they were wondering, you know, generally, about my attitude. Now, anything I say and everybody jumps right on in. Tell you the truth, I'd forgotten what they're like."

"How do they seem to you?"

"Angry. Underneath it all, they're pissed. I keep feeling the anger coming up inside me, too. It's all I can do to keep a lid on it."

"Why bother? Why not blow? The three of them certainly don't hesitate."

"I know, but if I flip my lid that's only going to make matters worse. I'm trying to show 'em I've changed and then I find myself feeling like I always did. Like I want to smash lamps, throw a chair through a window, get stoned or drunk or something bad like that."

"That must be a trial."

"I'll say. I mean, literally. All I can think about is maybe this is some kind of test of my faith."

"Oh, it is *not*," I said. "It may be a test of your patience, but not your faith in God."

He shook his head, pressing his hands down between his knees. "Let's talk about something else. This is making me so tense I could fart."

I laughed and changed the subject. For a while we chatted about inconsequential matters. Hunched there in the front seat, I was reminded of the occasional dates I had in high school where the only hope of privacy was remaining closed away in some kid's car. On chilly evenings, the front windshield would fog up even if all we did was talk. On warm nights like this, we'd sit with the windows rolled down, radio tuned to some rock and roll station. It was Elvis or the Beatles, clumsy moves and sexual tension. I don't even remember now what we talked about, those lads and I. Probably nothing. Probably we drank purloined beer, smoked dope, and thought about the incredible majesty of life.

"So what else's going on? Aside from interminable meetings?" I asked. Like a rough place on a fingernail, I couldn't resist going back to it. Apparently, Guy couldn't resist it either because we fell right into the subject again.

This time he smiled and his tone seemed lighter. "It's nice to see the house. I found some letters of my mother's and I read those today. She's the only one I ever missed. The rest of 'em are a waste."

"I don't want to say I told you so, but I did predict this."

"I know, I know. I thought we could just sit down like grown-ups and clean up some old business, but it doesn't really happen like that. I mean, I keep wondering if there isn't some kind of defect in me because everything I do just seems to come out wrong. Whatever I say seems 'off,' you know? They look at me like I'm speaking in tongues and then I see them exchange these looks."

"Oh, I know that one. Jack and Bennet are big on flicking looks back and forth."

"That's the easy part, but there's worse."

"Like what?"

"I don't even know how to describe it. Something under the surface. Something slides right by and no one owns up to it, so then I start questioning my own thought process. Maybe I'm nuts and it's not them after all."

"Give me an example."

"Like when I told 'em I'd like to give something to the church? I honestly don't want the money for me. I mean that. But Jubilee Evangelical saved my life and I want to give something back. To me, that doesn't seem so wrong. Does it seem wrong to you?"

"No, not at all."

"So, I say that and all of a sudden we're in the middle of a power play. Bennet's saying how it really doesn't seem fair. You know how he talks with that slightly pompous air of his. 'Our family's never been religious. Dad worked for the good of us all, not for the benefit of some church he never heard of.' He says it all in this completely rational tone and pretty soon I wonder if what I want to do is right after all. Maybe they have a point and *my* values are screwed up."

"Sure they have a point. They want you to relinquish all claim so they can divide up your portion among themselves. They know perfectly well you're entitled to a quarter of his estate. What you do with your share is none of their business."

"But how come I end up the magnet for all that rage?"

"Guy, stop. Don't do that. That's the third time you've said that. Don't get into self-blame. The gamesmanship has obviously been going on for years. That's got to be why you left in the first place, to get away from that stuff. I swear they were behaving the same way before you showed up."

"You think I should leave?"

"Well, of course I do! I've said it all along. You shouldn't take their abuse. I think you should get the hell out while you have the chance."

"I wouldn't call it 'abuse.' "

"Because you're used to it," I said. "And don't get sidetracked. Your brothers aren't going to change. If anybody goes down for the count, it's going to be you."

"Maybe so," he said. "I don't know. I just feel like I have to stay since I've come this far. If I cut and run, we're never going to find a way to work this through."

"I can tell you're not listening, but please, *please,* don't agree to anything without talking to an attorney first."

"Okay."

"Promise me."

"I will. I swear. Well, I gotta go before somebody figures out I've escaped."

"Guy, you're not sixteen. You're forty-three years old. Sit here if you want. You can stay out all night. Big whoop-dee-do. You're an adult."

He laughed. "I *feel* like I'm sixteen. And you're cute."

He leaned over quickly and brushed my cheek with his lips. I could feel the soft scratch of his whiskers against my face and I caught a whiff of his aftershave.

He said, "Bye-bye and thanks." Before I could respond, he was out of the car, shoulders hunched up against the wind as he moved to the gate. He turned and waved and then he was swallowed up by the dark.

I never saw him again.

13

Guy Malek was killed sometime Tuesday night, though I didn't actually hear about it until Wednesday afternoon. I'd spent most of the day over at the courthouse sitting in on the trial of a man accused of embezzlement. I hadn't been associated with the case—undercover cops had nailed him after seven months of hard work—but some years before, I'd done surveillance on him briefly at the request of his wife. She suspected he was cheating, but she wasn't sure with whom. Turned out he was having an affair with her sister and she broke off relations with both. The man was dishonest to the core and I confess I found it entertaining to watch the legal system grind away at him. As often as I complain about the shortage of justice in this world, I find it infinitely satisfying when the process finally works as it should.

When I got back to the office after court adjourned, there was a message from Tasha waiting on my machine. I noticed, in passing, it was the Maleks' number she'd left. I called, expecting to have Myrna pick up. Instead Tasha answered as if she'd been manning the phones. The minute I heard her, I realized how irritated I was that she'd gone out of town just as Guy arrived. If she'd been doing her job, she might have steered the family off their campaign of pressure and harassment.

Smart mouth that I am, I launched right in. "At long last," I said, "it's about time you got back. All hell's broken loose. Have you heard what's going on? Well, obviously you have or you wouldn't be there. Honestly, I adore Guy, but I can't stand the rest of 'em—"

Tasha cut in, her voice flat. "Kinsey, that's why I called. I cut my trip short and flew back from Utah this afternoon. Guy is dead."

I was silent for a beat, trying to parse the sentence. I knew the subject . . . *Guy* . . . but the predicate . . . *is dead* . . . made no immediate sense. "You're kidding. What happened? He can't be *dead.* When I saw him on Monday he was fine."

"He was murdered last night. Somebody smashed his skull with a blunt instrument. Christie found him in bed this morning when he didn't come down for breakfast. The police took one look at the crime scene and got a warrant to search the premises. The house has been swarming with cops ever since. They haven't found the murder weapon, but they suspect it's here. They're still combing the property."

I kept getting hung up about two sentences back. "Somebody killed him in bed? While he *slept?*"

"It looks that way."

"That's disgusting. That's awful. You can't be serious."

"I'm sorry to spring it on you, but there isn't any nice way to put it. It *is* disgusting. It's terrible. We're all numb."

"Has anybody been arrested?"

"Not at this point," she said. "The family's doing what they can to cooperate, but it doesn't look good."

"Tasha, I don't believe this. I'm sick."

"I am, too. A colleague called me in Utah this morning after Donovan called him. I left everything behind and got myself on a plane."

"Who do they suspect?"

"I have no idea. From what I've heard, Jack and Bennet were both out last night. Christie went to bed early and Donovan was watching TV upstairs in their sitting room. Myrna's apartment is off the kitchen in back, but she says she was dead to the world and didn't hear anything. She's currently down at the station being interviewed. Christie came in a little while ago. She says the detectives are still talking to Donovan. Hang on."

She put a hand across the mouthpiece and I heard her in a muffled discussion with someone in the background. She came back on the line, saying, "Great. I just talked to the homicide detective in charge of things here. He wants to keep the phone line open, but says if you want to come over, he'll tell the guys at the gate to let you in. I told him he ought to talk to you since you were the one who found Guy in the first place. I told him you might have something to contribute."

"I doubt that, but who knows? I'll be there in fifteen minutes. Do you need anything?"

"We're fine for the moment. If no one's at the gate, the code is 1-9-2-4. Just punch the number in at the call box beside the drive. See you shortly," she said.

I grabbed my blazer and my handbag and went out to my car. The day had been mild. The high winds had moved on, taking with them the unseasonable heat. The light was waning and as soon as the sun set, the temperatures would drop. I was already chilled and I shrugged into my blazer before I slid beneath the wheel. Earlier in the day, I'd tried to use my wipers and washer fluid to clean the dust off my windshield and now it was streaked in a series of rising half moons. The hood of my car was covered with the same fine layer of dust, as pale as powder, and just as soft by the look of it. Even the seat upholstery had a gritty feel to it.

I put my hands together on the steering wheel and leaned my forehead against them. I had absolutely no feeling. My interior process was held in suspended animation, as if the Pause button had been pushed on some remote control. How was it possible Guy Malek was gone? For the past week, he'd been such a presence in my life. He'd been both lost and found. He'd occupied my thoughts, triggering reactions of sympathy and exasperation. Now I couldn't quite remember his face—only a flash here and there, the sound of his "Hey," the whiskery brush of his chin on my cheek. He was already as insubstantial as a ghost, all form without content, a series of fragmented images without permanence.

What seemed so odd was that life just went *on*. I could see traffic passing along Cabana Boulevard. Two doors away, my neighbor raked brittle leaves into a pile on his lawn. If I turned on the car radio, there'd be intervals of music, public service announcements, commercials, and news broadcasts. Guy Malek might not even be mentioned on some stations. I'd lived my entire day without any intuition that Guy had been murdered, no tremor whatsoever in my subterranean landscape. So what's life about? Are people not really dead until we've been irrefutably informed? It felt that way to me, as though Guy had, just this moment, been jettisoned out of this world and into the next.

I turned the key in the ignition. Every ordinary act seemed fraught with novelty. My perceptions had changed, and with them many of my assumptions about my personal safety. If Guy could be murdered, why not Henry, or me? I drove on automatic pilot while the street scenes slid past. Familiar neighborhoods looked odd and there was a moment when I couldn't recall with any certainty what town I was in.

Approaching the Maleks', I could see that traffic had increased. Cars filled with the curious cruised by the estate. Heads were turned almost comically in the same direction. There were cars parked on both sides of the road out front. Tires had chewed into the grass, plowing down bushes and crushing the stray saplings. As each new car appeared, the assembled crowd would turn, craning and peering to see if it was someone of note.

My car didn't seem to generate a lot of interest at first. I guess nobody could believe the Maleks would drive a VW bug, especially one like mine, with its dust and assorted dings. It was only when I pulled up at the gate and gave my name to the guard that the reporters surged forward, trying to catch a glimpse of me. They seemed to be fresh troops. I didn't recognize anyone from my earlier trip over.

Somehow the national media had already managed to get camera crews assembled, and I knew that by seven the next morning, someone closely associated with the Maleks would be seen in a three-minute interview. I don't know how the major networks make arrangements so quickly. It was one of the miracles of technology that less than twenty-four hours after Guy Malek's death, somebody would do a close-up of a tear-stained face, maybe Christie's or Myrna's or even Enid's, the cook I'd yet to meet.

There was a black-and-white patrol car parked to one side, along with a vehicle from a private firm. I spotted the security guard pacing along the road, trying to keep the crowd from moving in too close. A uniformed police officer checked my name on his clipboard and waved me in. The gate swung inward by degrees and I idled the engine until the gap was sufficient to ease through. In that brief interval, there were strangers knocking on my car window, yelling questions in my direction. With their various handheld mikes extended, they might have been offering gimcracks for sale. I kept my eyes straight ahead. When I pulled forward through the gate, two male reporters continued to trot alongside me like cut-rate Secret Service agents. The security guard and the cop both converged, cutting off their progress. In my rearview mirror, I could see them begin to argue with the officer, probably reciting their moral, legal, and Constitutional rights.

My heart rate picked up as I eased up the driveway toward the house. I could see five or six uniformed officers prowling across the property, eyes on the ground as if hunting for four-leaved clovers. Light tended to fade rapidly at this hour of the day. Shadows were already collecting beneath the trees. Soon they'd need flashlights to continue the search. There was a second uniformed officer posted at the front door, his face impassive. He walked out to meet my car and I rolled down my window. I gave him my name and watched him scan both his list and my face. Apparently satisfied, he stepped away from the car. In the courtyard to my left, there were already numerous cars jammed into the cobblestone turnaround. "Any place in here all right?"

"You can park in the rear. Then come around and use the front door to go in," he said, and motioned me on.

"Thanks."

I pulled around to the left and parked my car at the far end of the three-car garage. In the diminishing light, a cluster of three floods, activated by motion sensors, flashed on to signal my presence. Except for the kitchen on this end of the house and the library on the other, most of the windows along the front of the house were dark. Around the front, the exterior lighting seemed purely decorative, too pale to provide a welcome in the accumulating gloom.

The uniformed police officer opened the door for me and I passed into the foyer. The library door was ajar and a shaft of light defined one pie-shaped wedge of the wood parquet floor. Given the quiet in the house, I was guessing the technicians were gone—fingerprint experts, the photographer, the crime scene artist, coroner, and paramedics. Tasha appeared in the doorway. "I saw you pull in. How're you doing?"

I said "Fine" in a tone that encouraged her to keep her distance from me. I noticed I was feeling churlish, as much as with her as with circumstance. Homicide makes me angry with its sly tricks and disguises. I wanted Guy Malek back and with some convoluted emotional logic, I blamed her for what had happened. If she hadn't been my cousin, she wouldn't have hired me in the first place. If I hadn't been hired, I wouldn't have found him, wouldn't even have known who he was, wouldn't have cared, and would have felt no loss. She knew this as well as I did and the flicker of guilt that crossed her face was a mirror to mine.

For someone who'd flown back from her vacation in haste, Tasha was flawlessly turned out. She wore a black gabardine pantsuit with a jacket cropped at the waist. The slim, uncuffed trousers had a wide waistband and inverted pleats in front. The jacket had brass buttons and the sleeves were trimmed with a thin gold braid. Somehow the outfit suggested something more than fashion. She looked crisp, authoritative, and diminutive, the dainty MP of lawyers here to keep matters straight.

I followed her into the library with its clusters of dark red cracked leather chairs. The red Oriental carpets looked drab at this hour. The tall leaded glass windows were tinted with the gray cast of twilight, as chilly as frost. Tasha paused to turn on table lamps as she crossed the room. Even the luster of the dark wood paneling failed to lend coziness to the cold stone hearth. The room was shabby and smelled as musty as I remembered it. I'd first met Bennet here just a week ago.

I left my handbag beside a club chair and circled the room restlessly. "Who's the chief investigator? You said there was someone here."

"Lieutenant Robb."

"Jonah? Oh, terrific. How perfect."

"You know him?"

"I know Jonah," I said. When I'd met him, he was working Missing Persons, but the Santa Teresa Police Department has a mandatory rotation system and detectives get moved around. With Lieutenant Dolan's retirement, there was an opening for a homicide investigator. I'd had a short-lived affair with Jonah once when he was separated from his wife, a frequent occurrence in the course of their stormy relationship. They'd been sweethearts since seventh grade and were no doubt destined to be together for life, like owls, except for the intervals of virulent estrangement coming every ten months. I suppose the pattern should have been evident, but I was smitten with him. Later, not surprisingly, she crooked her little finger and he went back to her. Occasionally now, the three of us crossed paths out in public and I'd become an expert at pretending I'd never dallied with him between my Wonder Woman sheets. This probably accounted for his willingness to have me on the scene. He knew he could trust me to keep my mouth shut.

"What's the story?" she asked.

"Nothing. Just skip it. I feel bitchy, I guess, but I shouldn't take it out on you."

I heard footsteps on the stairs and looked up as Christie came in. She wore bulky running shoes and a warm-up suit in some silky material, the blue of the fabric setting off the blue in her eyes. She wore scarcely any makeup and I wondered if this was the outfit she was wearing when Guy's body was discovered. The library, like the living room, was equipped with a wet bar: a small brass sink, a minirefrigerator, an ice bucket, and a tray of assorted liquor bottles. She moved over to the fridge and removed a chilled bottle of white wine. "Anybody want a glass of wine? What about you, Kinsey?"

I said, "Alcohol won't help."

"Don't be absurd. Of course it will. So does Valium. It doesn't change reality, but it improves your attitude. Tasha? Can I interest you in a glass of Chardonnay? This is top of the line." She turned the bottle so she could peer at the price tag on the side. "Nice. This is $36.95."

"I'll have some in a bit. Not just yet," Tasha said.

Mutely, the two of us watched while Christie cut the foil cap from a wine bottle and used a corkscrew. "If I smoked, I'd have a ciggie, but I don't," she said. She poured herself some wine, the bottle clinking clumsily on the rim of the Waterford crystal. "Shit!" she said, pausing to inspect the damage. A jagged crack ran down the side. She dumped the contents in the sink and tossed the glass in the trash. She picked up a second glass and poured again. "We need a fire in here. I wish Donovan were home."

"I can do that," I said. I moved over to the hearth and removed the fire screen. There were six or seven hefty pieces of firewood in a brass carrier. I picked up one and chunked it onto the grate.

"Make sure you don't destroy any evidence," she said.

I looked up at her blankly.

"Ted Bundy killed one of his victims with a hunk of wood," she said, and then shrugged with embarrassment. "Never mind. Not funny. What a day," she said. "I can't figure out how to handle it. I've felt drunk since this morning, completely out of control."

I stacked two more logs on the grate while she and Tasha talked. It was a relief to be involved in a task that was basic and inconsequential. The wood was beautifully seasoned oak. Most of the heat would go straight up the chimney, but it would be a comfort nonetheless. I flicked on the electric match, turned the key in the gas starter, and listened to the comforting *whunk* as the jets ignited. I replaced the fire screen, pausing to adjust the height of the flame. Belatedly, I tuned into their conversation.

Tasha was saying, "Did you ask to have an attorney present?"

"Of course I didn't ask for an attorney. I didn't *do* anything. This was just routine," Christie said irritably. She remained standing behind the bar, leaning against its leather surface. "Sorry. What's the matter with me? I'm completely frazzled."

"Don't worry about it. Who's still down there?"

"Jack and Bennet, I think. They kept everybody separated like they did here. So absurd. What do they think, Donovan and I aren't going to discuss it in detail the minute we can put our heads together?"

"They don't want to risk your influencing one another," I said. "Memory's fragile. It's easily contaminated."

"None of us have anything much to report," she said. "I drank too much at dinner and fell asleep by nine. Donovan was watching TV in the sitting room off our bedroom."

"What about Guy?"

"He went up to bed about the same time I did. He was drunk as all get-out thanks to Bennet's martinis." She caught sight of her fingertips and frowned to herself. She turned away from us and ran water in the sink. "They took prints for comparison."

Tasha directed a brief comment to me. "After the body was removed and the fingerprint techs were finished, the homicide investigator had one of the Maleks' housecleaning crew come over and walk through Guy's room with him describing the usual position of furniture, lamps, ashtrays, that sort of thing."

"Did they find anything?"

"I have no idea. I'm sure she was cautioned to keep her mouth shut. I know they tagged and bagged a bunch of items, but I don't know exactly what or why they were significant. Now they've brought in additional officers and started a grid search of the grounds. Apparently, they spent a lot of time down in the pool house earlier."

Christie broke in. "I could see them from up in my room checking perimeter gates, any point of entrance or exit."

"They're still out there on the property. I noticed that when I came in. But why check the exterior? It almost had to be someone in the house."

Christie bristled. "Not necessarily. What makes you say that? We have people all over. Maybe fifteen a week, with the gardeners and the car washers, housecleaners, and the woman who takes care of the plants. We have no idea where those people come from. For all we know, they're convicted felons or escapees from a mental institution."

I wasn't going to speak to her flight of fancy. If the notion gave her comfort, let her hang on to it. "It's always possible," I said, "but I'm assuming none of them have access to the house at night. I thought you had an alarm system."

"Well, we do. The police were interested in the system as well, but that's the problem," she said. "With all the high winds we've had here the past couple of days, windows were blowing open and the alarm kept going off. It happened twice Monday night after we'd all gone to bed. Scared the shit out of me. We finally turned it off so it wouldn't happen again. Last night, the system wasn't on at all."

"When do they think Guy was killed?" I asked.

"Around ten, I gather. Between ten and eleven. The detective didn't actually say that, but I noticed that was the period that seemed to interest him. Bennet and Jack were both out until late."

A woman in a housekeeper's uniform, with an apron tied over it, peered in at the door. She was short and round, and looked like someone whose eating habits had long ago outstripped any fat-burning activities. She was probably in her mid-forties, with dark hair pulled back neatly under a red-and-white bandanna she'd wrapped around her head. I wasn't sure if the purpose was ornamental or meant to keep falling hair from seasoning the food. "Excuse me. I'm sorry to interrupt, but I'm wondering what time you want dinner served."

Christie made a face. "My fault, Enid. I should have talked to you. Donovan's not back yet and I'm not really sure about Jack and Bennet. What are we having? Will it hold?"

"Baked chicken breasts. I stopped off at the market on my way in to work. I went ahead and changed the menu, so there's plenty if you're having extra people. I did up some oven-roasted potatoes and a casserole of sweet-and-sour cabbage. I can wait and serve if you like." Somehow she managed to indicate without a word that waiting around to serve dinner was the last choice on her list.

"No, no, no. I don't want you to do that. Just leave things in the oven and we can help ourselves. As soon as you're ready, go ahead and take off. I know you were in early."

"Yes, ma'am. Myrna called me. I came as soon as I heard."

"Have the police talked to you? I'm assuming they have. They talked to everyone else."

Enid picked at her apron uncomfortably. "I talked to Lieutenant Bower shortly before you did, I believe. Do you want me tomorrow at the usual time?"

"I don't know yet. Call me in the morning and we'll see what's going on. I may want you here early if that's all right with you."

"Of course."

As soon as she withdrew, Christie said, "Sorry for the interruption. That's Enid Pressman. She's the cook. I guess I could have introduced you. I didn't mean to be rude. Tasha's met her before."

"That's perfectly all right," I said. I made a quick mental note to have a chat with Enid at some point. She'd neatly avoided relating much in the way of information.

Tasha said, "Maybe I will have that drink. Here, let me get it. You look exhausted. We need to sit."

Christie had put the wine bottle in a cooler and now grabbed two more glasses. Tasha moved over to the bar and took the cooler from her, setting it down on a table between two chairs. Christie quizzed me with a gesture, asking if I was ready to have wine.

"I'm fine for now, but go ahead," I said.

Christie curled up in one of the leather chairs. She tucked her legs under her and crossed her arms.

I took the chair closest to the fireplace while Tasha perched on the arm of the chair next to Christie's. Tasha said, "What about Bennet? Where was he last night?"

"I'm not really sure. You'd have to ask him about that."

"And Jack?"

"Over at the country club with a hundred other fellows. There's a pro-am tournament coming up this weekend. Practice rounds start on Thursday. He went to the pairings' party with a friend of his."

"That should be easy enough to verify," Tasha said.

"Would you quit talking like that? He didn't kill Guy and neither did I."

"Christie, I'm not accusing you. I'm trying to analyze your position here. Given the situation, suspicion's bound to fall on one of you. I don't mean you specifically, so don't take offense. Other people may have access to the property, but who'd have a better motive than the family? There's a lot of money at stake."

"But Tasha, that's ridiculous. If one of us were going to kill him, why do it here? Why not somewhere else? Make it look like an accident or random violence."

I raised my hand like a student. "Think of the convenience. If you kill a man in his sleep, you don't have to worry about him putting up a fight."

Jonah Robb appeared in the doorway, his gaze fixed on Christie. "We'll be taking off shortly. The bedroom's still sealed pending the coroner's report. It's strictly off-limits until you hear from us. We'll be here early tomorrow morning to finish things up."

"Of course. Will there be anything else?"

"I understand your brother-in-law received some mail . . ."

"We gave that to the other detective, Lieutenant Bower."

Jonah nodded. "Fine. I'll check with her."

"Do you have any idea what time we can expect my husband? When I left the station, he was still being interviewed."

"I'll have him call if he's there when I get back to the station. With luck, he'll be done and on his way home."

"Thanks."

Jonah's gaze came to rest on mine and he tilted his head. "Can I see you out here?"

I got up and crossed the room. He held the door open and we went into the hall.

He said, "Donovan tells us you were the one who located Guy on behalf of the estate."

"That's right."

"We're going to want to talk to you in the morning, picking up background information."

"Of course. Glad to help. I can stop by at nine on my way into work," I said. "What's this business about the mail?"

"I haven't seen it yet," he said obliquely, meaning *none-of-your-beeswax*. We looked at each other for perhaps half a moment longer than was absolutely essential. I'd always thought Jonah was good looking. Black Irish, I think they call them. Blue eyes, coal black hair. He looked worn-out and tense, his eyes surrounded by a lacework of fine lines, his skin looking coarser than I remembered. Perhaps as a side effect of my renewed sexuality, I found myself sizing up the men in my life. With Jonah, there was a dark radiance in the air. I felt like a fruit fly, wondering if the pheromones were mine or his.

"How's Camilla?"

"She's pregnant."

"Congratulations."

"It's not mine."

"Ah."

"What about you? You involved with anyone these days?"

"Could be. It's hard to know."

His smile was brief. "See you in the morning."

That you will, I thought.

14

Once Jonah was gone, I found myself reluctant to return to the library. I could hear Christie and Tasha talking together companionably, their voices light, the conversation interspersed with nervous laughter. The subject had obviously changed. The ego is ill-prepared to deal with death for long. Even at a wake or a funeral, the topic tends to drift to safer ground whenever possible. I scanned the empty foyer, trying to get my bearings. Across from the library was the living room. I'd been in there, but I'd never seen the rest of the ground floor.

I passed under the stairs to an intersecting corridor that branched off in both directions. I caught a glimpse of a powder room across the hall. I saw two doors on the right, but both were closed. Under the circumstances, I thought it unwise to snoop indiscriminantly. In the unlikely event I encountered a cop, I was roaming in the guise of someone looking for the kitchen so I could offer my help.

Before, the house had felt comfortable despite the touches of shabbiness that appeared throughout. Now I was acutely aware of the imprint of Guy's murder. The very air seemed heavy, the gloom as languorous as a dense fog drifting through the rooms.

I took a left, moving toward the unhappy scent of cooked cabbage at the end of the hall. In a sudden glimpse of the future, I could envision the day when this house would be sold to a private boys' school and the smell of cruciform vegetables would overpower all else. Young lads in hard shoes would clatter through the halls between classes. The room where Guy had been bludgeoned to death would be turned into a dormitory where adolescent boys would abuse themselves surreptitiously after lights out. Always, there would be rumors about the pale apparition gliding down the corridor, hovering on the landing at the turn of the stairs. I found myself walking quickly, anxious for human company.

Beyond the dining room and butler's pantry, the swinging door to the kitchen stood open. The room looked vast to me, but then my entire culinary kingdom would fit in the rear of a moderately priced station wagon. The floors were pale, glossy pegged oak planks stretching out in all directions. The custom cupboards were dark cherry and the counters were topped with mottled green marble. There were sufficient cookbooks, utensils, and small appliances in view to furnish one small section of a Williams-Sonoma retail outlet. The stove top looked bigger than the double bed in my loft and the refrigerator had clear doors with all the contents on view. To the right, there was the equivalent of a little sitting area; and beyond, there was a glassed-in porch that extended the entire length of the room. Here the lush scent of roast chicken and garlic overrode the odor of cooked cabbage. Why does someone else's cooking always smell so much better than your own?

Myrna had come back from the police station. She and Enid were standing together near one of the two kitchen sinks. Myrna's face looked puffy and the prickle of red around her eyes suggested she'd been crying, not within the last few minutes, but perhaps earlier in the day. Enid had pulled on a poplin raincoat and the yards of tan fabric gave her the hapless form and shape of a baked potato. She'd removed her bandanna. Bareheaded, she had a wiry bird's nest of hair that was dark strands streaked with gray. Tea mugs in hand, they must have been having a few last words about the murder because both looked up guiltily as I came in. Given their proximity to events, the two of them must have been privy to just about everything. Certainly, the family wasn't shy about airing their conflicts. God knows they'd squabbled in front of me. Enid and Myrna must have picked up on plenty and probably compared notes.

Enid said, "Can I help you?" She was using the same tone museum guards take when they think you're about to reach out and touch something on the far side of the rope.

"That's what I came to ask," I said. "Can I do anything to help?" Little Miss Goody Two-shoes working on a Girl Scout merit badge.

"Thanks, but everything's under control," she said. She emptied her mug in the sink, opened the dishwasher, and set it in the top rack. "I better go while I can," she murmured.

Myrna said, "I can walk you out if you want."

"I'll be fine," Enid replied. "I can turn on the lights in back." And then with a look at me, "Can I fix you a cup of tea? The water's hot. I'm just on my way out, but it won't take but a minute."

"I'd like that," I said. I'm not that fond of tea, but I had hoped to prolong the contact.

"I can do it," Myrna said. "You go on."

"Are you sure?"

"Absolutely. We'll see you tomorrow."

Enid reached out and patted Myrna on the arm. "Well. Bye-bye. I want you to talk to my chiropractor about that bursitis and you call if you need me. I'll be home all evening." Enid took up a wide canvas tote and disappeared through the utility room, moving toward the backdoor.

I watched Myrna plug in the electric tea kettle. She opened a cabinet nearby and took down a mug. Wincing, she reached for a canister and removed a tea bag that she placed in the mug. Meanwhile, outside, I could hear a car door slam shut and moments later, the sound of Enid starting her car.

I moved over to the counter and perched on a wooden stool. "How're you doing, Myrna? You look tired," I said.

"That's my bursitis flaring up. It's been bothering me for days," she said.

"The stress probably contributes."

Myrna pursed her lips. "That's what my doctor says. I thought I'd seen everything. I'm used to death. In my job, I see a lot of it, but this . . ." She paused to shake her head.

"It must have been hellish around here today. I could hardly believe it when Tasha told me," I said. "You've worked for the Maleks, what . . . eight months?"

"About that. Since last April. The family asked me to stay on after Mr. Malek died. Somebody had to take responsibility for running the house. Enid was tired of doing it and I didn't mind. I've managed many a household, some of 'em a lot bigger than this."

"Couldn't you be making a lot more money as a private-duty nurse?"

She took down a sugar bowl and found a creamer that she filled from a carton of half-and-half in the refrigerator. "Well, yes, but I needed some relief from all the terminal illness. I become attached to my patients and where does that leave me when they pass? I was living like a Gypsy, moving from job to job. Here I have a small apartment of my own and the duties are largely supervisory. I do light cooking occasionally on Enid's nights off, but that's about it. Of course, they complain. They're hard to please sometimes, but I don't let it bother me. In some ways, I'm used to it. The sick are often difficult and it doesn't mean anything. I let it roll right off me."

"I take it you were here last night."

The tea kettle began a hoarse whisper that rapidly turned into a shriek. She paused to unplug it and the shrill sound subsided as though with relief. I waited while she filled the mug and brought it over to me. "Thanks."

I could see her hesitate, apparently debating with herself about her next comment. "Is something bothering you?" I asked.

"I'm not sure what I'm allowed to say," she hesitated. "The lieutenant asked us not to talk to the press . . ."

"Not surprising," I said. "Have you seen 'em out there?"

"Like vultures," she remarked. "When I came back from the station, they were all yelling and vying for my attention, pushing microphones in my direction. Made me want to pull my jacket right up over my face. I felt like one of those criminals you see on the television."

"It's probably only going to get worse. This started out as a minor human-interest story. Now it's big news."

"I'm afraid so," she said. "But to answer your question, yes, I was here, but I didn't hear anything. I've had trouble sleeping lately with this arm of mine. Ordinary analgesics don't begin to touch the pain, so I'd taken a Tylenol with codeine and a prescription sleeping pill. I don't do that often because I dislike the effect. Leaves me feeling logy the next morning, like I never quite wake up. Also, I find the sleep so deep it's almost not restful. I went to bed about eight-thirty and didn't stir until nearly nine this morning."

"Who discovered the body?"

"I believe it was Christie."

"What time was this?"

"Shortly after ten. I'd made myself a cup of coffee and I was back here in the kitchen, watching the morning news on that little TV set. I heard all the commotion. They were supposed to meet for breakfast to talk about the will, and when Guy didn't come down, I guess Bennet got furious. He thought Guy was playing games, at least that's what Christie told me later. Bennet sent her upstairs to fetch him.

Next thing I knew they'd dialed 9-1-1, but I still wasn't sure what was going on. I was just on my way out there when Donovan came in. He looked awful. He'd lost all his color and was white as a sheet."

"Did you see the body?"

"I did, yes. He asked if I'd go up. He thought there might be something I could do, but of course there wasn't. Guy must have been dead several hours by then."

"There's no doubt?"

"Oh, none. Absolutely. He was cold to the touch and his skin was waxen. His skull had been crushed and there was blood everywhere, most of it dried or congealed. Given his injuries, I'd say death must have been quick, if not instantaneous. Also, messy. I know the police have been puzzled by that aspect of the murder."

"Which aspect?"

"What the killer did with his own clothes. Not to be gross about it, but there would have been quite an area of splatter. Blood and brain material. There's no way you could leave the premises without attracting attention. The detectives were interested in a number of articles of clothing. They asked for my help since I take items to the cleaners."

"Did they find anything significant?"

"I don't know. I gave them everything that was going out today. They talked to Enid at length, but I'm not sure what they wanted with her."

"You have any idea what the weapon was?"

"I wouldn't hazard a guess. That's not an area where I feel qualified to comment. There was nothing in the room, at least as far as I could see. I did hear one of the detectives say the autopsy was scheduled first thing tomorrow morning. I imagine the medical examiner will have an opinion," she said. "Have you been hired by the family to investigate?"

I could feel the lie form, but then thought better of it. I said, "Not yet. Let's hope it doesn't come to that. I can't believe anybody in the family is going to turn out to be responsible."

I expected her to pipe up with protests and reassurances, but the quiet that followed was significant. I could sense a desire to confide, but I couldn't imagine what. I let my gaze rest on hers with an expression I hoped appeared trustworthy and encouraging. I could almost feel my head tilt like a dog trying to decipher the direction of a high-pitched whistle.

She'd become aware of a dried speck on the counter and she

worked at it with her fingernail, not looking at me. "This is really none of my business. I had only respect for Mr. Malek . . ."

"Absolutely."

"I wouldn't want anyone to think badly of me, but I can't help but hear things while I'm going about my business. I'm paid well and God knows, I enjoy the work. Or at least I did."

"I'm sure you're only trying to help," I said, wondering where she was going with this.

"You know, Bennet never agreed to share the money. He wasn't convinced that was Bader's intention and neither was Jack. Of course, Jack sided with Bennet in just about everything."

"Well, maybe they weren't convinced, but given the missing will, I don't know what choice they had, short of court action. I gather nothing was settled."

"Not at all. If they'd settled their business, Guy would have gone home. He was miserable here. I could see it in his face."

"Well, that's true. When I talked to him on Monday, he admitted he'd been drinking."

"Oh, especially last night. They started with cocktails and went through four or five bottles of wine with dinner. And then, port and liqueurs. It was still going on when I went off to bed. I helped Enid with the dishes and she could see how exhausted I was. Both of us heard them quarreling."

"Bennet and Guy quarreled?"

She shook her head, lips moving.

I cupped a hand to my ear. "Excuse me. I didn't hear that."

She cleared her throat and raised her voice half a notch. "Jack. Guy and Jack quarreled before Jack went off to his country club. I told the lieutenant about it and now I'm wondering if I should have kept my mouth shut."

"The truth is the truth. If that's what you heard, you had to tell the police."

"You don't think he'll be mad?" Her tone was anxious, her expression almost childlike in its apprehension.

I suspected the entire family would have fits when they heard, but we all had an obligation to cooperate with the police investigation. "Maybe so, but you can't worry about that. Guy was *murdered* last night. It's not up to you to protect anyone."

She nodded mutely, but I could see she remained unconvinced.

"Myrna, I mean this. Whatever happens, I don't think you should feel responsible."

"But I didn't have to volunteer the information. I like Jack. I can't believe he'd hurt anyone."

"Listen, you think I'm not going to end up in the same position? The cops are going to talk to me, too. I have to go down there tomorrow and I'm going to end up doing exactly what you did."

"You are?"

"Of course. I heard them quarrel the night I came here for drinks. Bennet and Donovan were going at it hammer and tongs. Christie was the one who told me they did it all the time. That doesn't make 'em killers, but it's not up to us to interpret the facts. You have to tell the cops what you heard. I'm sure Enid will back you up. Nobody's going to be arrested on that basis anyway. It's not like you saw Jack coming out of Guy's room with a bloody two-by-four."

"Not at all. Of course not." I could see some of the tension begin to leave her face. "I hope you're right. I mean, I can see what you're saying. The truth is the truth. All I heard was a quarrel. I never heard Jack threaten him."

"Exactly," I said, with a glance at my watch. It was nearly six by then. "If you're through for the night, I better let you go. I probably ought to get on out of here myself, but first I want to have a little chat with Christie."

Anxiety flickered in her eyes. "You won't mention our conversation?"

"Would you quit *worrying?* I won't say a word and I don't want you saying anything either."

"I appreciate that. I believe I would like to go wash my face."

I waited until Myrna had disappeared through the utility room, moving toward her apartment. My tea was untouched. I emptied my cup and left it in the sink. Despite Enid's good example, I've never owned a dishwasher and don't know the first thing about loading one. I pictured one false move and every dish would go flying, crashing in a heap of rubble. I returned to the library. Christie and Tasha had turned on the television set. Christie held the remote and she was switching from channel to channel to see if she could catch the news. She pressed the Mute button when I came in, turning to look at me. "Oh, there you are. Come in and join us. Tasha thought you were gone."

"I'm on my way," I said. "I went out to the kitchen to see if I could help out there. Could I ask you a question before I take off? I heard you mention the mail when you were talking to Lieutenant Robb. Can I ask what that was?"

"Sure. Uhm, let's see. I guess late Monday afternoon someone put an unsigned letter in the mailbox. The envelope had Guy's name on it, but there was no return address. He left it on the hall table when he went to bed last night. I thought the police might want to take a look."

"Was it typed or handwritten."

"The envelope was typed."

"Did you read the letter?"

"Of course not, but I know it bothered Guy. He didn't say what it was, but I gather it was something unpleasant."

"Did he ever mention a Max Outhwaite? Does the name mean anything to you?"

"Not that I remember." She turned to Tasha. "Does it ring a bell with you?"

Tasha shook her head. "What's the connection?"

"That's how the reporter first heard Guy was back. Someone named Max Outhwaite dropped off a letter at the *Dispatch,* but when Katzenbach checked it out, there was no one by that name and no such address. I double-checked as well and came up blank."

"Never heard of him," Christie said. "Is there any chance he's connected to one of Guy's old sprees? Maybe Outhwaite was somebody Guy mistreated back then."

"Possible," I said. "Do you mind if I check Bader's file upstairs?"

"What file?" Tasha asked.

Christie answered before I did. "Bader kept a folder of newspaper clippings about Guy's various arrests and his scrapes with the law. It goes back quite a way."

"I'll tell you something else crossed my mind," I said. "This Outhwaite, whoever he is, certainly put Jeff Katzenbach on the trail of Guy's criminal history. I'm not sure Jeff would have known about it otherwise. The minute I saw the letter, I remember wondering if it was really Bennet or Jack who tipped him off somehow."

"Using Outhwaite's name?"

"It seems possible," I said.

"But why would either of them do that? What's the point?"

"That's the problem. I don't know. Anyway, I could be off base on this one," I said. "I do like the idea that Outhwaite's someone Guy sinned against in the old days."

"Take the file if you want. It was still on the desk in Bader's office last I saw."

"Let me pop upstairs and grab it. I'll be right back."

I moved out of the library and crossed the foyer. Maybe when I talked to Jonah, he'd level with me about the letter. I went up the steps two at a time, studiously avoiding a look down the hall. I had no idea which room Guy had been in, but I didn't want to go near it. I took a hard left at the head of the stairs and went straight to Bader's room, where I opened the door and flipped on the overhead light. Everything seemed to be in order. The room was cold and smelled slightly musty from disuse. The overhead illumination was dim and the pale colors in the room looked flat. I passed through to the office beyond, hitting switches as I went. Bader's life force was being systematically erased. Closets had been emptied, all the personal items removed from his desktop.

I surveyed the surrounding area. I spotted the folder with all the newspaper articles about Guy's past behavior, relieved that the cops hadn't swept through and taken it. On the other hand, the search warrant probably wasn't that broad. The list of property to be seized might have been directed only toward the murder weapon itself. I leafed through the clippings, speed-reading for content, looking for the name *Outhwaite* or anything close. There was nothing. I checked through some of the stray folders on the desk, but found nothing else that seemed relevant. One more dead end, though the idea was sound —someone with a grudge making Guy's life difficult. I pressed the file under my arm and left the room, turning off the lights as I went.

I pulled the door shut behind me, pausing in the hallway outside the master suite. Something felt wrong. My first urge was to scurry down the stairs toward the lighted rooms below, but I found myself slowing. I could hear a crackling sound and I peered to my left. The far end of the corridor was enveloped in shadow, except for an X of crime scene tape across three doorways. As I watched, the tape seemed to become nearly luminous, vibrating audibly as if rattled by wind. I thought for a moment the tape would break free, clicking and snapping as though a current were moving through it. The air on the landing was chilly and there was the faint scent of something animal— wet dog or old fur. For the first time, I allowed myself to experience the horror of Guy's death.

I began to descend, one hand on the railing, the other clutching the file. I pivoted, reluctant to turn my back on the darkness behind me. For a moment, I scrutinized the stretch of corridor I could see. Something hovered in my peripheral vision. I turned my head slowly, nearly moaning with fear. I could see sparkles of light, almost like dust motes materializing in the stillness. I felt a sudden flush of heat and I could hear ringing in my ears, a sound I associated with childhood fainting spells. My phobia about needles had often inspired such episodes. When I was young, I was often subjected to a typhoid inoculation, a tine test for tuberculosis, or a periodic tetanus injection. While the nurse took the time to pooh-pooh my fears, assuring me "big girls" didn't put up the fuss I did, the ringing would begin, building to a high pitch and then silence. My vision would shrink, the light spiraling inward to a tiny point. The cold would rush up and the next thing I'd know, there'd be anxious faces bending over me and the sharp scent of smelling salts held under my nose.

I leaned back against the wall. My mouth flooded with something that tasted like blood. I closed my eyes tightly, conscious of the thudding of my heart and the clamminess in my palms. While Guy Malek slept, someone had crept along this hallway in the darkness last night, toting a blunt object of sufficient brute matter to extinguish his life. Less than a day ago. Less than a night. Perhaps it had taken one blow, perhaps several. What troubled me was the notion of that first bone-crushing crack as his skull shattered and collapsed. Poor Guy. I hoped he hadn't wakened before the first blow fell. Better he slept on before the last sleep became final.

The ringing in my ears went on, mounting in intensity like the howling of wind. I was weighted with dread. Occasionally in nightmares, I suffer from this effect—an overpowering urge to run without the ability to move. I struggled to make a sound. I would have sworn there was a presence, someone or something, that hovered and then passed. I tried to open my eyes, almost convinced I'd see Guy Malek's killer passing down the stairs. My heartbeat accelerated to a life-threatening pitch, thrumming in my ears like the sound of running feet. I opened my eyes. The sound ceased abruptly. Nothing. No one. The ordinary noises of the house reasserted themselves. The scene before me was blank. Polished floor. Empty hall. Incandescent light from the chandelier. Glancing back down the corridor, I could see that the X's of crime scene tape was simply tape again. I sank down on the stairs. The whole of the experience had surely taken less than a minute, but the rush of adrenaline had left my hands shaking.

Finally, I roused myself from the step where I'd been sitting for God knows how long. From somewhere downstairs, I could hear a mix of male and female voices, and I knew without question that Donovan, Bennet, and Jack had returned from the police station, arriving while I was still in Bader's office. Below me, the library door stood open. Tasha and Christie must have gone to join them. Faintly, from the direction of the kitchen, I could hear the clatter of ice cubes and the clink of bottles. Drink time again. Everybody in the house seemed to need alcohol along with extended psychiatric care.

I completed my descent, anxious to avoid encountering the family. I returned to the library, peering in with caution, relieved to see the room empty. I grabbed up my handbag and shoved the file down in the outside pocket, then headed for the front door, heart still pounding. I pulled the door shut behind me, careful to soften the sound of the latch clicking into place. Somehow it seemed important to slip away undetected. After my experience on the stairs—whatever it was —I was incapable of making superficial conversation. It didn't seem unreasonable to suppose that someone in this household had murdered Guy Malek and I'd be damned if I'd make nice until I knew who it was.

15

Back in my neighborhood, parking spaces were at a premium and I was forced to leave my VW almost a block away. I locked the car and trotted to my apartment. It was fully dark by then and a chill shivered in the trees like wind. I crossed my arms for warmth, clutching the strap of my handbag as it bumped against my side. I used to carry a handgun as a matter of course, but I've given up that practice. I moved through the gate, which gave its usual welcoming squeak. My place was dark, but I could see the lights on in Henry's kitchen. I didn't want to be alone. I headed for his backdoor and rapped on the glass.

He emerged moments later from the living room. He gave a half wave when he saw me and crossed to let me in. "I was just watching the news. The murder's on all channels. Sounds bad."

"Awful. It's vile."

"Have a seat and get warmed up. It's gotten nippy out there."

I said, "Don't let me interrupt. I'll be fine sitting here."

"Don't be silly. You look cold."

"I'm freezing."

"Well, wrap up."

I put my bag down and grabbed his afghan, folding its weight around me like a shawl as I slid into his rocking chair. "Thanks. This is great. I'll be warmer in a minute. It's mostly tension."

"I'm not surprised. Have you eaten supper yet?"

"I think I had lunch, but I can't remember what I ate."

"I've got beef stew if you want. I was just about to have a bowl myself."

"Please." I watched as Henry adjusted the flame under the stew. He took out a loaf of homemade bread, sliced it thickly, and placed it in a basket with a napkin folded over it. He assembled bowls and spoons, napkins, and wine glasses, moving around the kitchen with his usual ease and efficiency. Moments later, he set bowls of stew on the table. I left his rocking chair and shuffled over to the kitchen table still wrapped in his afghan. He pushed the butter in my direction as he settled in his chair. "So tell me the story. I know the basic details. They've been blasting that across the TV screen all afternoon."

I began to eat as I talked, realizing how hungry I was. "You may know more than I do. I'm too smart to stick my nose in the middle of a homicide investigation. These days it's hard enough to put a case together without an outsider interfering."

"You're not exactly an amateur."

"I'm not an expert either. Let the techs and forensic specialists give it their best shot. I'll keep my distance unless I'm told otherwise. My stake's personal, but it's really not my business. I liked Guy. He was nice. His brothers piss me off. This is great stew."

"You have a theory about the murder?"

"Let's put it this way This is not a case where some stranger broke in and killed Guy in the middle of a robbery. The poor man was asleep. From what I heard, everybody'd been drinking, so he more than likely passed out. He wasn't used to hard liquor, especially in massive quantities, which is how the Maleks go at it. Somebody knew where his room was and probably knew he was in no condition to defend himself. I tell you, with the possible exception of Christie, I've developed such an aversion to that family I can hardly bear to be under the same roof with them. I feel guilty about Guy. I feel guilty about finding him and guilty he came back. I don't know what else I could have done, but I wish I'd left him in Marcella where he was safe."

"You didn't encourage him to return."

"No, but I didn't argue that strenuously either. I should have been more explicit. I should have detailed their attitude. I thought the danger was emotional. I didn't think anyone would go after him and bludgeon him to death."

"You think it was one of his brothers?"

"I'm tempted by the idea," I said reluctantly. "It's a dangerous assumption and I know I shouldn't jump to conclusions, but it's always easier to pin suspicion on someone you dislike."

By eight-thirty that night, I was back in my apartment with the door locked. I sat at the kitchen counter for what felt like an hour before I worked up the courage to call Peter and Winnie Antle, who'd been following the story on the Santa Maria news station. The entire church congregation had come together earlier that evening, shocked and saddened by the murder. I hoped to cushion their loss, though in reality their faith provided them more comfort than I was able to offer. I told them I'd do what I could to keep in touch, and I broke the connection feeling little or no solace. Once the lights were turned out, I lay in my bed with a stack of quilts piled over me, trying to get warm, trying to make sense of what had happened that day. I was weighted with dread. Guy's death had generated something far worse than grief. What I experienced was not sorrow, but a heavy regret that was wedged in my chest like an undigested lump of hot meat. I didn't sleep well. My eyes seemed to come open every twenty minutes or so. I changed positions and adjusted the covers. First I was too hot, then too cold. I kept thinking the next arrangement of limbs would offer sufficient comfort to lure me to sleep. I lay on my stomach with my arms shoved under my pillow, turned on my back with my shoulders uncovered. I tried my left side, knees pulled up, arms tucked under, switched to my right side with one foot sticking out. I must have set the alarm without thinking about it because the next thing I knew, the damn thing was going off in my ear, bringing me straight up out of the only decent sleep I'd managed all night. I turned off the alarm. I refused to run. There was no way I was budging from the chrysalis of heat-generating quilts. Next thing I knew, it was nine-fifteen and I felt compelled to drag myself out of bed. I had a date with Jonah Robb down at the police station. I checked my reflection in the bathroom mirror. Nice. My color was bad and I had bags under my eyes.

As it turned out, it wasn't Jonah I spoke to but Lieutenant Bower. She kept me waiting for fifteen minutes, sitting on a little two-person bench in what I suppose would be referred to as the lobby at the police station. Under the watchful gaze of the officer at the desk, I shifted in my seat and stared at the rack of crime prevention pamphlets. I also eavesdropped shamelessly while six whining drivers came to complain about their traffic tickets. Finally, Lieutenant Bower peered around the door from the Investigative Division. "Miss Mill-hone?"

I'd never met Betsy Bower, but I'd been curious about her. The name suggested someone perky and blond, a former varsity cheer-leader with terrific thighs and no brains. To my dismay, Lieutenant Bower was the least perky woman I'd had the pleasure to meet. She was the police equivalent of an Amazon: statuesque, eight inches taller than I, and probably fifty pounds heavier. She had dark hair that she wore skinned straight back, and little round, gold-rimmed glasses. She had a flawless complexion. If she wore makeup at all, it was artfully done. When she spoke, I caught sight of endearingly crooked teeth, which I realized later might have explained her reluctance to smile. It was also possible she didn't like me and longed to squash me like a bug.

I followed her into a small cubicle with two wooden chairs and a scratched wooden table that had a tendency to wobble if you tried to rest your arm on it, pretending to be relaxed. She had nothing with her—no pen, no legal pad, no file, no notes. She looked directly at me, offering a few brisk sentences after which it was my turn. Somehow I had the feeling she'd remember every word I said. More likely our conversation was being recorded surreptitiously. I would have done a furtive feel-check for wiring along the underside of the table, but I was worried about the wads of old chewing gum and dried boogers parked there.

She said, "We appreciate your coming in. I understand you were hired by the estate to locate Guy Malek. Can you tell me how you went about that?" Her gaze was watchful, her manner subdued.

The question caught me by surprise. I felt a sudden flash of fear, color rising in my cheeks as if I'd just emerged from a tanning booth. I stalled like a little airplane with a tank full of bad fuel. Too late, I realized I should have prepared for this. Ordinarily, I don't lie to police officers because that would be very naughty, wouldn't it? At heart, I'm a law-and-order type. I believe in my country, the flag, paying taxes and parking tickets, returning library books on time, and crossing the street with the light. Also, I'm inclined to get tears in my eyes every time I hear the National Anthem sung by somebody who really knows how to belt it out. Right then, however, I knew I was going to have to do a little verbal tap dance because how I "went about" finding Guy Malek wasn't exactly legitimate. Neither Darcy Pascoe nor I had any business dipping into CFI's computer system to do a DMV check on a matter completely unrelated to an insurance claim. I'd probably violated some kind of civil ordinance or penal code number something-something. At the very least, the two of us were in serious breach of company policy, department regulations, common decency, and proper etiquette. This might well go down on my permanent record, something my elementary school principal had threatened me with every time I fled school with Jimmy Tait in the fifth and sixth grades. I didn't think what I'd done was a jailable offense, but I was, after all, sitting at the police station and I did have my private investigator's license to protect. Since I'd now hesitated a conspicuous five seconds, I thought it was wise to launch in on *something*.

I said, "Ah. Well. I met with Donovan, Bennet, and Jack Malek last Wednesday. In the course of those conversations, I was given Guy Malek's date of birth and his Social Security number. So late in the day on Thursday, I went over to the DMV offices and asked the clerk if there was any record of a driver's license in Guy Malek's name. The information that came back was that his license had been surrendered in 1968, but that he'd been issued a California identification card. His mailing address was listed in Marcella, California. I reported that to Tasha Howard, the attorney for the estate, and to Donovan Malek, who authorized me to drive up to Marcella to verify the address. Marcella's a small town. I wasn't there ten minutes before I got a line on Guy. Frankly, I didn't think he should come down here."

"Why is that?"

Hey, as long as my butt wasn't on the line, I didn't care who I ratted out here. "His brothers were upset at having to give him a share of their father's estate. They felt he'd been paid all the monies he was entitled to. There was the issue of a second will, which came up missing when the old man died. Bennet was convinced his father had disinherited Guy, but since that will was never found, the prior will was the one being entered into probate." I did a little detour at that point, giving Lieutenant Bower the gist of the business about Max Outhwaite, whose letter to the *Dispatch* had set all the adverse publicity in motion. She didn't leap up with excitement, but it did serve to distract her (I hoped) from the issue of my illegal computer access.

She took me through a series of questions related to the Maleks' attitude toward Guy, which I characterized as hostile. I told her about the outburst I'd witnessed between Donovan and Bennet. She asked me a number of pointed questions about Jack's statements regarding Guy, but I honestly couldn't think of anything he'd said that suggested a homicidal bent. In our initial conversation, he'd expressed bitterness at Guy's defection, but that had been almost eighteen years ago, so I wasn't convinced it was relevant. Though I didn't say so to her, I'd pegged Jack as the family mascot, someone harmless and doglike, trained to distract others with his antics. I didn't feature him as a prime player in any ongoing domestic drama.

"When did you last talk to Guy?" she asked.

"He called Monday night. He needed a break so I drove over to the house and met him near the side gate. I was glad to hear from him. I'd been worried because I knew the media had picked up the story. Peter Antle, the pastor of his church up north, had been trying to get in touch with him. The house was literally under siege and it wasn't possible to get a call through. I'd driven over there once before, hoping to make contact, and I'd just about given up."

"Why were you so interested in talking to him?"

"Largely, because Peter and his wife, Winnie, were concerned."

"Aside from that."

I stared at her, wondering what she had in mind. Did she think I was *romantically* involved? "You never met Guy," I said, stating it as fact and not a question.

"No." Her face was without animation. Her curiosity was professional and had an analytic cast to it. That was her job, of course, but I found myself struggling to articulate his appeal.

"Guy Malek was a beautiful man," I said in a voice suddenly fragile. Inexplicably, I found myself pricked by grief. My eyes stung with tears. I could feel my face get puffy and my nose turn hot. It seemed odd that in Henry's company I'd felt nothing while there, but in the face of Betsy Bowers's cold authority, all my unprocessed sorrow was surfacing. I took a deep breath, trying to cover my emotions. I was avoiding her eyes, but she must have picked up on my distress because she produced a tissue from somewhere that suddenly appeared in my field of vision. I took it with gratitude, feeling vulnerable and exposed.

Within moments, I was fine. I have strong self-control and managed to get my emotions back in the box again. "Sorry. I'm not sure where that came from. I really haven't felt much sorrow since I heard about his death. I should have guessed it was down there. He was a good person and I'm really sorry he's gone."

"I can understand that," she said. "Would you care for some water?"

"I'll be fine," I said. "It's funny—I really only saw him three times. We talked on the phone, but we weren't exactly best friends. He seemed boyish, a young soul. I must have a weakness for guys who never quite manage to grow up. I'd already given Donovan an invoice and I figured my job was done. Then Guy called on Saturday. Donovan had called him, urging him to come down so they could talk about the will. Personally, I didn't think the visit was such a hot idea, but Guy was determined."

"Did he say why?"

"He had emotional accounts to pay. At the time he left home, he was messed up on drugs. He'd been in a lot of trouble and alienated just about everyone. Once he was settled in Marcella, he cleaned up his act, but he'd left a lot of unfinished business. He said he wanted to make his peace."

"When you last spoke to him, did he mention contact with other people from his past?"

"No. I know a letter was delivered—Christie mentioned it last night —but that came on Monday and Guy never said a word about it when I saw him. As far as I know, there was nothing else. Was it significant?"

"We'd rather not discuss the content until we check it out."

"Who wrote it? Or would you rather not discuss that either?"

"Right."

"Was it typed?"

"Why do you ask?"

"Because of the letter to the *Dispatch* that generated all the hype. If the papers hadn't been tipped off, no one would have known he was back in town."

"I see what you're saying. We'll follow up."

"Can I ask about the autopsy?"

"Dr. Yee hasn't finished yet. Lieutenant Robb is there now. We'll know more when he gets back."

"What about the murder weapon?"

Her face went blank again. I was wasting my breath, but I couldn't seem to let go. "You have a suspect?" I asked.

"We're pursuing some possibilities. We're doing backgrounds on a number of people associated with the family. We're also checking everybody's whereabouts to see if all the stories add up."

"In other words, you won't say."

Chilly smile. "That's correct."

"Well. I'll do what I can to help."

"We'd appreciate that."

She made no move to close, which was puzzling. From my perspective, we'd pretty much wound up our chat. She'd asked all her questions and I'd told her what I knew. In the unspoken structure of a police interview, Detective Bower was in charge and I'd have to dance to her tune. In the unexpected pause, I could see that it was suddenly her turn to stall.

She said, "Rumor has it you're involved with Lieutenant Robb."

I squinted at her in disbelief. "*He* told you that?"

"Someone else. I'm afraid this is a small town, even smaller when it comes to law enforcement. So it's not true?"

"Well, I *was* involved, but I'm not now," I said. "What makes you ask?"

The look on her face underwent a remarkable alteration. The careful neutrality fell away and in one split second, she went from blank to blushing.

I sat back in my chair, taking a new look at her. "Are you *smitten* with him?"

"I've been out with him twice," she said cautiously.

"Ohhh, I see. Now I get it," I said. "Listen, I'm fond of Jonah, but it's strictly over between us. I'm the least of your worries. It's the dread Camilla you'd better be concerned about."

Detective Betsy Bower had abandoned any pose of professionalism. "But she's living with some guy and she's *pregnant.*"

I raised a hand. "Trust me. In the continuing saga of Jonah and Camilla, the mere fact of this infant has no bearing on their relationship. He may act like he's cured, but he isn't, believe me. Camilla and Jonah are so enmeshed with each other I don't know what it would take to split up their act. Actually, now that I think about it, you probably have as good a shot at it as any."

"You really think so?"

"Why not? I was always too caught up in my own abandonment issues, I hated being a minor player in their little theater production. We're talking seventh-grade bonding. Junior high school romance. I couldn't compete. I lack the emotional strength. You look like you could tackle it. You have self-esteem issues? Are you a nail biter? Bed wetter? Jealous or insecure?"

She shook her head. "Not a bit."

"What about confrontation?"

"I like a good fight," she said.

"Well, you better get ready then because in my experience, she's indifferent to him until someone else comes along. And for God's sake, don't play fair. Camilla goes for broke."

"Thanks. I'll remember. We'll be in touch."

"I can't wait."

On the street again, I felt as if I was emerging from a darkened tunnel. The sunlight was harsh and all the colors seemed too bright. Nine black-and-white patrol cars were lined up along the curb. Across the street, a row of small California bungalows were painted in discordant pastel shades. Flowering annuals in fuchsia, orange, and magenta stood out in bold relief against the vibrant green of new foliage. I left my car in the public parking lot and walked the remaining blocks to work.

I entered Kingman and Ives by the unmarked side door. I unlocked my office and let myself in, glancing down at the floor. On the carpet, there was a plain white business-size envelope with my name and address typed across the front. The postmark was Santa Teresa, dated Monday P.M. Distracted, I set my bag on the desk, took out Bader's file, and set it on top of the file cabinet. I went back to the letter and picked it up with care. I centered it on my desk, touching only the corners while I lifted the handset and dialed Alison in reception.

"Hi, Alison. This is Kinsey. You know anything about this letter that was slipped under my door?"

"It was delivered yesterday afternoon. I held on to it up here, thinking you'd be back and finally decided it was better to go ahead and stick it under your door. Why, did I do something wrong?"

"You did fine. I was just curious."

I put the phone down and stared at the envelope. I'd picked up a fingerprint kit at a trade show recently and for a moment I debated about dusting for latents. Seemed pointless to tell the truth. Alison had clearly handled it and even if I brought up a set of prints, what was I to do with them? I couldn't picture the cops running them on the basis of my say-so. Still, I decided to be cautious. I took out a letter opener and slit the flap of the envelope, using the tip to slide the note onto my desk. The paper was cheap bond, folded twice, with no date and no signature. I used a pencil eraser to open the paper, anchoring opposite corners with the letter opener and the edge of my appointment book.

Dear Miss Milhone,

I thought I should take a moment to inlighten you on the subject of Guy Malek. I wonder if you rilly know who your dealing with. He is a liar and a theif. I find it sickning that he could get a second chance in life threw the acquisition of Sudden Riches. Why should he get the benefitt of five million dollars when he never urned one red cent? I don't think we can count on him making amens for his passed crimes. You better be carefull your not tared with the same brush.

I found a transparent plastic sleeve and slid the letter inside, then opened my desk drawer and took out the copy of the letter Max Outhwaite had written to Jeffrey Katzenbach, placing the two side by side for comparison. On superficial examination, the typefont looked the same. As before, my name was misspelled. Thanks, it's two *l*'s, please. The sender seemed to have a problem distinguishing *your* from *you're* and consistently reversed the two. The use of *threw* for *through* was the same, but there were other oddities of note. My letter was less than half the length of the one to Katzenbach, yet it had more spelling mistakes. To my untutored eye, the two sets of errors were curiously inconsistent. If the writer were relying strictly on phonetics, why would words like *acquisition, aforementioned,* and *besieges* be spelled right? Certainly in my letter, there were far fewer commas, exclamation points, and Capitalizations! It was possible there was a certain level of carelessness at work, but I also had to wonder if the writer weren't simply *pretending* to use language badly. There was something vaguely amusing about the use of the word *amens* instead of *amends,* especially in the context of a born-again.

From another angle, why affix the name *Max Outhwaite* to the first letter, tacking on the embellishment of a phony address, and leave mine unsigned? I had to guess that *Outhwaite* imagined (quite correctly, as it turned out) that an unsigned letter to the *Dispatch* would get thrown in the trash. It was also likely the sender had no idea I'd end up with both. While I understood the reasoning behind the letter to the *Dispatch,* why this one to me? What was Outhwaite's intent?

I took out my magnifying glass and cranked up my three way bulb to maximum illumination. Under magnification, other similarities became apparent. In both documents, the letter *a* was twisted on its axis, leaning slightly to the left, and on the lowercase *i* a portion of the serif was broken off along the bottom. Additionally, the lowercase *e, o, a,* and *d* were dirty and tended to print as filled dots instead of circles, suggestive of an old-fashioned fabric ribbon. On my portable Smith-Corona, I'd been known to use a straight pin to clean the clogged typewriter keys.

I left the letters on my desk and took a walk around the room. Then I sat down in my swivel chair, opened my pencil drawer, and pulled out a pack of index cards. It took me fifteen minutes to jot down the facts as I remembered them, one piece of information per card until I'd exhausted my store. I laid them out on my desk, rearranging the order, shuffling them into columns, looking for connections I hadn't seen before. It didn't amount to much from my perspective, but there'd soon be more information available. The autopsy was done by now and the medical examiner would have a concrete opinion about the manner and cause of death. We were all assuming Guy died from blunt-force trauma to the head, but there might be some underlying pathology. Maybe he'd died of a heart attack, maybe he'd been poisoned, expiring in his sleep before the first blow was struck. I couldn't help but wonder what difference any of it made. Guy would be laid to rest, his body probably taken back to Marcella for burial up there. The various forensic experts would go on sifting through the evidence until the case was resolved. Eventually, the story would be told in its entirety and maybe I'd understand then how everything fit. In the meantime, I was left with all the unrelated fragments and a sick feeling in my stomach.

I took the letters down the hall, the one still encased in its plastic sleeve. At the Xerox machine, I made a copy of each so that I now had two sets. The copies I placed in my briefcase, along with the notes I'd made on my index cards. The originals I locked away carefully in my bottom drawer. When the phone rang, I let the answering machine pick up. "Kinsey, this is Christie Malek. Listen, the police were just here with a warrant for Jack's arrest—"

I snatched up the receiver. "Christie? It's me. What's going on?"

"Oh, Kinsey. Thank God. I'm sorry to bother you, but I didn't know what else to do. I put a call through to Donovan, but he's out in the field. I don't know where Bennet's gone. He left about nine, without a word to anyone. Do you know the name of a good bail bondsman? Jack told me to get him one, but I've looked in the Yellow Pages and can't tell one from the other."

"Are you sure he's in custody? They didn't just take him to the station for another interview?"

"Kinsey, they put him in *handcuffs*. They read him his rights and took him off in the back of an unmarked car. We were both in shock. I don't have any money—less than a hundred bucks in cash—but if I knew who to call . . ."

"Forget about the bondsman. If Jack's being charged with murder, it's a no-bail warrant. What he needs is a good criminal attorney and the sooner the better."

"I don't know any attorneys, except Tasha!" she shrieked. "What am I supposed to do, pick a name out of a *hat?*"

"Wait a minute, Christie. Just calm down."

"I don't want to calm down. I'm scared. I want help."

"I know that. I know. Just wait a minute," I said. "I have a suggestion. Lonnie Kingman's office is right next door to mine. You want me to go see if he's in? You can't do better than Lonnie. He's a champ."

She was silent for an instant. "All right, yes. I've heard of him. That sounds good."

"Give me a few minutes and we'll see what we can do."

16

I caught Lonnie's secretary, Ida Ruth, on her way back from the kitchen with a coffeepot in hand. I hooked a thumb in the direction of Lonnie's door. "Is he in there?"

"He's eating breakfast. Help yourself."

I tapped on the door and then opened it, peering in. Lonnie was sitting at his desk with an oversized plastic container of some kind of chalky-looking protein drink. I could see bubbles of dried powder floating on the surface and the barest suggestion of a milky mustache on Lonnie's upper lip. From assorted bottles, he'd emptied out a pile of vitamins and nutritional supplements, and he was popping down pills between sips of a shake so thick it might have been melted ice cream. One of the gel caps was the size and the color of a stone in a topaz dinner ring. He swallowed it as though he were doing a magic trick.

Lonnie more nearly resembles a bouncer than an attorney. He's short and stocky—five feet four, two hundred four pounds—bulging with muscles from his twenty years of power lifting. He's got one of those revved-up metabolisms that burns calories like crazy and he radiates high energy along with body heat. His speech is staccato and he's generally amped up on coffee, anxiety, or lack of sleep. I've heard people claim he's on the sauce—shooting anabolic steroids in concert with all the iron he pumps. Personally, I doubt it. He's been manic for the whole nine years of our acquaintance and I've never seen him exhibit any of the rage or aggression allegedly generated by extended steroid use. He's married to a woman with a black belt in karate and she's never once complained about testicles shriveled to the size of raisins, another unhappy side effect of steroid abuse.

His usually shaggy hair had been trimmed and subdued. His dress shirt was pulled tightly across his shoulders and biceps. I don't know his neck size, but he claims a tie makes him feel he's on the brink of being hanged. The one he was wearing was pulled askew, his collar unbuttoned, and his suit jacket off. He'd hung it neatly from a hanger hooked through the handle of a file drawer. His shirt was spanking white, but badly wrinkled, and he had rolled up the sleeves. Sometimes he wears a vest to conceal his rumpled state, but not today. He swallowed the last of a palmful of pills, holding up a hand to indicate that he was aware of me. He chugged off the balance of his protein drink and shook his head with satisfaction. "Whew, that's good."

"Are you tied up at the moment?"

"Not at all. Come on in."

I entered the office and closed the door behind me. "I just got a call from Christie Malek. Have you been following that story?"

"The murder? Who hasn't? Sit, sit, sit. I'm not due in court until two P.M. What's up?"

"Jack Malek's been arrested and needs to talk to an attorney. I told Christie I'd see if you were interested." I took a seat in one of two black leather client chairs.

"When was he picked up?"

"Fifteen or twenty minutes ago, I'd guess."

Lonnie began to screw the lids back on the motley collection of bottles sitting on his desk. "What's the deal? Fill me in."

I brought him up to speed on the case as succinctly as possible. This was our first conversation about the murder and I wanted him to have as thorough an understanding as I could muster on short notice. As I spoke, I could see Lonnie's gears engage and the wheels start to turn. I was saying, "Last I heard—this was from the housekeeper—Guy and Jack quarreled after hours of heavy drinking and Jack went off to a pairings' party at the country club."

"I wonder how the cops are gonna bust that one. You'd think at least half a dozen people would have seen him there." Lonnie shot a glance at his watch and began to roll his sleeves down. "I'll pop on over to the station house and see what's going on. I hope Jack has sense enough to keep his mouth shut until I get there."

He pushed away from his desk and took his suit jacket from the hanger. He shrugged himself into it, secured his collar button, and slid his tie into place. Now he looked more like a lawyer, albeit a short, beefy one. "By the way, where does Jack fit? He the oldest or the youngest?"

"The youngest. Donovan's the oldest. He runs the company. Bennet's in the middle. I wouldn't rule him out if you're looking to divert suspicion. He was the most vocal in his opposition to Guy's claim on the estate. You want me to do anything before you get back?"

"Tell Christie I'll be in touch as soon as I've talked to him. In the meantime, go on over to the house. Let's put together a list of witnesses who can confirm Tuesday night. The cops find the murder weapon?"

"They must have. I know they did a grid search of the property because I saw 'em doing it. And Christie says they carted off all kinds of things."

"Once I finish with Jack, I'll have a chat with the cops and find out why they think he's good for this. It'd be nice to have some idea what we're up against."

"Am I officially on the clock?"

He looked at his watch. "Go."

"The usual rates?"

"Sure. Unless you want to work for free. Of course, it's always possible Jack won't hire me."

"Don't be silly. The man's desperate," I said. I caught Lonnie's look and amended my claim. "Well, you know what I mean. He's not hiring you because he's desperate—"

"Get out of here," Lonnie said, smiling.

Briefcase in hand, I hiked back over to the public parking lot, where I retrieved my car. My attitude toward Jack Malek had already undergone a shift. Whether Jack was guilty or innocent, Lonnie would hustle up every shred of exculpatory evidence and plot, plan, maneuver, and strategize to establish his defense. I was no particular fan of Jack's, but working for Lonnie Kingman I'd be kept in the loop.

As I approached the Maleks', I was relieved to see that the roadway on either side of the estate was virtually deserted. The shoulder was churned with tire prints, the ground strewn with cigarette stubs, empty cups, crumpled paper napkins, and fast-food containers. The area outside the gate had the look of abandonment, as if a traveling circus had packed up and crept away at first light. The press had all but disappeared, following the patrol car taking Jack to County Jail. For Jack, it was the beginning of a process in which he'd be photographed, frisked, booked, fingerprinted, and placed in a holding cell. I'd been through the process myself about a year ago and the sense of contamination was still vivid. The facility itself is clean and freshly painted, but institutional nonetheless; no-frills linoleum and government-issue furniture built to endure hard wear. In my brush with them, the jail officers were civil, pleasant, and businesslike, but I'd felt diminished by every aspect of the procedure, from the surrender of my personal possessions to the subsequent confinement in the drunk tank. I can still remember the musky smell in the air, mixing with the odors of stale mattresses, dirty armpits, and bourbon fumes being exhaled. As far as I knew, Jack had never been arrested and I suspected he'd feel as demoralized as I had.

As I drove the VW up to the gate, a hired security guard stepped forward, blocking my progress until I identified myself. He waved me on and I eased up the driveway into the cobblestone courtyard. The house was bathed in sunlight, the grounds dappled with shade. The old, sprawling oak trees stretched away on all sides, creating a hazy landscape as if done in watercolors. Tones of green and gray seemed to bleed into one another with the occasional spare sapling providing sharp contrast. I could see two gardeners at work; one with a leaf blower, one with a rake. The sounds of machinery suggested that branches were being trimmed somewhere out of sight. The air smelled of mulch and eucalyptus. There was no sign of the search team and no uniformed officer posted at the front door. To all intents and purposes, life had reverted to normal.

Christie must have been watching, perhaps hoping for Donovan. Before I was even out of the car, she'd come onto the porch and down the steps, walking in my direction. She wore a white T-shirt and dark blue wraparound skirt, her arms folded in front of her as though for comfort. The sheen in her dark hair had faded to a dull patina, like cheap floor wax on hardwood. Her face showed little of her emotions except for a thin crease, like a hairline crack, that had appeared between her eyes. "I heard the car on the drive and thought it might be Bennet or Donovan. Lord, I'm glad to see you. I've been going crazy here by myself."

"You still haven't gotten through to Donovan?"

"I left word at the office, saying it was urgent. I didn't want to blab all our business to his secretary. I've been waiting by the phone, but so far I haven't heard a word from him. Who knows where Bennet is. What about Lonnie Kingman? Did you talk to him?"

I filled her in on Lonnie's intentions. "Have the police unsealed the bedroom?"

"Not yet. I meant to ask about that when they showed up this morning. I thought they came to *do* something up there. Take photographs or measure or move the furniture. I never imagined they were here to arrest anyone. I wish you could have seen Jack. He was scared to death."

"I'm not surprised. What about you? How are you holding up?"

"I'm antsy. And feel my fingers. They're as cold as ice. I catch myself pacing, half the time jabbering away. This is all so unreal. We may have problems, but we don't kill one another. It's ridiculous. I don't understand what's going on. Everything was fine and now this." She seemed to shudder, not from cold, but from tension and anxiety. In the wake of Jack's arrest, she'd clearly erased all her earlier complaints.

I followed her around the front and into the house. The foyer felt chilly and again I was struck by the shabbiness. A wall sconce hung awry. In the hanging chandelier, several flame-shaped bulbs were missing and some were tilted like crooked teeth. The tapestries along the wall were genuine, faded and worn, depicting acts of debauchery and cruelty picked out in thread. I felt my gaze pulled irresistibly toward the stairs, but the landing above was empty and there was no unusual sound to set my teeth on edge. The house was curiously quiet, given events of the past few days. These people didn't seem to have friends rushing in with offers of help. I wasn't aware of anyone bringing food or calling to ask if there was anything to be done. Maybe the Maleks were the sort who didn't invite such familiarities. Whatever the reason, it looked like they were coping without the comfort of friends.

Christie was still chatting, processing Jack's arrest. I've noticed that people tend to drone on and on when they're unnerved. "When I saw Detective Robb on the doorstep, I honestly thought they were coming with information and then they asked if Jack was in and I still didn't think anything about it. I don't even know what's supposed to happen next."

We moved into the library, where I sank into a club chair and Christie paced the floor. I said, "I guess it depends on what he's charged with and if bail's been set. Once he's booked in, the DA has twenty-four hours to file his case. Jack has to be arraigned within forty-eight hours, excluding Sundays and holidays, of course. So this is what, Thursday? They'll probably take him before a magistrate today or tomorrow."

"What's arraignment? What does that mean? I don't know the first thing. I've never known anyone who's been arrested, let alone charged with *murder*."

"Arraignment's the process by which he's formally charged. They'll take him into court and identify him as the person named in the warrant. He'll be told the nature of the charges against him and he'll be asked to plead guilty, not guilty, or no contest."

"And then what?"

"That's up to Lonnie. If he thinks the evidence is weak, he'll demand a preliminary hearing without waiving time. That means within ten court days—two weeks—they'll have to have him in there for a prelim. For that, the prosecuting attorney's present, the defendant and his counsel, the clerk, and the investigating officer, blah, blah, blah. Witnesses are sworn in and testimony's taken. At the end of it, if it appears either that no public offense has been committed or that there's not sufficient cause to believe the defendant's guilty, then he's discharged. On the other hand, if there's sufficient evidence to show the offense has been committed and sufficient cause to believe the defendant's guilty, then he's held to answer. An information's filed— that's a formal, written accusation—in Superior Court, he enters a plea, and the matter's set for trial. There's usually a lot of bullshit thrown in, but that's essentially what happens."

She paused in her pacing and turned to stare at me, aghast. "And Jack's in *jail* all this time?"

"He's not allowed to post bail on a homicide."

"Oh my God."

"Christie, I've been in jail myself. It's not the end of the world. The company's not that great and the food's off the charts when it comes to fat content—hey, no wonder I liked it," I added in an aside.

"It isn't funny."

"Who's being funny? It's the truth," I said. "There are worse things in life. Jack might not like it, but he'll survive."

She reached out and placed a hand on the mantelpiece to steady herself. "Sorry. I'm really sorry. I didn't mean to snap at you."

"You better have a seat."

She did as I suggested, perching on the edge of the chair next to mine. "You must have come for some reason. I never even asked what it was."

"Lonnie was hoping you'd know who was at the club that night. We need someone who can verify Jack's presence at the pairings' party."

"That shouldn't be too hard. I guess the police are already talking to people at the country club. I'm not sure what the deal is on that. I've gotten two calls this morning, one from Paul Trasatti, who says he needs to talk to Jack, like pronto."

"Were they together Tuesday night?"

"Yes. Jack picked him up and took him to the club. I'm sure they sat at the same table. Paul can give you the names of the other eight sitting with them. This is all so crazy. How can they possibly think Jack's guilty of anything? There must have been tons of people there that night."

"What's Paul's number?"

"I don't know. It's got to be in the book. I'll go look it up."

"Don't worry about it. I can check that out in a bit. Once he confirms Jack's alibi, it should go a long way."

Christie made a face. " 'Alibi.' God, I can't stand the word. Alibi implies you're guilty and you've cooked up some story to cover your ass."

"Can I use your phone?"

"I'd prefer it if you'd wait until Donovan or Bennet check in. I want to keep the line free until I hear from them. I hope you don't mind."

"Not at all," I said. "You mentioned the police picking up some items. Do you have any idea what they took?"

She leaned her elbows on her knees and put her hands across her eyes. "They left a copy of the warrant and a list of items seized. I know it's around here somewhere, but I haven't seen it yet. Donovan went down to the pool house as soon as they left. He says they took a lot of sports equipment—golf clubs and baseball bats."

I winced, thinking of the impact of such items on the human skull. Switching the subject, I asked, "What about Bennet? Where was he that night?"

"He went back to the restaurant he's remodeling, to see what the workers had done that day. Construction's been a nightmare and he spends a lot of time down there."

"Did anybody see him?"

"You'd have to ask him," she said. "Donovan and I were here. We'd had quite a lot to drink at dinner and I went straight to bed." There was a marked tremor in the hand Christie was running through her hair.

"Have you had anything to eat?"

"I couldn't touch a bite. I'm too anxious."

"Well, you ought to have *something*. Is Enid here yet?"

"I think so."

"Let me check in the kitchen and have her make you a cup of tea. You should have a cookie or a piece of fruit. You look awful."

"I feel awful," she said.

I left her in the library and headed down the hall. I couldn't believe I'd put myself on tea detail again, but simply being in the house made me tense. Any activity helped. Besides, I didn't want to pass up the chance to talk to Enid if she was on the premises.

"Me again," I said when I entered the kitchen.

She was standing at the island with a cutting board in front of her, smashing garlic with the blade of a Chinese cleaver. She was wrapped in a white apron with a white cotton scarf around her head, looking as round and as squeezable as a roll of toilet paper. While I watched, she laid down assorted sizes of unpeeled cloves, placed the wide blade on top of them, and pounded once with her fist. I could feel myself flinch. If the blade were angled incorrectly, she was going to end up whacking down on it with the outer aspect of her own hand, hacking straight to the bone. I stopped in my tracks. With her eyes pinned on me politely, she repeated the process, fist smashing down. She lifted the blade. Under it, the hapless garlic had been crushed like albino cockroaches, the peel sliding off with the flick of a knife tip.

"I thought I'd fix Christie a cup of tea," I said. "She needs something in her system—do you have a piece of fruit?"

Enid pointed at the refrigerator. "There are grapes in there. Tea bags up in the cabinet. I'd do it myself, but I'm trying to get this sauce under way. If you set up a tray, I'll take it in to her."

"No problem. You go right ahead."

She leaned to her left and slid open a compartment in which the trays were stored, pulling out a teak server with a rim around the edge. She placed it on the marble counter next to six big cans of crushed tomatoes, two cans of tomato paste, a basket of yellow onions, and a can of olive oil. On the stove top, I noticed a stainless steel stockpot.

I moved over to the cabinet and removed a mug, pausing to fill the electric kettle as I'd seen Myrna do. I glanced at Enid casually. "You have paper napkins somewhere?"

"Third drawer on the right."

I found the napkins and placed one, along with a teaspoon, on the tray. "I take it you heard about Jack's arrest."

She nodded assent. "I was coming in the gate just as they were taking him away. I wish you could have seen the look on his face."

I shook my head regretfully, as if I gave a shit. "Poor thing," I said.

"It seems so unfair." I hoped I hadn't laid it on too thick, but I needn't have worried.

"The police were asking about his running shoes," she said. "Something about a pattern on the soles—so there must have been bloody footprints in the bedroom where Guy was killed."

"Really," I replied, trying to disguise my startlement. Apparently, she felt no reluctance about discussing the family's business. I'd thought I'd have to be cunning, but she didn't seem to share Myrna's reservations about tattling. "They picked up the shoes yesterday?"

"No. They called me this morning at home. Before I left for work."

"Lieutenant Robb?"

"The other one. The woman. She's a cold fish, I must say. I hope she's not a friend of yours."

"I only met her this morning when I went in to be interviewed."

She flicked me a look as if taking my measure. "Myrna tells me you're a detective. I've seen 'em on the TV, of course, but I never met one in real life."

"Now you have," I said. "In fact, I work in the same firm as Jack's attorney, Lonnie Kingman. He's on his way over to the station house to talk to Jack." I was anxious to press her on the matter of the shoes, but worried she would clam up if I seemed too intent.

She dropped her eyes to her work. She was tapping the Chinese cleaver in a rapid little dance that reduced all the garlic to the size of rice grains. "They searched for the shoes all day yesterday. You've never seen anything like it. Going through all the closets and trash cans, digging in the flowerbeds."

I made a little mouth noise of interest. It was clear Enid had an avid interest in all the trappings of police work.

She said, "They told me I was actually the one who put 'em on the right track. Of course, I had no idea the shoes would turn out to be Jack's. I feel terrible about that. Myrna's beside herself. She feels so guilty about mentioning the quarrel."

"It must have been a shock about the shoes," I prodded.

"Jack's my favorite among the boys. I came to work here twenty-five years ago. This was my first job and I didn't expect to stay long."

"You were hired as a nanny?"

"The boys were too old for that. I was more like a companion for Mrs. Malek," she said. "I never trained as a cook. I simply learned as I went along. Mrs. Malek—Rona—was beginning to fail and she was in and out of the hospital all the time back then. Mr. Malek needed someone to run the house in her absence. Jack was in junior high school and he was pretty much at loose ends. He used to sit out in the kitchen with me, hardly saying a word. I'd bake a batch of cookies and he'd eat a whole plate just as fast as he could. He was really like a little kid. I knew what he was hungry for was his mother's praise and attention, but she was much too sick. I did what I could, but it nearly broke my heart."

"And Guy was how old?"

She shrugged. "Eighteen, nineteen. He'd already given them years of aggravation and grief. I never saw anything like him for the trouble he made. It was one scrape after another."

"How did he and Jack get along?"

"I think Jack admired and romanticized him. They didn't pal around together, but there was always a certain amount of hero worship. Jack thought Guy was like James Dean, rebellious and tragic, you know, misunderstood. They never had all that much to do with one another, but I can remember how Jack used to look at him. Now, Bennet and Jack, they were close. The two younger boys tended to gravitate to one another. I never had much use for Bennet. Something sneaky about him."

"What about Donovan?"

"He was the smartest of the four. Even then he had a good head for business, always calculating the odds. When I first came to work, he'd already been off to college and was planning to come back and work for his dad full-time. Donovan loves that company more than any man alive. As for Guy, he was the troublemaker. That seemed to be his role."

"You really think Jack might have been involved in Guy's death?"

"I hate to believe it, but I know he felt Guy broke faith with him. Jack's a fanatic about loyalty. He always was."

"Well, that's interesting," I said. "Because the first time I was here, he said much the same thing. He was off at college when Guy left, wasn't he?"

Enid was shaking her head. "That wouldn't have mattered. Not to him. Somehow, in Jack's mind, when Guy went off on his great adventure, he should have taken him along."

"So he saw Guy's departure as betrayal."

"Well, of course he did. Jack's terribly dependent. He's never had a job. He's never even had a girl. He has no self-esteem to speak of and for that, I blame his dad. Bader never took the time to teach them they were worth anything. I mean, look at the reality. None of them has ever left home."

"It couldn't be healthy."

"It's disgraceful. Grown men?" She opened the can of olive oil and poured a short stream in the stockpot while she turned up the flame. She moved the cutting board from the counter and balanced the edge of it on the pot, sliding garlic across the surface. The sound of sizzling arose, followed moments later by a cloud of garlic-scented steam.

"What's the story on the shoes? Where did they turn up?"

She paused to adjust the flame and then returned the board to the counter, where she picked up an onion. The peeling was as fragile as paper, crackling slightly as she worked. "At the bottom of a box. You remember the cartons of Bader's clothing Christie packed away? They were sitting on the front porch. The Thrift Store Industries truck stopped by for an early-morning pickup first thing yesterday."

"Before the body was discovered?"

"Before anyone was even up. I don't know how I connected it. I saw the receipt lying on the counter and didn't think much about it. Later, it occurred to me—if the shoes weren't on the premises, they must be somewhere else."

"How'd you figure out where they were?"

"Well, that's just it. I was loading the dishwasher, you know, humming a little tune, and boom, I just knew."

"I've done the same thing. It's almost like the mind makes an independent leap."

Enid flashed me a look. "Exactly. He must have realized he left a shoe print on the carpeting upstairs."

"Did you see it yourself?"

"No, but Myrna says she saw it when she went in Guy's room." She paused, shaking her head. "I don't want to think he did it."

"It *is* hard to believe," I said. "I mean, in essence, he must have killed Guy, seen the footprint, slipped off his shoes, and shoved them in the box on his way out of the house. He was lucky—or thought he was."

"You don't sound convinced."

"I just have trouble with the notion. Jack doesn't strike me as that decisive or quick. Doesn't that bother you?"

She thought about that briefly and then gave a shrug of dismissal. "A killer would have to depend on luck, I guess. You can't plan for everything. You'd have to ad-lib."

"Well, it backfired in this case."

"If he did it," she said. She picked up a can and tilted it into the electric opener. She pressed a lever and watched as the can went round and round, rotating blades neatly separating the lid from the can. Kitchens are dangerous, I thought idly as I looked on. What an arsenal—knives and fire and all that kitchen twine, skewers, meat pounders, and rolling pins. The average woman must spend a fair portion of her time happily contemplating the tools of her trade: devices that crush, pulverize, grind, and puree; utensils that pierce, slice, dissect, and debone; not to mention the household products that, once ingested, are capable of eradicating human life along with germs.

Her eyes came up to mine. "Do you believe in ghosts?"

"No, of course not. What makes you ask?"

She glanced toward the corner of the kitchen where I noticed, for the first time, a staircase. "Yesterday I went upstairs to put some linens away. There was a Presence in the hall. I wondered if you believed in them."

I shook my head in the negative, remembering the chill in the air and the roaring in my ears.

"This one smells of animal, something damp and unclean. It's very strange," she said.

17

I left the Maleks' shortly after one o'clock. Driving home, I spotted a pay phone at a corner gas station. I pulled in and parked. Outside the service bay, a group of kids from the local alternative high school had organized a car wash. According to the hand-lettered sign, the price was $5.00 and proceeds were being used to pay for a trip to San Francisco. There was not a customer in sight. Buckets of soapy water waited at the ready and the kids milled around in a manner that suggested they were about to spray one another down with hoses. With luck, I wouldn't end up in the line of fire.

I looked up Paul Trasatti in the telephone book. There were two numbers listed; one a residence on Hopper Road, the other—with no address—simply said Paul Trasatti, Rare Books. I found a handful of loose change at the bottom of my handbag and fed coins into the slots. I dialed the business number first, thinking it more likely I'd catch him at his desk. Trasatti answered before the phone on his end had finished ringing the first time.

"Trasatti," he said, tersely. He sounded like a man who'd been waiting for a call regarding drop-off instructions for the ransom money.

"Mr. Trasatti, my name is Kinsey Millhone. I'm a private investiga-

tor, working with Jack Malek's attorney. You knew he'd been arrested?"

"I heard about that this morning. I called to talk to Jack and his
sister-in-law told me they'd just taken him away. Did she tell you to
call?"

"Well, no. Not really. I—"

"How'd you get my number?"

"I looked you up in the telephone book. I need information and I
thought maybe you could help."

"What kind of information?"

"I'll be talking to Lonnie Kingman and I know he'll want to hear
about Jack's activities that night."

"Why can't he ask Jack?"

"I'm sure he will," I said, "but we're going to need someone who
can verify Jack's claims. Christie says he drove you over to the country
club Tuesday evening. Is that true?"

There was a fractional hesitation. "That's right. He picked me up
after dinner. Truth is, I ended up trading places with him, so I was the
one driving. He was too tipsy. This is strictly off the record, right?"

"I'm not a journalist, but sure. We can keep it off the record, at
least for now," I said. "Tipsy, meaning drunk?"

"Let's just say I was the designated driver in this case."

I closed my eyes, listening for the subtext, while cars passed back
and forth on the street behind me. "Were you seated at the same
table?"

"Tables were reserved. We had assigned seats," he said. He was
being as cagey as a politician. What was going on here?

"That's not what I asked. I'm wondering if you can verify his presence at the pairings' party."

A brief, most curious silence ensued. "Can I ask you a question?"
he said.

"What's that?"

"If you're working for this attorney . . . what'd you say his name
was?"

"Lonnie Kingman."

"Okay, this Kingman fellow. I know he can't repeat anything said
between him and Jack, but what about you? Does the same thing
apply to you?"

"Our conversation isn't privileged, if that's what you want to know.
Anything relevant to Jack's defense, I'll be reporting to Lonnie. That's
my job. I *can* be trusted with information. Otherwise, I'd be out of
business by now," I said. "Were you sitting with Jack?"

"See, that's what the police have been asking me," he said. His mouth must have been dry because I could practically hear him lick his lips before he spoke. "Jack's a good friend and I don't want to get him in any more trouble than he's in. I've done everything I could short of telling lies."

"You don't want to lie to the cops," I said. Maybe the line was tapped and they were checking my attitude.

"Well, no, I wouldn't. And that's just it," he said. "I didn't come right out and say so, but there was a stretch when Jack was, you know, uhm, off somewhere. What I mean is, I couldn't say he was right there in my line of sight."

"Uhn-hun. How long a stretch?"

"Might have been as much as an hour and a half. I didn't think anything of it at the time, but you know, later—like when this other business came up—I did wonder about the time frame. I wouldn't want to be quoted, but just between us."

"Do you know where he was?"

"I know where he *said* he was. Out walking the tenth hole."

"In the *dark?*"

"That's not as odd as it sounds. I've done the same thing myself. Smokers go outside to have a cigarette sometimes. Most club members know the course by heart so it's not as if you're likely to get lost or fall down a hole."

"But why would he do that in the middle of a pairings' party?"

"He was upset—I'd say real upset—when he came to pick me up. That's another reason I insisted on driving. Jack tends to be careless about things like that."

"Did he say what upset him?" I waited. "I can keep it to myself," I said.

"He said him and Guy got into an argument."

"About what?"

"Probably the money. I'd say the money."

"You're talking about the money Guy was due to inherit."

"That's right."

"So Jack was drunk and upset and when the two of you arrived at the club, he disappeared."

"Uhn-hun."

"Did you believe him?"

"About taking a walk? More or less. I mean, it makes sense—you know, if he was trying to sober up and cool off."

"And *did* he seem cooler when he got back?"

For a moment, I thought the line went dead. "Mr. Trasatti?"

"I'm here. See, the thing is, he didn't actually get back in time to give me a ride. I had to find someone else."

"And that's what you told the police?"

"Well, I had to. I felt bad, but they were real persistent and it's like you said, I couldn't *lie.*"

"Was his car still there?"

"I think so. I couldn't swear to it. I thought I saw it in the parking lot when I was set to go, but I might have been mistaken."

"But you're sure there was no sign of Jack?"

"That's right. A friend of mine said he saw him take off across the fairway at the first hole. Then this other fellow ended up giving me a ride home."

"Can I have both those names?" I cocked one shoulder, anchoring the handset against my ear while I fumbled in my bag for a pen and a scrap of paper. I made a note of the names, neither of which rang a bell. "And how did you find out where Jack had been?"

"He called first thing the next morning to apologize and that's when he explained."

"He called Wednesday morning?"

"I just said that."

"I wanted to make sure I understood you correctly. Do you remember what time he called?"

"About eight, I guess."

"So this was before anyone knew Guy Malek was dead."

"Must've been. I know Jack never mentioned it. You'd think if he knew he'd have spoken up."

"Is there anything else you remember from your conversation with him?"

"Not that I can think of. I probably got him in enough trouble as it is. I hope you won't tell him I told you all this."

"I doubt I'll have occasion to talk to Jack," I said. "I appreciate your help. You may hear from Lonnie Kingman or me again on this." You're certainly going to end up on the witness stand, I thought.

"I guess it can't be helped," he said glumly, as if reading my mind. He disconnected before I could press him for anything else.

I checked the pile of change I'd laid on the shelf near the coin box. I dropped more coins in the slot and dialed Lonnie's private line. He picked up on his end without identifying himself.

"This is Kinsey," I said. "How'd it go?"

"Don't let me handle any sharps. I might open a vein."

"You heard about the shoes?"

"Did I ever," he said. "Lieutenant Robb delivered the happy news with glee."

"I take it the pattern on the sole matched the print at the scene."

"Oh, sure. And to make things even better, he says the lab found bits and pieces of Guy Malek's brain spattered on the instep. I mean, Jesus, how's Jack going to explain a fleck of brain matter buried in the eyelet of his shoes? This is not like 'Oh gee fellas, Guy-accidentally-cut-himself-and-must-have-bled-on-me.' "

"What'd Jack have to say?"

"I haven't had a chance to ask. Once he invoked, the cops hustled him out to County Jail for booking. I'm going out there later and have a long chat with him. He'll probably tell me the shoes were stolen. Oh yeah, right."

"What about the murder weapon?"

"They found a baseball bat shoved in with a bunch of sports equipment down at the pool house. Somebody'd made a clumsy attempt to wipe it clean, but traces of blood were still on the hitting area. At least there were no prints, so we can thank God for small favors. What about his alibi? I hope you're going to tell me a hundred club members had an eye on him at all times."

"No such luck," I said. I laid out the sequence of events as Paul Trasati had reported them.

I could hear Lonnie sigh. "Too bad Jack wasn't out there screwing somebody's wife. You have a theory, I'm sure."

"He could have left the club on foot. There are half a dozen places near the road where he could've climbed the fence."

"And then what?" Lonnie said. "The country club is miles from the Malek estate. How's he going to get from there to the house again without somebody seeing him?"

"Lonnie, I hate to tell you this, but the man has a Harley-Davidson. He could have hidden his motorcycle earlier. The house might be an hour away on foot, but it's only ten minutes by car."

"But so what? Where was Bennet that night? And what about Donovan. He was right there on the premises when the murder occurred."

"I can talk to Bennet this afternoon."

"Did anybody see Jack climb the fence? I doubt it. Anybody see the Harley during the period we're discussing?"

"I can check it out," I said.

"I know the line the cops are taking. They're saying Jack's room adjoined Guy's. All he had to do was slip from one room to the other, bash his brains out, and slip back again."

"Not that simple," I said. "Don't forget he's got to hide the shoes at the bottom of the thrift box, wipe the blood off the bat, and return it to the pool house before he hightails it back to the country club."

"Good point. Is there a guardhouse at the club? Someone might have noted what time he left."

"I'll pop over there and check. I can also clock the time it takes to get from there to the house and back."

"Hold off on that. We'll get to that eventually. For now, let's focus on finding someone else to blame."

"That shouldn't be too hard. I mean, Jack's not the only one with access to Guy's room. Anybody in the house could have entered the same way. The cops have the murder weapon, but from what you've said, they don't have Jack's fingerprints."

"Yeah, they can't find anybody else's either."

"So how are they going to prove Jack was wielding the damn thing? Maybe he was framed."

Lonnie snorted in my ear. "Somebody'd have to take a pair of forceps and fuckin' *tweeze* up brain material, then tiptoe into Jack's room, find the shoes in the closet, and deposit all the little brainy bits."

"It's always possible, though, isn't it?"

"It's possible Santa Claus came down the chimney and did the deed himself. Stinks. The whole thing stinks."

"I like the idea about eyewitnesses. So far it doesn't sound like there's anyone who can place him at the murder scene."

"Not so far, no, but I'm sure the cops are out scouring the neighborhood."

"Well, then we'll scour some, too."

"You're such an optimist," he said.

I laughed. "Actually, I can't believe I'm standing here defending him. I don't even like Jack."

"We're not paid to like him. We're being paid to get him out of this," Lonnie said.

"I'll do what I can."

"I know you will."

Before I left the service station, I paused long enough to pull up to the pump so I could fill my gas tank. On the hood of my car, the early-morning dew had now combined with the dust from Monday's Santa Ana winds. My former VW was dingy beige and never showed dirt. With this snappy 1974 model, the streaks were more conspicuous, rivulets of pale blue cutting through a speckled patina of soot. A bird had passed its judgment on the hood as well. I paid for the gas and then turned the key in the ignition, peered over my right shoulder, and backed up into the area where the car wash was being held. The kids began to whistle and clap, and I found myself smiling at their enthusiasm.

I stood to one side while one of them crawled inside with a bottle of window cleaner. Another fired up the Shop-Vac and began to suck grit off the floor mats. A crew of three were sudsing down the outside, all of them towering over the vehicle. The kid with the Shop-Vac finished cleaning the interior and I watched him approach from the far side of the car with an envelope in hand. He held it out to me. "Have you been looking for this?"

"Where did that come from?"

"I found it beside the passenger seat in front. Looks like it slipped down in the crevice."

"Thanks." I took the envelope, half expecting to see the now-familiar typeface. Instead, my name was scrawled across the front in ballpoint pen. I waited until the kid had moved away and then I opened the envelope and removed the single sheet of paper. The message was handwritten in black ink; the penmanship distinct, a peculiar blend of cursive and printing. I flicked a glance at the signature. *Guy Malek.* I could feel ice crystals forming between my shoulder blades.

> *Monday night. Waiting for you to show.*
>
> *Hey K . . .*
>
> *Sure hope I have the nerve to pass you this note. I guess I must have if you're reading it. I haven't asked a girl on a date since I was fifteen years old and that didn't work out so hot. I got a big zit on my chin and spent the whole evening trying to think up excuses to keep my face turned the other way.*
>
> *Anyway, here goes.*
>
> *Once this family mess is settled, would you like to take off for a day and go to Disneyland with me? We could eat snowcones and do Pirates of the Caribbean and then take the boat ride through Small World singing that song you can't get out of your head for six months afterward. I could use some silliness in my life and so could you.*
>
> *Think on't and let me know so I can stock up on Clearasil.*
>
> *Guy Malek*

P.S. Just for the record, if anything should happen to me, make sure my share of Dad's estate goes to Jubilee Evangelical Church. I really love those folk.

By the time I finished reading, my eyes had filled with tears. This was like a message from the dead. I stared off across the street, blinking rapidly. I could feel pain in my chest and my facial features were instantly defined by heat as my nasal passages seized up. I wondered if grief had the capacity to suffocate. In conjunction with the sorrow came a rush of pure rage. I sent Guy my thoughts across the Ether. I'm going to find out who killed you and I'm going to find out why. I swear I will do this. I swear it.

"Miss? Your car's ready."

I took a deep breath. "Thanks. It looks great." I gave the kid ten bucks and took off with the radio cranked up full blast.

When I got home, I spotted Robert Dietz's little red Porsche parked out in front of my apartment. I set my briefcase on the pavement while I stood at the curb and studied it, afraid to believe. He'd told me he was going to be gone two weeks. This was just coming up on one. I circled the car and checked the license plate, which read DIETZ. I picked up my briefcase and let myself in the gate. I rounded the corner and unlocked my door. Dietz's suitcase was sitting beside the couch. His garment bag was hooked across the top of the bathroom door.

I said, "Dietz?"

No response.

I left my handbag and the briefcase on the counter and crossed the patio to Henry's, where I peered in the kitchen window. Dietz was sitting in Henry's rocking chair, his pant leg pulled up to expose his injured knee. The swelling had visibly diminished and from various gestures he was making, it seemed safe to guess he'd had the fluid drained out of it. Even his pantomime of a hypodermic needle being stuck into his flesh made my palms start to sweat. At first he didn't see me. It was like watching a silent movie, the two men earnestly engrossed in medical matters. Henry, at eighty-five, was so familiar to me—handsome, good-hearted, lean, intelligent. Dietz was constructed along sturdier lines—solid, tough, stubborn, impulsive, just as smart as Henry, but more streetwise than intellectual. I found myself smiling at the two of them. Where Henry was mild, Dietz was restless and rough, without artifice. I valued his honesty, distrusted his concern, resented his wanderlust, and yearned for definition in our relationship. In the midst of all the heaviness I felt, Dietz was leavening.

He glanced up, spotting me. He raised a hand in greeting without rising from the chair.

Henry crossed to the door and let me in. Dietz lowered his pant leg with a brief aside to me about a walk-in medical clinic up in Santa Cruz. Henry offered coffee, but Dietz declined. I don't even remember now what the three of us talked about. In the course of idle chitchat, Dietz put his hand on my elbow, setting off a surge of heat. Out of the corner of my eye, I caught his quizzical look. Whatever I was feeling must have been transmitted through the wires to him. I must have been buzzing like a power line because even Henry's easy flow of conversation seemed to falter and fade. Dietz glanced at his watch, making a startled sound as if late for an appointment. We made our hasty excuses, moving out of Henry's backdoor and across to my place without exchanging a word.

The door closed behind us. The apartment felt cool. Pale sunlight filtered through the shuttered windows in a series of horizontal lines. The interior had the look and the feel of a sailboat: compact, simple, with royal blue canvas chairs, walls of polished teak and oak. Dietz undid the bed in the window bay, easing out of his shoes. I slipped my clothes off, aware of flickering desire as each garment was removed. Dietz's clothes joined mine in a heap on the floor. We sank together, in a rolling motion. The sheets were chill at first, as blue as the sea, warming at contact with our bare limbs. His skin was luminous, as polished as the surface of an abalone shell. Something about the play of shadows infused the air with a watery element, bathing us both in its transparent glow. It felt as if we were swimming in the shallows, as smooth and graceful as a pair of sea otters tumbling through the surf. Our lovemaking played out in silence, except for a humming in his throat now and then. I don't often think of sex as an antidote to pain, but that's what this was and I fully confess—I used intimacy with the one man to offset the loss of the other. It was the only means I could think of to console myself. Even in the moment, what seemed odd to me was the flicker of confusion about which man I betrayed.

Later, I said to Dietz, "Are you hungry? I'm starving."

"I am, too," he said. Gentleman that he was, he'd padded over to the refrigerator where he stood buck naked in a shaft of hot light, contemplating the interior. "How could we be out of food? Don't you eat when I'm gone?"

"There's food," I said defensively.

"A jar of bread-and-butter pickles."

"I can make sandwiches. There's bread in the freezer and half a jar of peanut butter in the cupboard up there."

He gave me a look like I'd suggested cooking up a mess of garden slugs. He closed the refrigerator door and opened the freezer compartment, poking through some cellophane-wrapped packages of meat products covered in ice crystals and suffering from freezer burn. He closed the freezer, returned to the sofa bed, and got under the sheets. "I'm not going to last long. We have to eat," he said.

"I couldn't believe you came back. I thought you were taking the boys off on a trip."

"Turns out they had plans to go camping with friends in Yosemite and didn't know how to tell me. When I read about the murder in the Santa Cruz papers, I told them I needed to drive back. I felt guilty as hell, but they were thrilled to death. Given the perversity of human nature, it pissed me off somehow. They could hardly get me in the car fast enough. I pull away and I'm looking in the rearview mirror. They don't even stop to wave. They're galloping up the outside stairs to grab their sleeping bags."

"You had a few days together."

"And that was good. I enjoyed them," he said. "So tell me about you and what's been happening down here."

Having been through the drill with Lonnie, I laid out events with remarkable efficiency, faltering only slightly in my account of Guy. Even the sound of his name touched a well of sorrow in me.

"You need a game plan," he said, briskly.

I waggled my hand, maybe so maybe not. "Jack will probably be arraigned tomorrow if he hasn't been already."

"Will Lonnie waive time?"

"I have no idea. Probably not."

"Which means he'll insist on a prelim within ten court days. That doesn't give us much time. What about this business of Max Outhwaite? We could try chasing that down."

I noted the "we," but let it sit there unacknowledged. Was he seriously proposing help? "What's to chase?" I asked. "I tried the hall of records and voter registration. Also the city directories. The name's as phony as the address."

"What about the crisscross?"

"I did that."

"Old telephone books?"

"Yeah, I did that, too."

"How far back?"

"Six years."

"Why six? Why not take it all the way back to the year Guy Malek left? Even before that. Max Outhwaite could be the victim of a rip-off during his teen crime years."

"If the name's a fake, it's not going to matter how far back I go."

"In other words, you were too lazy," he said, mildly.

"Right," I said, without taking offense.

"What about the letters themselves?"

"One's a fax. The other's typed on ordinary white bond. No distinguishing marks. I could have dusted for prints, but there didn't seem to be much point. We've got no way to run them and nothing for comparison even if a latent turned up. I did put the one letter in a plastic sleeve to protect it to some extent. Then I made copies of both letters. I left one set at the office, locked away in my desk. I get paranoid about these things."

"You have the other set here?"

"In my briefcase."

"Let's take a look."

I pushed the sheet back and got up. I retrieved my briefcase from the kitchen counter and sorted through the contents, returning to the sofa bed with my pack of index cards and the two letters. I slid between the sheets again and handed him the paperwork, turning over on my side so I could watch him work. He put his glasses on. "This is really romantic, you know that Dietz?"

"We can't screw around all day. I'm fifty. I'm old. I have to save my strength."

"Yeah, right."

We propped up the pillows and settled in side by side while Dietz read the two letters and thumbed through my index cards. "What do you think?" I asked.

"I think Outhwaite's a good bet. Seems like the object of the exercise is to find another candidate, divert attention from Jack if nothing else."

"Lonnie said the same thing. The evidence looks damning, but it's all circumstantial. Lonnie's hoping we can find someone else to point a finger at. I think he favors Donovan or Bennet."

"The more the merrier. If the cops think Jack's motivation was Guy's share of the inheritance, then the same case could be made for the other two. It would have been just as easy for one of them to slip into Guy's room." He was thumbing through the index cards. He held a card up. "What's this mean? What kind of scam are you referring to?"

I took the card and studied it. The note said: *widow cheated out of nest egg.* "Oh. I'm not sure. I wrote down everything I could remember from my first interview with Donovan. He was talking about the scrapes Guy'd been in over the years. Most sounded petty—acts of vandalism, joyriding, stuff like that—but he was also involved in a swindle of some kind. I didn't ask at the time because I was just starting my search and I was focusing on ways to track him down. I didn't care what he'd done unless it somehow pertained."

"Might be worth it to take a good hard look at his past. People knew he was back. Maybe somebody had a score to settle."

"That crossed my mind, too. I mean, why else would Max Outhwaite notify the paper?" I said. "I've also toyed with the idea that one of Guy's brothers might have written the letters."

"Why?"

"To make it look like he had enemies, someone outside the family who might have wanted him dead. By the way, Bader kept a file of newspaper clippings, detailing Guy's escapades."

Dietz turned and looked at me. "Anything of interest?"

"Well, nothing jumps right out. I've got it at the office, if you want to see for yourself. Christie offered to let me take it when I was at the house."

"Let's do that. It sounds good. It might help us develop another lead." He went back to the two letters, analyzing them closely. "What about the third one? What did Guy's letter say?"

"I have no idea. Lieutenant Bower wouldn't tell me and I couldn't get much out of her. But I'd bet money it's the same person in all three cases."

"Cops probably have their forensic experts doing comparisons."

"Maybe. They may not care about Max Outhwaite now that Jack's in custody. If they're convinced he's good for it, why worry about someone else?"

"You want some help with the grunt work?"

"I'd love it."

18

I dropped Dietz at the public library while I drove out the freeway to Malek Construction. I hadn't expected to be gone long, but as I turned into the parking lot, I spotted Donovan getting into a company truck. I called his name and gave a quick wave, pulling into a visitor's space two spots away from his. He waited while I approached and then leaned over and rolled down the window on the passenger side.

Donovan's face creased with a smile, his dark eyes all but invisible behind dark sunglasses. "How are you?" he asked. He slid his glasses up on top of his head.

"Fine. I can see I caught you on your way out. Will you be gone long? I have some questions."

"I've got some business at the quarry. I'll only be gone about an hour if you want to come along with me."

I thought about it briefly. "Might as well," I said.

He moved his hard hat from the passenger seat to the floor, then opened the truck door for me. I hopped in. He wore blue jeans and a jean vest over a blue plaid sportshirt with the sleeves rolled up. His feet were shod in heavy-duty work boots with soles as waffled as tire treads.

"Where's the quarry?"

"Up the pass." He fired up the pickup and pulled out of the parking lot. "What's the latest word from Jack?"

"I haven't talked to him, but Lonnie Kingman had a meeting with him before they took him off to jail. You talked to Christie?"

"I took a late lunch," he said. "I must have gotten home about ten minutes after you left. I had no idea this stuff was going on. How's it looking at this point?"

"Hard to say. Lonnie's in the process of working out his strategy. I'll probably take a run over to the country club later to start canvassing members who were there on Tuesday. We'd love to find someone who could place Jack at the club between nine-thirty and eleven-thirty."

"Shouldn't be too hard."

"You'd be surprised," I said.

I'm about as perky as an infant when it comes to riding in trucks. Before we'd even reached the narrow highway that snaked up the pass, I could feel the tension seeping out of me. There's something lulling being a passenger in a moving vehicle. In Donovan's pickup, the combination of low grinding sound and gentle bumping nearly put me to sleep. I was tired of thinking about murder, though I'd have to bring the subject around to it eventually. In the meantime, I asked him about the business and took inordinate pleasure in the length of his reply. Donovan steered with one hand, talking over the rattle of the truck.

"We've gotten into recycle crushing where we take broken concrete and asphalt. We have a yard in Colgate where we collect it and we have a portable plant—well, we have two portable plants now—one in Monterey and one in Stockton. I think we were one of the first in this area to do that. We're able to crush the materials into road base that meets the specifications. It costs more to haul the materials here than it does the material itself, so you have a cost advantage in the haul."

He went on in this vein while I wondered idly if it might be worthwhile to verify his claims about the company's solvency. When I tuned back in, he was saying, "Right now, we produce about the same quantity out at the rock quarry as we do out at the sand and gravel mine. By far the majority of the sand and gravel operation goes into the production of asphalt concrete. We're the closest asphalt concrete plant to Santa Teresa. We used to have one in Santa Teresa where we hauled in the sand and the gravel and the liquid asphalt and we made it there, but again, it was more economical to make the product here and haul it into Santa Teresa. I'm probably the only man alive who rhapsodizes about road base and Portland Cement. You want to talk about Jack."

"I'd rather talk about Guy."

"Well, I can tell you Jack didn't kill him because it makes no sense. The first thing the cops are going to look at is the three of us. I'm surprised Bennet and I aren't under scrutiny."

"You probably are, though at the moment, all the evidence seems to point to Jack." I told him about the running shoes and the baseball bat. "You have any idea where the Harley-Davidson was that night?"

"Home in the garage, I'd guess. The Harley's Jack's baby, not mine. I really didn't have occasion to see it that night. I was upstairs watching TV."

We headed up the pass on a winding road bordered by chaparral. The air was still, lying across the mountains in a hush of hot sun. The woody shrubs were as dry as tinder. Farther up the rocky slopes, weeds and ornamental grasses—ripgut and woodland brome, foxtail fescue and ryegrass—had spread across the landscape in a golden haze that softened the stony ridges. Scarcely a breeze stirred outside, but late in the day, the warm descending air would begin to blow down the mountainside. Relative humidity would drop. The wind, squeezing through the canyons, would start picking up speed. Any tiny flame from a campfire, burning cigarette, or the inadvertent spark from weed abatement equipment, might be whipped up in minutes to a major burn. The big fires usually struck in August and September after months under high-pressure areas. However, lately the weather had been moody and unpredictable and there was no way to calculate the course it might take. Below us and at a distance, the Pacific Ocean stretched away to the horizon in a haze of blue. I could see the irregularities of the coastline as it curved to the north.

Donovan was saying, "I didn't see Jack that night once he left for the club so I can't help you there. Aside from his whereabouts, I guess I'm not really sure what you're looking for."

"We can either prove Jack didn't do it or suggest someone else who did. Where was Bennet that night? Can he account for his time?"

"You'd have to ask him. He wasn't home, I know that much. He didn't come in until late."

"The first time we met you told me about some of Guy's bouts with the law. Couldn't someone have a grudge?"

"You want to go back as far as his days in Juvenile Hall?"

"Maybe. And later, too. You mentioned a 'widder' woman he cheated out of money."

Donovan shook his head. "Forget it. That's a dead end."

"How so?"

"Because the whole family's gone."

"They left town?"

"They're all dead."

"Tell me anyway."

"The widow was a Mrs. Maddison. Guy was gone by then and when the old man heard what Guy'd done, he refused to make good. It was one of the few times he got tough. I guess he'd finally gotten sick of cleaning up after him. He told the woman to file charges, but I'm sure she never got around to it. Some people are like that. They don't take action even when they should."

"So what's the story?"

We reached the summit and the road opened out to a view I love, a caramel-colored valley dotted with dark green mounds of live oak. Ranches and campgrounds were woven into the land, but most were invisible from up here. The two-lane highway widened into four and we sped across the span of the Cold Spring Bridge. "Guy got involved with a girl named Patty Maddison. That's two *d*'s in Maddison. She had an older sister named Claire."

I heard a dim clang of recognition, but couldn't place the name. I must have made some kind of sound because Donovan turned and gave me a quick look. "You know her?" he asked.

"The name's familiar. Go on with the story. It'll come to me."

"Their old man never had a dime, but he'd somehow acquired some rare documents—letters of some kind—worth a big chunk of change. He'd been sick and the deal was, when he died the mother was supposed to sell 'em to pay for the girls' educations. The older sister had graduated from a college back East and she was waiting around to go to medical school. Some of the money was earmarked for her and some for Patty's college.

"The Christmas before he took off, Guy knocks on this woman's door. He says he's a friend of Patty's and presents himself as an appraiser of rare documents. He tells her there's some question about the authenticity of the letters. Rumor has it, says he, these are fakes and he's been hired by the father to take a look at them."

"This was while the father was still alive?"

He shook his head. "He'd been dead a month by then. He died at Thanksgiving time. Mom's feeling very nervous because the letters are really all she has. She doesn't know beans about an appraiser being hired, but it all sounds legitimate—like something her husband would have done toward the end—so she hands the letter over to Guy and he takes them away."

"Just like that?" I asked. "She didn't ask for ID or credentials?"

"Apparently not. He had some business cards done up and he handed her one, which she took at face value. You have to understand, this was all pieced together months afterward. What the hell did she know? She needs an appraisal done anyway in preparation for selling."

"I can't believe people are so trusting."

"That's what keeps con artists in business," he said.

"Go on."

"Well, Guy keeps the letters for two weeks. He claims he's subjecting them to a number of scientific tests, but what he's really doing is making copies, elaborate forgeries. Or, not so elaborate as it turns out. At any rate, he's putting together a set of fakes good enough to pass superficial inspection. After two weeks, he takes the copies back and gives her the bad news. 'Golly, gee, Mrs. Maddison, these really *are* fakes,' he says, 'and they're not worth a *dime.*' He tells her to ask any expert and they'll tell her the same. She nearly drops dead from shock. She takes 'em straight to another expert and he confirms what Guy's said. Sure enough, the letters are completely worthless. So here's this lady whose husband's dead and she suddenly has nothing. Next thing you know, she's knocking on Dad's door demanding restitution."

"How'd she figure out it was Guy?"

"He'd been seeing Patty Maddison . . ."

I said, "Ohhh. That Patty. I get it. Guy told me about her the day we walked the property. He said he'd broken up with her. Sorry to interrupt, but I just remembered where I'd heard the name. So how'd they know it was him? Did Patty point a finger?"

Donovan shook his head. "Far from it. Patty tried to protect him, but Guy had just taken off and Mrs. Maddison put two and two together."

"Mrs. Maddison hadn't met him?"

"Only the one time when he showed up for the appraisal. Obviously, he didn't use his own name."

Donovan slowed and turned left off the main highway. We followed a two-lane paved road for a mile until it turned to gravel, small rocks popping as the truck bounced upward. Ahead, I could see white dust, like smoke, drifting across the road as it curved around to the left where it widened to reveal the quarry site. Massive benches of raw soil and rock had been cut into the hillside. There were no trees and no vegetation in the area. The din of heavy machinery filled the still mountain air. Much of the area was a flat, chalky gray contrasting sharply with the surrounding gray-green hills and a sky of pale blue. The mountains beyond were cloaked in dark green vegetation interspersed with the gold of short dry grassy patches. Tiers had been cut into the side of the hill. Everywhere there were steep piles of earth and gravel, shale and sandstone, eroding raw earth and rock. Conveyor belts trundled rock upward toward the crusher, where rocks as big as my head were being shaken down into vibrating jaws that reduced them to rubble. Rugged horizontal and inclined screens and feeders sorted the crushed rock into various sizes.

Donovan pulled up close to a trailer, turned off the ignition, and set the hand brake. "Let me take care of business and I can finish the story on the way back. There's a hard hat in the back if you want to take a walk around."

"You go ahead. I'll be fine."

Donovan left me in the pickup while he conferred with a man in coveralls and a hard hat. The two disappeared into the trailer while I waited. From a distance, the machinery was the size of Matchbox toys. I watched as a conveyor belt moved loose rock in a steady stream that poured off the end into a cascading pile. I lifted my chin, shifting my sights to the countryside stretched out in a pristine canvas of hazy mountain and low-growing dark green. I let my gaze drift across the site, trying to make sense out of what Donovan had said. As nearly as I remembered Guy's passing reference to Patty, he saw his discretion with her as his one decent act. He'd described her as unstable, emotionally fragile, something along those lines. It was hard to believe he'd try to convince me of his honor when he'd gone to such lengths to rip her mother off. In truth, he'd ripped Patty off too since the money from the letters was supposed to go to her.

The sun was beating down on the cab of the pickup. Donovan had left the windows open so I wouldn't cook to death. White dust clouded the air and the growling of heavy equipment battled the quiet. I could hear the clank of metal, the high whine of shifting gears as a wheel loader grumbled across flat ground as barren as a moonscape. I unsnapped my seat belt and slouched down on my spine with my knees propped on the dashboard. I didn't want Guy to be guilty of a crime of this magnitude. What was done was done, but this was bad, bad, bad. I was prepared for pranks, willing to accept minor acts of mischief, but grand larceny was tough to overlook, even at this remove.

I didn't realize I'd been dozing until I heard the crunch of work boots and Donovan opened the truck door on the driver's side. I awoke with a start. He kicked the sides of his boots against the floor frame, knocking gravel loose before he slid in beneath the steering wheel. I sat up and refastened my seat belt.

"Sorry it took so long," he said.

"Don't worry about it. I was just resting my eyes," I said dryly.

He slammed the door, clicked his seat belt into place, and turned the key in the ignition. Within moments, we were bouncing down the road toward the highway again. "Where was I?" he asked.

"Guy switched a set of forged letters for the real ones and then disappeared. You were saying your father refused to make good."

"I'll say. The letters were worth something close to fifty thousand dollars. In those days, Dad didn't have that kind of money and wouldn't have paid anyway."

"What happened to the letters? Did Guy sell them?"

"He must have, because as far as I know, they were never seen again. Paul Trasatti could tell you more. His father was the appraiser brought in once the switch was made."

"So he was the one who confirmed the bad news to Mrs. Maddison?"

"Right."

"What happened to her?"

"She was a lush to begin with and she'd been popping pills for years. She didn't last long. Between the alcohol and cigarettes, she was dead in five years."

"And Patty?"

"That was unfortunate. In May of that year—this was two months after Guy left—Patty turned up pregnant. She was seventeen years old and didn't want anyone to know. She'd had a lot of mental problems and I think she was worried they'd put her away, which they probably would have. At any rate, she had an illegal abortion and died of septicemia."

"What?"

"You heard me right. She had what they referred to as a 'back-room' abortion, which was more common than you'd think. Procedure wasn't sterile—just some hack down in San Diego. She developed blood poisoning and she died."

"You're kidding."

"It's the truth," he said. "We weren't down on Guy for nothing. I know you think we're nothing but a bunch of hostile jerks, but this is what we've had to live with and it hasn't been easy."

"Why wasn't something said before now?"

"In what context? The subject never came up. We all knew what happened. We discussed it among ourselves, but we don't run around airing our dirty laundry in front of other people. You think we like owning up to his part in it?"

I brooded about it, staring out at the passing roadside. "I'm really having trouble believing this."

"I'm not surprised. You don't want to think Guy would do a thing like that."

"No, I don't," I said. "Guy told me Patty was hung up on him. He considered it his one decent act that he didn't seduce her when he had the chance. Now why would he say that?"

"He was hoping to impress you. Stands to reason," he said.

"But there wasn't any context. This was passing conversation, something he brought up. He didn't go into any detail. What's to be impressed about?"

"Guy was a liar. He couldn't help himself."

"He might have been a liar back then, but why lie about the girl all these years later? I didn't know her. I wasn't pressing for information. Why bother to lie when he had nothing to gain?"

"Look, I know you liked him. Most women did. You start feeling sorry for him. You feel protective. You don't want to accept the fact he was twisted as they come. This is the kind of shit he pulled."

"It isn't that," I said, offended. "He'd undergone a lot of soul-searching. He'd committed his life to God. There wasn't any point fabricating some tall tale about Patty Maddison."

"He was busy revising history. It's something we all do. You repent your sins and then in memory, you start cleaning up your past. Pretty soon, you're convinced you weren't nearly as bad as everyone said. The other guy was a jerk, but you had good reason for anything you did. It's all bunk, of course, but which of us can stand to take a look at ourselves? We whitewash. It's human nature."

"You're talking about the Guy Malek of the old days. Not the one I met. All I know is, I have a hard time picturing Guy doing this."

"You knew him less than a week and believed everything he said. He was a bad egg."

"But Donovan, look at the nature of his crimes. None of them were like this," I said. "As a kid, he was into vandalism. Later, he stole cars and stereos to pay for drugs. Forgery's too sophisticated a scheme for someone who spent his days getting high. Trust me. I've been high. You think you're profound but you're barely functional."

"Guy was a bright boy. He learned fast."

"I better talk to Paul," I said, unwilling to concede.

"He'll tell you the same thing. In fact, that's probably what put the idea in Guy's head in the first place. You have a good friend whose dad deals in rare documents, it doesn't take any great leap to figure it out when you've got access to something valuable."

"I hear what you're saying, but it isn't sitting right."

"You know anything about liars?" Donovan asked.

"Sure, I think I can say so. What about 'em?"

"A liar—a truly dedicated liar—lies because he can, because he's good at it. He lies for the pure pleasure, because he loves getting away with it. That's how Guy was. If he could tell you some lie—even if it meant nothing, even if there was nothing to be gained—he couldn't resist."

"You're telling me he was a pathological liar," I said, restating his claim in a tone of skepticism.

"I'm saying he enjoyed lying. He couldn't help himself."

"I don't believe that," I said. "I happen to think I'm a pretty good judge of liars."

"You know when some people lie, but not all."

"What makes you such an expert," I said, beginning to take offense. Donovan was just as annoyed with me.

He made a dismissive gesture. I suspected he wasn't used to having women argue with him. "Forget it. Have it your way," he said. "I can tell I'm not going to persuade you of anything."

"Nor I you," I said tartly. "What happened to the older sister?"

Donovan grimaced with exasperation. "Are you going to take my word for it or is this an excuse for another round of arguments?"

"I'm arguing about Guy, not the Maddisons, okay?"

"Okay. Claire—the older one—abandoned her plans for med school. She had no money and her mom was sinking like a stone. For a while she came back to take care of her. That was maybe six months or so. Once mom was gone, she went back to the East Coast—Rhode Island or some place. Might have been Connecticut. She got married to some fellow, but it didn't work out. Then about a year ago, she offed herself. Or so I heard."

"She committed suicide?"

"Why not? Her whole family was gone. She had no one. The family was a bit dicey to begin with—bunch of manic-depressives. I guess something must have finally pushed her over the edge."

"What'd she do, jump off a building?"

"I don't know how she did it. I wasn't being literal. There was a notice in the local paper. It happened back east somewhere."

I was silent again. "So maybe one of the Maddisons killed Guy. Wouldn't that make sense?"

"You're fishing. I just told you, they're all gone."

"But how do you know there isn't someone left? Cousins, for instance? Aunts and uncles? Patty's best friend?"

"Come on. Would you really murder someone who wronged a relative of yours? A sibling, maybe. But a cousin or a niece?"

"Well, no, but I'm not close to my relatives. Suppose something like that happened to your family."

"Something did happen to my family. Guy was killed," he said.

"Don't you want revenge?"

"Enough to kill someone? Absolutely not. Besides, if I cared enough to kill, I wouldn't wait this long. You're talking eighteen years."

"But Guy was missing all that time. You notice, once he came home, he was dead within days."

"True enough," he said.

"Does the name Max or Maximilian Outhwaite figure into this in any way? It could even be Maxine. I can't swear to gender."

Donovan turned and looked at me with surprise. "Where'd you come up with that one?"

"You know the name?"

"Well, sure. Maxwell Outhwaite's the name Guy used on the business cards he made to cheat Mrs. Maddison."

I squinted at him. "Are you sure?"

"That isn't something I'd forget," he said. "How'd you come across it?"

" 'Max Outhwaite' was the one who wrote the letters to the *Dispatch* and the L.A. *Times* That's how the press knew Guy was home."

19

Once back at Malek Construction, I left Donovan in the parking lot and picked up my car. I was feeling anxious and confused. This Max Outhwaite business made no sense at all. Maybe Dietz had come up with a line on him. Throw the Maddisons into the mix and what did it add up to? I glanced at my watch, wincing when I saw how late it was. The trip up the pass had taken more than an hour and a half.

Dietz was waiting in front of the public library. I pulled over to the curb and he slid into the passenger seat. "Sorry I'm late," I said.

"Don't worry about it. I got news for you. Outhwaite's a myth. I checked the city directories for the last twenty-five years and then went across the street and checked the County Clerk's office. No one by that name was ever listed in the phone book or anywhere else. No marriages, no deaths, no real property, building permits, lawsuits, you name it. Everybody alive leaves a trail of some kind. The name has to be phony unless we're missing a bet."

"There *is* a connection, but it's not what you'd expect," I said. I filled him in on my conversation with Donovan while we headed for home. I'd forgotten how nice it was to have someone to consult. I told him about the Maddisons and Guy's alleged involvement in the family's downfall. "Maxwell Outhwaite was the name used by the fictitious appraiser who stole fifty thousand dollars worth of rare documents. I'm not convinced it was Guy, but Donovan seems to take it for granted. Now, honestly," I said. "If you'd known about the Maddisons, wouldn't you have told someone?"

"Namely you?"

"Well, yes, me," I said. "Donovan could have *mentioned* it. Same with Max Outhwaite. The name pops up again years later—why didn't he tell someone?"

"Maybe Katzenbach never told him there was a letter and that Outhwaite was the name of the sender."

"Oh. I see what you're saying. I guess it's possible," I said. "It still annoys me no end. I wish we could find the typewriter. That would be a coup."

"Forget it. There's no way."

"What makes you say that? It has to be around here somewhere. Someone typed both those letters on the same machine."

"So what? If I were writing poison-pen notes, I'd hardly sit at my desk and use my own IBM. I'm too paranoid for that. I'd use one of the rental typewriters at the public library. Or maybe find a place selling typewriters and use one of theirs."

"This machine isn't new. The typeface has an old-fashioned look to it and a lot of the letters are clogged. It's probably got a fabric ribbon instead of carbon film."

"Those typewriters at the library aren't exactly hot off the assembly line."

"Pick me up some samples and we'll do a comparison. There are a couple of typeface defects that should help us pin it down. I'm sure a document expert could find others. I've only eyeballed it."

"The clogged letters don't mean much. Go after 'em with cleaning fluid and poof, those are gone."

"Sure, but don't you think the majority of people who write anonymous letters assume they're safe from discovery?"

"They might assume they're safe, but they're not," Dietz said. "The FBI maintains extensive files of anonymous letters. Plus, they have samples of type from most known machines. Post Office does, too, and so does the Treasury Department. They can determine the make and model of almost any machine. That's how they nail cranks, especially people who send threatening letters to public officials. The only way to play it safe is to dismantle the machine."

"Yeah, but who's going to trash a typewriter? If you thought you were safe enough to use your own machine, you wouldn't turn around and toss it in the garbage afterward. And in this case, why bother? Those letters were a nuisance, but hardly actionable."

Dietz smiled. "What, you picture it sitting out on someone's desk?"

"Maybe. It's possible."

"Keep an eye out."

"I know you're just saying that to humor me," I said.

"What else did Donovan have to say about the Maddisons?"

"Not much. He claims they're all gone, but I don't think we should take his word for it."

"It's worth pursuing," Dietz said. "As stories go, it's not bad."

"What do you mean, 'it's not bad'? I think it's fabulous. I mean, talk about a motive for murder. It's the best lead we've had—"

"The only lead," he pointed out.

I ignored the obvious. "On top of that, we have Outhwaite, who seems to tie right back to them."

"Shouldn't be too hard to track down the name Maddison with two *d*'s. Even if they're not local, they had to come from somewhere."

"Donovan says the father died around Thanksgiving of 1967 and Patty followed, probably in May or June of 1968. The mother died five years later, but that's as much as I know. You may not find Claire at all. He says she moved back to the East Coast and married. He does remember reading about her death in the local paper, so there must have been a notice in the *Dispatch*. Maybe she kept her maiden name?"

"I'll get on it first thing."

"You will? I can't believe you're volunteering. I thought you hated doing this stuff."

"Good practice. It's nice to keep a hand in. This way I know I haven't lost my touch," he said. "We might try the newspaper morgue if we can get Katzenbach's cooperation. They might have old clips on the Maddisons along with the obits."

"That's a sexy suggestion."

"I'm a sexy guy," he said.

When we got home, I changed into my sweats in preparation for jogging. I had slept through my usual six A.M. run and I was feeling the effects. I left Dietz in the living room with his leg propped up, icing his bum knee while he flipped from channel to channel, alternately watching CNN, talk shows, and obscure sporting events. I headed out the front door, thankful for the opportunity to spend time alone.

There was scarcely any breeze coming off the ocean. The late-afternoon sun had begun to fade, but the daylong baked beach was still throwing off heat saturated by the smell of kelp and brine. The

fronds of the palm trees looked like construction paper cutouts, flat
dark shapes against the flat blue sky. I lengthened my stride, running
at a pace that felt good. The stiffness and fatigue gradually gave way
to ease. My muscles became liquid and sweat trickled down my face.
Even the burning in my chest felt good as my body was flooded with
oxygen. At the end of the run, I flung myself down on the grass, where
I lay panting. My mind was a blank and my bones were washed clean.
Finally, my breathing slowed and the run-generated heat in my body
seeped out. I did a series of stretches and then roused myself. As I
headed for home, I could feel the return of the Santa Ana winds
lufting down the mountainside. I showered and changed clothes,
throwing on a T-shirt and jeans.

Dietz and I had dinner up at Rosie's. William was working behind
the bar again. At the age of eighty-seven, this was like a whole new
career for him. Since their marriage, the two of them had settled into
a comfortable routine. More and more, Rosie seemed to be turning
management over to him. She'd always maintained tight control of the
day-to-day operation, but William had persuaded her to pay decent
wages and as a consequence, she'd been able to hire better employees.
And she'd begun to delegate responsibility, which gave her more time
to spend with him. William had given up some of his imaginary illnesses and she'd surrendered some of her authoritarianism. Their affection for each other was obvious and their occasional spats seemed
to blow over without incident. Dietz was talking to William about
Germany, but I was only half attentive, wondering if the two of us
would ever reach an accommodation. I pictured Dietz at eighty-seven,
me a comparatively youthful seventy-two; retired from the stresses of
private-eye work, riddled with arthritis, bereft of our teeth. What
would we do, open a private-detective school?

"What are you thinking? You look odd," he said.

"Nothing. Retirement."

"I'd rather eat my gun."

At bedtime, Dietz offered to hobble up the spiral stairs. "My knee's
killing me again so I'm probably not much good except for company,"
he said.

"You're better off downstairs. My bed's not big enough, especially
with that knee of yours. I'd just lie there worrying I'd bump you
wrong."

I left him below opening up the sofa bed while I ambled up the
stairs, talking to him over the rail.

"Last chance," he said, smiling up at me.

"I'm not sure it's smart getting used to you."

"You should take advantage while you can."

I paused, looking down. "That's the difference between us in a nutshell, Dietz."

"Because I live in the moment?"

"Because for you that's enough."

First thing Friday morning, Dietz took his car and headed over to the *Santa Teresa Dispatch* offices while I drove to Paul Trasatti's house. Hopper Road was located midway between the Maleks' and the country club. The neighborhood was small, the street lined with elm trees and dappled with shade. The house was built in the style of an English country cottage, the sort you'd see pictured on a deck of playing cards; gray stone with a thatched roof that undulated like an ocean wave where the gables appeared. The windows were small-paned, leaded glass, the wood trim and the shutters painted white. Two narrow stone chimneys bracketed the house like a pair of matching bookends. The yard was enclosed with a white picket fence, pink and red hollyhocks planted along the front. The small yard was immaculate, thick grass bordered in dark ivy with small flowerbeds along the brick walk leading to the door. Birds twittered in the young oak growing at the corner of the property.

I'd called the night before, of course, wanting to be certain Trasatti would be home. Even on the porch, I could smell bacon and eggs and the scent of maple syrup. My whimper probably wasn't audible above the sound of the mower two doors down. In response to my ring, Trasatti came to the door with his napkin in hand. He was tall and thin, as bald as a lightbulb. He had a large nose, thick glasses, and a jutting chin. His chest was narrow, slightly sunken, swelling to a thickened waistline. He wore a white dress shirt and a pair of stovepipe pants. He frowned at me, looking at his watch with surprise. "You said nine."

"It is nine."

"This says eight." He held his watch to his ear. "Shit. Come on in. You caught me at breakfast. Have a seat in here. I'll be back in a second. You want coffee?"

"I'm fine. Take your time," I said.

The living room was small and perfectly appointed, more like a doctor's office than a place to put your feet up. The furniture had a vaguely Victorian air, though to my untutored eye, it didn't appear to be the real thing. The chairs were small and fussy, rimmed with carved wooden fruit. There were three dark wood tables topped with pink-veined marble slabs, an array of Sotheby's catalogs neatly lined up on

one. The carpeting was a short-cut wool pile, pale blue with a border
of Chinese dragons and chrysanthemums. Two cloisonné vases were
filled with artificial pink and blue flowers of some generic sort. A clock
on the mantel had a second hand that clicked distinctly as it inched its
way around. I leafed through a Sotheby's catalog, but didn't see much
of interest except a letter from the Marquis de Sade, which was being
offered at two thousand dollars. The passage quoted was in French
and seemed petulant. There was also a pretty little greeting from Erik
Satie to Mme Ravel with "decorated borders and raised blind relief
heading showing in colour two hands held in front of a rose . . ."
Lots of talk about *"jolies fleurs"* and *"respecteusements."* My thoughts
exactly. I've often said as much.

I strolled the perimeter, taking in numerous framed letters and
autographs. Laurence Sterne, Franz Liszt, William Henry Harrison,
Jacob Broom (whoever he was), Juan José Flores (ditto). There was a
long, incomprehensible letter bearing the signature S. T. Coleridge,
and some kind of receipt or order blank signed by George Washington. There was another letter written in a crabbed hand, dated August
1710, fraught with brown ink and cross-outs and looking crumpled and
stained. Who'd had the presence of mind to save all this litter? Were
there people with foresight going through the dustbins back then?

Across the hall, I could see what must have been a dining room
done up as an office. There were bookshelves on every wall, some
extending across the windows, which greatly diminished the incoming
light. Every surface was stacked ten deep, including tables, chairs, and
floors. No typewriter on the premises as far as I could see. I had no
reason to think Trasatti was involved, but it would have been nice to
have a piece of the puzzle fall into place. The air smelled of old dust
and book mold, glue, aging paper, and dust mites. A large tortoiseshell cat picked its way daintily across a desk piled with books. This
creature had only a stump for a tail and looked like it might be searching out a place to pee.

"Making yourself at home?" came the voice behind me.

I started, making ever so slight a leap.

"I was admiring this enormous cat," I said casually.

"Sorry if I startled you. That's Lady Chatterley."

"What happened to her tail?"

"She's a Manx."

"She looks like a character," I said. Animal people seem to love it
when you say things like this. Trasatti didn't seem to warm to it. He
gestured me into the office, where he took a seat at his desk, pushing
aside an irregular stack of hardback books.

"No secretary?" I asked.

"Business isn't big enough for clerical help. Anything I need done, I use the Mac upstairs. Go ahead and make a space for yourself," he said, indicating the only chair in the room.

"Thanks." I placed some books, a briefcase, and a pile of newspapers on the floor, and sat down.

"Now what can I help you with? I really can't add to what I've already given you in regard to Jack," he said.

"This was in regard to something else," I said while the fifteen-pound cat hopped onto my lap and settled between my knees. Up close, Lady Chatterley smelled like a pair of damp two-week-old socks. I scratched that little spot just above the base of its tail which made the back end of the cat rise up until its rosebud was staring me in the face. I pushed the back end down. I peppered my preface with lots of reassuring phrases—"off the record," "just between us," and other felicitous expressions of confidentiality—before getting down to business. "I'm wondering what you can tell me about the Maddisons—Patty and her sister, Claire."

He seemed to take the question in stride. "What would you like to know?"

"Anything you care to tell," I said.

Paul straightened the stack of books in front of him, making sure all the edges were aligned and the top right-hand corners matched. "I didn't know the sister. She was older than we were. She was off at college by the time the family moved into the area and Patty started hanging out with Guy."

"The Maddisons were new in town?"

"Well no, not really. They'd been living out in Colgate and bought a house closer in. They never had the kind of money we did, the rest of us—not that we were wealthy," he added. "Bader Malek did well back in those days, but he wasn't what you'd call rich."

"Tell me about Patty."

"She was pretty. Dark." He put his hand at eye level, indicating bangs. "Hair down to here," he said. "She'd kind of peer out like this. She was strange, lots of phobias and nervous mannerisms. Bad posture, big tits. She chewed her nails to the quick and liked to stick herself with things." Trasatti put his hands in his lap, trying not to touch the items on his desk.

"She stuck herself? With what?"

"Needles. Pencils. Safety pins. I saw her burn herself one time. She put a lighted cigarette on her hand—casually, like it was happening to someone else. She never even flinched, but I could smell cooked flesh."

"Was Guy serious about her?" I pushed the cat's hind end down again and it began to work its claws into the knees of my jeans.

"She was serious about him. I have no idea what he thought of her."

"What about the others? Donovan and Bennet."

"What about them?"

"I just wondered what they were up to during this period."

"Donovan was working for his dad, as I remember. He was always working for his dad, so that's a safe bet. Jack was back at school by then, so he was only home on occasion. Christmas and spring break."

"And his mother's funeral," I said. I extracted the cat's claws from my knee and held its right paw between my fingers. I could feel its claws protrude and retract, but the cat seemed content, probably thinking about mice. "What about Bennet? Where was he?"

"Here in town. He and I were both finishing at UCST."

"Majoring in what?"

"My major was art history. His was economics or business, maybe public finance. He switched around some. I forget."

"Did it surprise you when Patty turned up pregnant?"

Trasatti snorted, shaking his head. "Patty would screw anyone. She was desperate for attention and we were happy to oblige."

"Really," I said. "Donovan never said she was promiscuous."

"She wasn't the only one. There was lots of screwing in those days Free love, we called it. We were all smoking dope. Bunch of small-town hippies, or as close as we could get. We were always horny and hungry. Half the girls we hung out with were as fat as pigs. Except for Patty, of course, who was gorgeous, but whacked out."

"Nice of you boys to help yourselves to a minor," I said. "Given her loose ways, how'd you know the baby was Guy's?"

"Because she said it was."

"She could have lied. If she was crazy and stoned, she might have made things up. How do you know the baby wasn't yours?"

Trasatti shifted uncomfortably. "I had no money to speak of. Where's the benefit in claiming it's mine. The Maleks had class. She might have been crazy, but she wasn't stupid. It's like the old joke—"

"I know the old joke," I said. "Was there ever any proof? Did anybody run blood tests to establish paternity?"

"I hardly think so. I'm sure they didn't. This was sixty-eight."

"How do you know Guy wasn't blamed because it was convenient?

He was gone by then. Who better to accuse than a chronic screwup like him?"

Trasatti picked up a pencil and then put it down. His expression had gone blank. "What does this have to do with Jack? I thought you were working to try to get him off."

"That's what I'm doing."

"Doesn't sound like that to me."

"Donovan told me about Patty yesterday. I thought the story might pertain, so I'm following up. Did you ever see the letters Guy allegedly forged?"

"Why put it that way? It's what he did."

"Did you actually see him do it."

"No, of course not."

"Then it's all supposition. Did you ever see the letters?"

"Why would I?"

"Your father did the appraisal when the forgeries were discovered. I thought he might have showed you the copies, if he was training you to follow in his footsteps."

"Who told you that?"

"He handed the business over to you, didn't he?"

Trasatti smiled at me, blinking. "I don't understand where you intend to go with this. Are you accusing me of something?"

"Not at all," I said.

"Because if you are, you're out of line."

"That wasn't an accusation. I never said you did anything. I'm saying Guy Malek didn't. I'm saying someone else did it all and blamed him. What about 'Max Outhwaite'? How does he fit in?"

"Outhwaite?"

"Come on, Trasatti. That's the name Guy supposedly used on his fake business cards."

"Right, right, right. I remember now. Sure thing. I knew it sounded familiar. What's the link?"

"That's why I'm asking you. I don't know," I said. "I think the story of Patty Maddison ties in somehow. Her death, the forged letters. I'm just fishing around."

"You better try something else. The family's gone."

"What makes you so sure?"

Paul Trasatti was silent. He began to arrange a row of paper clips on the side of a magnetized holder on his desk. Each one had to be exactly the same distance from the one above it and the one below.

"Come on. Just between us," I said.

"I tried to find them once."

"When was this?"

"About ten years ago."

"Really," I said, trying not to seem interested. "What was that about?"

"I was curious. I thought there might be other rare documents. You know, passed down to other members of the family."

"How'd you go about it?"

"I hired a genealogist. I said I was trying to find some long-lost relatives. This gal did a search. She took months. She traced the name back to England, but on this end—the California branch—there weren't any male heirs and the line died out."

"What about aunts, uncles, cousins . . . ?"

"The parents were both the only children of only children. There was no one left."

"What happened to the copies of the documents?"

"The forgeries were destroyed."

"And the originals?"

"No one's ever seen them again. Well, I haven't in any case. They've never come up for sale in all the years I've done business."

"Do you know what they were?"

"I have the itemized list. My dad kept meticulous records. You want to see it?"

"I'd love to."

Trasatti got up and crossed to a closet. I caught a glimpse of a wall safe and four gray metal file cabinets. Above them, on shelves, there was a series of old-fashioned card files. "I'm going to get all this on computer one of these days." He seemed to know right where he was going and I wondered if this was something he'd done recently. He extracted a card, glanced at it briefly, and then closed the drawer again. He left the closet door ajar and returned to his desk, handing me the card as he passed my chair. The cat had gone to sleep, lying across my knees like a fifteen-pound bag of hot sand.

The list detailed six documents: a framed Society of Boston Membership Certificate and a personal letter, both signed by George Washington and valued at $11,500 and $9,500, respectively; a judicial writ signed by Abraham Lincoln, dated December 1847, valued at $6,500; a wartime document signed by John Hancock, valued at $5,500; a ten-page fragment from an original manuscript by Arthur Conan Doyle valued at $7,500; and a letter signed by John Adams, valued at $9,000.

"I'm impressed," I said. "I don't know beans about rare documents, but these seem fabulous."

"They are. Those prices you're looking at are twenty years out of date. They'd be worth more today."

"How did Patty Maddison's father get his hands on items like these?"

"Nobody really knows. He was an amateur collector. He picked some up at auction and the rest, who knows? He might have stolen them for all I know. My father'd heard about 'em, but Francis—Mr. Maddison—would never let him examine them."

"His widow must have been an idiot to hand 'em over the way she did."

Trasatti made no comment.

"How did Guy hear about the letters?" I asked.

"Patty probably told him."

"Why would she do that?"

"How do I know? Showing off. She was nuts. She did all kinds of weird things."

I saw him glance at his watch. "You have an appointment?" I asked.

"As a matter of fact, I'm hoping we can wrap this up. I have work to do."

"Five minutes more and I'll be on my way."

Trasatti shifted restlessly, but motioned me on.

"Let me try out a little theory. None of this came to light until after Guy took off, right?"

Trasatti stared at me, without offering encouragement.

I was forced to go on, feeling like Perry Mason in a courtroom confrontation, only this wasn't going as well as his always did. "So maybe Jack was the one who got Patty knocked up. I heard Jack was the randy one. According to Guy, he screwed anything that moved."

"I told you he was off at college. He wasn't even here," Trasatti said.

"He came back for his mother's funeral and again for spring break. That was March, wasn't it?"

"I really don't remember."

"As I understand it, Guy had hit the road by then. Jack felt betrayed. He was crushed that Guy'd left without him so maybe he turned to Patty for consolation. At that point, she must have needed comfort as much as he did."

Trasatti kept his face expressionless, his fingers laced together on the desk. "You're never going to get me to say anything about this."

"Jack could have forged the letters. You two were buddies. Your father was an appraiser. You could have cooked up the scheme your-self and showed Jack how to do it."

"I'm finding this offensive. It's pure speculation. It doesn't mean a thing."

I let that one slide, though what he said was true. "Everything was cool until Guy came home again."

"What difference would that make?"

"In the old days, Guy took the blame for everybody's sins, so it just stands to reason everyone felt safe until he showed up again."

"I'm not following."

"Maybe the motive for Guy's murder was never money," I said. "Maybe Jack was just trying to protect himself."

"From what? I don't get it. There's really nothing at stake. The theft was eighteen years ago. The statute of limitations has run out. There's no crime on the books. Even if your guess is correct, Jack's the one who ends up with his ass in a sling. You said you were here to help, but it's blowing right back on him."

"You know what? Here's the truth. I don't really give a shit what blows back on him. If he's guilty, so be it. That isn't my concern."

"Well, that's nice. You want me to pick up the phone and call Lonnie Kingman? He's going to love your attitude and so will Jack. As far as I know, he's the one paying your bills."

"You go right ahead. Lonnie can always fire me if he doesn't like what I'm doing."

20

I stopped at a pay phone and put a call through to Lonnie, who had the good grace to laugh when he heard my account of the conversation with Paul Trasatti. "Forget it. The guy's a prick. He was just on the phone to me, whining and complaining about harassment. What a jerk."

"Why's he so worried about Jack?"

"Forget Jack for now. I'll take care of him. You better go talk to Bennet; I couldn't get to him. According to the grapevine, he's talking to an attorney in case the hairy eyeball of the law falls on him next. He's still got no alibi, as far as I've heard."

"Well, that's interesting."

"Yeah, people are getting nervous. That's a good sign," he said. He gave me the address of Bennet's restaurant, which was located downtown on a side street off State. The neighborhood itself was marked by a tire store, a minimart, a video rental shop, and a billiard parlor where fights erupted without much provocation beyond excess beer. Parking didn't seem to be readily available and it was hard to picture where the restaurant trade would be coming from.

Apparently, the place had once been a retail store, part of a chain that had filed for bankruptcy. The old sign was still out, but the interior had been gutted. The space was cavernous and shadowy, the floor bare concrete, the ceiling high. Heating ducts and steel girders were exposed to view, along with all of the electrical conduit. Toward the rear, an office had been roughed in: a desk, file cabinets, and office equipment arranged in a bare-framed cubicle. The back wall was solid and through a narrow doorway, I could see a toilet and a small sink with a medicine cabinet above it. It was going to take a lot of money to complete construction and get the business on its feet. No wonder Bennet had been so eager to get his hands on the second will. If Guy's share was divided among his brothers, each would be richer by more than a million, which he could clearly use.

To the right, a huge rolling metal door had been opened onto a weedy vacant lot. Outside, the sun was harsh, sparkling on the broken bottles while its heat baked a variety of doggy turds. There was not a soul in sight, but the building was wide open and I kept thinking Bennet, or a construction worker, would show up before long. While I waited, I wandered into the office area and took a seat at Bennet's desk. The secretarial chair was rickety and I imagined he made his phone calls upright with his hip resting on the desk, which seemed sturdier. Everything in the office had an air of having been borrowed or picked up on the cheap. The calculator tape showed a long series of numbers that didn't add up to anything. I could have checked in the drawers, but I was too polite. Besides, my recent clash with Paul Trasatti had chastened me some. I didn't want Lonnie getting two complaints in a single day.

There was a manual typewriter sitting on a rolling cart. My gaze slid across it idly and then came back. It was an ancient black Underwood with round yellowed keys that looked like they'd be hard to press. The ribbon was so worn it was thin in the middle. I looked over at the rolling door and then surveyed the whole of the empty restaurant space. Still no one. My bad angel was hovering to my left. It was she who pointed out the open packet of typing paper sitting right there in plain sight.

I pulled out a sheet and rolled it into the machine, settling myself on the wobbly typing chair. I typed my name. I typed that old standby: *The quick brown fox jumps over the lazy dog.* I typed the name *Max Outhwaite.* I typed *Dear Miss Milhone.* I peered closely. The vowels didn't appear to be clogged, which (as Dietz had pointed out) didn't mean that much. This could still be the typewriter used for the notes. Maybe Bennet had simply made a point of cleaning his keys. I pulled the paper out and folded it, then stood up and slipped it in the pocket of my jeans. When I got back to the office, I'd see if the defective *a* and *i* were visible under magnification. I still hadn't seen the anonymous letter Guy had received the Monday before he died, but maybe Betsy Bower would relent and let me pirate a copy.

The telephone rang.

I stared at it briefly and then lifted my head, listening for footsteps heading in my direction. Nothing. The phone rang again. I was tempted to answer, but I really didn't need to because the answering machine kicked in. Bennet's voice message was brief and very businesslike. So was the caller.

"Bennet. Paul here. Give me a call as soon as possible."

The machine clicked off. The message light blinked off and on. My bad angel tapped me on the shoulder and pointed. I reached out and pressed DELETE. A disembodied male voice told me the message had been erased. I headed for the front door, breaking into a trot when I reached the street. Trasatti was a busy boy, calling everyone.

A Harley-Davidson rumbled into view. Shit. Bennet was back just when I thought I'd escaped. I slowed my pace, as if I had all the time in the world. Bennet rolled Jack's motorcycle up to the curb less than ten feet away. He killed the engine and popped the kickstand into place. He peeled off his helmet and cradled it under his arm. I noticed his hair was tightly frizzed and matted with sweat. Despite the heat, he was wearing a black leather jacket, probably protection in case he flipped the bike and skidded. "Working again?"

"I'm always working," I said.

"Did you want to talk to me?" His jacket creaked when he walked. He headed into the restaurant.

I followed. "How goes construction? It's looking pretty good," I said. It looked like a bomb crater, but I was kissing butt. Our footsteps echoed as we crossed the raw concrete floor.

"Construction's slow."

I said, "Ah. What's your target for opening?"

"April, if we're lucky. We have a lot of work to do."

"What kind of restaurant?"

"Cajun and Caribbean. We'll have salads and burgers, too, very reasonably priced. Maybe jazz two nights a week. We're really aiming for the singles' market."

"Like a pickup bar?"

"With class," he said. "This town doesn't have a lot going on at night. Get some dance music in here weekends, I think we're filling a niche. A chef from New Orleans and all the hot local bands. We should pull crowds from as far away as San Luis Obispo."

"That sounds rowdy," I said. We'd reached the office by then and I saw him flick a glance at his answering machine. I was only half listening, trying to think how to keep the conversation afloat. "Any problem with parking?"

"Not at all," he said. "We'll pave the lot next door. We're in negotiations at the moment. There's room for thirty cars there and another ten on the street."

"Sounds good," I said. He had an answer for everything. Mr. Slick, I thought.

"I'll comp you some tickets for the grand opening. You like to dance?"

"No, not really."

"Don't worry about it. We'll get you in and you can cut loose. Forget your inhibitions and get down," he said. He snapped his fingers, dipping his knees in a move meant to be oh so hip.

My least favorite thing in life is some guy encouraging me to "cut loose" and "get down." The smile I offered him was paper thin. "I hope this business with Jack has been resolved by then."

"Absolutely," he said smoothly, his expression sobering appropriately. "How's it looking so far?"

"He can't account for his time, which doesn't help," I said. "The cops are claiming they found a bloody print from his shoe on the carpet up in Guy's room. I won't bore you with details. Lonnie wanted me to ask where you were."

"The night of the murder? I was club-hopping down in L.A."

"You drove to Los Angeles and back?"

"I do it all the time. It's nothing. Ninety minutes each way," he said. "That night, some of the time I was on the road."

"Did you have a date?"

"This was strictly business. I'm trying to get a feel for what works and what doesn't, sampling menus. You know, listening to some of the L.A. bands."

"I'm assuming you have credit card receipts to back you up."

A fleeting change of expression suggested I'd caught him out on that one. "I might have a few. I'll have to look and see what I've got. I paid cash in the main. It's easier that way."

"What time did you get in?"

"Close to three," he said. "You want to come in the back? I've got some beer in a cooler. We could have a drink."

"Thanks. It's a bit early."

"Where you going?"

"Back to the office. I have a meeting," I said.

•   •   •

On the way back to the office, I stopped off at a deli and picked up some soft drinks and sandwiches. Dietz had said he'd be joining me as soon as he'd finished his research. I stashed the soft drinks in the little refrigerator in my office and dumped my handbag on the floor beside my chair. I put the sack of sandwiches on the file cabinet and grabbed the folder full of clippings, which I tossed on my desk. I sat down in my swivel chair and assembled my index cards, the typewritten letters, and the sample I'd just taken from Bennet's machine, lining everything up in an orderly fashion. In the absence of definitive answers, it's good to look organized.

I turned on the desk lamp and pulled out my magnifying glass. The type was no match. I was disappointed, but I wasn't surprised. I took Guy's last letter from my handbag and read the contents again. Aside from his invitation to Disneyland, which I'd have accepted in a flash, I realized that what I was looking at, in essence, was a holographic will. The letter was written entirely by hand and he'd specified in the post-script what he'd wanted done with his share of his father's estate. I didn't know all the technicalities associated with a holographic will, but I thought this might qualify. The handwriting would have to be verified, but Peter Antle could do that when I saw him next. I knew Guy had received a disturbing letter late that Monday afternoon, and whatever its contents, he must have been sufficiently alarmed to want to make his wishes clear. I got up and left the office, taking his letter with me to the copy room. I ran a Xerox and then locked the originals with the others in my bottom drawer. The copy I slid in the outer pocket of my handbag.

I tried to picture Guy, but his face had already faded in my mind's eye. What remained was his sweetness, the sound of his "Hey," the feeling of his whiskers when he'd brushed my cheek with his lips. If he'd lived, I'm not sure we would have had a very strong relationship. Kinsey Millhone and a born-again was probably not a combination that would have gone anywhere. But we might have been friends. We might have gone to Disneyland once a year to experience some silliness.

I went back to my index cards and began to make notes. Every investigation has a nature of its own, but there are certain shared characteristics, namely the painstaking accumulation of information and the patience required. Here's what you hope for: a chance remark from the former neighbor on a skip-trace, a penciled notation on the corner of a document, an ex-spouse with a grudge, the number on an account, an item overlooked at the scene of a crime. Here's what you expect: the dead ends, bureaucratic bullheadedness, the cul-de-sacs, trails that go nowhere or simply fade into thin air, denials, prevarications, the blank-eyed stares from all the hostile witnesses. Here's what you know: that you've done it before and you have the toughness and determination to pull it off again. Here's what you want: justice. Here's what you'll settle for: something equivalent, the quid pro quo.

I glanced down at my desk, catching sight of the label on the file of clippings. The label had been neatly typed: *Guy Malek, Dispatch Clippings.* The two letters from Outhwaite were lined up with the label itself, which is what made me notice for the first time that the lowercase *a* and the lower case *i* were both defective on all three documents. Was that true? I peered closely, picking up my magnifying glass again and scrutinizing the relevant characters. It would take a document expert to prove it, but to me it looked like the letters had been typed on the same machine.

I reached for the phone and called the Maleks. In the tiny interval between punching in the number and waiting for it to ring, I was scrambling around in my imagination, trying to conjure up a reason for the call I was making. Shit, shit, shit. Christie picked up on her end, greeting me coolly when I identified myself. I figured she'd talked to Paul Trasatti, but I didn't dare ask.

I said, "I was just looking for Bennet. Is he home, by any chance? I stopped by the restaurant, but he was out somewhere."

"He should be here in a bit. I think he said he was coming home for lunch. You want him to call you?"

"I'm not sure he'll be able to reach me. I'm down at the office, but I've got some errands to run. I'll call back later."

"I'll pass the message along." She was using her good-bye tone.

I had to launch in with something to keep the conversation afloat. "I talked to Paul this morning. What an odd duck he is. Is he still on medication?"

I could hear her focus her attention. "Paul's on medication? Who told you that? I never heard that," she said.

I let a beat pass. "Uhh, sorry. I didn't mean to breach anybody's confidence. Forget I said anything. I just assumed you knew."

"Why bring it up at all? Is there a problem?"

"Well, nothing *huge.* He's just so paranoid about Jack. He actually sat there and accused me of undermining Jack's credibility, which couldn't be further from the truth. Lonnie and I are working our butts off for him."

"Really."

"Then he turned around and called Lonnie. I think he's probably on another phone rampage, hounding everyone he knows with those wild stories of his. Ah, well. It doesn't matter. I'm sure he means well, but he's not doing anybody any favors."

"Is that what you wanted to talk to Bennet about?"

"No, that was something different. Lonnie wanted me to verify Bennet's whereabouts Tuesday night."

"I'm sure he'll be happy to talk to you. I know he's told the police and they seem satisfied. I can leave him a note."

"Perfect. I'd appreciate that. Can I ask you about something? You remember the file I borrowed?"

"With all the clippings?"

"Exactly. I wondered about the label. Did you type that yourself?"

"Not me. I never took typing. My mother warned me about that. Bader probably typed the label or he gave it to his secretary. He thought typing was restful. Shows how much he knew."

"That must have been a while ago. I don't remember seeing a typewriter in his office when I was there."

"He got himself a personal computer a couple of years ago."

"What happened to the typewriter?"

"He passed it on to Bennet, I think."

I closed my eyes and stilled my breathing. Christie's attitude had changed and she was sounding friendly again. I didn't want to alert her to the importance of the information. "What'd Bennet do with it? That's not the one he's using at the restaurant, is it?"

"Nuhn-uhn. I doubt it. It's probably in his room. What's this about?"

"Nothing much. No big deal. Just a little theory of mine, but I'd love to see it sometime. Would it be all right with you if I stopped by to take a look?"

"Well, it's all right with me, but Bennet might object unless he's here, of course. His room is like the inner sanctum. Nobody goes in there except him. We're just on our way out. We have an appointment at eleven. Why don't you ask Bennet when you talk to him?"

"I can do that. No problem. That's a good idea," I said. "And one more quick question. The night of the murder, could you really see Donovan? Or did you just assume he was watching television because the set was turned on in the other room?"

Christie put the phone down without another word.

The minute I hung up, I wrote a hasty note to Dietz, put a couple of pieces of blank paper in the file, and shoved it in my handbag. I headed out the side door and took the stairs down to the street, skipping two at a time. I wasn't sure which "we" had an appointment at eleven, but I was hoping it was Christie and Donovan. If I could get to the Maleks' before Bennet came home, I could probably bullshit my way upstairs and take a look at the machine. It had occurred to me more than once that Jack or Bennet might be behind the letters and the leak to the press. I couldn't pinpoint the motivation, but getting a lock on the typewriter would go a long way toward shoring up the connection. I was also thinking tee-hee on you, Dietz, because I'd told him whoever wrote the letters wouldn't trash the machine. It's the same way with guns. Someone will use a handgun in the commission of a crime and instead of disposing of the weapon, he'll keep it in his closet at home or shove it under the bed. Better to pitch it in the ocean.

I reached the Maleks' in record time, burning up the route I'd driven so many times before. As I approached the estate, I could see the front gates swing open and the nose of a car just appearing around the curve in the drive. I slammed on my brakes and slid into the nearest driveway, fishtailing slightly, my eyes pinned on my rearview mirror for a moment until the BMW sped past. Donovan was driving, his gaze fixed on the road ahead. I thought I caught sight of Christie, but I couldn't be sure. I heard a car horn toot and looked out through my windshield. The Maleks' neighbor, in a dark blue station wagon, was waiting patiently for me to get out of his driveway. I made lots of sheepish gestures as I put my car in reverse. I backed out of the driveway and pulled over to let him pass. I mouthed the word *Sorry* as he turned to look at me. He smiled and waved, and I waved back at him. Once he was out of sight, I pulled out, crossing the road to the Maleks' entrance gates.

The security guard had been relieved of his duties. I leaned out toward the call box and punched in the gate code Tasha had given me. There was a happy peeping signal. The gates gave a little wiggle and then swung open to admit me. I eased up the driveway and around the curve. Vaguely, it occurred to me that Christie might have stayed home. I'd have to think of a whopper to account for my arrival. Oh, well. Often the best lies are the ones you think up in a pinch.

There were no cars in the courtyard, a good sign I thought. Two of the three garages were standing open and both were empty. I had to leave my vehicle out front, but there didn't seem to be any way around that. If my purpose was legitimate, why would I bother to conceal my car? If the Maleks returned, I'd find a way to fake it. I bypassed the front door and hiked around to the kitchen, pulling the file from my handbag as I rounded the house. Enid was visible through the bay window, standing at the sink. She spotted me and waved, moving toward the backdoor to let me in. She was still drying her hands on a towel when she stepped back, allowing me to precede her into the room.

I said, "Hi, Enid. How are you?"

"Fine," she said. "What are you doing coming to the backdoor? You just missed Christie and Donovan going out the front." She was wearing a big white apron over jeans and a T-shirt and her hair was neatly tucked under a crocheted cap.

"Really? I didn't see them. I rang the front doorbell twice. I guess you couldn't hear me so I thought I'd come around. I can't believe I missed them. My timing's off," I said.

I could see the ingredients for a baking project laid out on the counter: two sticks of butter with the paper removed, a sixteen-ounce measuring cup filled with granulated sugar, a tin of baking powder, and a quart container of whole milk. The oven was preheating and a large springform pan had already been buttered and floured.

She returned to the counter where she picked up her sifter and began sifting cake flour into a mountain that had a perfect point on top. While I watched, she used a spatula to scoop more flour. I seldom bake anything and when I do, I tend to assemble the items as needed, not realizing I'm missing some essential ingredient until I get to the critical moment in the recipe. "Quickly fold in whipped egg whites and finely minced fresh ginger . . ." Enid was methodical, washing up as she went along. I knew she wouldn't bake anything from mixes and her cakes would never fall.

"Where'd everybody go? I didn't see any cars in the garages," I said.

"Myrna's lying down. I imagine she'll be up in a bit."

"What's wrong with her? Is she ill?"

"I don't know. She seems worried and I don't think she's been sleeping that well."

"Maybe I should talk to her. Where's everyone else?"

"Christie says Bennet's coming home at lunchtime. She and Donovan went over to the funeral home. The coroner's office called. The body's being released this afternoon and they've gone to pick out a casket."

"When's the funeral? Has anybody said?"

"They're talking about Monday, just for family and close friends. It won't be open to the public."

"I should think not. I'm sure they've had their fill of media attention."

"Can I help you with anything?"

"Not really. I talked to Christie a while ago and told her I'd be returning this file. She said to stick it in Bader's office. I can let myself out the front door when I'm done."

"Help yourself," she said. "Take the back stairs if you want. You know how to find the office?"

"Sure. I've been up there before. What are you making?"

"Lemon pound cake."

"Sounds good," I said.

I trotted up the back stairs, folder in hand, slowing my pace when I reached the top landing. The back hall was utilitarian, floors uncarpeted, windows bare. This mansion was built in an era when the wealthy had live-in servants who occupied nooks and crannies squeezed into wings at the rear of the house, or wedged into attic spaces that were broken up into many small rooms. Cautiously, I opened a door on my left. A narrow stairway ascended into the shadows above. I eased the door shut and moved on, checking into a large linen closet and a cubicle with an ancient commode. The corridor took a ninety-degree turn to the right, opening into the main hall through an archway concealed by heavy damask drapes on a wrought-iron rod.

I could see the polished rail of the main stair at the midpoint in the hall. Beyond the stair landing, there was another wing of the house that mirrored the one I was now in. A wide Oriental runner stretched the length of the gloomy hall. At the far end, damask drapes suggested an archway and yet another set of stairs. The wallpaper was subdued, a soft floral pattern repeated endlessly. At intervals, tulip shaped crystal fixtures were mounted on the walls. They'd probably been installed when the house was built and converted at some point from gas to electricity.

There were three doors on my left, each sealed with an enormous X of crime scene tape. I had to guess that one door led to Guy's bedroom, one to Jack's, and one to the bathroom that connected the two. On the right, there were two more doors. I knew the second was Bader's suite: bedroom, bath, and home office. The door closest to me was closed. I flicked a look behind me, making sure Enid hadn't followed. The whole house was silent. I put my hand on the knob and turned it with care. Locked.

Well, now what? The lock was the simple old-fashioned type requiring a skeleton key that probably fit every door up here. I scanned the hall in both directions. I didn't have time to waste. Bader's suite was closest. I did a racewalk to his bedroom and tried the knob. This room was unlocked. I peered around the door. There was a key protruding neatly from the keyhole on the other side. I extracted it and hurried back to Bennet's room. I jammed the key in the lock and tried turning it. I could feel the key hang, but there was some tolerance to the lock. I applied steady pressure while I jiggled the door gently. It took close to thirty seconds, but the key gave way suddenly and I was in.

21

I scanned the room quickly, taking in as much as I could. Two table lamps had been left on. This had to be Bennet's bedroom. He was still in possession of all the paraphernalia from his boyhood hobbies. Model airplanes, model cars, stacks of vintage comic books, early issues of *MAD* magazine, Little League trophies. He'd framed a paint-by-numbers likeness of Jimmy Durante and a color snapshot of himself at the age of thirteen wearing spiffy black dress pants, a pink dress shirt, and a black bolo tie. His bulletin board was still hanging on the back of his closet door. Tacked to the cork were various newspaper headlines about the assassinations of Martin Luther King, Jr., and Bobby Kennedy. There were photographs of the *Apollo 8* spacecraft the day it was launched from Cape Kennedy. A framed movie poster from *The Odd Couple* still hung above his unmade bed. It wasn't hard to pinpoint the peak year in his life. There was no memorabilia beyond 1968.

I flicked on the overhead light and crossed the room, placing my handbag on the floor near my feet. His desk was built-in and ran along the front wall from one side of the room to the other, punctuated by two windows. Bookshelves had been hung on the wall above the desk. Most of the books looked dated, the titles suggestive of textbooks accumulated over the years. I let my gaze skip across the spines. *Ring of Bright Water,* Maxwell; *No Room in the Ark,* Moorehead; *Stalking the Edible Life,* Gibbons; *The Sea Around Us,* Carson. Little or no fiction. Not surprising somehow. Bennet didn't strike me as intellectual or imaginative. A personal computer occupied his desk at center stage, complete with an oversized printer. The machine had been shut down and the glassy gray screen of the monitor reflected distorted slices of the light from the hall door. Everything was a jumble; bills, loose papers, invoices, and stacks of unopened mail everywhere. I spotted the typewriter to the left, covered with a black plastic typewriter "cozy" complete with dust. A stack of books had been placed on top.

I backed up and stuck my head out into the hallway. I did a quick survey, seeing no one, and then closed myself into Bennet's room. If I were caught, there was no way I was going to explain my presence. I went back to the desk, lifted the stack of books from the typewriter, and removed the cover. The machine was an old black high-shouldered Remington with a manual return. Bader must have hung on to the damn thing for forty years. I reached into my bag and removed a piece of blank paper from the folder. I rolled it into the machine, typing precisely the phrases and sentences I'd typed before. *The quick brown fox jumps over the lazy dog.* The typewriter made a racket that seemed remarkably noisy, but it couldn't be helped. With the door to the hall closed, I thought I was safe. *Dear Miss Milhone. Max Outhwaite.* Even at a glance, I knew I was in business. The *a* and the *i* were both askew. This was the machine I'd been looking for. I rolled the paper from the machine, folded it, and slipped it in my pocket. Out of the corner of my eye, the name Outhwaite suddenly popped into view. Was I seeing things? I checked the line of textbooks again, squinting as I pulled out the two books that caught my attention. *Ring of Bright Water,* Gavin Maxwell, was the first in that row. In the middle, about six books down, was *Atlantic: History of an Ocean.* The author was Leonard Outhwaite. I stared, feeling rooted in place. Gavin Maxwell and Leonard Outhwaite. *Maxwell Outhwaite.*

I slipped the cover over the typewriter and put the stack of books back in place. I heard a low rumble, like thunder. I paused. Empty coat hangers began to ring, tinkling together in the closet like wind chimes. All the joints in the house began to squeak quietly and the window glass gave a sharp rattle where the putty had shrunk away from the panes. Nails and wood screws chirped. I put a hand on the bookshelf to steady myself. Under me, the whole house shifted back and forth, perhaps no more than an inch, but with a movement that felt like a sudden gust of strong wind or a train rocking on a track. I didn't feel any fear, but I was alert, wondering if I'd have time to clear the premises. An old house like this must have survived many a temblor, but you never quite knew what was coming with these things. So far, I pegged it in the three- or four-point range. As long as it didn't go on and on, it shouldn't do much damage. Lights flickered faintly as if wires were loose and touching one another intermittently. The strobe effect sparked a series of jerky pale blue images, in the midst of which a dark shape appeared across the room. I peered, blinking, trying to see clearly as the shadow moved toward one corner and then blended into the wall.

I made a small sound in my throat, paralyzed. The trembling gradually ceased and the lights stabilized. I clung to the bookshelf and leaned my head weakly on my arm, trying to shake off the frosty feeling that was creeping down my spine. Any minute, I expected to hear Enid calling from the kitchen stairs. I pictured Myrna on her feet, the three of us comparing notes about the earthquake. I didn't want either one of them coming up to search for me. I snagged my handbag and crossed the room. I moved out into the hall, looking quickly in both directions. I locked the door behind me, cranking the key in the lock so hard it nearly bent under my hand.

I ran down the hall on tiptoe, making a hasty detour into Bader's room. I put the key back in the door where I'd found it, then crossed swiftly into his home office. I opened a file cabinet and shoved the folder between two unrelated files where I could find it later. I crossed the room again and went out into the corridor. I walked quickly toward the heavy drapes at the end of the hall, pushed my way through the arch, and hurried along the back corridor. I clattered down the stairs and into the kitchen. There was no sign of Myrna. Enid was calmly pouring a thick yellow batter into the springform pan.

I put my hand on my chest to still my breathing. "Jesus. That was something. I thought for a minute there we were really in for it."

She looked up at me blankly. I could tell she didn't have the faintest idea what I was talking about.

I stopped in my tracks. "The temblor," I said.

"I wasn't aware of any temblor. When was this?"

"Enid, you're kidding. Don't do this to me. It must have been at least four points on the Richter scale. Didn't the lights flicker down here?"

"Not that I noticed." I watched her use a rubber spatula to sweep the last of the batter from the bowl into the pan.

"The whole house was shifting. Didn't you feel *anything*?"

She was silent for a moment, her gaze dropping to her bowl. "You hang on to people, don't you?"

"What?"

"You have trouble letting go."

"I do not. That's not a bit true. People tell me I'm too independent for my own good."

She was shaking her head before I reached the end of the sentence. "Independence has nothing to do with hanging on," she said.

"What are you talking about?"

"Ghosts don't haunt us. That's not how it works. They're present among us because we won't let go of *them*."

"I don't believe in ghosts," I said, faintly.

"Some people can't see the color red. That doesn't mean it isn't there," she replied.

When I reached the office, Dietz was sitting in my swivel chair with his feet up on the desk. One of the sandwich packets had been opened and he was munching on a BLT. I still hadn't eaten lunch so I reached for the other sandwich. I removed a soft drink from the refrigerator and sat down across from him.

"How'd you do at the *Dispatch*?"

He laid the four Maddison obituaries on the desk so I could study them. "I had Jeff Katzenbach dig through the files. Mother's maiden name was Bangham, so I went over to the library and checked the city directory for other Banghams in the area. None. Three of those obits I've verified at the Hall of Records, checking death certificates. Claire's still a question mark."

"How so?" I popped the top on my soda can and began to pick at the cellophane and plastic packet in which my sandwich was sealed.

Dietz was saying, "There's no suggestion how she died. I'd be interested in seeing if we can get the suicide confirmed just to put that one to bed. I got the name of a PI in Bridgeport, Connecticut, and left a lengthy message with her service. I'm hoping someone will return my call."

"What difference does it make how she died?" I tried biting the seal on the cellophane. Was this kiddie-proof, like poison? Dietz held his hand out for the wrapped sandwich and I passed it across the desk to him.

"Suppose she was murdered? Suppose she was the victim of a hit-and-run accident?" He freed the sandwich and gave it back to me.

"You've got a point," I said. I paused to eat while I reread the information. The obits were in date order, starting with the father's death in late November 1967. Dietz had had all four of them copied onto one page.

MADDISON, Francis M., 53,
departed suddenly on Tuesday, November 21. Loving, adored husband of 25 years to Caroline B. Maddison; beloved father to daughters, Claire and Patricia. He was a service manager at Colgate Automotive Center and a member of the Community Christian Church. He was much loved and will be missed by family and friends. Funeral: 11:30 A.M. Friday. In lieu of flowers, donations to the American Heart Association would be appreciated.

I glanced up at him and said, "Fifty-three. That's young."
"They were all young," Dietz said.

MADDISON, Patricia Anne, 17,
died Thursday, May 9, at Santa Teresa Hospital. She is survived by her loving mother, Caroline B. Maddison, and a devoted sister, Claire Maddison. At the family's request, services will be private.

MADDISON, Caroline B., 58,
died Tuesday, August 29, at her home after a lengthy illness. She was born on January 22 to Helen and John Bangham, in Indianapolis, Indiana, graduating from Indiana University with a degree in home economics, Caroline was a devoted wife, mother, a homemaker, and a Christian. Preceded in death by her husband, Francis M. Maddison, and her daughter Patricia Anne Maddison. Survived by loving daughter Claire Maddison of Bridgeport, Connecticut. No services are planned. Contributions may be made to Hospice of Santa Teresa.

MADDISON, Claire, 39,
formerly of Santa Teresa, died Saturday, March 2, in Bridgeport, Connecticut. Daughter of the late Francis M. and Caroline B. Maddison, Claire was preceded in death by her only sister, Patricia. Claire graduated from Santa Teresa High School in 1963 and the University of Connecticut in 1967. She pursued her secondary teaching credential and M.A. in Romance Languages at Boston College.

She taught French and Italian at a private girls' academy in
Bridgeport, Connecticut. Service, Tuesday in the Memorial
Park Chapel.

I read Claire's death notice twice. "This was just last year."

"Thank goodness she'd gone back to her maiden name," he said. "I
don't know how we'd have found her if she'd been using her ex-
hubby's moniker."

"Whoever he was," I said. "She'd probably been divorced for ages.
There wasn't much family to speak of. You watch the names of the
survivors diminish until there's no one left. It's depressing, isn't it?"

"I thought the mother might have surviving family members in
Indiana, but I can't seem to get a line on them," Dietz said. "I tried
directory assistance in Indianapolis. There weren't any Banghams
listed, so at least on the face of it, we're not talking about a large
close-knit clan. Just to be on the safe side, I checked the CALI Directory and put a call through to an Indianapolis private investigator. I
asked him to check Caroline Bangham's birth records to see if that
nets us anything. We might not glean much, but he said he'd get back
to us."

I made a face. "You know what? I think we're spinning our wheels
on this one. I just don't buy the idea that some distraught family
member would seek revenge eighteen years later."

"Maybe not," he said. "If it weren't for Bader's death, there
wouldn't have been a reason to look for Guy at all. He might have
gone on living in Marcella for the rest of his days."

"It wasn't strictly Bader's death. It was the will," I said.

"Which brings us back to the five million."

"I guess it does," I said. "I'll tell you what hurts. I feel like I was
part of what happened to Guy."

"Because you found him."

"Exactly. I didn't cause his death, in any strict sense of the word,
but if it hadn't been for me, he'd be safe the way I see it."

"Hey, come on. That's not true. Tasha would have hired herself
some other detective. Maybe not as good as you . . ."

"Don't suck up."

"Look, someone would have found him. It just happened to be
you."

"I suppose," I said. "It still feels like shit."

"I'm sure it does."

The phone rang. Dietz answered and then handed me the handset,
mouthing the name *Enid*.

I nodded and took the phone. "Hi, Enid. This is Kinsey. How are you?"

"Not so good," she said, fretfully. "Did Myrna call you?"

"Not as far as I know. Let me check my messages." I put a hand across the mouthpiece. "Did the Maleks' housekeeper call or leave a message for me?"

Dietz shook his head and I went back to Enid. "No, there's nothing here."

"Well, that's odd. She swore she was going to call you. I made her promise she would. I went to the supermarket and I was only gone fifteen or twenty minutes. She said she'd be here when I got back, but she's gone and there's no sign of her. I thought you might have asked her to come in."

"Sorry. I never heard from her. What'd she want to talk to me about?"

"I'm not sure. I know something's been bothering her, but she wouldn't be specific. Her car's still out back. That's what's so strange," she said.

"Could she have gone to the doctor's? If she really wasn't feeling well, she might have called a cab."

"It's always possible, but you'd think she would have waited to have me take her. This is just so unlike her. She told me she'd help me with dinner. I have a meeting at seven and I have to be out of here early. We discussed it in detail."

"Maybe she's out walking somewhere on the property."

"I thought of that," she said. "I went out there myself, calling, but she's disappeared."

"Enid, let's be realistic. I don't think being gone less than an hour constitutes a disappearance."

"I'm worried something's happened."

"Like what?"

"I don't know. That's why I called you. Because I'm scared."

"What's the rest?"

"That's it."

"No, it's not. You're leaving something out. I mean, so far this doesn't make sense. Do you think she's been abducted by aliens, or what?"

I could hear her hesitation. "I got the impression she knew something about the murder."

"Really. She said that?"

"She hinted as much. She was too nervous to say more. I think she saw something she wasn't supposed to see that night."

"She told me she was sleeping."

"Well, she was. She'd taken some pain medication and a sleeping pill. She slept like the dead, but then she remembered later that she woke up at one point to find someone standing at the foot of her bed."

"Wait a minute, Enid. You're not talking about this woo-woo stuff . . ."

"Not at all. I promise. This is what she said. She said she thought she'd been dreaming, but the more she thought about it, the more convinced she was that it was real."

"What was?"

"The person she saw."

"I gathered that, Enid. Who?"

"She wouldn't tell me. She felt guilty she hadn't said anything before now."

"Myrna feels guilty about everything," I said.

"I know," Enid said. "But I think she was also worried about the consequences. She thought she'd be in danger if she opened her mouth. I told her to tell the police, in that case, but she was afraid to do that. She said she'd rather talk to you first and then she'd talk to them. It's not like her to go off without a word."

"You did check her room?"

"That's the first thing I did. And that's the other thing that bothers me. Something doesn't seem right. Myrna's very fussy. Everything has to be just so with her. I don't mean to criticize, but it's the truth."

"Her room is messed up?"

"It's not exactly messed up, but it doesn't look right."

"Who else is there? Is anybody home besides you?"

"Bennet was here, but I think he's gone. He came in for lunch. I fixed him a sandwich and he took it up to his room. He must have left again while I was at the market. Christie and Donovan are due back any minute. I don't mean to be a bother, but I don't feel right about this."

Dietz was giving me an inquisitive look. Having eavesdropped on my end of the conversation with her, he was suitably mystified. "Hang on a second." I put a palm across the mouthpiece. "How long will you be here?"

"At least an hour," he said. "If you'd ever get off the phone, I might get this call from the East Coast that I've been waiting for. What's the problem?"

"It's Myrna. I'll tell you in a minute." I went back to Enid. "Why don't I come over there," I said. "She might have mentioned something to Christie before they left for the funeral home. You're sure she didn't leave a note?"

"Positive."

"I'll be there in fifteen minutes."

"I don't want you to go to any trouble."

"It's no trouble."

I took my sandwich and soda with me, driving with one hand while I finished my lunch. I kept the chilled soda can between my thighs. Shifting gears is a pain in the ass when you're trying to dine in style. At least I knew the route. I could have done it with my eyes shut.

Enid had left the gate open for me. I pulled into the courtyard and left my car in a spot I was beginning to think should be reserved for me. Donovan's pickup truck was parked to one side of the garage. At first, I thought he was back, but then I remembered that he'd been driving the BMW when he left. Both the open garages were still empty. The driveway angled up along the house on the left. For the first time, I noticed a separate parking pad nearby with spaces for three vehicles. Currently, I could see a bright yellow VW convertible and what looked like a Toyota, a pale metallic blue, maybe three or four years old.

Enid had the backdoor ajar and was standing in the opening. She'd taken off her apron to do the marketing and she now wore a jacket as though chilled by circumstance.

I moved into the utility room. "Still no sign of her?" I asked, following Enid through a door that opened into a rear hall.

"Not a peep," she said. "I'm sorry to be a bother. I'm probably being silly."

"Don't worry about it. You've had a murder in the house. Everybody's nerves are on edge. Is one of those cars out there hers?"

"The Toyota," she said. She paused in front of a door at the end of the hall. "This is hers."

"Have you tried knocking on her door since we talked?"

Enid shook her head. "I think I scared myself. I didn't want to do anything until you arrived."

"Geez, Enid. You're scaring me," I said. I knocked on the door, my head tilted against the panel, listening for sounds that might indicate Myrna was back. I was reluctant to barge right in. She might be napping or naked, just out of the shower. I didn't want to catch her with her dentures out or her wooden leg unstrapped. I tapped again with one knuckle. "Myrna?"

Dead silence.

"Yeah, that's what you call money in the bank right there."

Sampson gave me a look like he wanted to either puke or kill someone.

"Let's do this," he said, and we started up the hall.

TWO

"POLICE! WE'RE COMING IN!"

Sampson's voice boomed over everything else. He gave one hard pound on the paneled mahogany door—his own version of knock and announce—and then threw it open.

Elijah Creem was standing just inside, looking every bit as pulled together as the pictures I'd seen of him—slicked-back blond hair, square cleft chin, perfect veneers.

He and Bergman were fully dressed. The other three—not so much. Bergman had an iPhone held up in front of him, taking a video of the freaky little ménage à trois they had staged there on the king-size sleigh bed.

One girl was laid out flat. Her bra was open at the front, and her bright pink thong was down around her ankles. She was also wearing a clear breathing mask of

8

some kind, tethered to a tall gray metal tank at the side of the bed. The boy on top of her was buck naked except for the black blindfold around his eyes, while the other girl stood over him with a small digital camera, shooting more video from another angle.

"What the hell is this?" Creem said.

"My question exactly," I said. "Nobody move."

All of them were wide-eyed and staring at us now, except for the girl with the mask. She seemed pretty out of it.

"What's in the tank?" I said as Sampson went over to her.

"It's nitrous oxide," Creem said. "Just calm down. She's fine."

"Screw you," John told him and eased the mask off the girl.

The buzz from nitrous is pretty short lasting, but I didn't assume for a second that it was the only thing these kids were on. There were several blue tabs of what I assumed was more XTC on the nightstand. Also a couple of small brown glass bottles, presumably amyl nitrate, and a half-empty fifth of Cuervo Reserva.

"Listen to me," Creem said evenly, looking me in the eye. As far as I could tell, he was the ringleader here. "Do you see that briefcase in the corner?"

"Elijah? What are you doing?" Bergman asked, but Creem didn't respond. He was still watching me like we were the only two in the room.

"There's an envelope with thirty thousand dollars in that case," he said. Then he looked pointedly from a brown leather satchel on the antique setback cabinet, over to one of the three windows at the back of the bedroom. The fringed shades were all drawn, but it was pretty clear to me what he was going for.

"How much time do you think thirty thousand dollars is worth?" he said. He was unbelievably cool about the whole thing. And arrogant. I think he fully expected me to go for it.

"You don't seem like the climb-out-the-window type, Creem," I said.

"Ordinarily, no," he said. "But if you know who I am, then you know I've got quite a bit at stake here—a family, a medical practice—"

"Six and a half million in revenue last year alone," I said. "According to our records."

"And then there's my reputation, of course, which in this town is priceless. So what do you say, detective? Do we have a deal?"

I could tell he was already halfway out that window in his mind. This was a man who was used to getting what he wanted.

But then again, I wasn't a seventeen-year-old girl with a self-image problem.

"I think my partner put it best," I told him. "What was it you said, John?"

"Something like screw you," Sampson said. "How old are these kids, Creem?"

For the first time, Dr. Creem's superior affect seemed to crack right down the middle. His silly grin dropped away, and the eyes started moving faster.

"Please," he said. "There's more cash where that came from. A lot more. I'm sure we can work something out."

But I was already done with this guy. "You have the right to remain silent—"

"I don't want to beg."

"Then don't," I said. "Anything you say can and will be used against you—"

"For Christ's sake, you're going to ruin me! Do you understand that?"

The narcissism alone was kind of staggering. Even more so was the cluelessness about what he'd done here.

"No, Dr. Creem," I said as I turned him around and put the cuffs on. "You've already done that to yourself."

THREE

TWO MONTHS TO THE DAY AFTER ELIJAH CREEM'S UNFORTUNATE SCANDAL broke in the headlines, he was ready to make a change. A big one. It was amazing what a little time, a good lawyer, and a whole lot of cash could do.

Of course, he wasn't out of the woods yet. And the cash wasn't going to last forever. Not if Miranda had anything to say about it. She was only speaking to him these days through her own attorney, and he hadn't been allowed to see Chloe or Justine since the future ex–Mrs. Creem had packed them off to her parents' house in Newport. Word from the lawyer was that they'd be finishing out the school year there.

The silence from the girls had been deafening as well. All three of his blond beauties—Miranda, Justine, Chloe—had swiftly turned their backs on him, just as easily as closing a door.

As for the medical practice, there hadn't been a consult, much less a booking, since it had come out in the press that Dr. Creem (or Dr. Creep, as a few of the less savory rags were calling him) had traded surgical procedures for sex with more than one of Joshua Bergman's unfortunately underage protégées. Between that, and the little video collection Creem had accumulated on his home computer, there was still the very real possibility of a jail sentence if they went to trial.

Which was why Elijah Creem had no intention of letting that happen. What was the old cliché? *Today is the first day of the rest of your life?*

Yes, indeed. And he was going to make it count.

"I can't go to prison, Elijah," Joshua told him on the phone. "And I'm not saying I don't *want* to. I mean, I *can't*. I really don't think I'd make it in there."

Creem put a hand over the Bluetooth at his ear to hear better, and to avoid being overheard by the passersby on M Street.

"Better you than me, Joshua. At least you like dick."

"I'm serious, Elijah."

"I'm joking, Josh. And believe me, I'm no more inclined than you are. That's why we're not going to let it come to that."

"Where are you, anyway?" Bergman asked. "You sound funny."

"It's the mask," Creem told him.

"The mask?"

"Yes. That's what I've been trying to tell you. There's been a change of plans."

The mask was an ingenious bit of latex composite, molded from human forms. The very newest thing. Creem had been experimenting with it since the scandal broke, and his own famous face had become something of a social liability. Now, as he passed the plate-glass window in front of Design Within Reach, he barely recognized his own reflection. All he saw was an ugly old man—sallow skin, sunken cheeks, and a pathetic remnant of dry, silver hair over a liver-spotted scalp. It was spectacular, actually. Poetic, even. The old man in the reflection looked just as ruined as Dr. Creem was feeling these days.

Dark-rimmed glasses masked the openings around his eyes. And while the lips were tight and uncomfortable, they were also formfitting enough that he could talk, drink, eat—anything at all—with the mask on.

"I didn't want to let you know until I was sure this would work," Creem told Bergman, "but I've got a surprise for you."

"What do you mean? What kind of surprise?" Bergman asked.

"Joshua, do you remember Fort Lauderdale?"

There was a long pause on the line before he responded.

"Of course," he said quietly.

"Spring break, 1988."

"I said I remembered," Bergman snapped, but then softened again. "We were just a couple of fetuses then."

"I know it's been a while," Creem said. "But I've given this a lot of thought, and I'm not ready to just go quietly into the night. Are you?"

"God no," Bergman said. "But you were the one who—"

"I know what I said. That was a long time ago. This is now."

Creem heard his friend take a long, slow breath.

"Jesus, Elijah," he said. *"Really?"*

He sounded scared, but more than that he sounded excited. Despite the mousy tendencies, Bergman also had a wonderfully twisted streak. He'd always been more excited by the murders than Creem.

For Creem, they'd been cathartic as much as anything else. A means to an end. And this time around, he had a whole new agenda.

"So . . . this is really happening?" Bergman said.

"It is for me," Creem told him.

"When?"

"Right now. I'm waiting for her to come outside as we speak."

"And, can I listen?"

"Of course," Creem said. "Why do you think I called? But no more talking. Here she comes now."

FOUR

⚑

CREEM POSITIONED HIMSELF ACROSS THE STREET FROM DOWN DOG YOGA AS
the seven forty-five evening class let out. Among the first
to emerge onto Potomac Street was Darcy Vickers, a tall,
well-proportioned blonde.

He couldn't take credit for the tall or blond part, but as
for the well-proportioned elements, those were all thanks
to him. Darcy's ample bust, the perfectly symmetrical
arch of her brows and lips, and the nicely tapered thighs
represented some of Dr. Creem's best work.

Not that Darcy Vickers had ever expressed the first
drop of gratitude. As far as she was concerned, the world
was populated with her lackeys. She was a typical specimen, really—a K Street lobbyist with a steroidal sense of
entitlement and a desperate need to stay beautiful for as
long as possible.

All of it so very familiar. So close to home, really.

He waited outside Dean & Deluca while she ran in for whatever it was women like her deigned to eat these days. He watched while she held up the line at the register, talking obliviously away on her cell phone. Then he crossed the street again, to follow her down the quaintly cobblestoned alley toward the garage where Darcy's Bimmer was parked.

There was no need to keep too much distance. He was just some geezer in a windbreaker and orthopedic shoes—all but invisible to the Darcy Vickerses of the world. By the time they reached the deserted third level of the garage, he'd closed the gap between them to less than twenty feet.

Darcy pressed a clicker in her hand, and the Bimmer's trunk popped open with a soft click. That's when he made his move.

"Excuse me—Miranda?" he said, half timidly.

"Sorry, no," Darcy said, dropping her grocery bag and purple yoga mat into the trunk without even a glance.

"Funny," he said. "You look so much like her." When the woman didn't respond, he stepped in closer, crossing that invisible line of personal space between them. "Almost exactly like her, in fact."

Now, as she turned around, the annoyance on her face was clear, even through the Botox.

"Listen," she said, "I don't mean to be rude—"

"You never do, Miranda."

As he came right up on top of her, she put a hand out to deflect him. But Dr. Creem was stronger than the old man he appeared to be. Stronger than Darcy Vickers, too.

His left hand clamped over her mouth as she tried to call out.

"It's me, sweetheart," he whispered. "It's your husband. And don't worry. All is forgiven."

He paused, just long enough to see the surprise come up in her eyes, before he drove the steak knife deep into her abdomen. A scalpel would have been nice, but it seemed best to stay away from the tools of his own trade for the time being.

All the air seemed to leave Darcy Vickers's lungs in a rush, and she collapsed forward, bending at the middle. It was a bit of work to get the knife out, but then it came free all at once.

With a quick sweep of his leg, Creem kicked her ankles off the ground and lifted her into the trunk. She never even struggled. There were just a few gurgling sounds, followed by the glottal stoppage of several half-realized breaths.

He leaned in close, to make sure it would all reach Bergman's ears over the phone. Then he stabbed again, into the chest this time. And once more down below, opening the femoral artery with a swift, L-shaped motion, so there could be no chance of recovery.

Working quickly, he took a hank of her long blond hair in his hand and sawed it off with the serrated edge of the knife. Then he cut another, and another, and another, until it was nearly gone, sheared down to where the scalp showed through in ragged patches. He kept just one handful of it for himself, tucked into a Ziploc bag, and left the rest lying in tufts around her body.

She died just as ugly as she had lived. And Dr. Creem was starting to feel better already.

When it was done, Creem closed the trunk and walked away, taking the nearest stairs down toward M Street. He didn't speak until he was clear of the garage and outside on the sidewalk.

"Joshua?" he said. "Are you still there?"

Bergman took a few seconds to answer. "I'm...here," he said. His breath was ragged, his voice barely above a whisper.

"Are you..." Creem grinned, though he was also a little disgusted. "Joshua, were you masturbating?"

"No," his friend said, too quickly. Bergman had an ironic sense of modesty, all things considered. "Is it done?" he asked then.

"Signed, sealed, delivered," Creem said. "And you know what that means."

"Yes," Bergman said.

"Your move, old pal. I can't wait to see what you cook up."

Part One
WIN, LOSE, OR DRAW

CHAPTER

IN THE PREDAWN DARKNESS OF APRIL 6, RON GUIDICE SAT BEHIND THE WHEEL of his car, keeping an eye on the house across the way.

Alex Cross's place was nothing special, really. Just a white three-story clapboard on Fifth Street in Southeast DC. The shutters were ready for a coat of paint. There was a tidy little herb garden on the front stoop.

Cross lived here with his grandmother, his wife, and two of his three children, Janelle and Alex Jr., aka Ali. The oldest Cross child, Damon, was home for spring break, but he spent most of his time at boarding school these days. And there was a foster kid, too. Ava Williams. It wasn't clear whether she was on track for adoption, or what. Guidice still had some digging to do. He liked to know as much as possible about his subjects.

There were a dozen Metro police officers on his list, and he'd been keeping tabs on all of them, mostly as a point of comparison. But Cross was special. Alex was the one that Guidice wanted to kill.

Just not yet.

Killing a man was easy. Any half-wit with a gun could put a bullet in someone's head. But really *knowing* a man—learning his weak spots first, getting to know his vulnerabilities, and taking his life apart, piece by piece? That took some doing.

Meanwhile, whether Cross knew it or not, he had a big day ahead of him.

Guidice watched the front windows, waiting for a light to come on. It wasn't strictly necessary to spend this much time on a subject, but he enjoyed it. He liked the quiet of the early morning hours, even if it meant just sitting and absorbing the seemingly inconsequential details—the missing chunk of concrete on the stairs, the eco-friendly bulb in the porch light. It was all part of the larger picture, and you never knew which tiny piece might take on some kind of significance in the end. He passed the time scribbling observations into a spiral notebook on his lap.

Then, just after five, a soft stirring came up from the backseat.

"Papa? Is it time to get up?"

"No, sweetheart," he said. He kept his chin down and his eye on the house. "You can go back to sleep."

Emma Lee was cuddled up in an army sleeping bag with her favorite Barbie, Cee-Cee. Her pillowcase had Disney's Cinderella on it. She'd chosen it for the picture of the little helper mice, whom she adored, for whatever reason.

"Will you sing me something?" she asked. "'Hush, Little Baby'?"

Guidice smiled. She always called songs by their first words.

"'Hush little baby, don't say a word,'" he sang quietly. "'Papa's going to buy you a mockingbird....'"

The front hall light came on in Alex's house. Through the frosted glass of the door, Guidice could see the tall, dark shape of the man, descending the stairs.

Guidice continued to take it all down while he sang. "'If that mockingbird don't sing, Papa's gonna buy you a diamond ring....'"

"A real one?" Emma Lee interrupted. It was the same question, every time. "A real diamond ring?"

"You bet," he said. "Someday, when you're older."

He looked back over his shoulder into the soft, sleepy eyes of his daughter and wondered if it was even possible to love someone more than he did her. Probably not.

"Now go back to sleep, Baby Bear. When you wake up again, we'll be home."

CHAPTER

2

I GOT THE FIRST CALL AT HEADQUARTERS AROUND TWO O'CLOCK THAT afternoon.

A woman had been found dead in the trunk of her car, in a Georgetown parking garage. Pretty unusual for Georgetown, so my hackles were up more than usual. I took the elevator straight down to the Daly Building garage and headed out with an extra-large coffee in hand. It was going to be a long-ass day.

That said, I really do like my job. I like giving a voice to the people who can't speak for themselves anymore—the ones whose voices have been stolen from them. And in my line of work, that usually means through some kind of violence.

The responding officer's report was that a garage attendant at American Allied Parking on M Street had found what looked like a pool of dried blood underneath a BMW belonging to one Darcy Vickers. When the cops arrived, they'd forced open the trunk and confirmed what they already suspected. Ms. Vickers had no pulse, and had been dead for some time. Now they were waiting for someone from Homicide to arrive and take it from there.

That's where I came in. Or at least, so I thought.

It was a beautiful spring day. The best time of year in DC. The National Cherry Blossom Festival was on, and we hadn't yet gotten hit with the first wave of summer humidity—or summer tourists. I had my windows down and Quincy Jones's *Soul Bossa Nostra* up loud enough that I almost didn't hear my phone when the second call came in.

Caller ID told me it was Marti Huizenga, my sergeant at the Major Case Squad. I juggled the volume down on the stereo and caught the call just before it went to voice mail.

"Dr. C.," she said. "Where are you?"

"Pennsylvania and Twenty-First," I told her. "Why?"

"Good. Take a right on New Hampshire. Another body just popped up, and it sounds god-awful, to tell you the truth."

"So you thought of me."

"Natch. I need someone over there right away. It's a bad scene, Alex—a dead girl, hanging out of a sixth-floor window. Possible suicide, but I don't know."

"You want me on this instead of Georgetown?"

"I want you on both," Huizenga said. "At least for now. I need one set of eyes on both scenes, as fresh as possible.

And *then* I want you to tell me this is all just a coincidence, okay? I'm asking politely here."

Huizenga's sense of humor was as dark as mine could be sometimes. I liked working with her. And we both knew that the difference between two *unrelated* dead bodies and two *related* ones was the difference between not getting much sleep for the next forty-eight hours, and getting none at all.

"I'll do my best," I said.

"Vernon Street, between Eighteenth and Nineteenth," she said. "I'll tell Second District to get started without you at the garage in Georgetown, but try to be there as soon as you can."

That's kind of like telling the clouds when to rain. I had no idea how long I'd be at this new scene. You never do until you're there.

And this one turned out to be a nightmare.

3

VERNON STREET IS JUST A SINGLE TREE-LINED BLOCK OFF THE WEST END of U Street. It's a quiet residential area, but I could see a crowd of people pooled on the sidewalk as soon as I turned the corner from Eighteenth. Most of them were looking up and pointing at a mansard-roofed brick building on the south side of the street.

As soon as I got out of my car, I saw the girl. It was like a check in the ribs. She hung suspended by her neck on a length of rope, about three feet below one of the dormered sixth-floor windows. Her face was visibly discolored, and her hands seemed to be tied behind her back.

Jesus. Oh Jesus.

There were two cruisers and an ambulance parked out front, but the only personnel I saw was a single cop on the door of the apartment building. The rest of the sidewalk was filled up with looky-loos, snapping away on their phones and cameras. It pissed me off as much as it amazed me.

"Get this street roped off, right now!" I told the cop on my way into the building. "I don't want to see anyone on that sidewalk by the time I'm up there looking down, you got it?"

I knew he had his hands full, but I couldn't help feeling revved up by the whole thing. This girl was someone's daughter. She had a family. They didn't need her picture on some goddamn Facebook page for the world to see.

I left the cop to it and took the stairwell instead of the elevator. It seemed like a more likely exit, if this was in fact a murder we were talking about. And you only get one chance to see a crime scene for the first time.

When I came out into the sixth-floor hall, another cop and two EMTs were waiting outside an open apartment door. The building had three units on this level, all facing the street. Our dead girl was apparently in the center one.

"Door was locked when we got here," the police officer told me. "That splintering on the frame is us. We were inside just long enough to get a flatline on the girl, but it wasn't easy. I can't guarantee we didn't move anything in there."

The apartment was a small alcove studio. There was a closet kitchen to one side, an open bathroom door on the other, and a futon couch that looked like it doubled for a bed. As far as I could tell, there were no signs of a struggle. In fact, the only thing that looked out of place was the old-fashioned coat tree, braced sideways against the open window, with a loop of rope hanging down from the center.

I forced myself to enter the room slowly, checking for drag marks, or anything that might have been left behind. When I got to the window and looked down, I could see the top of the girl's head, just out of reach. Her heel had broken through the window of the apartment below, and the cord around her wrists seemed to be more of the same rope that had been used in the hanging.

That didn't rule out suicide, either. A lot of people will bind themselves just before they do the deed, to keep from trying to struggle free in the heat of the moment.

Down below, another cruiser had arrived and the street was clear. But now I had another problem. When I looked straight across, I could see at least a dozen people in the windows of the facing apartment building, looking my way—more phones, more cameras. I wanted to give them all the finger, but I held back.

Still, I wasn't going to let this go on for one second longer than I had to.

"Give me a hand over here!" I shouted toward the hall.

Technically, the body at any crime scene belongs to the medical examiner, not the cops. But I wasn't thinking about technicalities right now. I was thinking about this girl and her family.

I already had my own phone out, and I fired off a bunch of shots. I got the coat tree, the window frame, the rope, and the girl, from above. I needed to preserve as much detail as I could before I did what I was about to do.

"Sir?" a cop said behind me.

"Help me pull her in," I said.

"Um...don't you want to wait for the ME?"

"No," I said, pointing at the audience we had across the street. "Not anymore. Now give me a hand, or get me someone who will!"

WE LAID THE GIRL OUT AS CAREFULLY AS WE COULD ON THE FLOOR OF THE apartment, and left the rope around her neck. As long as she was out of the public eye, that's all I needed. The rest I could leave to the investigation.

Her name was Elizabeth Reilly. According to the driver's license I found in a purse by the front door, she was just two weeks shy of turning twenty-one. The apartment had all the signs of someone who lived alone, from the Lean Cuisines in the freezer to the single towel and washrag hanging neatly in the bathroom.

Obviously there was more to the story here, but I wasn't seeing it yet.

When the ME did arrive I was glad to see it was Joan Bradbury. Joan's an easygoing, sixty-something Texan. As far as I knew, she never came to work in anything but top-stitched cowboy boots, even after twenty years in

DC. She's opinionated, but also easy to work with, and didn't give me any big lectures when she saw what I'd done with the body. Joan has four daughters of her own; I think she instinctively got it.

While she started her initial exam, I got our team of investigators out knocking on doors, especially across the street. This hanging had gone down in broad daylight. Someone had to have seen something.

I also got some more info from Sergeant Huizenga on our victim. Elizabeth Reilly had been a nursing student at Radians College on Vermont Avenue until the previous December, when she'd dropped out. There was no word yet on recent employment, but other than one unpaid parking ticket her record was squeaky clean.

By the time I got back to Joan, they were ready to wrap and bag the body for transport to the morgue.

"I'm going to need a full autopsy," she told me, "but I'm thinking this girl was dead before she went out the window. Maybe strangled with the same rope."

She reached down and pointed at some dark, purplish marks on Elizabeth Reilly's lower neck.

"You see these contusions? These are all consistent with manual strangulation. But up here, higher, where the rope caught her? Just faint bruising. If there was any blood flow when she was actually hanged, those marks would be darker."

I rocked back on my heels and ran a hand over the bottom of my face.

"This is what I was afraid of," I said.

"There's more, Alex."

Normally Joan was pretty matter-of-fact, even at the roughest scenes, but there was a tightness in her voice I'd never heard before. This one was getting to her.

"The abdomen's still flaccid, and she's got obvious striations around her midsection and breasts," she told me. "As far as I can make out, our girl here had a baby recently. And, Lord help me, I mean *recently*."

CHAPTER

5

IT WAS LATE EVENING BY THE TIME I FINALLY GOT OVER TO THE AMERICAN
Allied Parking garage in Georgetown. The site was well
preserved, but Darcy Vickers's body had already been
removed. I'd have to fill in some blanks with the crime-
scene photography later and glean what I could for now.

Ms. Vickers's silver BMW 550i was parked on the third
level. That's where she'd been found. One of the Second
District detectives, Will Freemont, walked me through it.
He seemed like he wondered what I was doing so late to
the party, but that was the least of my worries right now.
My thoughts were still consumed by the Elizabeth Reilly
case.

"So, they found her in here," Freemont said, pointing
into the open trunk. "Stab wounds were here, here, and
here." He pointed with two fingers to his own chest, abdomen, and upper leg. "This lady didn't die too well, but

you can bet she died quick, for whatever that's worth. And just for shits and giggles, I guess, he cut off her hair, too."

Left behind were a yoga mat, a briefcase, a few shopping bags, and a garment bag, all covered in a combination of dried blood and a mess of loose blond hair, some of it matted with the blood.

There was also a good-size dark stain—more blood—pooled on the cement under the car.

"He would have needed it to be quick," I said. "It's a pretty risky site for a murder."

"He?" Freemont said.

"I'm guessing," I said. It was all about first impressions at this point. "What do we know about Darcy Vickers?"

The detective flipped open a small notebook, the same kind I carried, and looked down at it.

"Forty-two years old. Divorced, no kids. Works for Kimball-Ellis on K Street, mostly retainer work for a couple of the big tobacco companies. Supposedly she had a real cutthroat reputation, from what I've got so far."

In other words, Darcy Vickers had plenty of enemies. Most lobbyists do. But not every lobbyist ends up stabbed to death in the trunk of a car. Who, exactly, would want to do this? And why?

And for that matter, could this possibly have anything to do with Elizabeth Reilly's hanging?

Nothing obvious had been taken. Darcy Vickers's wallet, cash, phone, and jewelry were all still there, as far as anyone knew. That led me to believe that the killing itself was the motive, either to satisfy some impulse for violence or to get rid of this woman in particular—or maybe both.

In those respects, the two cases seemed the same. But the m.o. was completely different.

Assuming Elizabeth Reilly hadn't committed suicide, her killer wanted the body put on display for everyone to see. He would have had to go to some trouble for that. Whereas with Darcy Vickers, it was all about the act itself—the stabbing, and then for whatever reasons, the cutting of the hair.

My gut was telling me these were two different cases, but we still had a lot of background work to do. Maybe these two women shared some connection, somewhere.

"Any witnesses?" I asked Freemont.

"Not exactly," he said. "But security cameras picked up something interesting."

He unfolded several sheets from his pocket, and showed me a series of black-and-white screen captures.

"This is nine oh four last night. We've got Ms. Vickers, coming in the east entrance from the alley over there. Then, right behind her, we've got this guy."

The image showed a middle-aged, or maybe elderly, white male. The picture quality wasn't great, but it was clear enough for a few details. He was bald, with dark-rimmed glasses, and what looked like a Members Only jacket, with the snaps on the shoulders.

"At nine oh nine, we've got the same guy leaving a different way, out toward M Street, and still on foot," the detective went on. "What he was doing in here for five minutes is anyone's guess."

"What about cameras on this level?" I said.

"Right there." He pointed toward a badly battered unit in a corner of the ceiling. "Someone took it out just after eight o'clock last night. Threw a rock at it, or something."

"So, then…" I stopped to think about this. "If the old guy has anything to do with it, why just take out one camera? Why let himself be seen on two others?"

"I know," he said. "Good question. We've got a BOLO out on him right now. If we can get him in, we might start to put together some answers."

Maybe, I thought. But something told me it wasn't going to be that easy.

6

I GOT HOME AROUND FIVE THAT MORNING, HOPING TO CATCH A COUPLE HOURS of sleep.

And I guess that's what happened. I barely remember crawling into bed next to my wife, Bree. The next thing I knew, light was streaming in through the windows, and we were under attack by a small band of munchkins.

"Wake up, wake up, wake up! Doo-do-doo! It's a big day!"

Ali, my youngest, had already crawled right up the middle of the bed, and was kneeling there between us. My daughter Jannie stood at the end, all dressed and ready to go.

"It's seven thirty, Daddy," she said. "We're supposed to be there by nine!"

"Oh...right," I said.

"You didn't forget, did you?"

"No," I said. "Of course not. We'll be right down."

Of course—I had forgotten. I'd been planning on being at the ME's office first thing for the morning briefing, and then sitting in on Elizabeth Reilly's autopsy.

But the kids were right. Today was a *big* day.

This was lottery day at Marian Anderson Public Charter School, the best high school in Southeast, and one of the best in the city. Jannie, as well as Ava, who was living with us now, had both put in applications, along with four hundred and twenty other eighth graders, looking for one of the hundred and five spots available in that fall's freshman class. By law, charter schools have to hold a lottery when supply exceeds demand—which it always does—and we were hoping against hope to get both girls in.

"You know, you don't absolutely have to be there," Bree said, rubbing my back on the side of the bed. "I saw the news last night. I know you're buried at work. Nana and I can cover this."

"No," I said. "I'm coming. I just need to get this cement out of my head."

Over the past several months, I'd missed Christmas Eve, Ali's play, Damon's quarterfinals, and most Sunday mornings at church, to name a few. This felt like my last line in the sand, and I wasn't going to cross it. I'd call someone to cover for me at the ME's office until I could get there.

Downstairs at breakfast, Nana Mama had the griddle fired up, and all the kids had stacks of pancakes in front of them when Bree and I came in. It was a full house these days, with Damon home for spring break, and now Ava bringing our total up to seven.

"Good morning, children," Nana said, of course meaning me and Bree. She's the undisputed matriarch of our family, and the kitchen is her throne room. "Blueberries or no blueberries?"

I went straight for the coffee.

"What're you doing up? Didn't you just get home?" Nana muttered at me from the stove. I mumbled back something about *big day*. I wasn't thinking about a whole lot more than caffeine at that moment.

"So who's feeling lucky today?" Bree asked from the head of the table.

Everyone's hand went up but Ava's. She just kept shoveling her food in, eating fast like she always did.

"What about you, Ava?" I said. "Are you excited?"

She shrugged, and answered with a mouthful of pancakes. "S'not like I'm gonna get in."

"Don't be so gloomy, Gus," Nana said from the griddle. "Attitude is everything."

If I'm being honest, though, it wasn't hard for me to understand Ava's pessimism at all. She was far brighter than she let on—maybe even brighter than she knew. It wasn't about that, though.

She'd landed in our laps some months back after her mother, a junkie, had OD'd and left her to live alone on the streets of Southeast. There were still plenty of issues for Ava to work through, and I'd set her up with my own therapist, Adele Finaly. In the meantime, we had our good days and bad days.

Basically, Ava had been hardwired not to expect too much from life—and consequently, not to want too much. Every now and then I caught a smile, or an unguarded moment, and in a way it showed me the potential she had waiting for her, if we could just help her see it, too. The one thing she didn't have was hope. It's what I'd call an inner-city epidemic—and nothing holds a person back more than that.

If there was anything we could do to change the shitty hand life had dealt Ava so far, we were going to do it.

One good day at a time.

7

FILING INTO THE GYM AT MARIAN ANDERSON, YOU MIGHT HAVE THOUGHT THERE
was a carnival going on. There were balloons flying everywhere, and faculty and staff in bright yellow and green
T-shirts, greeting everyone with big smiles.

Inside, the bleachers were all pulled out and chairs
were set up on the gym floor. Between the kids who had
applied, their parents, siblings, and school staff, there
were nearly a thousand people in that gym, and the place
was buzzing with nervous tension.

Nana's lips were pursed from the second we got there.
She tried to stay upbeat, for the girls' sake, but she'd also
been a teacher for forty-one years. She had some definite
opinions about this particular ritual.

"*Mm-mm-mm,*" she said, looking around. "You know
why we're here today? Because we adults can't get off our

duffs to offer more than a random chance at a good education in this city, that's why."

I think the gridlock on education reform in Washington pisses Nana off more than anything else in life. There was no escaping the fact that three quarters of the people in that gym were going to leave disappointed today. Some of them—especially the poorer families—were going to be devastated. The only other free option for high school in our area was one of DC's so-called dropout factories, where less than sixty percent of entering freshmen graduate.

We found a block of seats on the floor and settled in. Jannie stayed on her feet, looking around for some of her friends, but Ava just sat quietly in her chair.

Finally, just after nine, the school's principal got up on stage to welcome everyone. And then they got right to it, pulling cards out of a rolling hopper and calling out the names, one by one.

"Monique Baxter ... Leroy Esselman ... Thomas Brown ..."

With every new draw, there was a shout, or a scream, or some flurry of movement from somewhere in the gym. It really was like winning the lottery. Each kid whose name was called got to walk up on stage, cheered along by the faculty, where they got a welcome packet, and then they were ushered back out again in a flurry of applause.

As the names went by, lots of people were making hatch marks on pieces of paper in front of them, or counting down on their fingers. I had Jannie on one side of me and Nana on the other. The tension coming off both of them was palpable.

Within about ten minutes, the lottery was already starting to wind down. We got up to name number eighty-two, eighty-three, eighty-four...and then—

"Janelle Cross!"

Just like that, we were the ones jumping up and hugging each other, swept along in the excitement of the whole thing. I'm not going to pretend I wasn't thrilled, because I was. This was a great opportunity for Jannie. But even as I headed up to the stage with her, I couldn't help looking back to see what Ava was doing.

She was just sitting there and staring at the floor like nothing had happened. Like she was made of stone—at least on the outside. Bree had an arm around her, and waved me on toward the stage. It was a tough bit of mixed feelings for me to juggle.

But maybe, just maybe, we could get lightning to strike twice before this whole thing was over.

8

NO SUCH LUCK.

By the time Jannie and I had circled all the way around and back to our seats, the lottery was over. Most of the people were on their feet now, milling around and getting ready to leave.

Ava was still in her chair, scuffing her feet back and forth. She looked numb, as much as anything else.

Nana looked angry. Bree looked heartbroken.

"I'm sorry, Ava," I said, sitting down next to her. "I wish it had come out differently."

"Wha'ever," she said. "I knew I wasn't gettin' in."

It was frustrating to me, when the world behaved exactly as Ava expected it to. If I had to guess, I'd say she wanted in just as badly as Jannie, if for no other reason than to feel like she'd won something for once.

Jannie came over and sat on the other side of her. Several families around us were holding each other, and a lot of their kids were crying. Some of the parents, too. It had all gone by so fast.

"This sucks," Jannie said. "Sorry, Ava."

"No, you ain't." Ava turned on her with a sudden glare. When Jannie tried to take her hand, she snatched it away and stood up fast. "Come on," she said. "It's time to go. The lottery's over." Then she started walking out ahead of the rest of us without looking back. There was nothing to do in the moment but soldier on and follow her out.

Nana took my arm as we went. I could feel her shaking with anger.

"It's insanity, is what it is," she said. "Why in God's name should children have to win a damn lottery to get a good education? And right here in the nation's capital! What does that say about our country to the rest of the world, Alex? What?"

Even the "damn" was unusual for her, but I knew how she felt. The problem was so big, and so intractable, it was hard to even know who to be mad at anymore. The school chancellor? The teachers' union? The mayor? God?

"I wish I had some answers for you, Nana. I really do," I said.

"Well, I'll tell you what," she went on. "Miss Ava Williams will not be falling through any cracks, thank you very much. That girl is going to get the education she deserves if I have to give it to her myself."

In other words, Nana Mama was going to get done

whatever the chancellor, teachers' union, mayor, and God hadn't seen fit to accomplish.

And I had every faith that she would. One hundred percent.

CHAPTER

9

RON GUIDICE SAT IN THE BLEACHERS AT MARIAN ANDERSON HIGH SCHOOL, taking notes as the school lottery played out. The place was jam-packed. Not too many white folks, but enough that he didn't stand out, anyway. Nobody would even notice that he didn't have a fourteen-year-old of his own in tow.

Emma Lee played quietly the whole time at his feet, undressing and redressing Cee-Cee without a peep. She had the patience of a little saint, that was for sure.

Maybe she got that part from me, he thought.

Meanwhile, he sat and watched the Cross family as the lottery wound down. Interestingly enough, he found himself glad to hear Jannie's name called out over the public address system. And then he was sorry when it became clear that Ava hadn't made it in.

Poor Ava. That girl couldn't catch a break, could she?

Unless you counted getting in with the Cross family to begin with. They were "good people," on paper. Guidice was even starting to like them a little more than he would have preferred. The grandmother and the kids, anyway. It happened all the time. He couldn't help getting involved with his subjects.

Would they be devastated when Alex was dead and gone? Of course they would. That was the part that couldn't be helped. The world was full of innocent victims.

He'd been one himself, once. Thanks to Alex.

But none of that mattered—not as long as he kept an eye on the bigger picture. Always the bigger picture.

That's where Alex Cross was a dead man walking.

CHAPTER

10

I SKIPPED LUNCH WITH THE FAMILY AND GOT MYSELF STRAIGHT OVER TO THE new Consolidated Forensic Lab at Fourth and School Streets. It's an amazing building—two hundred and eighty thousand square feet of facilities under one enormous roof. MPD finally had firearms, toxicology, DNA, fingerprint analysis, and the medical examiner's office all in one place.

As soon as I got there, I threw on a surgical gown and mask and pushed in through the swinging door of the examination suite where Joan Bradbury was already halfway through Elizabeth Reilly's autopsy.

"What have we got so far, Joan?" I asked.

"A lot," she said. "Come on in."

The body was open on the table, with a long Y cut down the middle of the torso, which had been flayed open by now. I've sat through more autopsies than I can remember, and my stomach's way past any kind of trouble with this stuff. At the same time, I never let myself forget the reason I'm there. I owed Elizabeth that much, at least.

"I did a tox screen on her blood last night, just to get a jump on things," she told me. "We got a positive read for antidepressants, and, get this—Pitocin."

"Pitocin? You test for that?"

"Not usually, but under the circumstances, I thought I might check. Glad I did, too. Pitocin doesn't stay in the system too long, only around forty-eight hours. Which means Elizabeth Reilly induced her labor less than two days before she died."

My mind started spinning around this new piece of information. So far there were no hospital records for Elizabeth Reilly in the area, and no record of any live births under that name, much less an induced labor.

Was it possible she'd done this on her own for some reason? She'd been a nursing student. She could have easily known how to get her hands on some Pitocin, and maybe even known how to administer it.

But why?

And meanwhile, was there a three-day-old baby out there somewhere? I needed to find out, ASAP.

"By the way," Joan went on. "We didn't find any rope fibers on her fingers or palms at all. Someone else put that noose around her neck. And if all that weren't enough, the break in the second and third vertebrae was definitely postmortem. I've got a few hours to go here, but I can tell you right now, my report's going to rule out suicide."

Ultimately, cause of death is the ME's to call. I hardly ever disagreed with Joan's conclusions, and I didn't have any reason to do it today, either. This was now officially a homicide investigation.

Maybe also a missing persons case.

I had my work cut out, that was for sure.

CHAPTER

11

THE FIRST THING I DID WHEN I LEFT THE MORGUE WAS FIND SAMPSON. HE WAS catching up on his reports at the Second District station house, and I pulled him outside for a talk.

I've known John all my life, and I trust him as much as anyone at MPD. He's also been around long enough that he knows people all over the city. More specifically, he knew which people at which agencies were going to be willing to talk to him about a missing baby without eighteen and a half signatures on two dozen forms first. I understand why we've got a lot of the paperwork we do, but there's a time and a place. This wasn't it. If speed was my number one priority right now, discretion was a close second.

We stood out by my car in the station house parking lot, downing some sandwiches and going over the details.

"All indications are that this was a vaginal birth. No signs of episiotomy, or any hospital intervention at all," I told him. "Given the Pitocin in Elizabeth's system, and the fact that nobody we've talked to said anything about any pregnancy, it seems pretty clear she was trying to keep this a secret."

"It's not so hard to hide a pregnancy," John said, flipping through the file I'd given him. "Especially if nobody's looking."

"Exactly. Her neighbors barely knew her, and she dropped out of school five months ago."

"What about family?" he asked. "Next of kin?"

"Not much. She's got two grandparents down in Georgia who raised her, and that's about it. According to them, she fell off the radar a while ago. They haven't heard from her since Christmas."

"In other words, this baby could be—"

"Anywhere. Yeah."

John chugged the last of his Diet Coke and obliterated the can in his huge hand. There's a reason we call him Man Mountain. "I'm going to need something stronger here," he said.

"Talk to Youth Division, see if any of this rings a bell," I told him. "Harry Keith over there will keep his mouth shut, if you need some help. Go district by district if you have to. Check the NCMEC database as often as you can, and talk to their people over in Alexandria. Just don't say anything about me or this case."

This was the thing. Elizabeth Reilly's pregnancy was the only card we were holding close anymore. If our killer had any connection to her baby, I didn't want him to see us coming, and I was already publicly attached to this very public story. That's where Sampson came in.

The other possibility was that there might not be a baby to find anymore. We didn't know if Elizabeth's pregnancy had been full term; if the baby was delivered stillborn; or God forbid, if it had been killed for some reason I didn't understand yet.

Right now, all of that was a question mark. But for the baby's sake, as well as the mother's, we had to assume that there was still someone out there to save.

CHAPTER

12

FOR THREE DAYS WE GOT NOWHERE. THERE WAS NO SIGNIFICANT MOVEMENT on the Darcy Vickers or Elizabeth Reilly murders, and the phone call I kept hoping to get from Sampson never came. You could just feel these cases going cold.

Then on that Saturday morning, we had a new development. The worst kind. Another body popped up in Georgetown.

I was home when I got the call from Sergeant Huizenga. She wanted me to keep going in the direction I'd been going, and monitor this homicide alongside the other two. The trick would be to see this scene on its own merit first, without comparing it to anything. Sometimes if you go looking for connections, you start to see what you want to see instead of what's really there.

I took Pennsylvania, and then M Street, all the way to the Key Bridge and parked just below it. Several cruisers were already on-site, and they'd strung an outer perimeter of yellow tape across Water Street, on the south side of the Potomac Boat Club.

A maintenance worker had found the boy's body that morning, lodged under one of their docks. By now someone had pulled him onto the shore and left him there, on a little spit of dirt and grass just beyond the white-clapboard-and-green-shingled building.

The first sight of him was a shock, even for me. The apparent cause of death was a gunshot to the face, with an ugly, wide-open entry wound that told me he'd been hit at close range. It was hard to know what kind of powder burns or stippling had washed away in the water, but there were still a few dark marks around the remains of his cheekbone. A couple of smashed teeth were exposed where the flesh had been blown away, and it gave him a kind of sideways grimace, almost as if he were still in pain.

That wasn't all. His jeans were stained dark all around the hips and crotch, presumably from stabbing. There were at least half a dozen ragged perforations in the denim of his pants, clearly centered around the genital area. It was a horrible proposition to think about what had happened to this poor kid. I could only hope for his sake that he'd been shot dead first, and mutilated after. Not much consolation there.

The most depressing part was how young he was. He didn't look any older than eighteen, and his waterlogged letterman's jacket was from St. Catherine's, a private high school in Northwest DC. How he had gotten here, like this, was anyone's guess.

My one clear hit was that this had been done in anger—possibly at the victim himself, but also maybe out of the killer's own sense of self-loathing. Mutilation can be a signifier of that, as often as not. Either way, our perpetrator obviously had some kind of demons to exorcise. You don't need a gun *and* a blade if your motivation is strictly murder.

In fact, it felt a little to me like this killer was getting out all of his ideas at once—stabbing, shooting, drowning. But why? What need did that satisfy?

After I'd taken in all the details I could, I slipped on some gloves and checked the boy's pockets. They were all empty, but I did find a name, Smithe, stenciled on the back of his jacket. I called it in right away.

It didn't take long to get word back, either. A few minutes later, a call from our Command Information Center told me that an eighteen-year-old senior at St. Catherine's, Cory Smithe, had been reported missing by his parents two days earlier. Six one, blond hair, and a small birthmark on his right wrist. Check, check, and check.

"Have you got an address?" I asked the dispatcher.

"Already sent it to your phone," she told me.

Because we both knew what I had to do next.

13

WHEN I HEADED BACK TO MY CAR ON THE FAR SIDE OF THE BOATHOUSE, I saw that the locust storm had descended—the kind with cameras, microphones, and broadcast towers.

Instead of the usual half-dozen reporters we might have seen by now, there were dozens of them, just waiting for the story. Trucks were lined up on Water Street, and without a designated press space everyone was right there on the tape line.

This was three bodies in less than a week, centered around one of DC's least violent neighborhoods. By comparison, the previous three murders anywhere west of Rock Creek had been spread out over a fourteen-month period. People were definitely sitting up and taking notice.

"Detective Cross, over here!"

"Who's the victim, Alex?"

"Are you considering this a serial investigation at this point?"

It's a little like being a rock star, without any of the fringe benefits. I gave them the bare minimum, which was all I could afford to do right now.

"Sergeant Huizenga will be out to brief you after the family has been notified," I told whoever was closest. "We won't be releasing any details in the meantime."

"Detective Cross, will you be overseeing all three of these cases?" Shawna Stewart from Channel Five asked me.

"I don't know yet," I told her.

"How are the Darcy Vickers and Elizabeth Reilly investigations coming along?"

"They're coming," I said, just as I reached my car.

"Hey, Alex, is it true you pulled Elizabeth Reilly's dead body out of that window before a proper examination?" someone else yelled out. "Doesn't that compromise the investigation?"

That one stopped me cold. Maybe I should have kept moving, but instead I turned around to see who had asked the question.

This guy struck me as a one-man operation from the first glance. I'd seen his type before—camera around his neck, a handheld recorder pointed my way, and a notebook sticking out of the pocket of his cargo shorts. He also had a full beard, and no press credentials that I could see. Everyone else around him had laminated badges from the city, clipped to their lapels or hanging on lanyards around their necks.

"I don't recognize you," I said. "Who are you with?"

"I'm just trying to get the facts, detective."

"That's not what I asked," I said. "I asked who you're with."

He raised his voice then, enough to make sure the microphones all around us were picking him up. "Am I a suspect, detective? Are you saying you want to detain me?"

He was baiting me. I've seen it a million times. If they can't get the story they want, they'll try to create one—especially the hacks and the wannabes.

"No, I'm not detaining you," I said. "It was just a simple question."

"Why? Am I required by law to identify myself?" he said.

Now he was just being a dick. The civilian in me wanted to shove that recorder right down his throat.

"No," I said again. "You're not required to identify yourself."

"In that case—no comment," he said, fighting back a smile. It got a laugh from a few in the crowd, but not from me. The best thing I could do right now was get in my car and leave.

I had somewhere more important to be, anyway. And it couldn't wait.

14

BY THE TIME I PULLED UP IN FRONT OF CORY SMITHE'S HOME, I FELT LIKE I HAD a fifty-pound bag of gravel sitting on my chest. Family notifications are the hardest part of my job, hands down.

The Smithes lived in one of the thousands of early twentieth-century row houses that line the streets of Northwest DC. This one was on Shepherd Street in Petworth, with a tiny, terraced stamp of green lawn halfway up the stairs to the front door. In the middle of the grass was a statue of the Virgin Mary, surrounded by a bed of spring tulips. Maybe the Lady would give these people some comfort when they needed it most.

I'd already notified the Fourth District missing persons unit. They had Victims Services on the way over, but this part was all on me. I climbed the stairs and rang the bell.

Cory's father answered the door almost right away. He

looked a lot older than I would have expected, and had a cane hooked over his wrist.

"Can I help you?" he asked, a little warily.

"Mr. Smithe? I'm Alex Cross from the police department," I told him. "I'm here to speak with you about Cory. May I come in?"

There are a few things you want to avoid in this kind of situation. One of them is mentioning up front that you're from Homicide. Notifications need to unfold at the right pace—not too fast, but not too slowly, either.

"Come in," he told me, and opened the screen door. "My wife's in the back."

He hobbled on ahead of me, and I followed him through to a screen porch off the kitchen. Mrs. Smithe was there, in slippers and a flowered housecoat. She clutched the neck of it closed and stood up as I came in. The cordless phone on her lap fell onto the floor, but neither of them seemed to notice.

"What is it?" she said. I could tell by her face that she'd already been contemplating the worst. I quickly reintroduced myself, and then got right to it.

"I wish there was an easy way to say this," I told them.

"Oh Lord. No . . ."

"I'm so sorry, but Cory's been killed. He was found this morning."

It was like her voice cracked the air. There weren't any words now, just a gut-wrenching expression of grief. Loss. Devastation. She sank down onto her knees and leaned against her husband, who was still holding the cane, trying not to go down himself, I think. He bent his head toward his wife's with his eyes squeezed shut, the cane shaking between the two of them.

"Where?" Mr. Smithe choked out. "Where was he?"

"In the Potomac," I said. "At the Georgetown water-front." There's no sense holding back information at this point. It was better for them to get it from me than some other version on the news later.

"Killed?" he said. "As in—"

"Somebody did this to him, yes," I said. "Again, I can't tell you how sorry I am."

I think a lot of people assume that's lip service when cops say it, but the truth was, I could have cried right there with them. The loss of a child is a tragedy, who-ever's it is. You learn to keep it inside.

I waited until I felt like they could hear more from me, and then moved on.

"I know how hard this is," I said, "but if you could give me a little information about Cory, it could be a big help."

Mr. Smithe nodded, still on his feet. His wife was back in her chair, quietly weeping.

"What do you need to know?" he asked.

"The kinds of things Cory liked to do, where he hung out, the friends he spent the most time with. That sort of thing," I said.

His mother looked up then. "Was he in some sort of trouble?" she asked.

"I don't know," I told them honestly.

"He was a good boy," Mr. Smithe said. "I know every parent must say that...or maybe they don't. But Cory walked hand in hand with God. He prayed with us every night. In fact, he's supposed to start at Catholic University in the fall. A theology major."

Later I'd learn that Mr. Smithe was a deacon at the family's church, and his wife had been a nun for twenty years. This had to feel to them like the cruelest possible blow from God.

I pressed them for as much as I could, and took down the names of Cory's closest circle. There was a girlfriend, Jess Pasternak, they said. She lived only a few blocks away. That was as good a next stop as any.

Then I gave the Smithes my card with my cell number written on the back, and left them to grieve in private. The best thing I could do for them now was keep moving.

As usual, time was not on my side.

15

"IS THAT WHAT THEY TOLD YOU? CATHOLIC U? ALTAR BOY, AND ALL THAT?"

Half an hour later, I was sitting in my car with Jess Pasternak. She had her legs pulled up on the seat, hugging her knees to her chest and crying bitterly while we talked.

When I'd shown up at her house, she'd asked to speak with me outside. Since she was eighteen, like Cory, that was her prerogative. After a tense exchange with her parents at the door, she'd followed me down to the curb.

Now, whatever it was she had to say, it wasn't coming easily.

"Why?" I asked her. "Is there something Cory's parents didn't know about?"

She pounded the seat with her fist, literally fighting back the tears. It was like she was two parts devastated, and one part pissed off about something.

"I warned him," she said. "I really did."

"Jess? What are we talking about?" I said. "I know this is hard, but you've got to tell me everything."

She sat up straighter and wiped her eyes. It left a dark streak of makeup on the back of her hand, and she absently wiped it onto the knee of her torn jeans.

She was a pretty girl, but not in the traditional, St. Catherine's kind of way. Her blond hair was cut short above her ears, and she wore a wifebeater with thin leather suspenders over it, along with calf-high black boots. She looked more rocker chick than cheerleader to me.

"Cory wasn't even going to college," she said. "We were going to travel in the fall. You know—France, Italy, la-la-la." She corkscrewed her hand in the air like it was all so much folly, now.

"How does that relate to what's happened?" I asked. I hadn't given her any of the specifics of Cory's murder, but she seemed to assume that something awful had been done to him. Which it had.

"I swore I'd never say anything," she told me, twisting the withered tissue in her hand. I could tell she was getting close, so I just sat quietly and waited.

Suddenly, she hitched up on the seat and pulled a silver phone out of her back pocket. I thought she was about to make a call, but instead she went onto the web and navigated to a page of some kind.

"There." She dropped the phone on the seat between us. "I didn't say a word, okay?"

When I picked up the phone, I saw she'd opened

up a site called Randyboys.com. More specifically, it was a profile for Cory Smithe—or Jeremy, as he called himself there. When I thumbed down the page, I saw there were pictures, too—Cory, with his shirt off; in his underwear; nude from behind, with his face obscured. The profile said he was available for outcalls only, no overnights, no travel. No Sundays either, I noticed.

"They told me you were his girlfriend," I said.

"Yeah, well..." Jess let out a scoff between her tears. "I mean, don't get me wrong. Mr. and Mrs. Smithe are super nice and everything. They're just kind of clueless about the whole gay thing. Much less"—she gestured at the phone without looking at it—"all that."

"Do you know anything about the men Cory was hooking up with?" I asked. "Were there regular customers?"

She held up her hands in a shrug. "He just said they were all letches and chicken hawks. Guys with money, I guess."

"Do you know where he'd meet with them?"

"Wherever they wanted," she said. "At a hotel, in the park, down by the waterfront..."

She rolled her eyes, and it seemed to hit her all over again that her friend was gone. Then the tears started back up.

"I told him to be careful. I really did, but he wouldn't listen. That asshole!"

I gave Jess my last tissue and let her cry. I didn't read too much into the anger, other than a defensive kind of reaction to feeling overwhelmed. As far as I could make out, she was telling me everything she could about Cory.

And, if I was lucky, she'd just given me a little bit about his killer, too.

CHAPTER

16

TALK ABOUT HAVING TO PULL IT TOGETHER. AFTER SPENDING THE DAY ON WHAT would be any parent's worst nightmare, I had to turn around and show up at home with something like a smile on my face. Especially tonight. This was Damon's last night before he had to go back to school for fourth quarter, and I was taking everyone out to dinner at Kinkead's.

For once I was glad to be running behind when I got home, if only as an excuse to grab a few minutes by myself. One shower, shirt, and blazer later, I was at least looking fit for public consumption.

By the time I was sitting down at my favorite restaurant, with my family chattering and laughing all around me, I was even starting to feel halfway human again. David Yarboro was on piano that night; I had a nice glass of pinot noir in front of me; and for just a little while, I could pretend that my biggest problem was deciding between the salmon and the New York strip with Kinkead's Scotch whiskey sauce.

Life was good. It really was.

After everyone ordered dinner, I pushed back my chair and stood up with my glass. It got some glances from around the room, and I noticed Jannie looking a little mortified—but if embarrassing your kids isn't one of the privileges of being a dad, I don't know what is.

"I'd like to make a toast," I said.

"White, wheat, or rye?" Nana joked, and got a laugh all around the table. My grandmother reads me as well as anyone. I'm pretty sure she could tell I needed a boost that night.

"To our guest of honor," I said. "Damon, you make me proud, every single day. We're going to miss you like crazy while you're gone, but in the meantime—here's to you. Here's to a great quarter at Chapin. And most of all, here's to summer vacation, when we get to see you again."

"Here's to summer vacation!" the kids chorused back.

"Close enough," Bree said, and we all clinked glasses around the table.

After that, Damon stood up to make a toast of his own. I could see all too well that my oldest boy, standing there at the head of the table in a jacket and tie, wasn't really a boy anymore. It didn't help that he was fifteen but looked twenty.

"Here's to Ava," he said, looking right at her. "I know you and I haven't really spent that much time together, but I just want to say, welcome to the family."

"Welcome to the family!" everyone echoed back.

I looked over at Ava and was a little shocked to see her grinning from ear to ear. Ever since the school lottery, she'd been scowling her way through the day, and spending long stretches of time alone in her room. Now it was like someone had turned on the lights for the first time in a long time.

And that's why my boy Damon is a star. With just a few words, he managed to get something out of Ava that I'd barely been able to do in four months. He may be the quietest of my kids, but that's the thing about the quiet ones. When they do speak up, it's usually for a good reason.

Or even a great one.

Suddenly, my eyes were stinging and the room went a little fuzzy. I never even saw it coming. It was like the whole day just washed over me in one big wave—all that stress on the way in, and everything I was so grateful for on the way out.

"Daddy?" Ali leaned over and looked up into my face. "Why are you crying?"

"I'm not," I said, wiping my eyes. "Well, maybe just a little." I pulled him up onto my lap and put my arms around his little string bean body. "But they're happy tears," I said.

"Don't mind him, children," Nana told everyone. "Despite appearances, Mr. Dragonslayer over here is just an old softie at heart."

"True that," I answered.

Then Nana gave me a wink and raised her glass to make one more toast. "Here's to old softie, who can cry all he likes, but he's still paying for dinner!"

CHAPTER

17

RON GUIDICE GOT HOME AROUND TEN THIRTY THAT NIGHT. AFTER GETTING up at five, and crisscrossing the city all day, he was exhausted. Still, there was plenty of work to do. It was probably going to be another all-nighter.

Just inside the door of his simple Cape house in Reston, he stepped out of his shoes. It was an old habit from growing up in New Hampshire, with its long winters and subsequent mud seasons. He set his Timberlands in the rubber tray by the door, alongside Emma Lee's little sneakers and his mother's old slip-ons.

"Hey, Mom, I'm home," he called out.

Lydia Guidice jerked awake on the couch, with a chubby hand to her chest. She'd been sacked out in front of *NCIS,* or *CSI,* or *SVU*—whatever it was. Guidice could never tell one of those shows from the other.

"Good Lord, you scared the bejesus out of me," Lydia

said. "I still can't get used to that beard of yours. Makes you look like some kind of terrorist."

"Uh-huh." Guidice leaned into the fridge and pulled out a Bud. "Emma Lee eat okay?"

"All her chicken nuggets and seconds on applesauce. She went down about eight thirty."

"Good, good. You want anything?"

"I wouldn't mind a little ice cream," his mother said.

In fact, ice cream was the last thing Lydia Guidice needed. She hadn't weighed herself since she slipped past the three-hundred-pound mark. But the ugly truth was, his mother was a lot easier to take when she was stuffing her face.

"Where were you tonight?" she asked, pushing herself up to sitting.

"Work," he said.

"You might have called."

"We've been over this, Mom. If I don't call, it means I'm working late. I don't understand what's so complicated about that."

"I just worry, that's all. Would it really kill you to pick up the phone?" she asked.

Guidice took a long hit of his beer. It was the same dance, every goddamn time.

"You know," he said, "if you want, I can just as easily take Emma Lee and find a smaller place—"

"No, no," his mother said.

"Take my benefit checks with me, too. I think they're hiring over at the Safeway right now. You want me to pick you up an application tomorrow?"

"Don't start," she said, and put out a hand for her dessert. Guidice stopped short, holding the quart of Breyers mint chip just out of her reach.

"Who's in charge, Mom?" he said.

"Oh, for pity's sake."

"Say it."

Lydia grunted testily and shifted her eyes up to meet his gaze. "You're in charge, Ronald. Always have been," she said. "Satisfied?"

Guidice handed her the ice cream and leaned down to kiss the top of her head.

"Then let's stop having this conversation, Mom, what do you say?"

The fact of the matter was, Lydia Guidice had never finished the tenth grade, never married Ron's father, and never held down a real job in her life. Now, at age sixty-two, three hundred and some pounds, and no Social Security coming in, she was about as marketable as a used condom, and they both knew it.

Guidice didn't enjoy making his mother squirm like this. That's why he only did it as often as necessary.

"I'm going to give Emma Lee a kiss, and then I'll be working in my room," he told her.

"Okeydoke."

"Love you, Mom."

"Love you, too, son," Lydia answered as she tucked into her ice cream. "Don't stay up too late."

CHAPTER

18

GUIDICE TIPTOED INTO EMMA LEE'S ROOM AND STOOD OVER HER BED. SHE WAS all curled up like a little hedgehog in one corner under the covers, sleeping peacefully.

There was nothing more precious than this. Nothing.

He leaned down and stroked his daughter's sweet little cheek. Brushed her sand-colored hair away from her eyes. Kissed her forehead.

Halfway out of the room, he changed his mind. He could just as easily work in here. He parked himself in the white-painted rocker by the door instead and listened to the metronome of Emma Lee's even breathing.

Once his laptop was powered up, Guidice plugged his earbuds into the computer's audio jack and started opening Windows. There were notes to transcribe from the day, sites to check, listservs to monitor—but first, he wanted to make sure everything was up and running at Alex's house.

With the family out to dinner that night, there had been plenty of time to install an Infinity transmitter on each level of the Cross home. Each one was hardwired behind an existing outlet so there would be no issues with battery life or losing power. There were also three corresponding match-head-size microphones tucked into the kitchen, the master bedroom, and Alex's office on the third floor. If anything, Guidice was going to net more information than he would ever have time to weed through, but too much was definitely preferable to not enough.

He opened all three channels now, and let them stream simultaneously in his ears while he worked. Mostly it was quiet over there. Someone was watching TV, and it seemed that maybe Alex was in his office, just from the sound of shuffling pages and the occasional clearing of a throat.

It was a bizarre mash-up, really—sitting here gathering source material from the privacy of his daughter's bedroom. A peaceful moment in the middle of the storm.

There was still Lydia to worry about, but so far she was more use to him than she was trouble. In a way, it was like his mother knew which questions she could get away with, and which ones to leave alone. Like how they were affording to live, for starters.

Guidice's reporting hadn't brought in any appreciable income for quite a while now. Not since everything had changed—and not since the cash settlement, after the cops had stolen his life away from him.

As if a wad of money could make up for what they'd done!

It was nothing more than routine incompetence, the way Theresa had been allowed to die that night, right there on the sidewalk like a common criminal.

And not just Theresa, either. No one else had known it at the time, but their unborn child had died that night, too, along with the only woman he'd ever loved. Both of them, murdered in cold blood.

And all on Alex Cross's watch.

CHAPTER

19

ELIJAH CREEM PREFERRED TO SECTION HIS OWN GRAPEFRUIT IN THE MORNING.
He liked the way the membranous flesh gave so easily,
but how it also demanded a certain element of precision
from the blade of his knife.

He took his time with it that morning, lingering over
his fruit, steak, and egg breakfast while he read the *Post*.
One story in particular had caught his attention there,
and he perused it twice through as he ate.

"Kate?" he called out to the housekeeper.

"Sir?" she said, poking her head through the swinging
kitchen door into the dining room.

"Would you bring me my phone, please? I think it's in
the hall."

"Certainly," she said, and disappeared again.

According to the paper, a boy from Northwest DC

had been shot, stabbed, and dropped into the Potomac, where his body had been found floating just the day before. The *Post*'s coverage, at least, indicated that the police had no leads whatsoever on who might have done this.

"Oh, I heard about that," Kate said, suddenly back with his phone and looking over Dr. Creem's shoulder. "It was on every channel last night."

"Was it?" Creem said. "Apparently, the boy died quite horribly."

He liked that she didn't turn away. Instead, she leaned closer to get a look at the black and white picture of the victim. Also, close enough for Creem to rest a hand gently on the curve of her ass.

"So young," she said, though she was barely older.

She hadn't flinched at his touch, either. Kate, with her green card problems and sick father, certainly knew which side her bread was buttered on.

"That's all, for now," Creem said, and winked at her as she freshened his coffee. She smiled pleasantly.

He watched her go and waited until she was back in the kitchen, out of earshot. Then he picked up his phone and called Josh Bergman.

"Elijah?" Bergman answered. "Is something wrong?"

"No," Creem told him. "I know we agreed to keep a little distance for the time being. But I'm looking at the paper here, and I just had to ask if you've been as busy lately as I think you have."

"Oh, that," Bergman said, feigning nonchalance.

"I thought so," Creem said. Joshie had really upped

his game since the last time around. It was impressive.

"And how are you, Elijah? I've been thinking about you."

"Never better," Creem told his friend—and it was true, to an extent. Maybe the old life had been burned down around him, but this new one was rising, phoenixlike, to take its place. "It turns out I hated my wife for the last sixteen years. I just didn't realize it until she was gone," he said.

"What about the girls?"

"I miss them terribly," Creem deadpanned. "But in the meantime, I wear what I like to the table, I don't have any of those soul-sucking dinner parties on my schedule anymore, and I'm seriously considering that little dark-eyed housekeeper of mine."

"You mean Kate? Nice choice," Bergman said. He'd always liked hearing about Creem's sex life, and only sort of tried to hide the fact. "What's stopping you?"

"Nothing, I suppose," Creem answered. "But Josh, listen. One more thing. I want you to know how much I appreciate you. How much I *have* appreciated you, through all of this."

"Elijah, have you been drinking?"

"I'm serious," he said. "I think you're the only real friend I've ever had."

"Okay, fine," Bergman said. "Then let me listen while you doink your maid."

Creem laughed it off. They kept each other entertained, that was for sure. "I'm hanging up now, Josh. Thanks for ruining the moment."

"Just remember—the ball's in your court," Bergman said.

"Yes, of course," Creem told him. "I can hardly wait."

Then he hung up the phone, picked up the small, serrated knife from the table, and headed off to the kitchen.

CHAPTER

20

KATE WAS DOING DISHES WHEN HE CAME IN.

"Can I get you something, Dr. Creem?" she asked.

"No, no, I'm fine," he said, coming to stand over by the sink. "I just meant to tell you before that you should help yourself to anything left in Miranda's closet upstairs. I think she was about your size."

"That's very nice. Thank you," she said.

"Also, there's really no need for the uniform anymore," he said, indicating the gray-and-white aproned dress she wore. "That was really Miranda's thing, not mine."

Kate kept washing the glass in her hand, but she smiled beautifully. For a girl who had obviously never had any work done, she was quite the specimen.

"How do you get anything done in this, anyway?" Creem asked. He reached over and fingered the hem of her uniform, letting his thumb brush against her thigh. "Looks awfully uncomfortable to me."

"I don't know," she said, looking down.

"I think you'd be much more comfortable"—Creem raised the knife in his hand, up to the white collar at the back of her neck—"like this."

He pulled the collar back and drew the blade straight down, cutting a ragged line all the way through to the skirt.

She squealed when he did it, and stiffened right up. So did Creem.

"It's all right," he said. "I'm a surgeon. You're in good hands."

Now she laughed nervously, but also pressed her body against his, grinding into him with her ass. She wanted him, didn't she? Of course she did. He was Dr. Elijah Creem. There were all kinds of things he could do for her.

And to her.

Creem reached around front and cut away the skin-thin fabric of her panties next. It wasn't the same as cutting actual flesh, but it had its appeal. Besides, his life was complicated enough right now. He couldn't afford to take out his own maid. What was the expression—don't shit where you eat?

Instead, he bent her over the sink, with the warm water still running, and entered her right there.

"Relax," he told her. "This should feel good."

With the very tip of his blade, he reached up again, and drew it softly down the exposed skin of her back.

Using only the slightest pressure, just enough to raise a few skin cells, it left behind a fine white line, like a tiny chalk mark. She shivered as he did it—either loving this, or displaying some killer acting skills. Creem didn't care which.

He didn't last long after that, either. The ruined uniform, and the sight of the girl bent over the sink, catching warm water in her hair, was enough to get him off. But then, with one fleeting mental image of the knife taking his place inside of her, Creem was quickly past the point of no return.

Up and over.

Fourth of July fireworks, and all that.

When he was done, he sent little Kate upstairs to pick out something else to wear. He even gave her a wad of cash to go shopping with afterward, and the rest of the day off.

"Thank you, Dr. Creem," she said in her quaint accent. "Thank you so much."

"No, thank *you*," Creem said. "What a lovely way to start the day."

He smiled as she scooted out, letting her enjoy herself for now.

By the end of the week, she'd be looking for another job.

CHAPTER

21

CREEM'S APPOINTMENT WITH HIS CRIMINAL ATTORNEY WAS SCHEDULED FOR nine thirty that morning. He showed up at the L Street offices of Schuman and Pace just after ten.

"Elijah," Bill Schuman said, coming around the desk to shake his hand. "Good to see you." He paused to let Creem apologize for his tardiness, but Creem only nodded. He'd probably be charged for the time, anyway.

"Have a seat. Please," the lawyer told him.

"Don't mind if I do."

He took the button-tufted tweed couch near the door instead of the leather swivel by Schuman's desk. Schuman seemed a little puzzled, but didn't say anything as he sat back down and started flipping through the file in front of him.

"Give it to me straight, doc. How long do I have to live?" Creem asked.

"You're in a good mood," Schuman said.

"Just got laid, if you want to know."

His lawyer looked at him with an expression somewhere between offended and envious. It was the look of a guy who hardly ever got laid himself.

"Anyway," Schuman went on, "things are moving along. We've got Lew Carroll coming down from New York for second chair, and I've already pinned down the two best jury consultants in the city for this trial."

"Fine, fine," Creem said. "Do we have a lot to go over?" Now that Joshie had thrown down the gauntlet with such determination, he had much more interesting things to think about.

"Well...yes," Schuman said. "Of course we do. Elijah, you've got to focus here. If you want to get your money's worth on this defense—"

"At eight hundred and twenty-five an hour, I don't know if that's possible," Creem said.

Schuman raised his voice. "—then you're going to have to show up. And I don't just mean physically. Now, this pandering charge is a nonstarter, but I want to talk about the pornography charge. That's where things start to get a lot stickier."

Creem wanted to say "No pun intended," but he kept his mouth shut.

"A worst-case scenario could be actual jail time," Schuman told him. "Five years for possession, or as much as fifteen if the DA starts talking distribution. Are you hearing me on that?"

"When do you expect to go to trial?" Creem asked, his first serious question.

"June fourth," Schuman said, "unless I can talk the DA into something more palatable."

"Such as?"

"Well, a plea bargain, for one."

"No," Creem said.

"Elijah, at least listen to the range of options—"

"No." Creem got up and paced over to the window. "I'm not taking a plea on this. I'll wait for the trial. You just do your goddamn job."

"I *am* doing my goddamn job!" Schuman said, showing his first bit of real spine. "I don't understand. Why aren't you—?"

He stopped short then, and dropped his head.

"Oh...cripes. Please don't tell me...."

Now Schuman stood up and walked over to where Creem was watching the traffic down on L Street. When he spoke again, it was in a needless hush.

"Elijah, please tell me you're not planning on doing something stupid, like fleeing the country. Just tell me that much, at least."

Creem smiled again, looking down at Schuman. Maybe this tightly wound little man was smarter than he looked.

"Now why would I need to do that, Bill?" he said. "I've got the best lawyer in the city working for me."

CHAPTER

22

AT THAT AFTERNOON'S MAJOR CASE SQUAD BRIEFING, SERGEANT HUIZENGA GOT the ball rolling by letting us know that word had come down from on high, approving all overtime requests until further notice.

That got a round of applause—it's not unusual for cops to work off the clock when things get as tight as they were these days. But of course, on the clock was better.

"One guess," I heard someone mutter behind me. "Al Ayla."

Just a few months earlier, Washington had taken several hard hits by the Saudi-based terrorist organization, also known as The Family. Both the mayor and the chief of police had caught hell over that one, with accusations of mishandled resources and slow response time to the crisis as it played out.

The one good thing that had come out of it, apparently, was that we now had the kind of resources we could really do something with. Patrol units in and around Georgetown had been doubled during daylight hours, and in some cases tripled at night. A dedicated tip line had been established, and our neighborhood outreach people were on the street every day.

Some of that was about increasing the scope of the investigation, to be sure, but some of it was also about heading off the inevitable public flogging you get, no matter how hard you work.

Each of our three homicides now had a lead detective assigned, along with a full squad of investigators. I'd be running between all three, along with whichever personnel I could pull in from the districts, as needed. Huizenga was happy to have me working with Sampson on the search for Baby Reilly, since the Major Case Squad was out flat right now. As long as these three cases were all grouped under one umbrella, I was the guy holding the umbrella.

When Huizenga handed the floor over to me, I started by putting the three victims' morgue photos on the screen at the front of the room for everyone to see. It wasn't easy to look at, but my whole focus right now was about trying to draw some lines between these cases.

"These are now officially in chronological order, left to right," I told everyone. "The autopsy puts Cory Smithe's time of death at twenty-four hours after Elizabeth Reilly's, and forty hours after Darcy Vickers's."

People started taking notes. A few just watched and

listened, absorbing the details, which is more my own style.

"Beyond the issue of timing," I said, "we've got a fair amount of common ground here, but mostly in pairs. Almost nothing I've found so far cuts across all three cases. Two of the victims were stabbed, for instance—although even there, Ms. Vickers's wounds were fatal, whereas Mr. Smithe was mutilated postmortem. In both cases it was done with a narrow, but not identical blade.

"Two of these victims, obviously, were women," I went on. "Two were found in Georgetown proper, although we don't know for sure where Smithe was put into the river, so the primary crime scene there is still an unknown."

The captain of our Homicide Branch, Frank Salazar, interrupted with a question—probably *the* question on everyone's mind.

"Alex, I know we're at the supposition phase, but what's your bottom line right now? How many perpetrators do you suppose we're looking at?"

I took a beat to think about it. The short answer was—*I wish to hell I knew.*

"Here's the problem," I said. "There's no scenario right now that doesn't defy logic, or at least, likelihood. We've never seen anything like this before, given the geography and the time frame. But I will say that it seems to me, a single killer is highly unlikely. The greater question in my mind is whether our perps are operating independently of each other, or not."

That went over like a lead balloon. People were getting anxious for answers, both inside and outside the department. But without more information than we currently had, we were still flying blind on all three of these murders.

Meanwhile, the whole time I'd been talking, I could feel my phone vibrating—once, twice, a third time, in quick succession. As soon as Huizenga started fielding a few of the questions, I took out the phone and checked messages. They were all from Sampson—two voice mails and a text. That seemed like a good sign to me.

Since I was still in the briefing room, I checked the text first, and sure enough, it was exactly what I'd been hoping for.

Alex—Package found. Give me a call, ASAP.

23

FIRST THING THE NEXT MORNING, SAMPSON AND I CAUGHT THE EARLIEST possible flight from DC down to Savannah, Georgia.

Elizabeth Reilly's baby had been found three days earlier, newborn and alone, in a rental cabin on the northern edge of the Okefenokee Wildlife Refuge. If it weren't for CODIS, the national DNA database, that little girl would have been absorbed into the system, put up for adoption, and probably never identified. Instead, as soon as her sample went online, it was only a matter of time before Sampson got a crossmatch to Elizabeth Reilly. With DNA, that meant a hundred percent certainty that this was her child.

A Charlton County sheriff's deputy, Joe Cutler, met John and me when we arrived late that morning, at the entrance to Oke-Doke Cabins and Campground. The place had a dozen rental units spread out over a thirty-acre parcel, and Cutler briefed us while we drove back toward the cabin in question. I wasn't even sure what I was hoping for here, just something to start clueing us in about what had happened to this poor girl.

"I was the one who responded to the call," Cutler told us. "Found that little butterbean all wrapped up in a towel and crying her head off. She probably wasn't more'n a few hours old, but we got her right over to the NICU at Charlton Memorial, and she checked out just fine. No thanks to whoever left her here, of course."

"And you don't know who called it in?" I asked.

"Just an anonymous ten twenty-one," he said. "But I'd put my money on the mother. Probably some teenage girl who didn't have the guts to admit getting knocked up, you know?"

Maybe, I thought. Cutler obviously had his own feelings about what had happened here, but I was trying to keep an open mind as we drove back through the woods.

Eventually we came into a clearing, where a single log cabin sat up against a stand of enormous kudzu-choked oak trees. The woods were fairly dense all around here, and if there were any other buildings nearby, I couldn't see them.

This cabin was one of the so-called deluxe units, which only meant that linens were provided and there was an indoor bathroom. Still, Elizabeth could have theoretically had everything she needed to deliver her own baby here, including plenty of privacy.

At the front door, Cutler stopped to point out some gouge marks around the hammered iron knob. "Didn't actually rent the place," he said. "Just kind of helped herself. You can check availability online, so it wouldn't have been too hard to know which one'd be empty."

Inside the cabin was sunny, clean, and basic. There was a knotty pine floor with a farm table made out of the same wood, a small kitchenette, a queen-size bed under the dormered window. A bookshelf in the corner had a couple of games and some discarded paperbacks—Dean Koontz, Patricia Cornwell, Stieg Larsson. Nothing to indicate what might have actually happened here.

I tried to imagine the scene. Did Elizabeth set up her own IV by the bed? Would she have administered the Pitocin right away? How long did the delivery take?

She had to have been terrified, but that only meant that something even more terrifying had motivated her to come all the way down here.

Something—or someone. Was it the father? The killer?

Were those one and the same? I had no proof either way, but that was the version of the story that made the most sense to me, as John and I poked around, trying to put together the pieces of this invisible puzzle.

"I'll tell you something else," Cutler said, watching us from the door. "I kind of hope that baby's daddy never turns up. Considering the mother, I can't imagine he's any prize either, you know? I mean, seriously—what the hell was that girl thinking? That's what I'd like to know."

I didn't say anything, but I was starting to think that Elizabeth Reilly just might have been trying to save her daughter's life by coming here.

Also, that she just might have succeeded.

CHAPTER

24

SHELLMAN BLUFF, ABOUT TWO HOURS NORTH OF OKEFENOKEE, IS A LOW country fishing town in Georgia, with tidal marshes all along the coast, once you get that far. On the map the whole area looks like a maze of tributaries feeding into Sapelo Sound, which itself feeds right into the Atlantic.

Sampson and I didn't have any trouble finding Tommy and Jeannette Reilly's place, a small stilt house overlooking the causeway at the dead end of a quiet road in the village. This was where Elizabeth Reilly had grown up—and now maybe where her daughter would, too.

It was eighty-five degrees when we got out of the car. Not unusual for Georgia, but a little ahead of DC's temperatures. I was sweating in my jacket and tie.

Down by the water I saw an older woman standing on the dock. She wore a loose white dress, and had a long gray braid down her back. When she turned around, I saw she had a small bundle in her arms, too. John and I walked down from the dirt driveway to meet her halfway, on the dry brown patch of a back lawn behind the house.

"Grow 'em tall up in Washington, don't they?" she said, craning her neck, especially at Sampson, who's six nine. We'd already spoken on the phone; there was no real need for introductions. "I'm going to guess you boys are hungry from your trip."

"We're fine, ma'am, thank you," Sampson said. "Looks like you've got your hands full there, anyway."

Mrs. Reilly beamed and turned to show us the tiny little girl. Baby Reilly, as I'd come to think of her.

"This is Rebecca," she said. "Our miracle child."

The baby was sleeping peacefully, wrapped up in a thin pink blanket. Her face was pink, too, from the heat, and her hair was the same sandy blond that her mother's had been. For me, there was a definite sense of relief, just laying eyes on her after all the searching and worrying about what might have happened. I think Sampson probably felt the same way.

Inside, we met Tommy Reilly, who looked to be in his early sixties, like his wife. I couldn't imagine taking on a newborn at that age, but he lit up just as brightly when he took Rebecca into his arms. It seemed clear to me that these people had already fallen deeply in love with their great-granddaughter. Maybe that's why they seemed so at peace here, all things considered.

Once we were settled around their kitchen table, I started in with some necessary business.

"Mr. and Mrs. Reilly, I don't mean to alarm you," I said,

"but I have to ask. Have you considered relocating for the time being, or even putting Rebecca into county custody until this can all be sorted out?"

"You mean, until they find out who killed our Lizzie," Mr. Reilly said.

"That's right," I said. "Just as a precaution."

"You know, this isn't Washington, detective," he said, bouncing the baby gently on his shoulder. "I don't mean to come off naive, but it's pretty quiet around here. And for that matter... well, let's just say I'm a firm believer in the Second Amendment. I think we'll be okay."

"But we do appreciate the concern," Mrs. Reilly added.

I nodded, and took my time answering. I could imagine that giving up Rebecca, even just for a little while, could be traumatic under the circumstances.

"What if we talked to your sheriff's office about setting up a unit outside?" I asked. "Just for overnights, until we know a little more. I'd feel a lot better if we erred on the side of caution here."

"For Rebecca's sake," Sampson added.

The Reillys looked at each other across the table again. Without saying anything, they seemed to come to some kind of silent agreement, the way couples can sometimes.

"You do what you have to do," Mr. Reilly said. "I still think you're going to be wasting Earl's time, but I won't chase him off. How's that sound?"

Once that was settled, we were able to move on to the subject of Elizabeth herself.

"I know you've probably been asked before," Sampson said, "but is there anyone we should be talking to in

Washington? Any friends, or boyfriends Elizabeth ever mentioned? Or for that matter, anyone who might have had some kind of grudge against her?"

Mr. Reilly shook his head and went to put Rebecca down in the raised bassinet by the window.

"I'm not sure Lizzie had a whole lot of friends up there," he said. "We kind of thought Washington was going to be a chance for her to spread her wings, and whatnot, but she never really did cotton to it. Or to the people, for that matter."

"There was one boy," Mrs. Reilly said. "I suspect he's the daddy, and maybe even—" She stopped, at a loss. "Maybe the one you're looking for. But honestly, I have no idea."

Sampson took out his pad and a pen. "Do you have a name?" he asked.

"Russell," she said, while John scribbled it down.

"Russell? Is that a first or last?"

"First," Mrs. Reilly said. "At least, I assume so. Lizzie only mentioned him in a few of her letters. Then he just kind of fell off the radar—last fall, I guess it was."

"I don't suppose you still have any of those letters?" I asked.

The smile I'd seen before came back onto Mrs. Reilly's face. "Oh, honey, I have all of them," she said. "Nobody writes real letters anymore, but Lizzie did. I figured those were worth saving. You just sit tight. I'll go get my Lizzie box."

CHAPTER

25

FOR THE NEXT HOUR, SAMPSON AND I SAT ON THE REILLYS' BACK DECK GOING through an old rosewood box, full of cards and letters Elizabeth had sent her grandparents during her two years in Washington. We put them all in order by postmark, and then started reading.

Most of the letters were on the same pink-and-gray stationery with Elizabeth's monogram at the top. They were usually decorated with funny little doodles and cartoons in the margins, and she always signed off with a heart dotting the i in her name.

At the same time, several of the letters were poignantly honest, about how lonely Elizabeth felt and how hard it was to meet people in the city. What I started to piece together here was a picture of a girl who had been a little naive about the world, a little young for her age, and probably all too vulnerable to a predator.

As for this Russell person, the first mention of him that we found was buried in the middle of a long letter from April of the previous year.

Want to hear something funny? I met a nice man the other day—at the Laundromat, of all places!! You never know, right? He talked to me the whole time I was there, and even offered to pay for my dryer. I thought that was cute, but I told him no thank you, maybe the next time.

And I'll tell you two a secret—I hope there IS a next time. Gentlemen aren't exactly easy to find in our nation's capital!!! Something tells me I'm going to have some extra-extra clean clothes over the next few weeks, ha-ha-ha.

The next mention came a month later, when she wrote to her grandparents that she'd run into "Laundromat guy (whose name is Russell, btw)" and that she'd accepted a dinner invitation this time. A subsequent letter described how Russell had driven her around to see the monuments at night. It was all very chatty, and never offered any other details about where this guy was from, what he did for a living, or who he actually was. Whether Russell had been keeping that information from Elizabeth, or if she was keeping it from her grandparents, I couldn't tell.

What I did know was that by early December, she was lying to them outright.

Dear Granny and Dodo,
I'm writing to tell you something that I'm too chicken

to call and say. It looks like I won't be home for Christmas, after all. We've got exams coming up after the break, and I promised my study group I'd meet three times a week in the meantime.

PLEASE DON'T HATE ME!! And don't even think about coming up here. Xmas wouldn't be the same in DC, and hotels are crazy expensive anyway. Just know that I love you, and I'll be down to visit when I can.

Sending buckets of love,

Lizzie

That letter was dated December 11, which was a full eight days after Elizabeth had already dropped out of nursing school. She also would have been five months pregnant by then—too far along to hide.

And she never did make it home again, either. The last letter she ever sent was a birthday card for Tommy, in late March, where she wrote about classes I knew she wasn't taking, and mentioned several times how much she was looking forward to seeing both of them that summer—presumably after the baby was born.

By the time John and I had read through Elizabeth's correspondence, it was time to go. We didn't have all the answers I might have liked, but what we did have was a new person of interest in this case. As soon as we were in the car and headed back to Savannah, I put out a call to Bree.

I didn't want to wait on this. I didn't want to wait on anything right now. Also, we'd already had one leak in the press about Elizabeth's pregnancy. There weren't a whole lot of people I trusted with these questions any-more.

"I've got a name I want to run through NCIC," I told Bree, while Sampson drove. NCIC is the National Crime Information Center, a database operated by the FBI. Anyone who's ever been arrested, convicted, or detained in the US is in there. It wasn't exhaustive for our purposes, but it was a good place to start. I'd also be going back through Elizabeth's phone records, looking at her mail, and reinterviewing her nursing school faculty—anything I could think of to get a line on this supposed boyfriend of hers.

"What's the name?" Bree said.

"Russell."

"Russell? Is that a first or a last name?"

I smiled in spite of myself. "First, I think, but we should try it both ways."

"You're joking, right?" Bree said. "Do you know how many records that's going to turn up?"

"I wish I was joking," I said. "For whatever it's worth, there's probably going to be a Washington area address sometime in the last two years. This guy may be the father of Elizabeth Reilly's baby. Maybe the guy who killed her, too."

"That's a lot of maybe," she said.

"I know, I know," I said.

But at this point, maybe was better than nothing.

CHAPTER

26

ELIJAH CREEM PICKED UP A SMALL HORSEHAIR BRUSH FROM HIS DESK AND added several dots of liver-colored pigment to his newest mask. The masks themselves came fully finished from the fabricator in Arkansas, but there was something to be said for putting on his own touches. Not a bad way to spend a Friday night, really, considering the pleasure it would get him in the long run. The older and uglier he could make these faces—which was to say, the more invisible on the street—the better.

When the phone rang in his pocket, Creem ignored it. There were very few people he was interested in speaking with these days, much less the variety of scum who bothered to call anymore—lawyers, creditors, and the occasional reporter looking for a new angle on his now fast-fading scandal.

Instead, he applied a thin layer of spirit gum to the mask's upper lip, and spread a mesh-backed mustache carefully into place. Later, when it was fully dry, he'd thread it with silvery gray to go with the wig he'd picked out.

It was only when the phone stopped ringing, then started right back up again that Creem even thought about checking the caller ID, which he did.

It was Josh Bergman. Of course. So much for keeping their distance from each other.

"Josh," he answered. "To what do I owe the dubious pleasure?"

"Hello, Dr. Creem, it's Joshua Bergman. How are you today?"

Bergman's voice was stiff, and ridiculously bright at the other end of the line.

"Ah," Creem said. "I take it you're not alone?"

"Good, good. Glad to hear it. Listen, I have a young lady here in my office. I'm considering signing her at the agency, but I'd like her to have a quick consult with you first," Bergman said. "If you're up for it, of course. I know it's a bit late."

Creem grinned broadly, even as he felt his own pulse start to rise.

Referrals were nothing new between his office and Josh's. Bergman had sent over a good million and a half in business in the past few years, including a handful of "prospects" who had found their way into Creem's bed.

But that was then. This was now. And *everything* had changed in the meantime.

Josh wasn't just upping his own game anymore, was he? Now he was trying to up Creem's as well. Either that, or he was eager to move things along and get the ball back into his own court. It didn't really matter which. The point was—Bergman knew exactly what Creem liked.

"This is a surprise," Creem said. "I assume she's the right type?"

"Yes, yes, lots of potential," Bergman said breezily. "Almost perfect, in fact. But that's where you come in, isn't it, doctor? How about if we swing by your home office around eight o'clock?"

And there it was. The *tour de salaud.* Josh's dirty little twist.

"I see," Creem said. "You want to be here when it happens. What is that, your commission?"

Bergman laughed. "This is why I like working with you, Elijah. You know me so well." He seemed to put his hand over the phone then, and addressed the girl. "Dr. Creem says he can't wait to meet you, sweetie."

It was a brilliant performance, really. There were few people as well trusted in the modeling world as gay men—and who else but Josh Bergman could play sister-friend with these Twiggies in one breath and offer them up for sport in the next?

Creem looked at his watch. It was just after seven.

"Make it eight thirty," he said. "And don't park in the street. I'll leave the garage open. And, Josh?"

"Yes?"

"If you're going to bring her here, you're going to have

to get rid of her. I'm not taking that on," Creem said. "Are we clear?"

"Crystal," Bergman said. "Nice chatting, doctor. We'll see you soon."

CHAPTER

27

AT EIGHT THIRTY EXACTLY, THE ELECTRIC CHIME OUTSIDE DR. CREEM'S LOWER-level waiting room rang. Bergman was almost always hyper-punctual, and tonight was no exception. When Creem opened the door, Bergman was standing there with a statuesque blond beauty on his arm.

He wore a simple two-button blazer over a white shirt, open at the collar. His "uniform," he called it. The young woman wore an LBD—the sort of little black dress that said, I'm a serious model, but I'm not opposed to giving a hand job or two on my way to the top.

"Was I right, or was I right?" Josh said.

"You were right," Creem said, gesturing them both inside. "You're a lovely girl, Miss...?"

"Larissa Swenson, Dr. Elijah Creem," Bergman said, making the introductions, even as his eyes darted around the room. "I don't suppose you have anything to drink down here, Elijah?"

"Thank you so much for seeing me," the girl said. Her hand was warm in his, her skin perfectly soft. "Mr. Bergman tells me you're the best there is."

"Mr. Bergman is a smart man," Creem said, his eyes locked on hers. "Joshua, try the console in the media room down the hall."

He'd already forgotten the girl's name, but she was, in fact, perfect. He could feel that creeping sense of adrenaline up his spine, and in the tension of his jaw. It was the feeling of coming back to life, he now knew. He'd felt the same way on the night of Darcy Vickers.

"My receptionist is off this week," he told the girl. "We'll worry about paperwork later, if it's all the same."

"Fine, fine," Bergman answered for her, coming back into the room with three glasses clutched in one hand and a cut crystal decanter in the other. "Larissa? Elijah? A little drink?"

"No, thank you," the girl answered politely.

"Maybe afterward," Creem said.

"Suit yourself." Bergman poured himself a two-finger shot and turned toward the examination room door. "In here, I assume?" He wasn't even trying to contain his excitement anymore. It was a little funny, and a little infectious, too.

"Are you...both coming in?" the girl asked. She seemed suddenly wary, but Creem gave her his best professional smile. Worked every time.

"It's really in your own best interest," he said. "Josh

will be handling the cost of any procedures, as I'm sure he told you. But if you'd rather decline the consult, now would be a good time to say so."

"No," the girl said quickly. "It's fine." She sounded as if she were convincing herself as much as anything. Talk about blind ambition!

"You're sure?" Creem asked, more for fun than anything. He knew he had her now.

Within a few minutes, all three of them were inside the examination room. Creem stood waiting with a clipboard in hand, as the girl stepped out from the changing cubicle in a thin blue hospital gown, while Josh watched expectantly from the rolling chair in the corner.

"So," Creem said, looking down at the blank intake form in front of him. "What are we thinking about here?"

"Breast augmentation, for sure," Bergman piped up. "We want to be able to book Larissa for print, runway, editorial—all of it. Isn't that right, sweetie?"

"Sure," the girl answered, with another determined smile.

Creem set the clipboard down behind her and took the stainless steel pointer out of his pocket.

"All right, stand up nice and tall for me, with your hands on your hips," he said. He untied the gown in front and stepped back to take a look, playing out the charade to its fullest.

"Nice symmetry. Good elasticity of the skin," he said. "All I'd really need to do is make a small incision, right along here."

He used the pointer to indicate a line under the girl's

breast to illustrate. Not for the girl, though. For Bergman. Josh had been nice enough to arrange this little home delivery. Might as well give him a good show.

"That's where I'd like to cut. Do you see?" Creem said.

"I see," Bergman said. The girl only nodded.

"But let's not limit ourselves," Creem went on. "Should I keep going?"

"Definitely," Bergman said, pouring himself another drink. "Tell me what you're thinking about, Elijah."

Creem stood to the side and used the pointer again, pressing the tip of it into the girl's well-toned obliques.

"Let's say we wanted to go for a little tummy tuck, while we were at it," he said. "In that case, I might try coming in right here, or maybe even here...." Now he plied the lower abdominals under her navel. There was more resistance there, but that meant more payoff—more purchase for his blade when it went in.

"Something like that?" Creem said, ostensibly for the girl, but again it was Bergman who answered.

"Yes," he said, his voice a little smaller than before. "Something like that."

"And how about the thighs?" Creem went on, turning his attention south. "It wouldn't be much to take those down a little." He drew another line, along the psoas, and came to a stop just over the femoral artery. His favorite. "That's where I'd like to cut. Right there."

"Mm-hm," Bergman said. The girl blinked a few times. She seemed confused by now, which was fine.

"I'm just going to make some notes," Creem said, and indicated the gown again. "You can close up there, Justine."

"It's Larissa," she said.

"Right. Sorry. It's just that…you look so much like my daughter. Almost exactly, really."

He put away his pointer and stepped over to the clipboard on the counter behind her. There, he opened a drawer and took out a number eighteen blade. It was perfect for deep cutting, and the custom handle made it feel like an extension of his own arm.

He probably should have stuck with the same cheap steak knife as before, he knew. In fact, it was right there in the drawer where he'd left it half an hour ago. But with skin like this girl had, that would have been like taking a chain saw to porcelain.

He'd just have to go back and rough up his work a bit afterward, to cover his tracks.

"So, what do you think, Josh?" Creem turned to face his friend. "Have you heard enough, or should I keep going?"

"Keep going," Bergman said right away. His eyes were focused on the scalpel in Dr. Creem's hand. He was sitting perfectly still by now, and his voice was little more than a hoarse whisper. "By all means, Elijah. Keep going. Please."

"Are you okay to keep going, too, Justine?" Creem asked.

"Um…Larissa," the girl said again.

"Shh," Creem told her. "It doesn't matter, Justine. Just stand nice and still for me like a good girl. We'll be done here before you know it."

CHAPTER

28

WHEN IT WAS OVER, CREEM AND BERGMAN HAD NO TROUBLE GETTING THE GIRL wrapped up and ready to go. They used latex gloves and a white nylon disaster bag to move her down the hall, a straight shot into the garage and then Bergman's waiting trunk.

It really was like spring break, 1988, all over again, Creem thought. One of those sweet little fillips of time, where the normal rules of the world didn't apply.

Not that they'd been better off with their piece of shit cars and four-digit bank accounts, trawling Fort Lauderdale for thrills. But it had, in fact, been a golden time.

"What's better than gold?" Creem said.

"Platinum, I guess," Bergman said. "Why?"

"That's what this is, Josh. These are our platinum days."

He held up his glass in a toast. They were leaning

against the hood of Bergman's Audi now, drinking sixteen-year-old Hirsch Reserve, while Creem enjoyed a cigar.

"I'll drink to that," Bergman said.

"You'll drink to anything," Creem said, and his friend shrugged at the truth of it. "What are you going to do with her, anyway?"

"Rock Creek Park," he said. "I know a place."

Creem tapped the ash of his Romeo y Julieta, watching it float down like snow onto the concrete garage floor. He felt calm and contemplative, not at all worked up the way Josh was. It pleased him to see Bergman so happy, but it made him a bit nervous, too, the way he seemed to enjoy this. Almost too much, if there were such a thing.

"Just be careful," Creem said. "We're not twenty-two anymore, Josh. We're better than that."

"I'm always careful," Bergman said.

"No," Creem said. "In fact, you're not."

"That's true," Bergman said, and they both laughed. "But I will be, Elijah. Cross my heart. We started this together, and when it's time, we'll end it together. That's a promise."

Creem wasn't entirely sure what Bergman meant. Maybe it was the bourbon talking. Or maybe it meant nothing at all. But for reasons of his own, he let it lie where it was. When the time was right, he'd pick it back up again.

In the meantime, he finished his drink and stood up, indicating it was time for Josh to leave. He was tired. He wanted to go to bed.

And tonight, he was going to sleep like a baby.

CHAPTER

29

WHEN THE PHONE RINGS AT TWO IN THE MORNING IN MY HOUSE, THERE'S A better than average chance that someone's dead. The only question is whose phone—mine or Bree's. She's with the Violent Crimes Branch at MPD, and I'm with Major Case Squad.

On this particular night, the wake-up call came from my side of the bed. I got the details from Sergeant Huizenga before I was even fully awake. Another body had turned up, in Rock Creek Park this time. White. Female. Multiple stab wounds. Hair all cut off.

Another Darcy Vickers.

"I'll be right there," I told Huizenga, and stood up with a Gordian knot in my stomach. If this homicide was what it sounded like, we'd just opened up a whole new dimension on an already-complicated case.

As I headed down the stairs a few minutes later, I was

surprised to see the light of the TV, flashing into the hall from the living room. Nana had her own set in her room, and as far as I knew, the kids were all tucked in.

What I found was Ava, asleep on the couch. She was slumped in a sitting position, with the remote in her hand, and her chin on her chest. The TV was muted while an episode of *Hoarders* played silently on the screen. She was still dressed, too, including the new suede boots Bree had just bought her.

Or maybe she was dressed again. Had she snuck out in the night?

"Ava, you need to go to bed," I said, with a hand on her shoulder from behind.

She didn't move.

"Ava?" I came around and gave her a shake. "Ava!" She stirred then, but barely. Her eyes opened halfway, and she looked at me like I was some kind of stranger.

"Wassup?" she said in a half slur that sent my heart sinking.

"Ava, are you high?" I said. When I turned on the lamp next to the couch, she put a hand up to shield her face. "Let me see your eyes."

"I ain't high," she said, and turned farther away.

But I wasn't messing around now. I sat down and squared her off by the shoulders to face me. "Look at me," I said. "Right now."

Her eyes weren't bloodshot, like I expected, but her pupils looked small, which was maybe even worse.

"Ava, what did you take?" I said.

"Nothin'."

"Was it Oxy? Something else?"

OxyContin is expensive, but there are also plenty of cheap, and more dangerous, knockoff drugs floating around out there. Ava was fourteen now, more than old enough to cross paths with any number of controlled substances on the street, especially considering her background. The few friends I knew about were street kids, who she used to crash with around Seward Square. Was that where she'd been tonight?

"What's going on in here?" Nana said, suddenly appearing in the archway from the hall. Her room is on the first floor of the house, and she's also the world's lightest sleeper.

Ava scooted away from me, to the far end of the couch. "He's saying I done something I didn't do. Why he's always gotta think I'm doing something bad? Damn!"

"Watch your mouth," Nana said. She parked herself on the cushion between us and turned to face Ava. "What is it you didn't do, honey?"

"He's saying I'm high, but I ain't."

"I'm *not*," Nana corrected her, probably because she couldn't help herself.

"And why are you up this late?" I asked. "Did you sneak out?"

"See?" Ava said, pointing at me. "I can't do nothing right for him."

I looked at Nana, feeling more than a little frustrated. I had a crime scene to get to, and it couldn't wait.

"I'm going to get Bree," I said.

"No. Let her sleep. I'll put Ava to bed in my room

and keep an eye on her," she said, eyeballing the keys and necktie in my hand. "You obviously have somewhere to be."

Nana hates my job, a lot of the time. But why was I suddenly feeling like the bad guy here?

"Nana," I said.

"Just go."

I looked Ava over one more time. Was she just sleepy—or something else?

"I'll be back first thing in the morning," I said. "We'll talk about this then."

She rolled her eyes at me but didn't answer. It wasn't until I was almost all the way out of the house that I heard her speak up at all, somewhere behind me.

"It *is* first thing in the morning," she said.

CHAPTER

30

I WASN'T THE FIRST ONE ON THE SCENE THIS TIME. BESIDES THE CRUISERS parked at the picnic area just off Beach Drive in Rock Creek Park, there were several unmarked cars in the lot when I got there.

The action was across the grass, at the edge of the woods, where Rock Creek itself runs through the park's seventeen hundred acres. We'd have kliegs up soon, but for now everyone was working with flashlights and head-lamps.

I found Sergeant Huizenga leaning against the edge of a picnic table, signing off on something for a uniformed officer and talking on the phone at the same time.

"Yes, sir, I know. Yes, yes, we're all over it. We will."

I figured it was either the chief or the mayor himself on the line. Not too many people get a willing "sir" out of Marti Huizenga. She's a good cop, but her temper gets in her way sometimes.

"We're screwed, Alex," she said, just as she hung up. "We could solve this tonight, and we're still screwed. I've got the mayor's command center so far up my ass, I can't even breathe. How did they even know about this yet?"

It was a rhetorical question more than anything. Not all mayoral administrations are created equally, and this one had a strong tendency to step in sooner rather than later. The fact that we were now getting a substantial boost in resources from the city only exacerbated the situation. Increased resources meant increased oversight, accountability, and yes, sometimes meddling. Just one of the reasons I tend to avoid upward mobility at the police department as much as I can. I like working the cases, not the politics, where I can help it.

I followed Huizenga into the woods and down to the creek bed where the body had been left.

Errico Valente was already there, along with Tom D'Auria. Valente was the lead investigator on the Darcy Vickers case, and D'Auria is MPD's Homicide Division captain. It didn't look like anyone was sitting this one out.

At their feet was a nude victim, facedown along the edge of the water. She'd been there long enough for postmortem lividity to set in, with a line of bright red coloration along the lower parts of the body, where her blood had settled by gravity since the time of death.

If the previous case was any indication, she would have also lost quite a bit of blood in the attack, but a quick scan of the ground around her didn't show any signs of it. No loose hair, either, even though she'd obviously been sheared nearly down to the scalp. That told me she'd been brought here from somewhere else.

"Do we have an ID?" I asked.

Valente shook his head. "Jane Doe, so far. Stab wounds are in the chest, abdomen, and upper thigh."

"Just like Darcy Vickers," I said.

"Yeah."

"Shit."

Psychologically speaking, we were looking at a whole new kind of perpetrator now. This was my worst nightmare—someone who seemed to be getting a taste for his craft. The first murder had gone sufficiently well, which meant there was no motivation to stop. Just the opposite. The resting period between Darcy Vickers and this young woman had been statistically very short. If he wasn't already thinking about what he wanted to do next, he would be soon.

Also, it seemed pretty clear now that our killer had a type. The nudity was a departure from the Vickers case, but the physical similarity between the two victims was striking. This girl looked like she could have been Ms. Vickers's daughter, with her pale white skin, remnants of blond hair, and well-proportioned, athletic body.

I thought about the old man we'd seen on the security video from the parking garage where Vickers was found. Could someone like him have gotten her all the way out here? Maybe. Was that what happened?

The girl's back and legs were streaked with mud. By all

appearances, she'd been brought to the top of the bank, rolled down, and left behind. But there was something about the way her right arm was cocked over her head that I didn't quite buy.

"Does that positioning look natural to you?" I asked the others.

"Why?" Huizenga said. "What are you thinking?"

I came around to get a better look, and shined my light down. The girl's hand on that side was closed in a loose fist, except for the index finger, which was extended. Or pointing, maybe, straight downstream.

"How wide's our perimeter so far?" I asked.

"Just what you see," Valente said. There were a handful of crime-scene techs scanning the banks around us, but it didn't look like any of them had gotten more than thirty feet from the body so far.

"What are you thinking, Alex?" Huizenga asked me.

"I'm not sure." Maybe I was thinking too much. Maybe not. "I'm just curious. Walk with me?"

Huizenga and I left Valente and D'Auria with the girl and started picking our way downstream.

It didn't take long, either. After a hundred feet or so, we came around a shallow bend and my light landed on something straight ahead.

It was another body, I realized all at once. It sent a fresh wave of dread straight through me. What the hell were we up against here?

"Oh...God," Huizenga said, and then shouted over her shoulder. "Let's get some backup over here! Now!"

I ran over to check vitals, but even before I knelt down

I could see there was no chance. It was a young man this time. White. Fully clothed. He'd taken a single gunshot to the face, and there were several fresh stab wounds, all around the groin.

Another Cory Smithe.

He'd been left at the water's edge, like our Jane Doe, with one arm extended out over his head. His hand on that side was clenched into a loose fist, and his index finger was pointed back upstream, the way we'd just come.

CHAPTER

31

BEFORE ANYONE REACHED US, HUIZENGA SWUNG AROUND AND SHINED HER light up into the woods on the opposite bank.

"What is it?" I said.

"Shh!"

She put a hand on my arm and pointed. That's when I heard it. Someone was moving through the woods, breaking twigs and going at a good clip over dead leaves and soft ground.

Huizenga started up that way a beat before I did.

"Whoever you are, this is the police. Stop right there! Don't *make* me chase you!"

I've got legs almost twice as long as hers, and by the time I was up the bank and past the tree line, I'd already left her behind. My Glock was out in one hand, my Maglite in the other. Maybe this was just some homeless person we were chasing, or a curious kid, but if not—I wanted this guy, bad.

About twenty yards in, I stopped and listened. Whoever it was, they'd been heading toward the Sixteenth Street side of the park, but now he—she? he?—had turned and was running parallel to the creek instead.

Meanwhile, I could hear Huizenga on the radio, somewhere behind me.

"—any available units to Sixteenth Street, north of Sherrill Drive. We've got an unsub, on foot, possibly headed out of Rock Creek Park—"

I took off at a sprint again, catching a few low branches in the face as I went. The adrenaline was driving me as much as anything right now.

Again, the footfalls ahead of me changed direction—but this time I caught him with the beam of my light. It was a man, anyway, in dark clothes. That's all I saw. He'd just disappeared up and over a small rise, straight ahead.

I was right behind him, and a few seconds later I spilled out onto the pavement of Sherrill Drive. The road curved here, in a hairpin turn on its way out of the park. There was no sign of the guy, though. Had he kept going, back into the woods? Turned and run up the road?

If I'd had another half second, I would have realized why I didn't hear him running anymore. But the next thing I felt was something hard, slamming into the back of my head. My knees buckled, and what little vision I had in the dark blurred out completely. Pain shot down my neck and back as I hit the pavement.

I tried to jump right up, but it was no good. Everything spun. The ground turned sideways, and I was down again.

"Alex?"

I heard Huizenga now, moving through the woods behind me.

"Sixteenth Street!" I shouted back. "Keep going!"

I wasn't even sure about that, but a guess was better than nothing at this point. All I could do was kneel there waiting for some sense of equilibrium to come back while the seconds ticked away—when seconds mattered.

By the time I finally caught up to Huizenga, our guy was gone, gone, gone.

CHAPTER

32

I MISSED A GOOD HALF HOUR WITH THE PARAMEDICS BEFORE HUIZENGA would let me get back to work. There was no concussion, just a gash and a bad headache. Even then she wanted me to go home, but she didn't insist.

By the time I was back in the loop, Chief Perkins was on-site, along with Jessica Jacobs as well. Jacobs was the primary investigator on the Cory Smithe murder. By all indications, we either had one very busy psychopath on our hands, or more likely, two cases that had more to do with each other than we'd previously imagined.

Neither of the latest victims had been identified yet, but it had already been decided that MPD was going to hold a major press conference later that morning, to report out on the situation.

"Are we sure that's a good idea?" I said. "I know I'm coming late to the conversation, but—"

"You also weren't on the receiving end of the mayor's calls," Huizenga told me. "It's done, Alex. This is our reality now. Let's move on. Tell us what you're thinking here."

For better or worse, I'm the go-to profiler in the Homicide Division, not that there's any official title to that effect. Either way, I'd already started working up a few new ideas.

"Assuming we're talking about two killers," I said, "I'd say they're both white, like their victims, just going by statistics. Also bright, and well organized—but angry, too. Not necessarily about the same thing."

It wasn't such a stretch that murder and anger would go hand in hand, but that was the quality that struck me the most about all four of these homicides. None of them were simple or straightforward, in terms of methods. The knife work in particular had gone above and beyond the necessary, in terms of strictly taking lives.

That meant there was some emotion to it. Maybe some level of fantasy playing out here as well. And almost certainly some kind of high-functioning psychosis, which is the slipperiest aspect of all when it comes to pinning down any perpetrator.

Much less two of them.

I gave the others my spiel, and then shut up and listened again while D'Auria divvied the work to be done in the coming hours. If nothing else, we had a pretty good investigative machine up and running.

Valente was going to work IDs on both victims. Jacobs would run the 6 a.m. briefing at headquarters. Chief

Perkins was going to be with the mayor's people for the next few hours, and then D'Auria would be the face of the department for our press conference, while the rest of us stood behind him in a show of force. Sometimes, it is about appearances, and Washington was going to need some reassurance that MPD was on this.

Huizenga and I were both going to start pulling teams together, to go back through every report and witness account, and reinterview every first responder on all four of these murders. We'd also need to start from scratch on our victims' profiles. Maybe there was some connection, some cross-reference we'd missed. There had to be.

Something was attaching these cases to each other. We just had to figure out what it was.

CHAPTER

33

JUST AFTER THE SUN CAME UP, I STOLE AN HOUR I DIDN'T HAVE AND SWUNG back by the house before Ava left for school. Jannie and Ali were already gone when I got there, but Bree had told Ava she'd write her a note for being late. We had to talk.

There were plenty of reasons to be concerned. The smiling, happy Ava from Kinkead's the other night had turned out to be a momentary bit of sunshine. Most of the time these days she was sullen, withdrawn, and al most impossible for me to get through to. What I'd just seen the night before only added another layer.

"I wasn't high," she insisted, almost as soon as we sat her down in the living room. "I wasn't! Serious."

"You were pretty out of it, Ava," I said.

"Whatcha want me to say? Swear to God, okay?"

I didn't know whether to believe her or not. I wanted to, desperately, if only to establish some kind of mutual trust. But Ava was also an easy liar, and that wasn't a pattern I wanted to reinforce. I wanted her to use those smarts of hers for something more than a quick lie and squirming out of trouble.

"Why were you still dressed, in the middle of the night? Did you sneak out?" Nana asked.

For the first time, some of the fire went out of Ava's eyes. She jutted out her jaw and looked at the floor, answering and not answering at the same time.

"We can't have that, Ava," Bree told her. "Not even a little."

"I know," Ava said. "But I wasn't on anything, if that's what you're thinking."

"Either way," Nana said, "things are going to change around here. No more running out to the store, or whatever it is you're doing with your friends around Seward Square. No more dawdling on the way home from school like you've been doing. And *absolutely* no leaving the house by yourself at night. Don't test me on that, Miss Ava."

"Whatever," she said, and started up. "Can I go now?"

"No, you can't go," Bree told her. "Sit down."

Ava sat back again and folded her long arms over her chest. She was two years younger than Damon but just as tall and lanky.

"Ava, do you understand where all this is coming from?" Bree said. "We love you. We don't want anything bad to happen to you. If it did, that would be like something bad happening to us. Does that make any sense?"

Ava tossed off another shrug, but I could see her getting smaller, the longer this went on. She was breathing through her nose, and if I wasn't mistaken, trying not to cry.

So far, I'd been holding back. The truth was, Ava responded better to Nana and Bree than she did to me. But I didn't want to stay silent anymore. I pulled the hassock around and sat down right in front of her. She *was* going to hear me.

"Do you *want* to be part of this family?" I asked her.

"Huh?"

"I'm not saying you have a choice about where you live right now. You're kind of stuck with us for the time being," I went on. "But what I am saying is that there's a *family* in this house, if you want one. Do you?"

Nana, Bree, and I had all agreed that we'd wait until the end of the school year to think seriously about adoption, either way. The foster system was still overseeing Ava's case, and maybe I shouldn't have said anything yet. But then again, I was the one who'd been dragging his feet.

Ava seemed to fold in on herself a little more, pulling her arms tight around her own thin frame. When I saw the first tear start down her cheek, I didn't think about it. I just wrapped her up in a hug and held on tight.

At first, she stiffened up. But then, all at once, she broke. It was like she'd turned into a rag doll in my arms, and she started sobbing like I'd never heard her before. Nana reached over and put a hand on Ava's back. Bree did the same from the other side, and none of us said anything for a long time.

In fact, Ava was the first one to speak.

"I miss my mom," she said against my chest. That was all she got out before she started crying, even harder, as if just saying it was its own kind of pain.

"Of course you do," I said, rocking her gently. "I would, too."

It was heartbreaking. Nobody had ever shown Ava what it meant to really be there for her. She'd had a nonexistent father, and a mother whose drug addiction was stronger than their own relationship had been. But she was also the only mother Ava had ever known. I would have been more concerned if she *didn't* miss her.

We still had a lot of talking to do, and a lot of issues to address together—eventually. For the moment, though, it seemed like what Ava needed more than anything was to cry.

Maybe it was even a step in the right direction.

CHAPTER

34

OUR PRESS CONFERENCE WAS SCHEDULED TO START AT TEN THAT MORNING. For something as big as this, we use the largest all-purpose space at headquarters, which also happens to be the lineup room. The only difference was that we were the ones lining up this time.

Everything was hopping when I got there. We had at least eighty reporters in chairs, and maybe twenty news cameras across the back wall. Channels Four, Five, Seven, and Nine were all going live, I was pretty sure. The nationals were probably here to test the waters, and see what might be worth putting on the teleprompter for Diane Sawyer or Brian Williams that night.

At the front, on a small, low stage, the podium was already covered with a sloppy bouquet of microphones. A heavy blue curtain had been drawn across the one-way glass.

It looked like D'Auria was getting ready to start, so I went and took my place behind him with the other primaries—Huizenga, Jacobs, Valente, and Chief Perkins. It was a deliberate image for the cameras, to be sure. Washington was going to need to know—and see—that MPD was on top of these murders.

At ten o'clock exactly, our public information officer, Joyce Catalone, closed the secure door to the hall and nodded at D'Auria to go ahead. He stepped up to the mikes and started right in.

"Good morning, everyone. I'm Commander Tom D'Auria with the Metropolitan Police Department. I've got a prepared statement regarding the events of the last twelve hours, and then we'll have some time for questions."

D'Auria quickly covered the basics, without getting too specific about methods, weapons, or the exact location where the bodies had been found. It was too early to make any of that publicly available. He did indicate both victims by name, though—Larissa Swenson and Ricky Samuels. That part was news to me. They'd been Jane and John Doe, the last I'd heard.

D'Auria also indicated that Mr. Samuels was a known sex worker, like Cory Smithe before him; but he didn't make any mention of the physical similarity between Ms. Swenson and her equivalent "partner victim," Darcy Vickers.

I would have made the same call. Gay hustlers are a specific group of people who might be able to use information like this to protect themselves. By the same token, there's no effective way to warn and protect a city's worth of attractive blond women. Protect them against doing what, exactly? It's a fine line between what's useful at this point, and what just stirs up panic. Sometimes you have to make your best guess and roll the dice.

As soon as D'Auria reached the end of his statement, the questions started flying. At first they were the usual logistical kind of inquiries. Were the bodies found near each other? Yes. How near? No comment. Did we have any evidence of a connection between the two victims? No comment. Would MPD be updating the press that afternoon? Yes, if there was anything to tell.

But then, after about five minutes, D'Auria called on Bev Sherman from the *Post,* and things took a turn.

"Commander, you mention two possible serial cases associated with these murders—"

"I didn't say serial," D'Auria cut in. "Let me be clear. We have what appear to be second homicides by the same perpetrators, in two previously unrelated cases."

"Fair enough," Bev went on. "My question is about a third incident. The Elizabeth Reilly murder?"

My ears pricked up at that one. Technically, all these cases were on my plate, but I'd just been down to Shellman Bluff. I'd met the Reillys. I'd held that baby girl.

"What about it?" D'Auria asked.

"A new blog by the name of *The Real Deal* has been quite critical of MPD lately, and the Elizabeth Reilly investigation in particular. Most specifically, *The Real Deal* has been focusing on Detective Cross, who I know is coordinating on all three of these cases. I was wondering if the detective himself would care to comment?"

All around the room, people started tapping away on phones and iPads, presumably looking up *The Real Deal*. I also felt a good number of eyes turning my way.

D'Auria held the floor, though. "Bev, I'm not going to respond to rumors on a blog I've never heard of," he answered. "That's something we'll have to look into."

"Let me be more specific," Bev jumped in before he could move on. "Detective Cross, would you be willing to comment on some of the allegations—for instance, that you violated department policy by moving Ms. Reilly's body before a proper examination? Or that you were out socializing on Saturday night while the investigation, arguably, should have been gearing up?"

I was stunned, and thrown off guard, and most of all, steaming goddamn mad. Where was this coming from? What was this blog I'd never heard about before? And who the hell had been watching me and my family go out to dinner?

I had about eighteen responses for Bev, none of them fit to print in her paper. Chief Perkins didn't look too pleased, either. He was giving Joyce Catalone a signal to wrap this thing up.

"I can only repeat what Commander D'Auria already said," I finally answered. "Until we get a look at the material in question—"

"So, you're not familiar with *The Real Deal*?" someone else asked.

"Believe me, I will be in about ten minutes," I said. It

got a few chuckles around the room, and then Joyce was there at the podium.

"Ladies and gentlemen, that's all we have time for this morning. The investigative team has other business to attend to, but we will be updating you throughout the day, if there's anything to tell."

It's a thin charade, but absolutely preferable to letting the press conference spiral out of control. We'd come in trying to play offense, and already we were back on our heels.

Things weren't looking so good for the department right now. And maybe even worse for me.

35

FIVE MINUTES AFTER THE PRESS CONFERENCE LET OUT, OUR CORE TEAM WAS up in Chief Perkins's office on the fifth floor.

"What the hell just happened down there?" Perkins wanted to know.

"We got coldcocked by some random blogger," D'Auria said. "A million nobodies tapping away out there, and you never know which one's going to blow up until you're picking shrapnel out of your ass."

Perkins didn't keep a computer in his office, so Huizenga opened her laptop on the big round conference table. After a quick Google, she had *The Real Deal* up in front of her, and we all gathered around.

"Oh God," she said. "One of these."

The blog had a simple masthead—THE REAL DEAL, in a plain black font. Beneath that was a subheading, "Who's Policing the Police?"

In the margin, there was a numbered list of twenty-three MPD officers, each one clickable to some other page. I recognized several names right away. They were all cops who had been arrested in the last year, for anything from petty theft to domestic abuse, and even one murder. There was also a small map of the city's police districts, with different colored dots, presumably corresponding to various types of crimes.

The most recent blog entry was dated that morning. Its title was "America's Most Dangerous City?" Beneath that, "Murder Season in DC." And then, "Detective Cross: Asleep at the Wheel?"

"Looks like this guy's got a crush on you," Huizenga said. My name was clickable, like the others, and she hovered her pointer over it. "You mind?"

"I can hardly wait," I said.

What opened up then was a whole page dedicated to yours truly. It included my CV with the department, an old ID photo, a list of current and previous cases, and several other small images.

The first of those was a picture that had been taken from below, on Vernon Street, just as I'd gone to pull Elizabeth Reilly's body out of the window where she'd been hanging. Her face was even fuzzed out, in some kind of twisted nod to journalistic propriety.

The other picture showed Kinkead's restaurant from the outside. Beneath that was a screen capture of a tweet that had apparently been sent to go with it:

Three dead, and where's DC's favorite cop? Out to dinner. More like out to lunch! Priorities, anyone? #incompetentcops

Finally, there was a long screed at the bottom, all about how I was the wrong one to be coordinating on these cases, and blowing it at every turn, apparently.

"Who the hell is this guy?" Valente asked.

The blog did have a contact page, but when Huizenga pulled it up, it gave us everything *but* a name. You could e-mail *The Real Deal* with questions, tips, or other thoughts about the job MPD was doing. There were invitations to follow *The Real Deal* on Twitter, or like it on Facebook, or "join the conversation" on something called NewsNet. For someone who had just gotten started, this so-called reporter was clearly going all in.

And I was starting to think I knew who he was. Or at least that we'd met.

"We need to get him out in the open," I said to Perkins. "Let me run a subpoena on the blog's ISP records, and see who's attached to the account."

I was remembering the bearded jag-off from the morning Cory Smithe's body had been found. This was the guy with no press credentials who had refused to give me his name.

Perkins shoved back in his chair.

"Alex, I've got to ask you. Did you pull Elizabeth Reilly's body before the ME reached that scene?"

"I did," I told him. I wasn't going to start tap dancing for the chief right now. It was all in the report, anyway.

"And, were you out to dinner that night, like it says?"

I could feel the heat coming up into my face. "I'm sorry, Chief, but what the hell does it matter?"

"In and of itself? It doesn't. But if he's telling the truth, he can say whatever he wants," Perkins told me. "The last thing I need is a questionable subpoena on a guy like this, especially if he's got any kind of audience."

"If he doesn't now, he will after that press conference," Huizenga said, closing her laptop. "Stand by for the shit storm, everyone."

"See what you can find out on your own," Perkins said. "Pull whoever you need for this, but please, Alex—step lightly. We're fighting a war of public perception right now. Approval of the department's at an all-time low."

Chief Perkins is no hysteric. He usually doesn't give a hoot about public perception, especially not at the expense of an investigation. But the reality was, we were operating at expanded levels these days, and that hinged on a good relationship with the mayor, who had his own political angles to consider. The fact that he and his people had stayed away from the press conference meant they were already feeling skittish about this.

"I'm sorry, Alex," Perkins said. "It is what it is."

"Not a problem," I told him. "I'll find him anyway."

That was the answer the chief needed right now, and hopefully the one that was going to keep me as far from under his thumb as possible.

I just hoped it was also true.

CHAPTER

36

PULL WHOEVER YOU WANT. **THAT'S WHAT THE CHIEF HAD SAID. SO I STARTED** close to home.

Even on my way down the stairs, I was on the phone with Bree, asking her to take a look at *The Real Deal,* and meanwhile, to keep digging on the Elizabeth Reilly case.

When I hit the third-floor hall, I called Sampson. He was in court that day, but I left a long message and asked him to swing by the house later on if he could. Both of them were already invested in Elizabeth's murder. I didn't see any reason not to make it official.

As soon as I was back at my desk, I pulled up *The Real Deal*'s contact page again and fired off a quick e-mail.

To whom it may concern: Please contact me at your earliest convenience. Thank you, Detective Alex Cross, MPD.

I was going to play it civil for the time being. I'd even play it nice if I had to, but only as a means to an end. This guy had been putting eyes on me and my family, and that's a line you don't cross.

Next up, I wound my way around the little warren of cubicles in our office to find Jarret Krause at his desk. Krause was one of Major Case Squad's newbies, a Flatbush, Brooklyn, boy whose wife had taken a job working in their congressman's DC office the previous fall. Already he'd made a name for himself, tracking down two very slippery violent offenders online—one serial rapist who connected with his victims on Facebook, and an eighteen-year-old thug from Shaw who had robbed and killed a seventy-year-old liquor store owner, then tried to sell a case of Cristal on Craigslist. Someday, these punks are going to wise up to their own virtual footprints. In the meantime, we've got guys like Krause to go around and scoop them up.

"'Sup, Alex?" he said, when I showed up over the wall of his ridiculously tidy cubicle. For that, I was giving him another six months.

"Have you heard of this blog, *The Real Deal*?" I asked.

"Yeah." His fingers hit the keyboard in front of him and he brought it up. "This guy sucks," he said. "And he's seriously hating on you, too. How can I help?"

I was a little surprised at how much Krause already knew, but maybe I shouldn't have been. Bad news travels about as fast as sound around that department.

"I need a name," I said. "The blog's hosted at DC Access, but Perkins doesn't want to do an admin subpoena if we can avoid it. I was hoping—"

Already, Krause was scanning pages. "Yeah," he said. "He's hitting all the major platforms. Shouldn't be too hard."

"I'd appreciate it," I said.

"You want me to stop there, or keep going?" he asked.

I wasn't going to say no. "Define 'keep going,'" I said.

"Well, for instance—this." He came back to the latest blog entry, and pointed at the screen. "Twenty-six comments since seven this morning. These are the people you want to keep an eye on. Ninety-nine percent of the time, they're going to be nobodies. But then once in a while, one of them will know something they shouldn't, like a bullet caliber, or time of death, or whatever. That can be gold."

"I'll take it," I said. "Anything you can do. But first— get me a name."

"A name, to the face, to the asshole," he said. "No prob. I'll get back to you by the end of the day."

CHAPTER

37

BY 9 P.M. I'D PUT IN A FULL WORKDAY, FOLLOWED BY A LATE DINNER WITH the family, homework with Ava, more homework with Jannie, and a chapter of *Percy Jackson* with Ali before bed.

I wasn't going to say no to the six-pack of Cigar City Brown Ale that Sampson showed up with, just as Nana Mama and the girls were settling in for an episode of *Once Upon A Time*. John, Bree, and I took the beer up to my office in the attic and got back to work.

"Catch me up," John said, twisting off a cap. "Where are we?"

Bree unwrapped the red figure-eight string from a big manila envelope and took out the case materials she'd picked up that afternoon. A tan clip folder and several black-and-white crime-scene photos spilled onto her lap.

"I've been cross-referencing cases all day, and I found

this. I can't say it's definitively tied to Elizabeth Reilly, but it seems like a red flag, anyway."

She picked up the crime report and looked it over as she kept talking.

"The name's Amanda Simms. Ran away from an abusive home in West Virginia at age fifteen. Then no sign of her at all for eleven months, until a maid found her body in the tub at an Econo Lodge in Takoma Park. That was four and a half years ago."

"Four and a half years?" Sampson said. "What's the supposed connection to Elizabeth Reilly?"

Bree turned one of the crime-scene photos around to show him. John looked like he felt sick to his stomach.

"She was pregnant," Bree said. "The autopsy showed heavy doses of Rohypnol and morphine. All indications are that she was drugged, cut open, and left for dead."

"And the baby?"

"Never found."

"Jesus." John scrubbed at his eyes with a thumb and forefinger. We'd all had long days.

"So basically," I said, "we've got a young girl, away from home for the first time, and pregnant. All of that's in line with Elizabeth Reilly."

"What about this phantom boyfriend, Russell?" John asked.

Bree shook her head. "I've got nothing. Presumably, that's not his real name."

"But let's assume he's part of the picture," I went on. "Maybe Elizabeth finds out about Amanda somehow. She figures out her boyfriend is a monster, and she's carrying his baby. That could go a long way to explain why she'd go all the way to Georgia to induce labor."

"For that matter, maybe Amanda's not the only other one," Bree said. "I'm still looking."

After a long stretch of silence, Sampson spoke up again.

"You said something else on the phone this morning. This blogger. What's his deal? And why's he hating on you?"

"Good question," I said, and pulled up *The Real Deal* on my desktop. There was a new entry now, "MPD Whiffs Its Own Press Conference." It had been posted at four that afternoon, and it already had ninety-two comments. Word was definitely getting out on this thing.

"He's either got a vested interest in Elizabeth Reilly, or against me," I said. "Or both."

"Or," Sampson said, "maybe he's just looking to make a name for himself—trying to establish the blog and get some attention with a couple of big stories."

"Yeah, well, he's got my attention," Bree said. She was at least as put out by the whole thing as I was—most especially by that picture of Kinkead's from the night we were there.

"Alex, let me take a run at this guy," John said. "You've got five homicides on the line. Six now, if we're counting Amanda Simms."

"Thanks. I'd welcome the help, actually," I said. "Not to mention, you can be damn scary when you want to be."

Sampson just grinned. "What's the name on the account?" he asked.

"Still waiting on that."

It wasn't until close to eleven, when John was just getting up to leave, that I finally heard from Krause. It was perfect timing, actually.

"Sorry to take so long," he said. "But I tracked a couple of tweets back to a phone number with a DC exchange. No real address on the account, just a PO box, but I do have a name for you."

I grabbed a pencil off my desk and the nearest piece of paper—a takeout menu from Fusion Grill.

"Go ahead."

"The name is Ron Guidice," he said, and spelled it for me, then gave me the number. "You want me to bring him in?"

"No, but thanks," I said. It seemed like everyone wanted a piece of this guy, which was fine with me. I tore off the corner of the menu and put it into Sampson's very large outstretched hand. "We've got it from here."

38

HOURS AFTER SAMPSON LEFT, I WAS STILL AWAKE. SOMETHING WAS BUGGING me, and I couldn't figure out what it was. That name, Ron Guidice, was sticking in my head for some reason. Was it familiar? Or did I just want to think so?

Finally, I got out of bed and headed back up to the office.

"Where are you going?" Bree asked me, still half asleep

"I just want to check something," I said. "I'll be right back."

Up at my desk, I got online and logged into the MPD case files. Members of Homicide have the highest level of clearance on investigative reports, which meant I could access the system from any departmental computer, including the laptop I had at home.

After a quick search, the only place I found Guidice's

name was in a police report from six years earlier. And in fact, he hadn't committed any crime. He was the named next of kin for a woman who had died during a police action in Chinatown.

I remembered the case now. It came back to me with a creeping sort of dread. This one was not a good memory.

I'd been heading up an investigation on a midlevel arms runner who'd been playing both sides of the fence, providing automatic weapons to rival gangs in Southeast and Northwest DC. Word had been coming down from more than one informant that a major brawl was on its way. When you're talking about automatic weapons, crossed with two crews who had a history of disregard not just for each other but for innocent bystanders as well, it's best not to take too many chances. Even though we were still hoping to ID this guy's upper-level contacts, I made the call to bring him in, ASAP.

Now, sitting there at my desk, I didn't need to reread the report in front of me to remember what happened next.

The thug's name was Marco Bruillo, with a last known address at an expensive studio apartment on H Street. On the night in question, Bruillo had been tracked there, and the plan was to make the arrest inside, as quietly as possible.

When we arrived, though, Bruillo was just on his way back out. We had no choice but to take him right there on the sidewalk, or risk losing him altogether.

What we couldn't know was that two of his own people were parked and waiting for him across the street. As soon as we had Bruillo up against the wall, they opened fire from their vehicle.

It was the fastest-moving shootout I've ever found myself in. Within fifteen seconds, it was over. Bruillo was dead, but so were three other bystanders, all of them waiting in line to buy movie tickets at the theater next to his building.

In the end, forensics had shown that two of those bystanders had been killed with automatic weapon fire. But the third—a woman by the name of Theresa Filmore—was accidentally shot and killed by one of my fellow MPD detectives. It was a tragedy, no two ways about it.

The city had taken full responsibility, and settled out of court with Ms. Filmore's named next of kin—her fiancé, a man by the name of Ronald F. Guidice.

I'd never forgotten about Theresa Filmore, but it wasn't until I looked back at that file that I realized why Guidice's name had rung a bell.

Now I knew. And everything was starting to make a little more sense.

Part Two
TIPPING POINT

39

NIGHT FISHING WAS ALL THE COVER RON GUIDICE NEEDED TONIGHT. THERE WAS no necessity for a pseudonym, or physical camouflage, or even keeping out of sight, for that matter. From the middle of the wide saltwater channel where he sat, he could watch the little stilt house on the shore all he liked. Even if the cop in the driveway happened to look over and notice him, all he'd see was some goober out trying to hook a few snapper in the dark.

It was a good time to be away from DC, too. Guidice had started to pull back the covers now, and chances were high that Alex Cross had begun to figure out who he was. Which was fine. As long as Guidice controlled the flow of information, then he controlled Alex, too.

In the meantime, he kept his rod in the water and his eyes on the house at the shoreline, waiting for his gut to tell him it was time to move.

The fishing gear was the cheapest he'd been able to find, at an Outdoor World near Savannah. The boat had been even easier to procure. Shellman Bluff wasn't the kind of place where folks locked up their stuff at night, much less a dinged-up old aluminum dory like this one.

On the floor of the boat was a black-market M16. The detachable night scope sat on Guidice's lap. In the pouch pocket of his gray hoodie pullover, he also had a small Kahr 9mm with six rounds in the magazine. If everything went to plan, that was four more rounds than he'd need.

The only real variable here was time. The lights in the house had gone out at eleven o'clock. They'd come back on briefly at twelve thirty, and then again just after two. Such was life with a newborn baby.

Finally, when the house went dark a third time, Guidice set down the rod and pulled the M16 onto his lap. He could feel the adrenaline sharpening his focus as he raised the rifle to his shoulder and pressed his cheek against the hollowed-out stock.

Through the green and black night-vision lens, the cop's face came clear. He was sitting behind the wheel of his McIntosh County cruiser, looking bored and drumming his fingers on his jaw while he watched the house.

Guidice took a deep breath. He centered his main targeting chevron over the man's forehead. Then he squeezed off one fast round.

The rifle's suppressor allowed a small pop of sound, nothing more. Simultaneously, to the eye, a snowflake-shaped hole opened in the cruiser's windshield. The man inside stiffened for a fraction of a second, before his head lolled softly to the side. It looked like he'd fallen asleep as much as anything else.

For another count of thirty, Guidice kept his eye pressed to the scope. When the cop didn't move, he lowered the rifle and let it slip over the side of the boat, into the water. Finally, he took up his oars and started in toward shore.

It wasn't far to row. Within a minute, maybe two, the little dory was scraping across soft sand and gravel at the water's edge. Guidice stepped over the bow and onto the property, keeping his boots dry as he pulled the 9mm out of his pocket.

He went straight for the police cruiser first. The cop inside was no issue, that much was clear. Instead, he went to the passenger side and took the man's hat off the seat, as well as the uniform jacket folded neatly over the headrest.

He slipped both of them on as he rounded the house toward the back. The front door had a line of sight to the neighbors, but the only view from the rear deck was out toward the yard, and the dark tidal marsh beyond that.

Guidice paused at the back kitchen door, just long enough to pull the cop's hat a little lower over his eyes, and to check the pistol's magazine—a quick tap with the butt of his hand. Then he rapped hard, several times on one of the door's small glass panes.

Almost right away, a light went on from somewhere inside. The Reillys were sleeping light these days, no doubt.

A moment later, another light came on, in the kitchen this time. Through the sheer curtain hanging over the glass, Guidice could see Tommy Reilly tying the belt of a plaid bathrobe around his considerable middle as he came around the corner.

"Mr. Reilly?" he called through. "Sorry to disturb you, but we've got a bit of a problem out here. Would you mind opening up for a second?"

CHAPTER

40

JOSH BERGMAN KEPT IT SIMPLE TONIGHT. JUST A DARK PAIR OF JEANS, a long-sleeved tee, and an excruciatingly boring Gap blazer. It was important to look presentable, but there was no sense in spending major cash to get it done. It was all going in the incinerator by the end of the night, anyway.

He kept his change of clothes—his *real* clothes—in the trunk. Ian Velardi dot-print shirt, Armani trousers, and the custom Italian slip-ons from Vicenza, along with a change of underwear, and his Rolex Submariner.

For after.

Just before ten o'clock, he pulled his silver Audi A7 off Water Street and into the fenced waterfront parking lot. As he came around to the back, he spotted a single silhouetted male figure standing against the chain link and looking out at the Potomac.

Bergman came to a stop and lowered the passenger window.

"Travis?" he said.

The boy turned around and came closer. "Are you Bill?" he asked.

"I sure am," Bergman said. "Get in."

He pointed at the bank envelope on the seat as the young hustler opened the door. There were two one hundred dollar bills inside, but the kid didn't check. He just stuck it in his back pocket and sat down.

"Nice car," he said.

"Isn't it?" Bergman said.

He was thin. Maybe a little too thin, but cute, with a sexy little gap in his smile. His clothes were preppy-slouchy, a half-tucked oxford in ripped jeans. But it was the bright green limited edition Nike kicks that gave him away. This boy was obviously pulling down more cash than his friends with their little jobs at Abercrombie and Pizzeria Paradiso.

Bergman pulled out of the lot and headed north, toward MacArthur. He had Elvis Costello on the stereo. "Pills and Soap." A bit of vintage gold to go with his great mood.

For a while, he drove upriver and they played small talk. The boy was from Maine. He hadn't seen any good movies lately. He thought Mumford and Sons were just *awesome*.

Eventually, the kid took a breath and looked around.

"Where are we going?" he said. "This is like, practically Maryland."

"It is Maryland," Bergman said. "I know a place. How do you feel about outside? Your profile didn't really say either way."

The kid shrugged. "I like outside," he said. He put a hand on Bergman's knee as he leaned in to bump up the stereo's volume. "Whatever you're into."

"Awesome," Bergman said.

At the little one-lane stone bridge, he took a left off MacArthur, crossed over, and doubled back, half a mile down Clara Barton Parkway. The parking lot was just off the road, but low enough to offer some privacy. The only time anyone used it was during the day, and not even that much then.

"Here we are," he said, killing the engine. "Let's go for a walk."

If the kid had any second thoughts, he was keeping them to himself. Probably thinking about his next pair of kicks instead.

They got out and headed down into the woods. Bergman walked just behind him on the little footpath, his hand in his pocket, touching himself through the cloth.

"Down here?" the boy asked.

"Actually, stop right there," Bergman said. They were at the midpoint in the woods, between the lot and the canal down the hill. "This is good."

The boy turned around in the dark and stepped up toward him. He reached out and ran a hand over Bergman's crotch.

"Dude. You're ready to go, aren't you?" the kid asked.

"I am," Bergman said. "I really am."

It was likely the boy never even saw the gun. Bergman took one quick step back to avoid any splatter, and pulled the trigger.

The kid's shadow dropped to the ground unceremoniously, like a sack of whatever. Bergman dropped, too, onto his knees.

The knife was out next. He drove it in—once, twice, three times, fast... then again—four, five, six... seven... eight...

He lost count somewhere after that, as the rising swirl of it all caught him up, and then seemed to reverse direction, funneling back down into a final, excruciating explosion of pleasure—literal and figurative.

It was done. Again.

Bergman fell back onto his elbows. His breath was ragged. The inside of his pants was wet.

One by one, his senses seemed to float back into place. There was the boy on the ground. The sound of traffic on the highway. A slight metallic taste in his mouth.

As his head cleared, logic moved back in. He couldn't stay here, of course. He had to keep moving.

It was just a quick drag down to the canal, where he emptied the boy's pockets and rolled him into the water.

Then he made his way back up to the parking lot, popped his trunk, and changed quickly, bagging everything else for disposal.

By the time he was behind the wheel of his car again, heading south into the city, Bergman had come full circle and then some. He felt better now than he could remember feeling, ever.

And the night was young. It was time to take this party somewhere else.

CHAPTER

41

BY MIDNIGHT, BERGMAN WAS BACK DOWNTOWN AND READY FOR THE NEXT PART
of his evening. He got out at the corner of Seventh and
D, handed his keys to the valet, and headed inside.

The three-tiered lobby of the Woolly Mammoth
Theatre was jumping, with the annual Fashion Fights
Hunger fundraiser. They had the whole place awash in
yellow light, with bright pink theatrical spots throwing
shards of magenta around the room. It wasn't exactly flattering, but it was festive, anyway. The deejay booth at the
far end was spinning salsa, and it was a hoot to see some
of these industry suits trying to shake the sticks out of
their asses on the dance floor.

Bergman hit the bar first, then worked his way up to
the third level, the better to take in the scene.

"Joshua!" a voice screamed out as soon as he hit the

landing. He turned around and saw a big pair of red lips coming at him, with his friend Kiki attached.

"Incoming!" she said, and kissed him full on the mouth. "How's my darling boy doing? It's been forever and a half!"

Bergman nodded at the mostly finished pink concoction in her hand. "I think I have some catching up to do," he said.

"Oh, you do," she said. "You totally do. Garth and Tina are going to want to know you're here, too."

Unlike with Elijah, Joshua Bergman's recent troubles in the press had only upped his stock. He was now Washington's bad boy of style and fashion, it seemed. Well, if the shoe fit, why not?

He downed the rest of his watered half-rate Scotch and wagged the glass at Kiki. "Would you?" he said. "I have to make a call."

"I would," she said. "And stand by for Garth and Tina. I'm going to bring them back up here. I think Tina has coke, which is so freaking retro, I can't stand it."

As soon as she was gone, Bergman took out his phone and hit speed-dial one. He stood at the rail, watching the party and waiting for Elijah to answer.

"Josh?"

"Why do you always say my name like it's a question?" Bergman said. "Don't you trust caller ID?"

"I don't trust my mother, Josh. Why would I trust my phone?"

Bergman loved the way they could just fall into it. Elijah acted like he didn't care, Josh acted like he did, and both of them knew where the other was coming from. It was comfortable.

"Well, guess where I am," he said.

"Someplace loud."

"It's the Fashion Fights Hunger thing. You should come down and have a drink with me. It's been a big night."

"Rain check," Creem said. "I'm working at my desk, and I don't want to put all of this away right now."

Bergman felt a bubble of excitement rise up from his belly, and into his throat. It came out as a giggle.

"Let me try that again," he said. "It's been a *very* big night, Elijah, and I mean that in a way that only you could appreciate. I thought it would be nice to have a drink together."

Elijah didn't answer, or say anything at all for a very long time. Kiki, Garth, and Tina were on their way up the stairs now, and Bergman gave them a just-a-minute finger before he walked farther up the mezzanine.

"Elijah?" he said. "Are you still there?"

"I'm here," Creem said. "And you need to slow down, my friend. This isn't a race."

"It's not an *anything*," Bergman said. "Isn't that part of the beauty? It's whatever we want it to be. Just like life."

He could feel the adrenaline, or endorphins, or whatever it was running through his veins as hot as that salsa music down below. He even did a few giddy steps while they talked. Back, forth, cha-cha-cha.

"Well, enjoy yourself," Creem said. "I'll catch up with you soon."

Bergman smiled. "I hope that's a double entendre," he said. "Because just for the record, Elijah—if this *were* a race? I'd be winning."

"Good night, Josh."

"Love you, Elijah. Talk soon."

CHAPTER

42

THE NEXT DAY WAS ONE OF THE WORST I'VE EVER HAD ON THE FORCE.

It started just before the 6 a.m. briefing at headquarters. With all three of these cases in full go mode, the brass had shifted our morning meetings up to the Joint Operations Command Center on the fifth floor. Everything to do with these homicides was now tracked in real time through the JOCC, so we would always know who was working which leads, and if anyone had made any progress. The briefings were a chance to cross-reference any police action from the overnight shift against our open investigations, to see if anything might prove relevant.

When I got there that morning, Tom D'Auria was waiting in the fifth-floor hall to head me off with some very bad news. Word had just come in that Jeannette and Tommy Reilly, as well as the sheriff's deputy assigned to their house in Shellman Bluff, had all been killed some-time in the last eight hours.

"All three of them were shot," D'Auria told me. "But they're reporting two different calibers, so some of this is a little up in the air. CIC just got it a few minutes ago."

I nodded, but I wasn't hearing much. My chest had gone tight, and I felt like I couldn't breathe until I got an answer to my next question.

"What about the baby?" I said.

"Missing," Tom told me.

It was a one-word punch in the stomach. D'Auria ducked his chin, just to give me a moment of space. He knew I was invested here.

"What can I do?" I said.

"Not much," he said. "FBI's already on it. They're working with McIntosh County, and the state troopers. The AMBER Alerts are up. Transportation hubs in all contiguous states are already covered."

"There has to be something," I said.

"You can give a call down to the Atlanta field office if you want, or the Savannah satellite office, if anyone's there. They may want to talk to you. But other than that, it's going to be a waiting game at this point."

They were coming at it aggressively. That was good. If and when they determined Rebecca had been taken across any state lines, it would automatically go federal, and they were already set up for that.

I just hoped it was all enough. Without knowing how long ago she'd been taken, it was hard to say.

Meanwhile, the shift change was filing past us into the

JOCC. I saw a lot of bleary-eyed cops, either because they were just finishing for the night, or just getting started for the day.

"I'm going to cover all of this inside," D'Auria told me. "I figured you'd want a heads-up."

"I appreciate it, Tom."

"If you need to talk—"

"I'm good," I said. "I'll be right in."

Every cop I know gets overwhelmed sometimes. It's nothing to be ashamed of. I always encourage my people to talk it out when they need to. We've got an employee assistance program for that, but there's also supervisors, coworkers, shrinks, clergy, whatever. You just have to choose someone, is what I tell people.

Sometimes I take my own advice, and sometimes I don't.

I walked down the hall and locked myself in the handicapped bathroom by the stairs. I just needed a minute to breathe.

This wasn't my fault. Not technically. I knew that. But it was also true that I'd had more of a chance to stop it from happening than just about anyone else. I could have pushed harder to get Rebecca into protective services. I could have worked more closely with McIntosh County.

But I didn't. I'd made a perfectly justifiable call, on paper. Now three more people were dead, and one very little girl was missing. Again.

I turned on the sink and splashed some water on my face, as cold as I could make it. When I looked up again, I guess I caught sight of myself too fast or something. I couldn't help it—my fist came up and smashed the mirror into shards. It was a dumbass move, the kind of thing I'd yell at anyone else for pulling. All it got me was a bunch of broken glass and some bloody knuckles.

And the kicker was—my crap day had only just begun.

43

I SPENT THE MORNING PULLING TOGETHER EVERYTHING I HAD ON THE REILLY family and faxing it down to the FBI in Atlanta. I gave them what we had on Amanda Simms as well, for whatever that was worth. We still didn't know if both of these "pregnant girl" cases were linked or not.

Beyond that, I spent way too much time trying to get someone to answer at the Bureau's Savannah satellite office, but that was just an exercise in frustration. Hopefully, they were all out in the field, getting the job done.

The one piece of relative good news was that Rebecca had been taken at all. Given the three homicides, it meant that the kidnapper—or someone—wanted to keep her. That was better than the alternative. At least it left open the possibility that she could still be found.

Then, while I was sitting on hold with Savannah for

the third time that morning, I heard my name called out from somewhere else in the squad room.

I stood up and looked around. Across the cubicles, Huizenga was standing in the door of her office with Jessica Jacobs. When she motioned me over to join them, I pointed at the phone in my hand.

"Hang up!" she yelled back, and headed inside.

I didn't have to think hard about what this might be. Jacobs was the lead investigator assigned to Cory Smithe and Ricky Samuels, the two young hustlers who had been killed. I felt numb walking over to Huizenga's office, like there wasn't room for anything else right now. Not that it mattered.

Huizenga had her head in her hands when I came in. Jacobs was on the phone, scribbling notes on a yellow legal pad.

"Marti?" I said.

"Number three," she said, without looking up. "Young white male, single gunshot, multiple stab wounds, no ID."

"A jogger found the kid," Jacobs said, with a hand over her phone. "Way up at Lock Seven on the C and O Canal."

"Lock Seven," I said. "That's Maryland, isn't it?"

Huizenga nodded. "Montgomery County's already on the scene. You may see the Bureau before the day's over, too. I'll talk to D'Auria. This is the chief's call, but I'd rather not open this up if we don't have to."

Three murders committed in a similar fashion put this case squarely into serial territory. That's usually when the

FBI starts asking questions. They can be hugely useful, given the resources the Feds have, but they can also be an impediment, especially if anyone starts getting turfy about this stuff. I've been on both sides of that fence, and I know.

In the meantime, before I headed up to Lock Seven, what I needed was a vending machine, a cup of coffee, and a reset button for my brain.

I got two out of three, anyway.

44

RON GUIDICE STOOD IN THE FRONT HALL OF THE OLD PLACE AND LOOKED around. The house was like some kind of time capsule from 1979. There was gray shag carpet on the floor. A powder-blue toilet in the bathroom.

Still, it was solid, with three bedrooms, a backyard, and plenty of privacy. Also just ninety minutes from the city. The perfect hiding place for his growing family.

"Don't mind all these boxes," the rental lady said. "I have one of those Got Junk trucks coming this afternoon. Unless you see anything you'd like to keep."

"Just the furniture. Everything else can go," Guidice told her.

The woman, Mrs. Patten, stopped to look down into the Snugli, where Grace was fast asleep against his chest. She'd been fussy in the car but had tired herself out by the time they got to Virginia.

And it was Grace now. Not Rebecca. Not ever again.

"They're just little gifts from God, aren't they?" Mrs. Patten said. "How old?"

"She's three weeks today," Guidice said. "And yes, they really are. I fell in love the second I laid eyes on her."

That much was true. Mrs. Patten smiled, the way women always did when men showed even a hint of softness. Like he'd just done her some kind of favor.

"Would you like to see the back?" she asked.

"Please."

He followed her into a large eat-in kitchen, with a picture window over the formica table. Outside there was a wooden swing set at the back of the overgrown yard. It didn't look fit to use, but he could fix it up. Beyond that, Guidice could see a horse paddock through the trees. Half a dozen brown mares were munching on the spring grass.

Emma Lee was going to love it here. They all were, even Lydia, once she got used to it.

"I hope you don't mind vintage," Mrs. Patten said, "if that's what you call all this. Mr. Schiavo seemed to have stopped shopping quite a while ago."

"It's fine."

"A pity, really, how he died so suddenly. But I think he'd be happy to know there was a young family moving in. What do you do, Mr. Henderson?"

"I'm a journalist," Guidice said. "But I'm looking to take some time off."

Like Grace, he had a new name here, too. He'd used pseudonyms before, never as a byline, but sometimes to cover his tracks when he was chasing down a story. Paul Henderson was the one he'd used the most often, and the one for which he had passable identification, including a rarely used credit card. It was enough to secure the house, in any case.

"How about your wife?" the rental agent asked brightly. "Will she be staying home as well?"

"My wife isn't with us anymore," Guidice said. "We lost her on the night Grace was born."

Mrs. Patten stopped and put a hand to her mouth, covering the little O that had just formed there. "Oh my lord. I'm so sorry. I had no idea."

"Of course," Guidice said. "I'm just looking for somewhere quiet where my mother, my daughters, and I can put our lives back together in private."

She looked like she might actually cry. Guidice hoped not.

"How old is your other daughter?" she asked.

"Emma Lee's four and a half. She misses her mama, but she's very excited about being a big sister."

"And you have your mother as well. That's a blessing. I'm sure she's wonderful with the girls."

"Yes," Guidice said. He glanced down at the soft little angel curls on the top of his daughter's head. "Because there's nothing more important than family. Isn't that right, Grace?"

45

LOCK SEVEN ON THE CHESAPEAKE AND OHIO CANAL IS ORDINARILY A LITTLE recreational area just off the Clara Barton Parkway. Today, it had a yellow tape fence around the entrance. Later on, this quiet spot was going to be all over the news.

Our latest victim had been found just before noon. His body was entangled in the old drop gate mechanism of what used to be an operating lock. The original purpose of the canal was to run material goods over a 184-mile stretch between Georgetown and Cumberland Park, Maryland. Now, it was mostly something to run, bike, or walk along, though very few people got this far up the tow path anymore. My guess was that the killer didn't expect the body to be discovered so soon.

The Montgomery County detective assigned to the case was an older guy I knew and liked, Bob Semillon.

He met Jacobs and me in the parking lot and walked us down through the woods.

"Our ME's already gone, but I assumed you'd want one of your folks to take a look," Bob said. "It all sounds like the same character you've been dealing with down there in the city. Pretty awful stuff."

That was one way of putting it.

All indications were that the murder itself had taken place up here on the trail. A dark patch of dried blood in the dirt had been found about halfway down the hill, and there were some pretty clear drag marks between that spot and the canal.

They had the body laid out on the grass when we got there, giving me a sickening sense of déjà vu. There was the one gunshot wound to the face, and then multiple stab wounds around the hips and genitals.

Also, there was a water factor. Cory Smithe had been found in the Potomac, Ricky Samuels in Rock Creek, and now this.

The only real difference I could see, besides location, was in the knife work. Each victim seemed to have been stabbed quite a few more times than the one before him. This boy's jeans were bloodstained all the way down to his neon green shoes.

Jacobs knelt next to the body. I could tell she was doing what I did sometimes—forcing herself to get close and absorb as much as she could, subconsciously or otherwise.

"What's this guy so pissed off about?" she said. "What's he trying to work out here, do you suppose?"

She seemed to be homing in on some of the same anger I'd been seeing in all these cases. That word kept coming up.

"I don't know," I said. "But it can be a vicious cycle. The harder he tries to scratch that itch, the more he's going to find out it can't be done, and the more desperate he's going to get."

"Or enthusiastic," she said, fingering one of the perforations in the kid's pants with a gloved finger. "Or both."

The gunshot was a means to an end, I felt pretty sure. It was the knife work where his emotions took over. In every other respect, he seemed to be extremely well disciplined about the whole thing. These weren't spontaneous murders. Each one of them required some forethought and planning.

And that brought up the other big question here.

The last time around, in Rock Creek, our victim hadn't been alone. There were two bodies that night, most likely from two different killers.

The Montgomery County CSI unit had already made a first pass up and down the canal, and they were still dragging the woods, but it seemed clear to me by now that this was another solo job.

But why? What had changed? Or changed back?

I had no idea, but even as I stood there taking it all in, some part of me was already bracing for what came next. Whatever game these people were playing, it wasn't over yet.

And the score was three to two.

CHAPTER

46

IT WAS JUST BEFORE DARK WHEN I FINALLY WRAPPED UP AT THE CRIME SCENE. I'd been there longer than I meant to be, but then again, I always am. I walked back up through the woods to the parking lot and toward my car.

When I got there, someone was waiting for me. It was dusk, and I couldn't see who it was at first, but then I recognized the beard. Even the hoodie and cargo shorts were the same as the last time.

"Ron Guidice?" I said.

Sure enough, he turned around. I'd been right all along. It was him.

"I've been trying to reach you," I said. "We need to talk."

"Oh, now you want to talk?" he said, immediately aggressive. "Last time I got the brush off."

I took a deep breath. Part of me wanted to cuff him and

throw him in the back of the car. But that wasn't going to get me anywhere. I pressed on instead.

"Listen, I'm not going to pretend that I understand exactly what you went through six years ago. But what you're doing now? It's not helping anyone."

"I guess that's a matter of opinion," he said.

"I want you to know that I'm sorry for your loss," I told him. "I really am, but—"

"But what, Alex? I should just shut up and go away? I already tried that, but it didn't help. You and your department are just as incompetent as you were six years ago."

I looked him in the eye, trying to gauge how put together this guy was—or wasn't. Were there emerging paranoia issues here? Was Guidice one hundred percent? I wasn't convinced.

"It's not just my life you're making difficult," I said. "You're potentially putting future victims' lives at risk here. Do you understand that?"

"That's funny," he said. "Because I write what I do to protect the people *you're* putting at risk."

"You've got the wrong idea," I said.

"Do I?" he said. "What about Rebecca Reilly, detective? Can you tell me where she is? Because as far as I know, she disappeared on your watch."

He was just baiting me now. That much was obvious. I wasn't going to be able to placate this guy, and I wasn't sure it was worth trying anymore.

But I did have one other thing to say.

"All right, fine," I told him. "You want to blog your bullshit, that's your right. But I'll tell you something else.

If I find you tailing me when I'm with my family again, we're going to have a very different kind of problem. Do you understand?"

He stepped a little closer. Guidice was a big dude, and obviously not intimidated by much. But neither am I.

"Are you threatening me, Detective Cross?" he asked. "Is that what's going on here?"

I hadn't even noticed the recorder in his hand until now. He'd been palming it, just out of sight. Before I thought too much about it, I snatched it out of his hand and threw it as far as I could into the woods. Probably a mistake. Another one for my resume.

"You think that's going to stop me?" he said. He laughed without smiling before he went on. "This is your other problem. You've started to believe your own publicity. Alex Cross, the Dragonslayer. Alex Cross, the Sherlock Holmes of MPD. Alex Cross, the second god-damn coming of Christ! You're a paper tiger, Alex. A phony! And people need to know about it."

I was already walking away.

"This isn't over," he called after me. "Not even close!"

"That's one place where we agree, Guidice," I said as I got into my car. "It definitely isn't."

It was time to hit this guy from another angle.

47

IT'S NOT LIKE I WAS COMPLETELY UNSYMPATHETIC TO GUIDICE. I LOST MY OWN
first wife to senseless violence. It was the worst day of my
life, and in a strange way it connected the two of us.

But that didn't mean I was going to let him keep going
unchecked. If he wouldn't talk to me, in a real way, then
I had to do whatever else I could to stop him.

I spent the evening pulling everything we had on
Guidice, and digging for anything else I could find. Commander D'Auria let me piggyback onto his LexisNexis access, and that turned up what was basically a bibliography
of Guidice's past work. It gave me a whole new lens on him.

What I already knew was that he'd been with the US
Army for several years before receiving an honorable
discharge in 2005. That was where he'd cut his teeth,
journalistically speaking.

Most of his work in the army had been with administrative and communications units, first at Fort Bragg, then in Newark, New Jersey, with one six-month deployment to Baghdad for the *Army Times*. Overseas, he'd written a series of PR pieces highlighting US humanitarian efforts and infrastructure projects in Iraq. All of that was a matter of public record.

Then there was everything that came after his discharge. I don't know what happened to Guidice in the army, but by the time he started writing freelance—and well before Theresa Filmore died—it was like he'd turned a one eighty. His focus at that point was almost entirely on the overreach of the US government, both at home and abroad.

He'd traveled back to the Middle East a few times for some small presses, and he even won a few obscure awards for his work. At the same time, he wrote pieces on everything from police brutality to time-card falsification in law enforcement, and several scathing articles about MPD's supposed mishandling of the Al Ayla terrorist attacks in DC in the fall.

The one thing he seemed to have never written about directly was the death of his fiancée. For whatever reasons of his own, he'd left that incident off the table, but I could only imagine the kind of fuel it would have poured onto the fire he already had burning.

Now, all of it seemed to be bubbling up to the surface, including the blame he was laying so squarely at my feet.

I didn't know what exactly to expect from him next, but it was clear to me that I hadn't seen the last—or the worst—of Ron Guidice yet.

48

BY TWO O'CLOCK THE NEXT AFTERNOON, I'D GRABBED THE FIRST APPOINTMENT I could get with the US Attorney's Office. It's not always the fastest-moving machine over there, and if they could do anything for me about Guidice, I wanted to find out sooner rather than later.

At one forty-five, I left my office and made the quick walk from headquarters, up Fourth Street to the Judiciary Center Building. My meeting was with one of their line assistants, Larry Kim, in his third-floor office.

Kim and I knew each other more by reputation than from actually working together. He was known as a solid prosecutor, with a good grasp of case law and a willingness to go to bat for something he believed in. We'd already spoken on the phone, and he knew the basics of why I was there.

"Honestly, I'm not sure there's much you can do," he

told me. "The fact is, citizens have every right to investigate government affairs and share what they learn with other people."

"What about the invasion of my own privacy? Or a public good mandate, for that matter? At some point he's going to represent a threat to the investigation. I'm not just talking about murders already committed. I'm talking about a missing baby, and more than one killer still active out there."

Kim shook his head. "First Amendment, man. Freedom of the press. It's a tough nut to crack—for good reason. And getting tougher all the time."

"He's not the press," I said. "He's some guy with a computer, a cell phone, and a grudge."

"This is my point." Kim set down the extra-large Starbucks he'd been drinking and leaned toward me, warming to the conversation. "It used to be major stories broke in the mainstream press first, and filtered down. Now, you're just as likely to see some guy with a smartphone or a blog out in front of this stuff. The courts are recognizing that.

"There was a national security blog out of Oregon last year. Same thing—just some guy operating off a laptop, with questionable sources. Well, guess what? His rights to privacy were upheld all the way to the state supreme court. If Oregon thought they had a case, they would have appealed to the Feds, but they let it drop." Kim sat back and picked up his coffee. "That's the new reality."

"That's one case," I said.

"No," he said. "One of several. I'm guessing this

Guidice person knows it, and he's taking full advantage. And frankly, the fact that he's been coming after you personally doesn't bolster your case. If anything, it muddies the water."

"I'm just asking you to run this up the flagpole," I told him. The US Attorney's Office had a full staff of legal research lawyers. I trusted Kim's expertise, but maybe there was some alternate precedent out there. "If I could get as far as filing a motion in court, it might get Guidice to back off."

Larry nodded several times and started shuffling the files on his desk. It was a not-so-subtle indication that he was out of time for me.

"I can do that," he told me. "But it's not much to work with. If you can find anything more specific on Guidice—if he's broken any laws—you might have a better chance at getting some traction here."

"Believe me," I said. "I'm working on it."

I just hoped nobody else wound up dead in the meantime.

CHAPTER

49

I LEFT THE MEETING WITH KIM AND WENT STRAIGHT BACK TO MY CAR, IN the parking garage under the Daly Building. Sometimes there's no better place to get some work done in private. Bree calls it my mobile office.

Mostly, I had calls to make. I flipped open a pad on my knee and dialed the first of several names on my list—Ned Mahoney.

Ned's a good friend, a great FBI agent, and the person over at the Bureau who I most trust to give me a straight answer. He ran the Hostage and Rescue Team out of Quantico, but I'd also been hearing murmurs that Mahoney was on his way up at the Bureau. I'd believe it when I saw it.

"Alex," he answered. "How's the hardest-working man in show business? Wait, don't tell me. Up to your ass, am I right?"

Ned also has a mouth that won't quit. He comes across as sarcastic a lot of the time, but the truth is, there just aren't many sacred cows in Ned's world. It's one of the things I like about him.

"I need some info," I told him. "It's about a kidnapping down in Georgia," I said. "The name's Rebecca Reilly."

"Reilly," he said. "Anything to do with that nasty windowsill action over on Vernon a few weeks ago?"

"Off the record? Yeah," I said. "Rebecca's the vic's baby. She was in her grandparents' custody down south when she was taken. The grandparents were killed, too. I can't get anyone in Atlanta or Savannah to talk to me about it."

Ned made a sound like he was sucking air through his teeth. "This business stinks, doesn't it? Why didn't we become accountants or something?"

"'Cause we care, Ned."

"Oh, right. That," he said. "Let me see what I can do. I'll get you back as soon as I can."

It didn't take him long, either. By the time I'd put in calls to Jarret Krause, Sampson, and Sergeant Huizenga, I had a voice mail waiting from Ned. He didn't want to leave any specific information on my phone, so I called him back right away.

"Not much to tell," he said. "The Bureau's still active with the case, so they probably have good reason to believe Rebecca was taken out of Georgia. But that's as far as I got. They're holding their cards pretty close."

"Thanks for trying," I said. It was more than I'd had before.

"How're you doing, anyway?" Ned asked. "Seems like

you've been getting spanked pretty bad in the press lately."

This was the one thing I didn't want to talk about, but curiosity got the best of me. It often does.

"Why?" I said. "What have you heard?"

"That whole *Real Deal* thing," Ned said. "Seems like I can't turn around without reading about it these days. Or you. Is it true you threw that guy's tape recorder into the woods?"

"I'll take the fifth," I told him. It wasn't like I thought Guidice's blog was a secret anymore, but it was no fun to be reminded of the fact. The longer this went on, the more I'd become a part of the story myself—and that's nowhere a self-respecting cop wants to be. "Bottom line, the guy's a major tool," I said.

"Don't sweat it too much," Ned told me. "This stuff's like herpes. It pops up, it goes away for a while, then it comes back. There's nothing you can do but keep your head down and stick to what's important."

I had to laugh. "Herpes, huh? Remind me to call you back the next time I need cheering up."

"Anytime, Alex. Meanwhile, just don't read that crap. It's only going to piss you off. Especially today."

It was probably good advice, but it was coming a little too late. As soon as I hung up with Ned, I opened the browser on my phone and went straight to *The Real Deal.*

For better or worse.

CHAPTER

50

A NEW LOW

Posted by RG at 11:52 p.m.

Sometimes I'm surprised at the depths to which the Metropolitan Police Department will sink. Yesterday evening was a good example. My own criticisms of Detective Alex Cross (see sidebar, *here*) are well known. Despite his reputation as a superior investigator which he may well be—Dr. Cross is also a prime example of the kind of wolf in sheep's clothing that pervades that department.

Click *here* for an audio recording of my encounter with Detective Cross just yesterday. See what you think for yourself. I was attempting to report on the latest in a series of murders, of young hustlers in and around Georgetown— the so-called River Killer case (for which the MPD has no reported progress, by the way). At the time of the incident, I was in the parking lot at Lock Seven of the C&O Canal, off of Clara Barton Parkway. I've Google mapped it *here,* and marked the police perimeter as it was established, along with the spot where my encounter with Detective Cross took place. As you'll see, I was well within the allowable area for press and other onlookers. There is no question of trespass in this case.

I will, however, admit to having a concealed recording device during our conversation. It's something I always do in my dealings with MPD, as a backup, but this was the first time it's ever proven necessary. Click *here* to listen to the encounter. What you'll hear is me interacting with Detective Cross, followed by a brief struggle in which he took the handheld recorder I was carrying and threw it deep into the woods, in the direction I've marked with an arrow on the above-mentioned map.

What I hope is coming clear here is a growing—I'd say overwhelming—body of evidence that the MPD is badly in need of a little housecleaning. This is the kind of police behavior I've heard about in places like Egypt, and Libya, and China. Is it really what we want here at home?

As always, I encourage you NOT to take my word on any of this. Look into it for yourself. See what other people are saying. See what you think. If you'd like to share a comment or observation about the work MPD is doing, click *here.*

And remember—the police work for you. Not the other way around.

51

WHEN I GOT HOME JUST BEFORE SEVEN THAT NIGHT, THE HOUSE WAS disconcertingly quiet. There was no Wii from the living room. No Nikki Minaj playing behind some closed door. No pounding feet on the stairs.

Instead, what I found was Bree sitting in the kitchen with Stephanie Gethmann, our social worker. Stephanie was the one from Child and Family Services assigned to Ava's case. Usually we saw her once a month for home visits, but the last visit had been just a week before.

Something was up.

"Alex, come sit down," Bree said. She looked tense, and touched my hand as I pulled out a chair to join them.

"What's going on? Where are the kids?" I said.

"Jannie and Ali are with Aunt Tia," Bree told me.

"What about Ava?" I said. "Is she okay?"

"A patrol cop brought her home this afternoon," Bree

said. "He found her in Seward Square, passed out on a park bench."

The news hit me like a punch in the gut, but one that I was already half expecting.

"Passed out?" I said.

"With pupils like pin dots."

That meant opiates. OxyContin, possibly, although Ava didn't have that kind of money. Maybe fentanyl, which was cheaper and easier to get but also harder to control. My cop's mind couldn't help running down a list of possibilities.

"Nana's upstairs with her now," Bree went on. "She's just sleeping. We'll have to do a urine test in the morning."

I nodded and looked down at the table. All of a sudden, it felt like July 1989 all over again. That was the last time drugs had haunted this house.

My brother Blake had been an addict. He'd shown up on Nana's doorstep one night, dope sick and begging for help. Nana called me in my dorm at Georgetown and asked me to come home, which I did. It was a long, sweaty twelve hours, but we got through it. Nana was like an angel of mercy. I just helped out where I could.

What I didn't know then was that it would be the last time all three of us were together. Blake promised to stick with the rehab program Nana found for him, but he quickly skipped out and disappeared. The next we heard was on the morning of September 2—another cop at the front door. Blake had been found in an Anacostia flophouse, dead from a heroin overdose.

Now, sitting here, I couldn't help feeling terrified for Ava. She wasn't Blake, obviously. But it was also true that Nana and I had done all we could for my brother, and it still wasn't enough.

"So, what now?" I asked Stephanie.

"Counseling, for sure," she said. "Maybe treatment. It depends on what Ava has to say for herself. We need to find out how long this has been going on, and if she's dealing with an addiction here. Also, if you can find out where she's getting her drugs, that could be a good step toward doing something about it."

"We've had her on a short leash," Bree said. "There's been a little trouble lately."

"Drug trouble?" Stephanie asked.

Bree and I looked at each other. "We weren't sure," she said. "But I guess we are now."

"Well, as long as you'll have her, Ava's best off staying right here. I'll let her rest tonight, but I'd like to see her tomorrow. And I'll be making more frequent visits to the house. How are Wednesdays and Saturdays for you?"

"Fine," Bree said.

I felt like I was still trying to catch up. My head was too crowded. When I looked up again, Stephanie and Bree were both looking back at me.

"I'm sorry—what?" I said.

"Wednesdays and Saturdays," Stephanie repeated. "Is that okay for you, Alex?"

"Yes. Of course," I said. "Whatever it takes. We'll make it work."

CHAPTER

52

"YES. OF COURSE. WHATEVER IT TAKES. WE'LL MAKE IT WORK."

Ron Guidice slid the headphones off his ears and sat back. He'd heard all he needed to. The rest of the conversation could go to the hard drive.

In the meantime, it sounded like Alex was getting it coming and going these days. This was exactly what the electronic surveillance was for. There was only so much of a story Guidice could build without some kind of inside line on Alex's home life. It was working out perfectly, in fact.

Guidice marked the time on a legal pad next to his computer and had just started typing up some thoughts when a knock came from the hall.

"Ronald, honey?"

"Come in," he said, flipping the laptop closed.

When his mother opened the door, she had baby Grace held in the crook of one arm. A white cloth diaper was draped over her shoulder. The nipple of a small Evenflo bottle showed over the top of her housecoat pocket.

"Emma Lee says she wants daddy to tuck her in tonight."

"No problem," Guidice said.

When he got to the door, though, Lydia didn't move. She just stood there, filling the frame with her considerable girth. It was her own version of passive-aggressive, putting herself in the way like a cow on the tracks. She obviously had something on her mind.

Guidice steeled his patience. It wasn't clear yet whether his mother was going to need a little stick, or a little carrot. Maybe both.

"What is it, Mom?" he asked.

"Did you call the police yet?"

"No," he said. "Don't worry about it."

"Well, I do worry about it," she said, absently rocking the baby. "I mean..." Now she dropped her voice to a whisper, as if anyone else were listening. "How do you even know she's yours?"

Guidice reached over and stroked his daughter's rosy cheek with one finger. Her little half-lidded eyes made him smile.

"Look at her," he said. "She looks just like me."

"Still. This is the baby's mother we're talking about," Lydia insisted.

"She was just some slut, Mom. A one-night stand."

His mother half turned her head and held up a hand.

"Too much information, thank you. I'm just saying, it's not right what she did."

"Exactly," he said. "Think about it, Mom. This is someone who leaves a baby in a car with a note and walks away. Do you really want that kind of person in Grace's life?"

Lydia held the baby a little closer. "Well, no, but—"

"That's why we moved. I didn't want her finding us. And frankly, I don't want to find her, either. I say Grace deserves better than that."

"I suppose," Lydia answered tentatively—either because she agreed with him, or because her tenth-grade education hadn't armed her for any kind of substantive debate in life.

"Don't *suppose*, Mom. Think about it," he told her. "Do you really want someone like that raising your granddaughter?"

"No," she answered, more resolutely this time.

"No," he said. "You don't. And neither do I."

He let it all sink in for a moment, and then softened his tone as he went on. Time for a little carrot.

"Believe me," he said. "You're a way better mother than she'd ever be. No contest, Mom."

Lydia Guidice was always easily flattered. She smiled as she blushed, and then finally stepped out of the way.

"Go on," she said. "Emma Lee's waiting."

Guidice kissed his mother on the cheek before he headed up the hall.

There were other solutions, of course. Lydia could be eliminated just as easily as anyone else, physically speaking. It would even be a relief to put the ultimate gag order on that incessant nagging.

But it was basically a cost-benefit situation at this point. Lydia played a vital role in the family. Like it or not, he needed her right now. It would be shortsighted to take her out just to shut her up.

No, Guidice thought. He couldn't do that. Couldn't even think about it.

Not unless it became absolutely necessary.

CHAPTER

53

I TRIED TO STAY FOCUSED AT THE NEXT MORNING'S BRIEFING, BUT IT WAS HARD to keep my mind in the room.

I was starting to wonder if I'd overextended myself. It's a question that comes up a lot. I had three cases on the books—plus Ava. She was the fourth case. Later in the day, we had a meeting at Child and Family Services. In the meantime, I had more than enough to keep me busy.

Too much, in fact, but how do you say no to something when the stakes are people's lives? We had nine dead so far, one missing, and, with three unknown suspects at large, the looming promise of more to come.

There's a good amount of disagreement about clusters, as they're called in serial homicide. Some people say they're nothing more than coincidence, and that we're bound to see concurrent activity from time to time. The United States is the world capital of serial murder, with somewhere between twenty-five and fifty active killers at any given time.

The most famous cluster I knew of had been in South LA, from the early eighties through 2007. LAPD had tracked down five separate cases then, including the Grim Sleeper and the Southside Slayer. By the time all five of those files were closed, a total of fifty-five people had died, all within a fifty-square-mile area.

There had also been some recent coverage about the three killers operating simultaneously in Nassau and Suffolk Counties, on Long Island. The last I'd heard, two suspects were in custody, with one still at large, and the body count was up to thirty.

Now, Washington had the makings of its own cluster. I spent virtually all my time turning over these three cases in my head—thinking about methods, victim profiles, possible motives, and most of all, wondering where one of these guys might strike next.

Killer number one was the man I thought of as "Russell," the supposed boyfriend of Elizabeth Reilly. He was the most unpredictable in a way, with four and a half years between his pregnant victims, and a probable kidnapping on his resume, too.

Number two was the one they'd dubbed the River Killer in the press. Three gay hustlers had been found dead so far, but my fear was that we just hadn't found them all yet. Under normal conditions, it can take weeks for a submerged, decomposing body to build up enough gas to become buoyant and rise to the surface.

Killer number three was the least established, but he

already had two different monikers. Some were calling him the Georgetown Ripper. Others were using the Barbie Killer, for the blond hair and perfect bodies on his two known victims. MPD had left those comparisons out of their official statements, but the media had picked up on it anyway.

That was the case that had me most on edge right now. Considering the apparent relationship between the River Killer and this guy, I couldn't help feeling as though our Barbie Killer had some catching up to do. In the plainest possible terms, it felt to me like we were overdue for another dead blonde.

Three days later, it turned out I was half right.

This time, it was two dead blondes.

CHAPTER

54

THE BODIES WERE FOUND BY A HOUSEKEEPER WHEN SHE ARRIVED FOR WORK that Monday morning. Time of death was later determined to be somewhere around ten o'clock on Saturday night, which meant that these women were dead in their house for a full thirty-six hours. More bad news for the investigation. I headed over as soon as I got the call.

The place was a pink brick townhome on Cambridge Place, a well-to-do but tightly packed block of Georgetown. Still, there had been no reports of any screams, or disturbances of any kind.

"We've got no signs of forced entry," Errico Valente told me at the front door. "The alarm system was disabled, too. Seems like he might have been admitted to the house."

"Are there neighborhood cameras?"

"Yeah. It's a private security firm," he said. "We're tracking down the logs right now."

The bulk of DC's municipal crime cameras are normally reserved for our most violent neighborhoods. The irony was that these two homicides had now put Second District, which is Georgetown, on par with anywhere else in the city, body for body.

From the home's center hall, I followed Valente up to the apparent crime scene, a master suite on the second of three floors. The victims in this case were a mother and daughter, Cecily and Keira Whitley, ages forty-three and nineteen. Mrs. Whitley was divorced, but her ex-husband still lived in DC, where they'd raised two daughters. Keira's twin sister was enrolled at UC Santa Barbara out in California.

Now the Whitley family had been cut in half.

Coming into the bedroom, I saw the mother first. She was laid out on the pale pink sheets of an unmade king-size bed. The covers had been pulled off and left in a heap on the floor.

Her daughter was on an overstuffed chaise longue in the corner, facing her mother. Marks in the carpet told me the chaise had been moved to that position recently.

Both victims were tall, attractive women, with the telltale signs of what had once been long blond hair. In fact, they looked quite a bit alike. Two more Barbies for the Barbie Killer. If there was any doubt on that front, the signature knife work clinched it. Both had incurred stab wounds to the left chest, abdomen, and right thigh, near the femoral artery. Dried blood formed a dark corona around each of their bodies on the mattress and chaise, respectively.

"Evil son of a bitch," Valente said. "Just killing for killing's sake."

That seemed to be the case. There were no signs of sexual assault, or robbery. Mrs. Whitley's blue leather purse sat clasped on a dresser by the window, and the heavy diamond studs in Keira's ears had been left untouched.

Age didn't seem to be a factor for this guy, either. The only real consistencies were the very clear physical type, the repetitive knife work, and of course, the chopped hair. It was virtually everywhere I looked—matted in with the blood on the furniture, but also lying in loose tufts, and endless random strands all over the room, and all over the victims themselves. It was as bizarre a scene as I'd been to in a long time.

But was one of those elements more important than the other? He was working something out, that was for sure. Maybe reliving a fantasy of some kind—over and over.

It was possible these women were surrogates for someone else, I thought. Someone whom our killer only wished he could get to. His dead mother, maybe. Or an ex of some kind. I didn't really see a clear path to figuring that one out yet, but somewhere in my gut, the question felt like it was pointing me in the right direction.

Who was this guy—and who was he trying to kill, over and over again?

CHAPTER

55

BY THE TIME VALENTE AND I MADE A GOOD PASS THROUGH THE HOUSE, WE heard from the sergeant on the front door that a rep from Baseline Security had arrived. Errico radioed back to keep whoever it was outside, and we made our way out to the street to meet with him.

A black Range Rover was parked halfway between the Whitley home and the barriers at the end of the block. The man waiting for us there introduced himself as John Overbey, the owner of Baseline. His company worked for various neighborhood associations, providing video surveillance and away-from-home coverage where the city's municipal cameras fell short.

It looked to me like business was good. Overbey's green silk tie probably cost more than my entire suit.

"We've got one hundred percent coverage on this block," he told us. "I started scanning the logs as soon as I heard the terrible news. And I'm pretty certain we've got your man."

He kept eyeing the Whitleys' town house while we talked. I'd want to get a look inside, too, if I were him, but Valente motioned for him to open his Toughbook right there on the hood of his car instead.

When the laptop screen flicked on, Overbey already had two side-by-side video images waiting. His time coding looked like a jumble to me, maybe some kind of in-house encryption, but he read it easily enough.

"That's nine forty-six on Saturday night," he said, pointing to the image on the left. "And the other is at ten fifteen. Both from the same unit, right over there."

He turned and pointed up the block, to the corner of Cambridge and Thirtieth Street. In fact, I could see a small black box mounted under the second-floor window of the house on that corner.

"Let's go chronologically," Valente said.

Overbey brought the first image up to full screen and let the video play.

Unlike the city cameras, this one recorded a crisp digital color picture. The limitation was the fact that it had been taken at night. Cambridge Place was only sporadically lit by a handful of old-style street lamps along the brick sidewalk.

After a few seconds of empty footage, a man walked into the frame, heading up the block with his back to the camera.

"That's him," Overbey said.

There wasn't much to see, except that he had a ball

cap on, and a dark, knee-length coat. When he reached the Whitley home, he stepped up onto the stoop and appeared to ring the bell.

It was chilling, knowing what was about to happen, and not being able to do anything about it.

The porch light came on. There seemed to be a brief exchange at the door, while the man pointed up the street several times. Finally, a blond woman stepped outside. It was too far away to tell if it was Mrs. Whitley or her daughter, but she put an arm around the man and helped him inside. As she did, he moved with a sudden, pronounced limp that hadn't been there before.

"Probably told her he'd been mugged," Overbey said, minimizing that recording and bringing up the other. "Now watch. This is twenty-nine minutes later."

Again, we saw the same street scene as before, from the same camera. After a moment, the man stepped outside and closed the door behind him. He turned left off the stoop, then started back up the block, moving easily with no discernible limp at all.

As he came near the camera again, we saw his face for the first time. He even looked up, right into the lens for a split second, as he passed under it and out of sight.

"Right there," I said.

"Yeah." Overbey stopped, rewound, and froze the image.

The man seemed to be looking right at us. Valente leaned in to see closer, and then cursed under his breath.

"Look familiar?" he said.

It did. The face was similar, but not exactly the same,

as the old man we'd seen on the security tape at the parking garage the night Darcy Vickers was murdered.

He looked about the same age, maybe seventy, but unlike the last time, this guy had a mustache and glasses. Two white shocks of curly hair showed under the ball cap as well. The last guy had been mostly bald.

"Those are prosthetics," I said, at the same moment I realized it.

Valente nodded. "Some kind of mask, right? Jesus. That could explain a lot."

"I don't think he cares if we know it, either," I added. "He obviously had a bead on that camera, the way he looked right into it. Maybe he even wanted us to see him."

That could cut both ways, I thought. It might have meant he was confident for a reason, and we were never going to see past that disguise enough to pin him down.

Or, maybe he was starting to feel cocky—maybe a little *too* cocky for his own good—and we'd just turned a corner on this thing.

I looked up at Overbey. "Can you piece together his movements?" I said. "Try and figure out where he went from here? Or where he came from?"

"I'll do what I can," Overbey said. "Our service area only goes as far as Q Street. But you could pull from the city as well."

"On it," Valente said, tapping a number into his phone.

"Hey, Detective Cross?"

Someone else was there now. I turned around to see a uniformed cop trying to get my attention.

"What is it?" I said.

"You've got a visitor, detective."

"A *what?*" That didn't make sense. This was a closed crime scene.

The cop shrugged. "He said you called and asked him to come right down. He's waiting over there."

I looked up the street the way the cop pointed. There, in his usual hoodie and cargos, was Ron Guidice.

"What the hell's that douche bag doing here?" Valente said. "You want me to get rid of him for you?"

"No," I said. "I'll take care of it. In fact, it's going to be my pleasure."

Somehow, Guidice had found his way into my crime scene. I was going to be sure to help him find his way out.

CHAPTER

56

I'VE GOT NO QUALMS TAKING A REPORTER BY THE COLLAR AND WALKING THEM back, if they're compromising a scene. I've never actually had to arrest one before. But there's a first time for everything.

"Hey! Guidice!" I said, heading right for him. "You've got to go."

He stepped off the brick sidewalk to stand between a couple of parked cars as I came closer.

"Detective Cross, are you high?" he said, loud enough to be overheard.

"Very funny," I said. I had no doubt this little head game was for my benefit. Guidice was too smart *not* to know he was trespassing on the scene at this point. But I was also determined not to get sucked into his bullshit.

"You've got five seconds to get back on the other side of those barriers." I pointed to the top of the block, where a crowd had gathered. Some of them were even carrying protest signs—KEEP GEORGETOWN SAFE, WHAT THE HELL, MPD? I'm sure Guidice was loving those.

His eyes narrowed, and his pupils danced back and forth, taking me in.

"You are high, aren't you?" he said. "I didn't want to write about this until I was sure, but—"

"Ronald Guidice, you're under arrest for trespassing on a designated crime scene," I told him. I already had the bracelets out. "Turn around and put your hands behind your back."

He was still between the cars, and I had to step in there to try to get him moving. But then, as I did, I felt a sharp, stabbing pain in my leg.

When I looked down, it was just in time to see Guidice pulling his hand back. He was holding something, but I couldn't see what it was.

My next response was automatic. I hit him, hard. My fist sent a shower of blood out of his nose and down over his mouth. I probably should have stopped there, but the adrenaline had me, and Guidice was still standing. I countered the right punch with a left hook.

This time, he went down.

He landed on his back, looking stunned. My knee was on his chest now, holding him in place. My thigh was throbbing with the pain. He'd gotten me right in the muscle.

"What the hell was that?" I yelled at him. "What'd you stick me with?"

I'd barely started reaching for his pockets before two

uniformed cops were pulling me off of him. A third cop knelt down next to Guidice and pulled him in the opposite direction, up onto the sidewalk.

Valente was there, too, and I saw Huizenga rushing over from her car.

"Alex? What's going on here?" she said.

"He's under arrest!" I pointed at Guidice. "Check his pockets! Book him!"

Guidice had gone slack, watching me as they held us apart. "Sergeant, your detective here is obviously on drugs. He just attacked me for no reason."

He wiped the blood off his mouth, keeping his hand up high for the cameras at the end of the block.

"Alex Cross did this to me!"

"Come here!" I yelled at him, but Huizenga put herself in the way and walked me back. Valente had me by the arm, too.

"Pull it together, Alex!" Huizenga said. "Now tell me there's a good goddamn reason for this."

"He just stuck me!" I said.

"What are you talking about?"

"I don't know...." I said. "I don't know what that... was."

It was hard to concentrate, and my thoughts were starting to swim. I felt a tingling all over my body. A warm sensation crawled up through my limbs and into my head.

"I think I'm..."

I meant to say, *I think I'm going to pass out,* but I never got that far.

It wasn't just a stab or an ordinary needle stick, I realized. It was something else. The last thought I can remember before I lost consciousness was that I'd just been poisoned.

Had Guidice killed me? Was I dying?

CHAPTER

57

I WOKE UP IN THE AMBULANCE. HUIZENGA WAS THERE. WE WERE MOVING.

None of it made sense at first, but quickly I remembered what had happened.

"Lie back," Huizenga said, pushing me onto the gurney when I tried to sit up.

Two paramedics were perched on either side. One of them had a blood-pressure cuff on my arm. The other was radioing my vitals, presumably to whatever hospital we were headed toward. Georgetown, maybe.

"He stuck me...."

"Just relax."

"He..."

I felt like Jell-O all over, except for a twitch in my hands. My head was still swimming. What the hell was this? I knew cognitively that something was terribly wrong, but somehow I couldn't quite *feel* that way. It was like a euphoric state more than anything, with the fear and dread somewhere way in the background. I felt like I was watching the movie of my own emergency more than I was actually in it.

My eyes rolled. A paramedic lifted one of my lids to have a look.

"He's nodding out," the guy said.

That was the last I heard.

58

THE NEXT TIME I WOKE UP, I WAS IN THE HOSPITAL. A FLUORESCENT BOX fixture was shining down on me. Instead of walls there was a blue curtain pulled around whatever examination room or cubicle they'd stuck me in.

Huizenga was still there. Bree now, too, I realized.

"Hey there," she said, squeezing my hand. "How do you feel?"

I was still groggy, and floating on the last of some kind of cloud. I smiled, in spite of everything else. It was all a little blurry.

"How long have you been here?" I asked her.

"A couple of hours. It's six o'clock."

"What happened?"

"They found opiates in your bloodstream," Huizenga said to me. "Mostly OCs."

"Mostly?"

"A little morphine."

"Ah." I let my head fall back on the pillow. "I knew I recognized something."

I'd been through my share of scrapes before—been given my share of morphine, too. The last time was when I'd been shot, tracking a case up to Vermont several years earlier.

Now, everything started coming back in pieces. I remembered the crime scene in Georgetown. The security company. Guidice—

I sat up all at once and threw off the thin blanket they had over me.

"Where's Guidice?" I said. "Is he in custody?"

"Whoa," Bree said. "Slow down, Alex. Take it easy."

"Where is he?" I repeated.

"I think they still have him over at the department," Huizenga told me. "But no. He's not arrested."

"What are you talking about? I was in the middle of putting the cuffs on him when he stuck me."

Marti took a deep breath and looked at Bree before she answered. They both knew something I didn't.

"There was nothing on him, Alex," she said. "Just ID, cash, and his camera."

"Well, he must have ditched the needle," I said. "I'm telling you—"

She cut me off. "Everything we found was on you. Including this." Huizenga held up a brown pharmacy bottle. "These were in your pocket when we got here. And his prints aren't on the bottle, either."

"*What?*"

"Guidice is claiming you were on drugs—which you were, one way or the other. Also, that you attacked him for no reason. If he stuck you, Alex, nobody saw it."

"Oh my God."

I lay back again. The full twisted reality of it all started to sink in. Huizenga wasn't done, either.

"He's also filing assault charges against you. A restraining order, too. He says you've been out to get him ever since he started writing about you."

I looked up into Huizenga's eyes. "I'm being set up here, Marti. Jesus—do you even believe me? You know the history on this guy, right?"

She stood back from the bed, hating every second of this, I could tell.

"I don't want to say too much, Alex. Not until we know more. But I am going to need your gun, badge, and ID." She took another deep breath. "And I'm going to have to take you in when we're done here."

"Like hell you are!" Bree stepped in now. "You heard the man. He was attacked. Are you seriously questioning his word on this? He's one of the best cops in DC."

"*I'm* not questioning anything," Huizenga told Bree. "But the department's circling the wagons. We've got a whole city screaming for police accountability these days, and the fact of the matter is that—for whatever reason—Alex assaulted this guy."

"I don't believe this," Bree said. "You people have lost your minds!"

For the first time, Huizenga raised her voice.

"Bree, you're here as a professional courtesy, and I *am*

your superior officer. You got that? Now dial it the hell back down, or I'm going to ask you to leave."

"Ask all you like," Bree said. "He's coming home with me."

"I can also have you removed, if necessary," Huizenga countered.

I couldn't believe everything I was hearing. Everything that Guidice seemed to be getting away with here.

"Marti, what do you mean—take me in?" I said.

It could have gone one of two ways. Either they needed to talk to me back at the office, or she was actually putting me under arrest.

Huizenga ducked her chin and answered without answering.

"I'll give you two a few minutes alone," she said.

In other words, I wasn't coming home that night.

59

I WASN'T PRIVY TO THE CONVERSATIONS HAPPENING BACK AT HEADQUARTERS, but by the time I got released from the hospital, word had been handed down. There would be no special treatment in this case. The department couldn't afford it. Not in the current environment. It was a game of political football, and right now, I was the ball.

Huizenga took me straight to headquarters. She bypassed the press gathered outside on Indiana and pulled into the parking garage without either of us talking about it. From the garage it's a straight shot down on the freight elevator to Central Cell Block in the basement.

The looks on the booking officers' faces when we got there were somewhere between dumbstruck and fascinated. I don't think they knew what I was doing there, but they certainly knew who I was. I'd brought hundreds of arrestees through that facility over the years.

Now the tables were turned in the worst possible way. I was printed and photographed. My pockets were emptied and their contents were catalogued in a plastic bag. I was given a thin sandwich and a blanket and was walked down the row to the cell where I'd be spending the night.

Central Cell Block is seventy years old. The cells are just about exactly what you might imagine—steel bar doors that clang shut, concrete floors, steel cots with no mattresses, and a steel toilet in the corner. More than once I've locked someone up and thought about how glad I was that I didn't have to spend the night down there.

Huizenga pulled enough rank to get me my own cell, and she offered to bring me some dinner from outside. But I couldn't even look at her by the time she was on the other side of those bars.

"We'll get this straightened out in the morning, Alex," she told me. "That's a promise."

I think she was desperate to leave me with some shred of optimism. The truth was, she couldn't possibly know how long this was going to take. When I didn't answer her, she said good night and left.

I sat down on my cot with my head in my hands. This whole thing was verging on the surreal—or at least, the nightmarish. I truly couldn't believe I'd landed here, much less for something I didn't do.

I wondered what Bree was telling the kids. I wondered how Ava was doing. What Jannie and Ali were making of all this. I even wondered what was up with the double homicide on Cambridge Place, and if Valente had made any progress.

We'd arrived at the cell block after lights out, so there was nothing to do until morning but sit there alone with my thoughts. God knows, I wasn't going to get any sleep.

In fact, every time I closed my eyes that night, I saw Ron Guidice's face. I kept thinking about that bloody palm of his. The way he'd held it up for the cameras. That was going to play beautifully for him, wasn't it? Especially alongside the stories about my arrest, which were no doubt all over the news by now.

If I could have wished that man dead, I just might have done it.

CHAPTER

60

IN THE MORNING I WAS ROUSED BY THE FIVE THIRTY CHANGEOVER, AS THEY brought in the overnight arrests from the districts and moved some others out for transport to the arraignment courts next door. Why they do that at five thirty, I've never been sure, but it wasn't like I was sleeping, anyway.

A few hours later they pulled me out of my own cell, for a 9 a.m. interview with Internal Affairs. IAD has a main office in the old homicide division at Penn Branch, but this meeting was in one of the interview rooms right there at the Daly Building—three floors down from my own desk in the Major Case Squad room. It was bizarre to be escorted around the building this way.

When the duty officer brought me into the room, I didn't recognize either of the investigators waiting for me. Neither of them moved to shake my hand. They just gestured to the empty chair on my side of the table.

It was a plain, small box of a room. A closed-circuit camera was mounted in the corner above the door, and on this particular morning, an AV cart had been wheeled in, with a DVD player and an old boxy television sitting on top.

The two suits introduced themselves as officers Wieder and Kamiskey from the Public Corruption and Police Misconduct Section. Even that was enough to set my teeth on edge, as if I weren't already pissed off enough. Police misconduct? Unbelievable.

Still, this was a chance to tell my side of the story. Once I'd signed and initialed my Miranda rights card, I was ready to get straight to it.

"So, Detective Cross," Wieder started in. "I understand that you're alleging you were deliberately drugged during the incident in question yesterday. Is that right?"

"That's right," I said. I pointed to my hip. "I was stuck with some kind of hypodermic needle. The ER report can confirm the puncture mark."

"Sure, but not who made it," Wieder interrupted right away. "And was this alleged needle stick before or after you struck Mr. Guidice?"

"Directly before," I said. "That was the reason I retaliated against him. The *only* reason."

"Twice."

"Excuse me?"

"You struck him twice. The first time, you broke his nose. Then you knocked him down."

My heart was thudding. I didn't like this guy's tone, or the way the interview already seemed to be going.

"Let's take a look, shall we?" Wieder said.

Kamiskey used a remote to start a video playback on the TV. It looked like a clip from Channel Five news. What it showed was Guidice and me, standing between the two parked cars on Cambridge Place.

There was no audio, but the two of us were obviously in the middle of a heated conversation. And then— seemingly out of the blue—my fists were up, and I was knocking Guidice to the ground, out of sight.

"That's one camera," I said. "There were at least a dozen others on-site."

"All showing the same thing," Wieder told me. He took a beat, long enough to give me a condescending look. "I'm not saying that your allegation about the needle stick is provably false, detective. And we do know about the case history between you and Mr. Guidice—"

"Technically, there is no case history," I said. "It was his fiancée. And it wasn't my bullet that killed her."

But Wieder wasn't about to let me take charge of the conversation.

"What I'm saying," he went on, raising his voice, "is that our job right now is to focus on the possibility of police misconduct in yesterday's incident. So far, we have no corroborating evidence to support your version of the events. But here's what we *do* have."

He opened his file. Inside there was an incident report clipped to the top of several other sheets. I didn't recognize the handwriting, or the signature at the bottom.

"We have a short but marked history of unflattering articles about you, by Mr. Guidice. We have a documented altercation, up at Lock Seven the other day, where by all appearances you behaved aggressively toward Mr. Guidice and threw a piece of his recording equipment. We have this, of course," he said, pointing at the frozen image on the TV. "And finally, we have a positive tox screen for opiates in your system, with a chemical match to the pills found in your pocket yesterday."

Wieder paused again and raised his eyebrows at me. He reminded me of every sanctimonious prick I've ever met—the ones who don't even try to hide how much they enjoy their own power.

"So let me ask you," he said. "You're an experienced detective. What conclusion would you draw if you were sitting on my side of the table?"

"If I were you?" I said. "I'd be asking myself *why* Ron Guidice is writing those articles in the first place. And I might be thinking—isn't this exactly what someone like him would like to see happen?"

The two investigators looked at each other.

"With all due respect, detective, that sounds like conspiracy theory to me," Wieder said, closing his file.

The gesture wasn't lost on me. These two weren't even interested in my story. They'd already interviewed their witnesses, they'd built their narrative, and this meeting was just—what? A formality? A necessary step toward the indictment they so obviously wanted?

In which case, there was no reason for me to be here. I pushed my chair back, stood, and pounded on the interview room door.

"Excuse me—" Wieder said.

"You want to build a case against me, you can do it on your own goddamn time," I said. "I'm ready to go back to my cell."

It was time to lawyer up.

CHAPTER

61

AS SOON AS I WAS LED OUT OF THE INTERVIEW ROOM, I FOUND CHIEF PERKINS waiting there in the hall. Not exactly the last person I might have expected—but not the first, either.

"Chief?"

"Come on," he told me and signaled to the duty officer that he'd take over from here.

Instead of heading back to the cell block, we walked around the corner, through a locked door, and out to the main elevator bank.

"Where are we going?" I said.

"You've been released," he told me. "The press has gotten their pound of flesh."

"What?" I wasn't following. "Did Bree post bail?"

The chief's features were set hard while he avoided my eyes. This wasn't easy for him.

"I'm just doing what I can, Alex."

I wasn't sure what to say to that. Perkins could have kept me from getting thrown into the cell block in the first place. Now, it seemed, he was pulling strings to save me from any more time down there.

"Thanks," I told him. "I guess." He didn't question my response, or say anything else until we were alone on the elevator. It was a strange vibe I was getting.

"Huizenga is expecting you back at the office. We've got you on noncontact status for the time being," he told me.

"Noncontact?" I said.

Whatever relief I'd been feeling had just been cut in half. Noncontact means that you come into work every day, sit at a desk, and answer the phones, or do the filing, or any of a hundred other things nobody else wants to do.

It also meant I was removed from all investigative duties at a time when the squad could least afford it.

"I don't suppose I can appeal to your better judgment," I said. "We've never been busier."

"Believe me, I wish you could," he said, shaking his head. "You're not out of the woods yet. You've still got these charges against you. If the US Attorney's Office decides to hand down an indictment, then it's out of my hands."

"As far as I can tell, Internal Affairs is gunning for it," I said.

"If the mayor had his way, you'd be sitting home without a paycheck. And not because he doesn't like you," Perkins said. "Dammit, Alex, I don't believe that druggie horseshit for a second—but I wish to hell you hadn't hit that guy."

"He deserved it," I said. "And then some."

"No doubt," the chief answered, just as the elevator doors opened onto the third-floor hall. "But that's justice. This is politics."

I think it might have been the most cynical thing I've ever heard from Perkins.

Which isn't to say that it wasn't also true.

CHAPTER

62

WHEN I WALKED INTO THE MAJOR CASE SQUAD OFFICE, I WASN'T EXPECTING much—a meeting with Sergeant Huizenga and a year's worth of backlogged filing to do. What I found instead was more like a surprise party.

"Here he is!" Valente shouted as I came through the door. Suddenly, everyone was on their feet, either prairie dogging out of their cubicles or coming my way. All of them were applauding and cheering, and slapping me on the back. And all of them were wearing the same yellow T-shirts pulled over their shirts.

The T-shirts all said FREE ALEX CROSS. It felt like the first laugh I'd had in days.

"Got any new tattoos?" Valente asked, with an arm over my shoulder. Jarret Krause handed me a cup of coffee.

"Good to see you, Alex. Welcome back."

"I wasn't even gone," I said.

"Close enough," Valente told me.

The truth is, I was deeply touched by the whole thing. Lying in that cell all night, I had no way of knowing who stood behind me on this, and who didn't. Now it seemed like a no-brainer. The Major Case crew is one of the best squads I've ever had the pleasure of working with. They gave me exactly the response I would have hoped for and the same support I would have given any of them.

Then I saw Sergeant Huizenga. She was standing in the door of her office, watching me as I came in. She wasn't smiling, and she wasn't wearing one of the T-shirts, either. But I did notice that she looked like hell. She was also wearing the same blazer and pants as the day before. It didn't look like Marti had gone home at all.

When I came into her office, the first thing she did was extend her hand across the desk.

"No hard feelings?" she asked.

I shook, gladly. "No hard feelings," I said. If anything, I respected her for locking me up herself and not passing it off to someone else.

"Have a seat," she told me. "We've got to do some technicalities here."

She gave me two release forms to sign and then returned my personal effects, with the exception of my Glock. Then she ran down the particulars of Guidice's restraining order. I wasn't to come within five hundred feet of him for as long as the temporary restraining order was in effect. If that went through, and it became permanent, I'd be informed accordingly.

It was one of the strangest twists of right and wrong I'd seen in a while. All things considered, wasn't it me who needed protection from Guidice?

"Have you seen the news?" Marti asked. "I think he gave a dozen 'exclusive' interviews last night. Plus, that goddamn blog of his."

"I'm sorry about all this," I said. "You're going to be down an investigator for a while."

"I don't think I'll be any worse off than you," she said. "I can tell, just looking at your face."

It was true. Maybe I was "free," but I was still in a holding pattern. Cop purgatory.

"Now, why don't you take the rest of the day off and go see your family?" Huizenga said.

"You sure?" I said. In fact, that's exactly what I needed.

"I'm sure," Marti told me, finally cracking a smile. "I think the filing can probably wait until tomorrow."

CHAPTER

63

IT'S LESS THAN A TWO-MILE WALK FROM HEADQUARTERS TO OUR HOUSE, BUT Bree insisted on picking me up that morning. My car was still in Georgetown, and I'd have to go get it later. For now I just wanted to go home, shower, and give my family whatever they needed for the rest of the day. The kids would be in school until three fifteen, so there was plenty of time to regroup with Nana and Bree.

So I thought.

When I got into Bree's white Explorer in front of the Daly Building, I expected her to be glad to see me but also still pissed about my arrest. What I got instead was tears.

She put her arms around me and we kissed. "Are you okay?" she said. I could see then how red her eyes were, and how long she'd been crying.

"I'm fine," I said. "Are *you* okay?"

She clearly wasn't. "I was going to try and get you home first, but—you have to know, Alex. They're removing Ava from the house. Today."

"What? Who's taking her?" I said.

"Child and Family Services. Stephanie called first thing this morning. Given that Ava's been using lately, and now these drug charges against you—"

I went straight from disbelief to anger. "This is bullshit," I said. "I've barely even been charged, much less convicted."

But it was just the anger talking. I knew better, and so did Bree.

"They don't have a choice. They have to err on the side of caution," she said. "And they're not waiting, either. Stephanie's coming at five o'clock to get her."

In other words, the whole guilty until proven innocent thing was now reverberating into my personal life. My *family* life. And Ron Guidice was to blame for all of it.

"Where's she going?" I said.

"For now? Into a group home, up in Northeast. They're moving her in tonight."

It just got worse and worse. DC's group homes are a random mix of kids who have nowhere else to go—orphans, thugs, bangers, all of it. Other than actually living on the street, a group home was the last place I'd want Ava to land.

Bree told me we had an eleven o'clock appointment with our family attorney, Juliet Freeman. That was good. We'd already consulted with Juliet on some preliminary adoption issues for Ava, and Bree had gotten her up to speed on the current situation. Now I just wanted to get home so we could turn around and start doing something about this.

The morning traffic was still aggravatingly thick. It took way too long to crawl up Constitution Avenue, past the white dome of the Capitol and into Southeast. By the time we were passing Seward Square, where we'd first found Ava, Bree and I had both fallen into a depressed silence.

Nana wasn't in any better shape, either. When I came into the house, she was tearing around the kitchen as fast as a ninety-year-old woman can do. She likes to keep busy when she's upset, and it looked to me like she'd been cooking all morning. I could smell fresh bread baking in the oven.

When she saw me, she stopped, and her arms dropped to her sides. I went over and hugged her tight.

"We were just getting somewhere with her," Nana said. "Just starting to crack that little shell of hers. And now—"

"Now, we're going to get Alex some breakfast," Bree said. "We're going to meet Juliet at eleven. And we're going to fight this."

She's a cop, all right. She knows how to shake off the stress and take charge of a situation when she has to. That included the eggs she'd already started whisking in a bowl.

"What are you doing?" I said. "Don't worry about that."

"You need a decent meal, after the night you just had,"

Bree said. "What did they give you this morning, a doughnut? And I'm guessing you didn't eat that, either."

"She's right." Nana patted my hand. "Go get cleaned up, and come back down here ready to eat."

"Yeah." Bree's whisk was going about a hundred angry miles a minute by now. "And ready to fight," she said.

CHAPTER

64

"COME IN, COME IN. PLEASE."

Juliet Freeman isn't the kind of person you might tag as an attorney if you saw her walking down the street. She's almost as short as Nana, is fairly big around the middle, and she doesn't exactly dress to impress when she's not in court.

Likewise, the inside of her Pennsylvania Avenue law office feels more like it's part of somebody's home. I liked that she kept a laundry basket of toys in the corner for her clients' kids, and that the books on her shelves covered everything from constitutional history to *Green Eggs and Ham*.

Juliet doesn't just know family law—she understands *family*, and what it takes to keep one together. As far as I'm concerned, she's impressive in all the right ways.

I got right to it, even as we were sitting down.

"I have three questions," I told her. "How do we get Ava back? What do we do in the meantime? And how does all of this play with the other charges I have hanging over my head?"

Juliet poured tea from an old ornate samovar on her sideboard as she answered. "In a way, that's really just one big question," she said. "But a complicated one. I assume you want me to be blunt."

"Of course," Nana Mama said, accepting a cup. "I'm an old lady, Juliet. I don't have time for a lot of false hopes."

"Okay, then. The fact that Ava's been using drugs, combined with these charges against Alex, makes this an uphill battle. And even without that, you still don't have any superior rights to her, or any foster child."

"No, but we have a relationship with her," Nana Mama said. "That has to be worth something, for a girl who has nobody else in the world. Ava's part of our family now."

Juliet nodded, but only to acknowledge what Nana said, not to agree with her.

"Legally speaking, she's not. If they end up placing her with another family, and it sticks, then that's it. She won't be coming back to you."

That news settled heavily over all of us. Bree squeezed my hand in the silence. "What do you suggest?" I asked.

"You need to make it clear to your social worker that whatever drugs Ava has been using, she hasn't been getting them from you," Juliet said.

"I've been over that with her already," Bree said.

"She needs to hear it from Ava. If you can make that conversation happen, it's a good first step."

I wasn't so sure. "Couldn't that be taken as some kind of tacit admission about my own drug use?" I said.

"One thing at a time," Juliet told me. "First and foremost, address Ava's situation, and then your own charges. When's your court date?"

"A week from today."

She went to her desk and scribbled a note. "See what you can do. In the meantime, I understand you've got a restraining order against you?"

"Yes, but I was set up," I told her. "I can't prove anything—not yet. I'll countersue, if I have to. Whatever it takes."

Juliet leaned forward and caught my eye over the top of her red-framed glasses. "Alex, listen to me. If you've ever had a reason to stay above board, this is it. Whatever you do, don't start bending the rules, or God forbid, breaking the law to expose this guy." She knew me, maybe a little too well. It was good advice. Still, somewhere in the back of my mind, I was resolved to keeping my options open.

That fact that Ron Guidice had injected me with the same class of drugs Ava had been taking was no coincidence. That much I knew. I had no idea how he'd found out about her—maybe by bribing someone for lab results, or chatting up the cop who had dropped her off at our house that day. In any case, it wasn't the first time he'd dug up confidential information. Maybe Guidice was more of a reporter than I'd given him credit for.

A reporter, and a vindictive son of a bitch.

Now I just had to prove it. One way or another.

CHAPTER

65

WHEN THE KIDS GOT HOME FROM SCHOOL, WE SAT THEM ALL DOWN FOR THE hardest talk I've ever had as a parent. We had to explain to Ava that she needed to pack her things, and we had to explain to all of them why.

I didn't go into details about the hot water I was in. I just told them that there had been some legal complications, and that we had to get those worked out before Ava could come back to live with us again.

Stephanie held off for as long as she could, but they had to check Ava into the group home by six. When she showed up at five, Ava's suitcase was next to the door, and our house was quiet as a morgue. We'd all settled into the living room, waiting for the inevitable.

Even Stephanie was upset. She had tears in her eyes when I answered the door. We'd already spoken about the drug charge, and asked her to please interview Ava about it the first chance she got. Stephanie had promised she would. Meanwhile, there was a forty-eight-hour waiting period before we could visit Ava in her new place. That meant we wouldn't know anything else for at least two days.

"Ava, honey, you ready to go?" Stephanie asked, trying to stay upbeat.

Ava just shrugged and shuffled over to the door. I could already see the hardness coming back into her eyes. It was like she'd been expecting this all along. The only constant in this girl's life up to now had been impermanence itself. Why would she expect this situation to be any different?

"Hold your horses there," Nana said. She unclasped the silver locket from around her neck as she followed Ava to the door. Inside, I knew the locket had a tiny picture of the whole family on one side, and a goofy little baby picture of me on the other.

"Here." Nana put the chain around Ava's neck. "This is a loan, so don't you dare trade it or sell it. I'm going to want it back the minute you're settled here again."

Ava raised and lowered one shoulder, staring at the ground. "Thanks for being nice to me," she said, without any discernible emotion. "I'm sorry I wasn't always so good."

At that, Nana's expression went dark. She reached up and took Ava by the shoulders with her own small, bony hands.

"Girl, you've got nothing to be sorry for," she said, her voice starting to shake. "You are *loved* in this home, Miss

Ava Williams. Do you hear me? Nothing you do is ever going to change that. Nothing!"

She wrapped Ava up in a big hug, and we all gathered around. I could feel Ava there in the middle of us, as stiff as a board. It was like she was trying to feel as little as possible. The girl who had cried in my arms a week ago was now packed up and put away, just like the rest of her things. To me, that felt like a tragedy.

"I'm sorry, everyone, but we really do have to get moving," Stephanie said. "It's getting late."

"Bye, Ava," Jannie said. "We're going to miss you so much!"

"Bye, Ava!" Ali said, crying in my arms, as we followed her down the front stairs.

By the time we got to the curb, where another woman from Child and Family Services was double-parked, Ava wasn't even looking at us anymore. She climbed into the backseat and took her suitcase from Bree.

"We love you, Ava," Bree said. "And we'll see you in two days."

Ava stared straight ahead, up Fifth Street, with dry eyes. "Bye," was all she said.

A moment later, they were gone.

CHAPTER

66

RON GUIDICE WATCHED HIS REARVIEW MIRROR AS THE LADY FROM SOCIAL services walked Ava down the front steps. He hadn't been able to overhear much from inside the Cross home. His listening mike on the first floor was in the kitchen. But still, this little scene spoke for itself.

There was a time when he might have felt sorry for the Crosses on a day like this. Now, it felt more like a checkmark. If he needed any reminder about why, every glance in the mirror showed him the bandages across his broken nose. He had a black eye, too, and his jaw was as stiff as concrete.

An undeniable line in the sand had been crossed. Alex was on the run now, and he knew Guidice was coming for him. But Guidice still had the upper hand. Anytime he felt compromised, all he had to do was pull the trigger—literally, and figuratively. That's what the Kahr

9mm was doing under the seat. From here on out, he'd keep it with him at all times.

Meanwhile, his thumbs jumped around the touchpad on his phone, finishing up a quick piece for *The Real Deal*. As Ava climbed into the tan minivan in front of Alex's house, he jotted down his last few thoughts for the day.

Then, as the car took off from the curb, and before Guidice pulled out to follow, he hit Send.

UNFORTUNATE, AND INEVITABLE
Posted by RG at 5:28 p.m.

It seems that Detective Cross of the MPD has gone off the rails. Anyone who has been following this story might call the events of the last twenty-four hours unsurprising. I call it an unfortunate inevitability.

Before anything else, let me reiterate that I am making this information available as a matter of public record. I have no intention to sell, package, or profit from my own story beyond what you see in this space.

In a nutshell: Detective Cross beat the s**t out of me yesterday. This was not the first unprovoked confrontation I've had with the detective, but it was certainly the most violent. (Click *here* for an overview of Cross's most recent lapses in judgment.)

From the moment I encountered him, outside the Georgetown Ripper's most recent crime scene, I suspected that Detective Cross was altered in some way—either drunk, high, or both. When I asked him about it, he quickly grew angry and belligerent.

As I pressed the question, it sparked a reaction that surprised even me. After six years of reporting on police practices both in and out of the US, I've never experienced anything like this. I received one punch to the face, where I sustained a broken nose; one punch to the jaw; and one kick to the stomach while I was on the ground. Click *here* for pictures (warning—graphic content, not suitable for children). I will be using these images as evidence in my civil suit against Detective Cross, against whom I have already filed a restraining order.

The story doesn't end there, either. Immediately following this incident, the detective was seen passing out, and was then taken away in an ambulance. (I know this because MPD attended to his medical needs before mine.) Given that I never hit him, or even touched him, I feel more certain than ever that he was, in fact, under the influence of some illicit substance.

The city seems to agree with me, too. Just this evening, the foster child in Detective Cross's care was removed from his home. Hopefully, that child will now be living in a safer and healthier environment.

Lastly, for the record, I fully admit to using this platform for making an example of Detective Cross over the past several weeks. After what happened yesterday, I wonder if anyone could blame me. If even one corrupt police officer is taken off the streets as a result of my investigations, then this work (and yes, my recently sustained injuries) will have been worth it.

Comments? Thoughts? Share them *here.*

Part Three
DROP DEAD, GORGEOUS

CHAPTER

67

ELIJAH CREEM STOOD ON A DARK STRETCH OF PALM BEACH, ADMIRING HIS OWN house from a distance.

"You know, I'm actually going to miss this place?" he said to Bergman over the phone.

"Don't worry about it. It's just a house," Bergman told him.

"Yeah, but it's a *nice* goddamn house, and I paid for it. Not her."

Even at night, and all closed up, the place fairly glowed from the pearlescent white finish on the sleek modern exterior. Miranda had insisted it be reclad that way when they bought it, to the tune of three hundred thousand dollars. It was a ridiculous bit of real estate vanity, but she'd been right in the end.

The bitch had good taste. There was no denying that.

She'd also made it clear through her mouthpiece of a

lawyer that she was coming after the Palm Beach place in the divorce. Absent a thriving private practice, and the cash flow that went with it, Miranda was taking her revenge in real estate. Creem wouldn't have expected anything less.

"Ah, well," he said. "I guess I'll have to make it up to myself somehow."

"You're wearing one of those crazy masks again, aren't you?" Bergman asked. "I can hear it in your voice."

They'd been talking for a full five minutes before Josh even noticed the slight aspiration that followed Creem's consonants, as they tripped over his latex lips. That was a good sign. These masks were an outstanding bit of business.

Even if someone did take notice of him down here, what would they see? An elderly white gentleman in a Members Only jacket. Not exactly a stellar lead, in a place like southern Florida.

This would be the last time Creem was using the old man prototype. Now that the DC police had gotten wise to the whole mask thing, they were running with it in the media—which was fine. All he had to do was change the template. Just be someone else the next time. Simple as that.

In the meantime, he realized, Josh was still talking.

"...not sure I like you running off like this," he said. His own voice was low and slow, and fairly soaked in Scotch. "This little field trip of yours wasn't part of the plan."

"What plan?" Creem answered. "You said it yourself.

This can be whatever we want it to be. Hell, I haven't felt this free since——"

"Fort Lauderdale. Yeah, I know. That's the whole point. I thought we were in this together," Josh said.

Creem took a deep breath. He loved Bergman, but the man could be a bit needy.

"We are, Josh. All the way to the end, I promise. Just don't start getting all vaginal on me. The last thing I need right now is another wife."

"Tha's funny," he half slurred. "Oh, and PS, I've already figured out how you can make this up to me. When are you coming back?"

"Soon," Creem said. "We'll talk then. But right now, I've got to get busy."

"Can I listen? Please? Pretty please?"

Creem smiled down at the sand in the dark. He would have been surprised if Josh *hadn't* asked.

"Of course," he said. "Just keep your mouth shut until I'm done."

CHAPTER

68

CREEM WATCHED THE BEACH AS A SHADOWED COUPLE WORKED THEIR WAY along the shore, arm in arm. Once they'd passed off into the dark, he crossed the sand and cut through the high grass to the back of his own property.

"What exactly are you doing, anyway?" Josh whispered over the Bluetooth.

"Something a little different this time," Creem told him. "Wait and see."

Bergman chuckled out his excitement, as a few more ice cubes dropped into his glass, a thousand miles away.

Inside the gate, Creem skirted around the pool enclosure to the house's side entrance. The stone chess set on the patio was exactly as he'd left it, nearly eight months ago. He'd played Roger Wettig from next door. Beaten him, too, if memory served. The set had gone untouched in the meantime. Chess was a little above Miranda and the girls' mental pay grade.

At the utility room door, he stopped and tried the knob. It was secure, of course, but the alarm system on this entrance had been fritzed out since two Christmases ago. He twisted the suppressor onto a small Beretta hand-gun from the inside pocket of his jacket, and shot the door handle right off. There was a fast, loud ping of metal. Nothing that would carry past the property line, anyway.

A moment later, he was in.

It was more than a little strange, sneaking into his own house like this. He left the lights off as he padded into the echoey back hall and up toward the kitchen. As he passed through the butler's pantry, Creem stopped to take a white kitchen garbage bag out of a drawer, and stuffed it in his pocket.

He continued on, making a quick circuit around the first floor, just to look around. The whole place was making him ridiculously sentimental. There had, in fact, been some decent times in this house. A few Christmases and such, back before everyone started hating each other.

And it wasn't the sex that had bothered Miranda. Not even close. She had her dalliances, and he had his.

No, it was the scandal in DC, and everything that had gone with it. There would be no more seven-figure in-come, no more white-cloth reputation, no more perfect imperfect life. It gave her all the excuse she needed to pull the trigger on something they both should have done a long time ago.

Except now, Miranda was pissed. And she was getting greedy, too.

Creem climbed the sculptural bamboo and steel staircase to the second floor. He took his time, opening doors along the hall. First was Chloe's suite, then Justine's. Neither of them had left much behind, but he did find a pair of diamond studs in Chloe's dresser, and the opal ring he and Miranda had brought Justine from Santorini a few years back.

He'd loved his little blond beauties, once. But it was painfully clear what kind of women their mother was turning them into. Neither one had called in over a month, not even to say hello. There had been exactly one text, when Chloe wanted an increase on the limit of her Amex card.

Yes, indeed—just a couple of chips off the old bitch block. It was too late to save them now.

Creem kept moving. He passed the upstairs gym and a guest room, then up another half level to the master suite.

Inside Miranda's dressing room, he opened every drawer, spilling her panties and knickknacks onto the carpet. He took what little of value was there, and a few old prescriptions from the medicine cabinet. It wasn't much—not that it mattered. Tonight was all about appearances.

Finally, he turned and headed back outside.

"Josh?" he said, halfway up the hall. "You still conscious?"

"Still here," Bergman answered. "Getting a little bored, though. What's going on?"

"Just hang on," Creem told him. "It's about to get much more interesting."

CHAPTER

69

FROM THE UTILITY ROOM DOOR, CREEM TRAVELED LATERALLY. HE SKIRTED THE side yard and pushed right through the ten-foot arborvitae between his own property and Roger Wettig's next door.

It was a little like passing through the looking glass. The house on this side of the hedge was all lit up, with a soft golden light showing through the expanses of glass on both levels.

And in fact, Roger and Annette Wettig themselves were like some kind of skewed mirror version of the Creems. Roger was twenty years older than Elijah, and Annette was at least ten years younger than Miranda—the prototypical Palm Beach trophy wife, all set to be rich and single as soon as Roger had that inevitable second heart attack of his.

As he came onto the Ipe-planked deck around Roger's

pool, Creem went into his bit. He dragged his right leg behind him and held a hand up to the back of his head, limping the last twenty yards to one of the Wettigs' back doors.

Inside, he could see Roger watching a Marlins game on an enormous television. His back was to the door, with his hands laced over the monk's cap of bald scalp on his head.

When Creem banged on the glass, Roger nearly fell out of his chair.

"Hello?" Creem called through.

Roger stared back, squinting, but not coming any closer. "Who the hell are you?" he shouted.

Creem gestured toward the beach. "I was just attacked," he said. "Could you please help me?"

From the way Roger was looking at him so intently, it was clear he had no idea who Creem was, inside the mask. Just some old stranger who'd had the nerve to be mugged on his spit of Palm Beach. He didn't even try to hide his annoyance as he came closer.

"Hang on, hang on," he said. He beeped out a code on the glowing keypad by the floor-to-ceiling sliders, and then pulled one open with a whoosh of air. The Marlins game inside was up at top volume.

"Reyes's been looking good in early season play...."

"Do you want me to call the police?" Roger said.

"No," Creem told him. "That won't be necessary."

"Whether we'll see last year's kind of batting remains to be seen...."

"Well...can I help you?" Roger said. "Are you hurt?"

"Hurt?" Creem said. "Just my feelings, I suppose. You know, you could have at least called."

Softly in the background, he could hear Josh laughing with a hand over the phone.

"What the hell are you talking about?" Roger demanded.

"A swing and a miss."

"It's me, Roger. Elijah Creem."

That was all the fun Creem allowed himself. He produced the handgun from behind his back and fired into Roger's left man boob before he could even try to turn away. So much for the heart attack. He dropped dead right there.

"Strike two! Maybe this isn't José's night, after all."

Creem kept moving. He stepped over Roger's heft and continued farther into the house. He'd been here for a few beers, a few dinner parties, and he knew the basic layout. The master bedroom was on the ground level, in its own wing off to the right.

As he left the great room behind, he could hear another TV up ahead, with whatever Annette was watching on her own back there.

"Roger?" she called out, just as Creem opened the bedroom door and fired his third shot of the night.

It caught her in the shoulder as she started to scramble off the bed. The next bullet hit her in the face, and she went down for good. She died in her husband's Dallas Cowboys jersey, with little white pieces of cotton between her toes and a fresh coat of red on the nails.

A little knife work would have been more to Creem's

liking—probably Josh's, too—but not tonight. There was no sense drawing any parallels for the police down here.

He emptied Annette's drawers quickly, and bagged the two velvet boxes that fell out as he did. He dumped her purse, took the wallet, and then took Roger's wallet as well, from the tall dresser in the closet.

That was enough. It didn't really matter what he might have missed, and it was best to keep moving.

But then halfway out the door, Creem's curiosity got the best of him. He turned around and went back to where Annette was laid out, all angles and wide eyes on the bed. With one gloved hand, he lifted up the hem of her nightshirt to have a look.

Sure enough, her breasts had a noticeable asymmetry, with the shadow of a scar still showing on either side. Roger had cheaped out on the one thing it made the least sense in the world to skimp on, and it showed. What a fool.

Two minutes later, Creem was back on the beach, walking north toward the lot where he'd parked his rental.

"That's it, Josh," he said. "It's done. I'm calling it a night."

"I still don't get it," Josh said. "What just happened?"

"Well, for one thing, I might have just single-handedly brought down the property values on this little stretch of Gold Coast. But more important? I made sure that Miranda and the girls are never going to want to use this place again."

Not bad for a night's work. Inside his mask, Dr. Creem smiled.

70

THE NEXT DAY AT WORK STARTED WITH SOME DECENT NEWS. I GOT MY GUN and badge back from Sergeant Huizenga. The chief himself had to sign off on the Glock, so that felt like a vote of confidence in the right direction.

Too bad it didn't change my work status. I was still stuck in the office, and basically spent the whole day doing three things—answering the phones, logging cold case reports in the file room, and taking the temperature of everyone I'd been working with up until now.

Technically I was off the Elizabeth Reilly case, off the Georgetown Ripper, and off the River Killer. But you don't just work a multiple homicide one day and then stop caring about it the next. I wanted to know what was going on.

I also still had Ava on my mind, and Ron Guidice as

well. In fact, my first detour that morning was over to Jarret Krause's desk.

"Alex. How's it hanging?" he said, sitting back as I came into his cube. I noticed he'd shut down whatever window he'd been working on, too.

"I'm fine," I told him. "Just wondered if you have anything new on Ron Guidice."

Krause leaned farther back, with his hands on top of his head, like he was trying to get them as far off the keyboard as possible.

"Jeez, I'm not sure what to say," he told me.

"Meaning what?" I asked, just to keep the pressure on. I knew what he meant.

"Huizenga was pretty specific. You're noncontact, right? And frankly, aren't you supposed to be laying off of Guidice?"

I wasn't going to answer that one. The truth was, I understood where Krause was coming from. He was a newbie, and probably more ambitious than he was bold. That can change over time, but right now he was working his way up by staying inside the lines. It wasn't up to me to change that for him. So I moved on.

The person who was the most open to me that morning was Errico Valente. The last we'd really talked was at the double homicide on Cambridge Place, right before my big blowout with Guidice. I still had access to the investigative files online, but Errico let me look through his notes as well.

What I learned was that the knife work on the mother and daughter victims was strikingly similar. The incisions were close enough to each other in placement and scope to indicate some level of expertise. Most of the seemingly random flesh tears were secondary, almost as if the cutter had deliberately gone back and added some messiness to the whole thing. At a minimum, our killer was getting better with practice.

Errico had also been researching mask fabricators. Based on the security camera footage, he'd narrowed it down to three possible companies, in North Carolina, Texas, and California. It seemed doubtful that the Barbie Killer, or Georgetown Ripper, or whoever he was, would do anything so obvious as to have these things shipped to a traceable address. But either way, MPD was now talking about the masks publicly, including at the press briefings.

It was a good move. If nothing else, it might put the killer on the defensive, and maybe even push him to make some kind of mistake. Anything you can do to upset a serial killer's pattern can be a potent tool, especially when you have nothing else to work with.

By the end of the day, I knew a lot more than I had when I walked in that morning. But I was still frustrated. I wanted to help. Instead, all I could do was pace around the outside of it all, just waiting to get back in.

And so far, there was no sign of that changing anytime soon.

71

ANOTHER ADVANTAGE TO WORKING THE SO-CALLED RUBBER GUN SQUAD WAS the hours. I went in at eight and signed out at five. There's only so much office work you can do.

For the first time in a while, I beat Bree home, and even better, sat down to dinner with the family. If there's one thing I could change about my life, it might just be all those dinners I miss.

After the ice cream was eaten and the dishes were washed, I was helping Jannie with some algebra, when Sampson came up onto the back porch.

"Knock knock," he said, coming in. We were all feeling pretty down about Ava, but Sampson's family. He's welcome anytime.

"How are you holding up, Nana?" he said, giving her a hug in her chair.

"I'm just fine," she said, but I think she'd been on the

same page of Madeleine Albright's new book for the last half hour. "You want some ice cream, dear?"

"Actually, I was hoping to grab Alex and Bree for a minute," he said, thumbing over his shoulder. "Maybe outside?" He leaned down to kiss Jannie on the cheek as we headed out to the picnic table in the yard.

"What's up?" I asked, once John had closed the back door behind him.

Sampson settled his bear-size frame across from us and clasped his hands on the table. It took him a second to figure out what he wanted to say, or at least, how he wanted to start.

"Let me give you a hypothetical," he said. "Suppose there's some guy pressing charges against someone else—charges he knows are false. And say this guy's gone to some lengths to set that person up, and make life difficult. Maybe he even breaks the law to get it done, but no one can prove it."

"Okay," I said. We were obviously talking about Guidice—but also *not* talking about Guidice. I knew enough to keep my mouth shut and follow John's lead for the moment. "Go on."

"I'm thinking that sort of guy might have a few skeletons in his closet," Sampson said. "The kind that don't show up on a regular background check."

I noticed Bree was sitting very still, not saying a word.

"What kind of skeletons?" I said.

Sampson leaned back and shrugged. "Drug habit? Bad debt? I don't know, maybe he's sleeping with his best friend's wife. But just for the sake of argument, let's say someone else finds out about it. Someone like me, for instance. That kind of information might be used to make a person reconsider these charges he's pressing. And maybe *that* makes life a little easier for the other guy. Him, and his family."

"Jesus, John," I said. If I weren't so on the rack about all this, the pretense might have almost seemed funny. "I couldn't ask you to do something like that—"

"If we were even talking about it," John said. "Which we're not. But just for the record, Alex, you *have* asked me to do that kind of thing before. More than once."

"Yeah, when I'm in on it," I said. "This is different."

Finally, Bree spoke up. Her voice was low, and I got the impression she'd been expecting this.

"My two cents?" she said. "I don't think John would have come over here if he didn't want to."

"That's true," Sampson told me.

I believed him, but it was also true that Sampson would do anything for us. The same way I'd do anything for him. That's not always a good thing. This was John's career we were talking about.

"I don't know, Sampson," I said.

"But I do," Bree told me. "There's a lot at stake here, Alex, and you're right in the middle of it. Let me call this one. Please."

When I looked into her eyes, I saw something else. There was something she wasn't saying—and I finally got the whole picture. Unless I was very much mistaken, this wasn't just John's idea. Bree had asked him to come over tonight.

I still felt conflicted about it all, but she was right. There was a lot at stake here, either way. I was the one with the restraining order, and they were doing whatever they could to protect me—but also Ava.

Under other circumstances, I might have also still been caught up on the loss Guidice himself had incurred, back in 2007. But he'd trumped that issue the minute he'd started messing with my family.

So instead of saying anything else, I just stood up from the table and started back inside.

"I'm going to finish helping Jannie with her homework," I said. "You two come on in when you're done talking."

CHAPTER

72

BY THE END OF THE NEXT DAY, WE WERE FINALLY PERMITTED TO GO VISIT Ava. Sampson's wife, Billie, was nice enough to come over and watch the kids, while Nana, Bree, and I drove up to Quarles Street in Northeast.

The home where Ava had been placed was on the fringes of one of the city's worst neighborhoods. It was a converted single-family house, called Howard House now. They had twelve girls living there, along with a house manager, a pair of overnight staff, and a couple of part-time counselors.

I don't expect miracles from the city, and I've got plenty of respect for the job these people are up against. Still, I had to keep my feelings in check as we walked up the cracked sidewalk and rang the bell.

Inside, the place reminded me of a few of my college

apartments. The furniture was old and mismatched, with a threadbare wall-to-wall carpet that looked like it had been new sometime in the seventies.

Several young women were hanging out in front of the TV in the living room, watching *Judge Judy* on a wall-mounted TV. I could hear cooking sounds from farther back, and half of a phone conversation, at full volume, from somewhere upstairs.

"Yes, I did. *Nuh-uh!* Don't start, Lamar. Don't even start with that shit!"

The truth was, Ava could be just as street as the next girl. I had no doubt she could stand up for herself, and even hold her own in a fight, if it came to that. But it made me sadder than I could say to know she was living here now. Just looking at Nana and Bree, I could tell they felt the same way.

Eventually, a middle-aged woman in braids came out from the back, drying her hands on a dish towel. The T-shirt over her enormous bosom had a portrait of James Baldwin, one of Nana's favorites. I chose to take that as a good sign—our first one of the day.

"Can I help you?" she said.

"We're here to see Ava Williams," I told her.

The woman threw the towel over her shoulder. "And you are?"

"We're her family," Nana said. There was a little edge of stress in her voice.

"Her foster family," Bree added quietly.

"Stephanie Gethmann from Child and Family Services said we could see her today after five," I told her.

The woman nodded and took a deep breath. I imagine she took a lot of deep breaths, in her job.

"Ava's had some issues today," she finally said. "Now's not a good time. Maybe you could come back tomorrow."

"Is she here?" Bree eyeballed the open staircase, where the loud phone talker was on her way down.

"*Damn*, Lamar, what you want from me?" she said into her cell, but then stopped between us and the woman we were talking to. "Can I go to the store?"

The woman held up five fingers, as in, you've got five minutes to be back. The girl continued out the door and down the steps, cursing Lamar the whole way.

"Sorry," the woman said. She stepped out of the foyer and into the empty dining room, which I guess was the closest thing to privacy around here. "Anyway—no. Ava's not here right now."

"What kind of issues are we talking about?" Bree said. "Is she hurt?"

"She'll be fine," the woman said.

"Is she high?" Bree asked.

At that the woman paused, and looked me in the eye instead of Bree. "I really can't talk about it," she said.

"She's high," Bree said. "Unbelievable. Two days here and she's using again."

I tried to step in before Bree's or Nana's temper got us into trouble.

"We can help, if you'll let us," I said. "How about if we wait for her?"

"I'm sorry," she said. "Visiting hours are over at seven,

and she won't be back until later. You should really call first."

There didn't seem to be anything more we could do. For a minute we all just stood there, not wanting to leave. It was incredibly disappointing.

"Well, you give her this," Nana said between clenched teeth. She handed over the tin she'd brought, filled with her homemade brownies and Ava's favorite butterscotch candies. "I want every single one of those to get to Ava. Do you understand?"

"Don't worry, ma'am. I'll make sure she gets them."

"Hey, lady, what's that?" someone called out from the living room. "Something good?"

"Shee-it, nobody be bringing me nothing. Who those people here to see, anyway?"

Nana looked over her shoulder. "You watch your mouth, young lady," she said. Then she reached over and took the tin out of the manager's hands. "I changed my mind. We'll bring these tomorrow," she said.

The manager was doing her best, she really was. I don't know anyone in the child welfare system who isn't over-worked, underpaid, and underappreciated.

Still, as we left the house, I'm pretty sure all three of us were thinking the same thing. If Ava was going to have any kind of chance, we had to get her out of there.

73

MY THIRD DAY OF DESK DUTY WENT PRETTY MUCH THE SAME AS THE FIRST two. I was starting to feel like some kid stuck with an in-school suspension.

Then, late in the afternoon, another call came in.

"Homicide," I answered, for the hundredth time that day.

"Yes, hello, this is Detective Penner from Palm Beach Police down here in Florida. I'm looking for Detective Cross."

"You've got him," I said. I've done a fair amount of collaborating with departments all around the country. It's not so unusual to get a call like this. My guess was that he wanted some kind of consult.

"First of all, can I just say I'm a fan of your book?" Detective Penner told me. "I'm hoping you're going to write something else one of these days."

"Sure, in my spare time," I deadpanned. "How can I help you?"

"We've got a double homicide investigation going on down here, from two nights ago. It's a husband and wife, with all indications of a simple robbery. The reason I'm calling is we just heard from the caretaker at the house next door to this one. Looks like it was hit, too, when no one was home."

"And you're calling me because..."

"I'm having a hard time locating the owner of that second house. As it turns out, this guy is someone you arrested a while back. A doctor by the name of Elijah Creem. Ring any bells?"

It sure did. There was no forgetting that name, just for the name's sake. But beyond that, the night of Creem's little underage sex party, and the bust we ran, was pretty hard to forget.

He'd also made a few headlines in the meantime. They'd been calling him Dr. Creep in the rags. I was pretty sure he and his friend, Bergman, had a trial coming up, where Sampson was going to be testifying.

"I was wondering if you might be able to send someone over to see if Dr. Creem is home, or even in town," Penner said. "He hasn't been answering any calls."

"Is he a suspect?" I said. The guy was such scum, I was prepared to believe anything about him.

"Depends on where he was two nights ago," Penner said. "At a minimum, I need to notify him of the robbery and ask a few questions."

Technically, it was a breach of my noncontact status to

start interacting with the public. But everyone else was flat out, and truth be told, some part of me wanted to see how far this guy had fallen since the night I put the cuffs on him. If it turned into anything, I'd pass it on to Sampson. He worked out of Second District, where Creem lived, anyway.

I waited until five, then clocked out and headed over to Creem's house.

CHAPTER

74

DR. CREEM LIVED IN AN IMPRESSIVE TUDOR ON A LITTLE CUL-DE-SAC IN Wesley Heights. The whole property butted up against Glover-Archbold Park, with plenty of privacy all around. From what little I knew of Creem's situation, I assumed his next address was going to be something a bit more downscale, with guards and a roommate.

Then again, money like his has been known to buy justice—and freedom—every once in a while. I hadn't been planning on following the trial, but now that he was back on my radar, maybe I would.

There was no answer at the front door when I rang, but the garage was open, with a midnight-blue Escalade parked inside. I let myself around through the side gate, toward the wooded back half of the property.

That's where I found him. He was standing with a cigar

clenched in his teeth, bent over a putter on a big kidney-shaped green that had been worked into the patio at the back of the house. A small yellow flag stuck up from each of the three cups sunk into the fake turf.

"Dr. Creem?"

He didn't seem to recognize me at first. I'm pretty sure all he saw was some black guy in a suit, standing there on his property.

"Don't you believe in ringing the bell?" he said.

"I did," I told him, and showed my badge. "I'm Detective Cross from MPD. We've actually met before."

A flash of recognition showed on his face then. I wondered if he remembered trying to bribe me, too.

Either way, he played it off. He took a ball from the pocket of his sweats, dropped it on the green, and put both hands back on the putter. The guy just oozed arrogance. I tried not to take too much pleasure from the fact that I was here with bad news.

"What exactly can I do for you?" he said.

"We had a call from Palm Beach," I said. "The police department's been trying to reach you."

"Yeah? What did I do now?" he said and executed a smooth, twenty-foot putt that just missed its mark.

"Apparently there was a robbery at your house the other night. Your place and the one next door. Unfortunately your neighbors were both killed by the intruder."

"You don't say." Creem dropped another ball onto the ground. "Are we talking about the Wettigs or the Andersons?"

"I'm sorry, but I don't know."

"Jesus, I hope it's the Wettigs," he said. "No disrespect, but that guy's an ass, and he plays his TV way too loud."

No disrespect? It was a little late for that. I knew I couldn't stand this guy for a reason.

I interviewed Creem a little bit and got his story. He'd been home the night of the Florida murders and said I could check it out with his friend, Josh Bergman, if necessary. I told him I'd pass it all on to the Palm Beach Police Department.

"Now, if that's all, I need to keep moving, detective. I've got a social engagement." He stopped and looked me in the eye, with a familiar grin. "Believe it or not, there are still some people in this town who will associate with me."

In a strange way, it made me think of Ava, the way Creem deflected any and all sense of real emotion—about himself, or anyone else for that matter. In his own way, the man was shut up tight against the world. Just like Ava.

The difference being that I wished Ava well.

CHAPTER

75

CREEM HAD BEEN EXPECTING SOME KIND OF NOTIFICATION FROM PALM BEACH PD. He just hadn't expected it to come from someone like Detective Cross. It was more disarming than actually alarming. A nasty little coincidence that he chose not to share that evening.

Supposedly, this was make-it-up-to-Josh night, for the imagined little infraction of running off to Florida without him. Whatever big surprise Josh had planned—and Creem was fairly sure he knew what it was—there was no sense in muddying the waters with paranoia. At least not beforehand.

Still, some cover was in order. He waited until they were halfway through dinner, and then brought it up as casually as he could.

"By the way, if anyone asks, you and I were at my place on Friday night," he said. "We grilled a couple of steaks, just like the ones we're having right now, and watched a movie. Let's say *Taxi Driver.* You left just before twelve."

Josh grinned. He liked this part of the game. It also helped that he was in such a good mood tonight—maybe even a little too hyped. Creem poured him another draught of cabernet, and dug back into his own excellent Montana *wagyu.* There was no better place for beef in Georgetown than Bourbon Steak, at the Four Seasons. Josh had picked the place, but he knew Elijah loved it.

"So, what's the big surprise, anyway?" Creem asked. "Where are we headed from here?"

Josh set down his fork and leaned in. "Elijah, I need you to stay open-minded about this, okay? It's nothing we haven't done before. It's just been a while. Like...twenty-five years."

Creem looked him in the eye, holding back for the moment, as the understanding settled silently between them.

"I don't ask for much," Josh said. That was debatable, but whatever. He was putting on the puppy dog's eyes now. Obviously, he'd already settled on what he needed Creem's answer to be.

"Please don't say no. They're meeting us upstairs. I gave them a wad of cash, and they booked the room themselves. All very high-end." Josh leaned a little closer and lowered his voice again. "I even had them pick up a rubber mattress cover for the session. They probably think I'm totally kinky, but that's okay. The point is—it's all taken care of, Elijah. Every last detail."

Creem let him hang for another few seconds, but then

shrugged nonchalantly. "What am I going to say?" he asked.

Josh fairly beamed, and sat back with his glass in his hand. "You won't be sorry," he said.

"Of course, I do have to ask—"

"Actually, you don't. This is me, remember? She's absolutely perfect," Josh told him. "So is he, if you care."

Creem nodded, and sniffed his wine. The bouquet in the glass was almost enough to get drunk on. He'd go slow. He wanted to stay sharp, no pun intended.

"What time?" he said.

"Ten o'clock."

It was nine thirty now. "We'll have to skip dessert," he said.

Bergman signaled to the waiter from across the room. He playfully twirled the wine in his glass with his finger, then licked it clean and downed the rest before he threw a white napkin over the half-finished meal in front of him.

"Hardly," he said.

CHAPTER

76

UPSTAIRS IN THE SUITE, JOSH INTRODUCED ELIJAH TO THE ATTRACTIVE YOUNG couple waiting for them.

"This is Richie. And this," he said, with a barely contained laugh, "is Miranda."

Creem looked twice at the girl. "Is that your real name?" he asked, but she only stared awkwardly over at Josh. "Never mind," he said. She was more of a Chloe than a Miranda, but he appreciated the sick little gesture, anyway. Josh was trying to make this special for him, and in any case, she was tall, lithe, blond, and yes, perfect.

It looked like Richie and "Miranda" had started in without them. A bottle of tequila was open on the bedside table, and even though there were no loose tabs in sight, the ready-to-ball looks on their faces told Creem they were all X'd up and good to go.

He poured himself a small shot of the tequila and settled into a comfortable chair by the bed. A stolen knife from the steakhouse downstairs was in the breast pocket of his blazer. To his own surprise, he was starting to feel quite into this. Maybe Josh knew him even better than he realized.

"So, Miranda," Creem said. "Tell me what turns you on."

With a little prodding, the prelubricated couple-for-hire got right into the swing of things. They sat perched on the edge of the king-size bed while Creem and Bergman directed them, and watched.

Soon, the boy was running his hand up the girl's skirt. The girl, in turn, put a well-manicured hand over the boy's crotch.

"Not too fast," Josh told her. "Just unsnap his pants, and then leave them like that for a while."

There was no need for cross talk. They'd been here before. Josh told the girl what to do to the boy, and Creem told the boy what to do to the girl.

"Put your finger in her. That's it. Very nice."

After a while, Creem started to wish they'd brought a camera. The little beauty didn't seem to have a single hair below her neck. He recorded it with his eyes instead, watching from the side while Bergman sat on the uphol-stered bench at the foot of the bed.

Over the course of several minutes, the two were un-dressed, and then eventually going at it, flagrante delicto. The girl reached up, pressing her hands against the head-board with her back arched and her eyes closed, while the boy did his thing.

When Creem had seen enough, he gave Josh a nod, to let him know he was ready.

Josh held up a finger. He wanted to see the boy finish. But he did take a pistol out of the briefcase he'd carried in, and laid it flat on his own bulging lap. The two little bunny rabbits on the mattress didn't even notice.

It wasn't such a bad way to go, actually.

Slowly, Josh got onto his feet. The thousand-volt look in his eyes was unmistakable. It was his killing face. Creem had only seen it once before—twenty-five years ago, in Fort Lauderdale. That was the last time they'd killed together.

"That's it, kids," Josh told them. "Exactly like that. Don't stop now. Please, whatever you do, don't stop."

The boy probably couldn't have if he wanted to. He thrust a few more times and then ground furiously into the girl, as she squealed underneath him. He squeezed his eyes shut, and threw his head back.

That's when Josh went for it.

With a muffled pop, he fired one bullet straight into the crown of the boy's head. It sent him collapsing back onto the girl, like a naked rag doll, already dead. She didn't even seem to notice what had happened at first.

By the time she did, Creem's knife was out and it was far too late for her to do anything about it.

CHAPTER

77

IT WAS COMING UP ON THREE IN THE MORNING WHEN CREEM AND BERGMAN decided to call it a night. They sat parked in the deserted lot next to Fletcher's Cove, looking out toward the river.

Both Richie and "Miranda" were on their way downstream by now. The bottle of tequila sat mostly empty on the car seat. Josh had even smoked a cigar with Elijah, though he'd clearly just pretended to enjoy it. Still posing, after all these years.

"There's something you should know," Creem told him. "I didn't want to say anything before, and it's not as bad as it sounds, but a detective came to see me today."

Josh kept his cool, which surprised Creem a little. "A detective?"

"Cross. One of the ones who arrested us that night. He came to tell me my place in Palm Beach had been burgled. The neighbors are dead, too. Imagine that."

"Why him?" Josh said.

"I have no idea, but it was all about the robbery. I'm not too concerned."

"Whatever you say, Elijah."

Creem was relieved to hear Josh speaking like this. Of course, he was also half-drunk, and still riding the high of the evening. He lolled back against the headrest and closed his eyes as the silence stretched on in the car.

"What would you do if the police *were* onto us?" Creem said finally. "If you knew they were coming after you?"

Bergman shrugged. "Whatever I had to."

"Would you run?"

"If I could, sure. I hear Vietnam is nice. Cute boys, good food. Or Argentina."

"And what if you couldn't get away? What then?" Creem asked. "There's still the trial to consider."

"Believe me, I've considered it," Bergman said. "And in the words of my alcoholic mother"—he stopped and put on a shaky, Katharine Hepburn voice—"always leave the party before the party's over, darling."

He raised his head then and looked across at Creem with a sudden seriousness.

"I meant it about not going to jail, Elijah. I'm sorry, but I don't need to turn fifty that badly. Nobody does."

Bergman's ready answers seemed to explain a few things. Maybe that was the upside of Josh's paranoid streak—always considering the exit plan, one way or another.

"You said something the other day," Creem reminded

him. "Something about how we'll finish this together, when the time comes. Is that what you were talking about?"

Bergman picked up the bottle between them and took a swig. "You ever see *Thelma and Louise*?" he asked.

"No."

"Well, never mind," he said. "But to answer your question—yes. That's what I was talking about. I love you, Elijah. You can make fun all you like, but I do. Without you...without all of this...I really don't have anything worth sticking around for. Not anymore."

There were tears in his eyes now. The conversation had shifted in a way that Creem hadn't anticipated. He even allowed himself to be hugged, which was not something he usually went in for.

"I feel the same way, Josh," he said. "About all of it. I wouldn't trade the last several weeks for anything."

"Me either, Louise," he said.

"I don't know what that means," Creem said.

"Never mind."

CHAPTER

78

AT THE END OF THE NEXT DAY, WE FINALLY GOT TO SEE AVA. I HAD ALL KINDS OF questions for her, but I knew we couldn't push too hard on this first visit. She'd been through a lot since we'd last seen her.

It was quiet at Howard House when we got there, and Ava herself answered the door. Whether or not she was happy to see us, we got a cool breeze of tolerance when we went to hug her—arms at her sides, and no smile at all. I found myself scanning the exposed skin on her arms, and even behind her ears, for puncture marks. It made me sad to even consider that Ava might be injecting, but I've seen junkies younger than her.

After that, we settled on the front porch in some old lawn chairs, with Cokes and the tin of Nana's day-old brownies. Nana did a lot of the talking at first, and told Ava about the KIPP school she'd already scoped out for her.

Bree and I gave her a homemade "We Miss You" card from Jannie and Ali. That got the first and only smile of the day. It was all kind of stilted and awkward, but better than being kept at a distance. I was glad just to see her.

Still, after fifteen minutes of nodding and one-word answers from Ava, I decided to address the elephant in the room. We knew from Stephanie that she'd been enrolled in a mandatory drug counseling program, but not a lot more than that.

"Ava, there's something we need to ask you about," I said.

She went perfectly still then, and rested the toes of her sneakers against the concrete. It reminded me of a sprinter in the blocks, ready to bolt.

"We know a little about what's been going on the past few days, and I want you to know how concerned we are about you," I said. "Not about what you did. About *you*."

Nana looked at me like I was going too fast, but Bree picked it up from there.

"Sweetheart, listen to me. It's really important that you tell us where you've been getting these drugs. Which corner, or dealer, or friend—"

"I don't gotta answer that," Ava said. "You two are police."

Even after months of living in our home, she saw us as a threat. That distrust of authority was in her DNA.

"We're not here to bust anybody," I said. "The problem is, you never know what you're getting out there. Kids accidentally overdose every single day, especially on the kind of stuff you've been taking."

"I ain't taking any drugs!" she said suddenly.

I knew her well enough to recognize the kneejerk lying she did when she felt cornered. It wasn't about being believable. It was about saying whatever she had to in the moment.

Before we could say anything else, the front door opened and another girl came outside. It was the loud phone talker from the other day. She was about Ava's age, but going on thirty, with low-slung jeans and a tight denim jacket.

"W'sup, Ava?" she said. "These your people?"

"I'm Alex," I said. "This is Bree, and Nana. We're Ava's foster family."

The girl's eye landed on the brownies, and Nana held up the tin.

"Thank you, ma'am," she said, taking two, with a little grin. "Ava tell you what she been up to lately?"

"Shut up, Nessa!" Ava blurted out. "You mind your own business."

"Whatever," the girl said. I assumed she was talking about the drug counseling, but either way, she didn't seem to take Ava too seriously. In fact, she held up her phone to snap a group shot of us, like nothing had happened. "Say cheese, y'all."

"Cheese," we said—except for Ava, of course. I gave the girl my number and she texted the picture right over before taking another brownie and disappearing back inside.

"She doesn't seem so bad," Nana said. "Is she a friend?"

"My roommate," Ava said. "She's a'ight."

We offered to take both girls out to dinner, if she wanted, but Ava said they were making tacos that night, and she wanted to stick around. We all nodded and acted like we understood, but we also left frustrated when the visit was over.

I didn't see Ava as ungrateful, or bratty. I saw her as broken, and unable to process everything she was feeling. It's the kind of void kids try to fill up with drugs all the time. Once you add in a history of neglect, like Ava had, and the pressure of living in the foster system, meaningful change can start to be nearly impossible.

It's all about baby steps, at best. And that's on the good days.

Today was not one of them.

79

MEANWHILE, THE HITS JUST KEPT ON COMING.

Back at work the next morning, I went to log into the case files, and the system spit back an unwelcome message.

Login ID not recognized.

I tried a few more times but kept getting back the same message. Clearly, my access to the system had been revoked sometime in the last twelve hours. My noncontact status at work was now complete.

I shouldn't have been surprised. All it took was a routine case review for anyone up the food chain from me to see my virtual fingerprints all over the River Killer, Georgetown Ripper, and Elizabeth Reilly files. Based on the rules of my suspension, I wasn't supposed to be poking around the system to begin with.

But that didn't stop me from going in to complain to Sergeant Huizenga.

"Don't start, Alex," she said, as soon as I showed up in her door. She knew why I was there. "I'm not in the mood."

"This isn't about me," I told her. "We've got three potentially active serials on the books right now. When was the last time we were stretched this thin?"

"Not the point," she said. "All Commander D'Auria saw when he caught this was something I should have already taken care of. Chewed my ass out about it, too, at ten o'clock last night, thank you very much."

"I'm not talking about getting back in the field," I told her. "I'm talking about reading files, so I can be up to speed when I'm reinstated."

"What don't you understand about noncontact status?" she shouted at me. "You think I *want* you on the sidelines? Jesus! Why are we even having this conversation?"

It was day eighteen of the crisis, and progress wasn't nearly what it needed to be. The longer these investigations went on, the more Huizenga was going to have management breathing down her neck, micromanaging her life and demanding results. That's usually when the yelling starts.

And it was about to get worse.

Just then, Detective Jacobs pushed past me into Huizenga's office. Whatever she had, it was big. I could tell just from the way she was moving.

"Bad news, sergeant," she said.

"Hang on." Huizenga put up a hand and turned her lasers back on me. "That's it, Alex. We're done here."

I hadn't been left out of a Major Case Squad conversation since I could remember. The whole thing had me steaming mad, but there wasn't much choice.

I didn't go far, though. Instead of heading back to my desk, I stopped right outside Huizenga's door and listened in. It's not a move I'm especially proud of, but like I said, it wasn't about me. It was about the victims, and their families, and maybe most of all, the potential victims still to come. All those people deserved every resource we had to offer, and at the risk of tooting my own horn, they weren't getting it.

"What is it, Jessica?" Huizenga asked.

"We just got word from CIC about two floaters in the Potomac. They washed up on Roosevelt Island about an hour ago. One young white male, shot in the head and stabbed all over the groin. One young white female—"

"Don't tell me. Blond. Three carefully placed stab wounds. Bad haircut."

"Unfortunately, yeah," Jacobs said.

"And you're saying they were found at the exact same time?"

"That's the freaky little kicker to the whole thing. The two vics were handcuffed together in the water. Whatever that means."

I took a deep breath. It meant that our two Georgetown killers were back in business together. More than ever, from the sound of it.

I heard Huizenga's chair push back, and some jangling keys. "Does Valente already know?" she asked.

"Not yet."

"Call him. I'll notify the chief. And tell whoever's on the scene not to touch a damn thing."

When Jacobs came out, she glared at me but kept moving. Ten minutes later, all off-duty Major Case Squad personnel had been called in, and the office was empty. Except for me, of course. I was left back to answer the phones and twiddle my thumbs, like some kind of lackey in a cage. Again.

I really wasn't sure how much more of this I could stand.

CHAPTER

80

AS SOON AS I HAD THE OFFICE TO MYSELF, I PUT IN A CALL TO BREE.

I knew she was working a gang shooting over at the Garfield Terrace projects in Northwest. She'd left the house early that morning when the call came in. Hopefully, she'd be wrapping up soon and could go take a look at the scene on Roosevelt Island—or at least, get a little closer to it than my radioactive ass was ever going to get.

"I've still got about an hour to go here," she told me. "But I can drive by after that, if it helps."

"Anything helps," I said. I was determined to track this case, one way or another. "See if you can find Errico Valente. He'll keep you in the loop, if anyone will."

Working the same homicide—much less several of them—was something Bree and I had set out to avoid when we got married. It only made family life that much harder, in terms of being around for the kids and keeping things running smoothly at home. But somewhere along the way, between the Ava situation, and Ron Guidice, and now my own troubles at work, the rules of the game had shifted.

And for better or worse, we make a pretty good team. I like working with her.

After that, I spent the next few hours alone on the desk, taking calls and mulling over everything I knew about these cases.

Whatever our killers were getting out of their double homicides, it was clearly working for them. Two hand-cuffed victims in the river was a step up from a body dump in Rock Creek Park. It was staged. They were getting into it now.

And *staged* seemed like the right word. It was as if they were putting on some kind of show with all of this. For us? For each other? For the world?

Who knew? It was all just questions in a vacuum, while I hung there on the desk, answering call after call.

Finally, around midafternoon, I heard back from Bree.

"I just got here," she said. "And I'm already back at the perimeter. D'Auria tagged me out before I could even get a look at the bodies."

"Did you tell him you've got a prior connection to the case?"

"He wasn't having it," she said. "They've got this place tied down tight."

"What about Valente?" I asked.

"He's down by the water. I'm going to hang out a little and see if he comes up for air, but I've got to be at the

ME's office before five, and then…" Bree's voice trailed off. "Oh, for crap's sake," she said then. "You've got to be kidding me."

"What is it?" I asked. I hated getting all of this second-hand.

"It's Ron Guidice. He's over on the line with the other reporters. Son of a bitch just took my picture," she said.

My face started burning, just thinking about it. Of course he was there. He was everywhere these days.

"Don't give him the satisfaction of a response," I said. "That's exactly what he wants."

"I'd like to wrap that camera strap around his throat."

"Believe me, I know how you feel," I said. "But don't do it, Bree. Ignore him."

I heard her take a deep breath. I did the same.

"Yeah, okay," she said. "I'll let him live. But listen, I've got to go. I'll call you if I get anything off of Valente. Love you."

"You too," I said, and then she was gone.

Usually, I can read Bree pretty well. Not this time. After we hung up, I sat there wondering if she'd told me what I needed to hear, or if she really was going to give Guidice some distance. She hated the guy just as much as I did.

For all I knew, she'd already punched his lights out before I'd even taken my next call.

81

JOHN SAMPSON WAS IN HIS CAR WHEN HE GOT BREE'S TEXT.

Eyes on Guidice. Go now if u can.

They'd been waiting for this opportunity. Instead of continuing down Mass Ave. to the police training he was supposed to hit that day, he took a hard right on K Street and headed off to Virginia instead.

Accurint records showed Ron Guidice's name on a house rental in Reston for the last three years. The place belonged to a developer out of Atlanta, with a management company based in DC, but none of those people had anything interesting to say about their tenant. Guidice had decent credit, paid his rent on time, and looked normal on paper.

The house itself was surprisingly suburban, for lack of

a better word. It was a simple little Cape, painted an ugly light blue, in the middle of a tightly packed neighborhood, Sampson saw as he drove in. It wasn't nearly the hole in the ground you might expect a bottom-feeder like Guidice to crawl out of.

At the front door, he rang the bell just in case. When no one answered, Sampson stepped off the low porch and did a quick half lap around to the back. There was no car in the driveway, no garage, either. Just a nonexistent scrub of fenced-in backyard.

If there was any concern at all, it was the lack of deadbolts on Guidice's doors. There weren't even shades or curtains on the windows. Going by first impressions, it didn't seem like the guy had anything to hide. But there was one way to find out.

Sampson slipped the license out of his wallet and easily carded his way past the cheap lock on the back door.

From there, it didn't take long to case out the first floor. Empty seemed to be the operative word. There wasn't much of anything in the fridge, and just a single recliner next to a folding TV table in the living room. A stack of newspapers by the front door went back about three weeks—*Post, New York Times,* and *Al-Sabah,* for whatever that was worth.

He continued upstairs and found a simple layout of three small bedrooms. One was completely empty. One had a futon on the floor, with a few piles of folded clothes against the wall.

The third bedroom seemed to be Guidice's makeshift office. There was a card table piled with Pendaflex files, and a cheap Lexmark printer on the floor. The files didn't seem to have much rhyme or reason. There were clippings about everything from police brutality to financial planning, car engine repair, and even the White House vegetable garden.

The whole place was kind of depressing, actually. It was pretty easy to imagine Guidice living out his pathetic nights here, working up his conspiracy theories, and writing his shitty little blog.

Still, Sampson had been hoping for something he could run with. He took another twenty minutes or so, checking the closets, the floorboards, and the air vents, just in case. But there was nothing.

Back outside, he was halfway to his car when he spotted one of the neighbors. He was an older man in golf pastels, wheeling his garbage out to the curb. It seemed worth a shot, anyway. Sampson stopped to take an empty interoffice envelope off his backseat, and headed over.

"Excuse me," he said. "I'm looking for Ron Guidice. Can you tell me if this is where he lives?"

The old man regarded the little blue Cape house and shook his head.

"Sorry. I know he's a tall fellow with a beard, but I don't know his name."

"That sounds like him," Sampson said. He held up the envelope. "He's got to sign for this. Any idea when he tends to be home?"

"Hard to say." The man stopped to lean on his mini-dumpster. He had lonely bachelor written all over him— the kind who liked to talk. "Ever since the old lady and that little girl moved out, he just kind of comes and goes. Mostly goes."

Sampson nodded, keeping a poker face. Old lady? Little girl? Why hadn't there been any mention of that in the background checks? And why didn't they live here anymore?

"So, I guess that's his family, huh?" he asked.

The man shrugged. "I think she was the grandma. Big fat lady, anyway. The little girl was cute as a bug, though. Same age as my granddaughter, just about. Five, maybe six, I'd say."

Sampson's mind was turning it all over while the neighbor talked. It explained a thing or two—like why Guidice might choose a place like this.

"I don't suppose you know where I could find them," he said, but now the man stepped back.

"Son, I don't even know who they are. How am I going to know where they got to?"

"Fair enough," Sampson said. "I'll just try back."

"If I see him, I'll tell him you're looking for him. What's your name?" the man called out as Sampson headed to his car.

"Joe Smith," he said. "But don't worry about it. I'm pretty good at finding someone when I want to."

82

ABOUT HALFWAY THROUGH THE AFTERNOON, I GOT A SECOND CALL FROM Detective Penner down in Palm Beach.

I'd already passed Elijah Creem's information on to Penner, and for all I knew Creem's alibi for the night of the Florida murders had checked out. So what was this?

"What can I do for you?" I said.

"Actually, I might have something for you," he said. "We've been seeing some of the coverage on your Georgetown serial cases up there. Sounds like some pretty crazy stuff."

"To say the least," I told him.

"So, these masks your perp is using. What can you tell me about them?" he asked.

Penner had no way of knowing about my restricted work status, and I wasn't in any hurry to clue him in. I wanted to see what he had to say. For that, I was going to have to share a little information.

"They seem to be fabricated from latex," I said. "Definitely high-grade, and convincing enough to pass on the street. If you look closely, you can pick up on a little bit of stiffness in the footage we've got, but not much."

"Yeah, that's what I thought," he said. "We've got a little security footage of our own down here. We picked up a guy getting into a dark sedan, a quarter mile north of our double homicide, and about half an hour after the estimated time of death for our two victims. There was just something about him—"

Penner hadn't gotten all the way through what he had to say, but I saw it coming.

"Older white guy? Maybe six feet, and a hundred and eighty, two hundred pounds?"

"So you know what I'm talking about," he said.

"I know that much," I told him.

"I was hoping we could do an image swap, and see if we aren't talking about the same guy," Penner said.

"And by same guy, you mean Elijah Creem."

"At a minimum, it's highly suspicious," he said. "He's got homes in Georgetown and Palm Beach, which just happens to be where these masks are popping up."

I was already on my feet, with the blood pumping in my ears. Considering the kind of sociopathic tendencies Creem had shown me both times we met, it all felt entirely plausible. Creem was also a surgeon, which meant a high degree of knife skill, whether that was with a scalpel, or with our killer's signature serrated blade.

In homicide, circumstantial evidence can be an easy trap. I've been around long enough to avoid getting carried away by how things *seem* to be sometimes. But even so, by the time I hung up with Penner, this didn't just feel like a theory to me.

It felt a whole hell of a lot like the solution.

CHAPTER

83

IT DIDN'T TAKE LONG TO CONFIRM WHAT DETECTIVE PENNER HAD SUSPECTED.
Other than a few cosmetic details, the old man mask in
the Florida surveillance image was a clear match to the
ones we'd seen in Georgetown. It was time to move on
Dr. Creem.

The first thing I did was call Errico Valente down at
his crime scene on Roosevelt Island to brief him. Then I
printed everything I had in hard copy and left it in a plain
envelope on Valente's desk. I'd already gotten enough
heat for one day. I didn't need an e-trail leading back to
me on any of this, and I knew Errico could handle it.
Also, that he'd be discreet. If he got the credit, that was
the least of my worries.

After that, all I could do was finish out my day, head
home, and wait to hear what they'd made of it all.

Of course, that didn't stop me, Bree, and Sampson from

putting our heads together that night, up in my office at home. There was still plenty to talk about.

It was starting to feel like we had our own PI firm running out of my attic. It was a little ridiculous, with all the secrecy—but also exciting. After three days on the desk, I felt like I was actually getting something done.

I caught Bree and John up on everything I'd learned that day, and we swapped a few theories. My best guess was that Elijah Creem would be in for questioning by morning, if not actually in custody. This also put a bright light on his friend, Josh Bergman, who was starting to look pretty good as our River Killer. Valente would be speaking with him, too, no doubt.

After that, we moved on to the Elizabeth Reilly case, and her phantom boyfriend—the man we knew of only as Russell. Bree had continued checking NCIC records, flagging any arrests for someone with that first or last name. So far, none of the hits she'd gotten had shown even a remote possibility of being related.

It was the same deal with Rebecca Reilly, Elizabeth's kidnapped daughter. I'd been checking in with Ned Mahoney at the FBI, but there was no movement on that front, either. The hard truth was that our best shot at finding this baby would be if "Russell" came out of the shadows to go after another pregnant girl. I hated to even think about it.

All of which left the subject of Ron Guidice on the table.

"What about our other friend?" I said. "The one we don't talk about."

Bree and Sampson looked at each other. Whatever they had going on Guidice, they'd been keeping it to themselves.

"Not much to tell," John said.

"Not much?" I said. "Or nothing at all?" I was too curious to leave it alone. Or maybe just sick of being out of the loop.

Sampson shrugged and killed the last of his beer. "Supposedly, there was an older woman and a little girl living with him until recently. The neighbor thinks they were Guidice's mother and daughter, but he couldn't say for sure. Either way, they're gone now. That place of his out in Reston is like a ghost house."

"I thought we weren't talking about this," Bree said.

"We're not," Sampson said, and laid himself across my old leather couch.

I gave John a thumbs-up by way of thanks. I wished I could be in on this, but as long as Guidice's restraining order was in place, I wasn't going to touch it. If that meant Guidice got to win a few battles along the way, so be it.

I was still determined to win the war.

CHAPTER

84

RON GUIDICE SLID HIS HEADPHONES OFF.

Son of a bitch! He almost wanted to turn the whole operation ninety degrees and go after John Sampson instead. No way that pathetic excuse for a cop was going to get any closer to his family than he already had. That was for damn sure.

Either way, the signs were unmistakable. It was time to make a big move. The only question was—what first?

When the phone in his pocket buzzed, Guidice gritted his teeth. He didn't have to look at the ID. His mother was the only person who had this number, and it was the fourth time she'd tried him in the last hour. It was getting ridiculous.

"*What,* Mom?" he finally answered. "I'm working."

"Daddy?"

Instead of Lydia, it was Emma Lee at the other end. Immediately, he regretted his tone.

"Hey, sweetheart," he said softly. "What are you doing up so late?"

"When are you coming home?" his daughter asked. Her little Virginia accent coaxed at him, pulling his heart right through the phone. He felt guilty as hell, but that couldn't be helped right now.

"Just a few more days," he said. "Not much longer."

"The baby's been crying a lot. I think she misses you."

"That's what babies do, sweet pea. Don't worry about it. Now, put Grandma on the phone, okay?"

"I love you, Daddy."

"I love you, too. More than the moon."

After a short pause, Lydia came on the line. "Ronald?" she said.

Guidice could feel his gut turn a one eighty at the sound of her voice. "What the hell is she doing up?" he said. "You're supposed to be looking after her."

"Don't you curse at me," his mother said. "Your daughter misses her daddy. Can you blame her? You move us all the way out here and then don't come around for days. And we're out of milk, by the way. I can't keep walking back to that store on these ankles."

Guidice gave himself a ten count. There was nothing to do but suck it up. He needed Lydia now more than ever.

"Mom, we've talked all about this," he said slowly. "As long as I've got this lawsuit going, I don't think it's safe for me to be around you and the girls too much. It's no secret the police are out to get me."

"But you're the victim! You're the one who got his nose broken."

"That's exactly what I'm talking about. The last thing you want is cops like that coming around, asking questions. Then it's just a matter of time before you've got reporters out there, trying to snap pictures of you and the girls. Right through the windows, even."

"Stop it," she said. "Now you're scaring me."

"I'm not trying to, Mom. I'm just explaining."

In fact, he *was* trying, a little. If there was one thing Lydia Guidice hated, it was seeing pictures of herself. The fat ones reminded her she was fat, and the skinny ones reminded her that she wasn't skinny anymore. Somewhere there was a box of family snapshots—including half a dozen of Guidice's old man, standing there with his arm around nobody anymore—where she'd torn herself right out.

It was too bad the old man had dropped dead instead of her. He might have actually appreciated what Guidice was trying to accomplish here.

"Don't trust anyone, Mom," he said. "You know your rights, don't you?"

"Yes, Ronald. You've told me a thousand times."

"If someone comes around asking questions, you tell them you're not required to identify yourself, and that you want to speak to your lawyer first."

"Oh, for pity's sake. I know, I know."

It was one of the best ways to get Lydia off the phone. She hated talking about this stuff.

"I'll try to get out there when I can," he told her. "I just need you and the girls to hang on a little longer without me, okay?"

"Do we have a choice?" she asked, edging back into that childish tone of hers—the one that made Guidice think maybe the old man had been the lucky one after all.

"No, Mom," he said before he hung up again, "I guess you don't."

CHAPTER

85

THE NEXT MORNING, VALENTE BRIEFED THE ENTIRE INVESTIGATIVE TEAM ABOUT Elijah Creem. At least, that's what I inferred. I wasn't permitted into the briefings, or the Joint Operations Center, where they took place.

But as soon as everyone started filtering back into the office, I could feel the buzz. Valente waved at me from across the room before he took off again, followed out the door by Huizenga and Jacobs. I didn't expect him to catch me up in front of everyone, but it was clear that this case was now moving forward.

Before I could start sorting anything out, I got an unexpected call. It was Chief Perkins's office telling me I was wanted upstairs. Perkins's assistant, Tracy, didn't offer any details. She just said to come right away.

I knew this summons could cut either way—good or bad news. Up to now, Perkins had been looking out for me as much as not. He'd let me spend the night in jail, but he'd also pulled me off the cell block early. He'd kept me on the sidelines all this time, but he also made sure I got my gun and badge back, which he didn't have to do.

So what now?

"Go on in," Tracy said, waving me past reception when I got there. "He's waiting for you."

Perkins's door was open and he was sitting behind his huge maple desk—Old Ironsides, we call it—signing a stack of paperwork when I came in.

"Have a seat if you like," he said.

I stayed on my feet while he signed a few more forms. When he finally looked up, he took a separate page out of his inbox and held it out for me.

"What's this?" I said.

"A letter of declination from the US Attorney's Office," he told me. "It looks like today's your lucky day. They're citing insufficient evidence for prosecution."

I felt like a weight had just been lifted off me. A letter of declination meant they were declining to advance my case to an indictment.

"I'm a little surprised, to be honest," I said. "Internal Affairs has been riding me pretty hard since this whole thing started."

"Let's just say you owe me one. Or two or three," Perkins said without a smile.

Whatever he'd done, it had tilted the scales in my favor—which I appreciated, but quite frankly it shouldn't have been that hard to do, since I was innocent on all counts.

"And you're still going to be taking piss tests for the next couple months," he added.

"I can live with that," I said.

There was also the possibility of administrative charges, and Guidice would undoubtedly move forward with his own civil suit. But none of that was going to stop me from finally getting back to work. I was four days out of the loop by now, and that's like dog years in homicide. I had some catching up to do.

"Anything else?" I said.

"Yes. Not everyone's going to be happy about this. We're going to take some heat," Perkins said. "I need you to keep your mouth shut about the whole thing. Don't defend yourself to the press, don't talk about Ron Guidice, nothing. Just keep your head down and go back to work."

"That's all I ever wanted, Lou," I said.

"Good," he said. "Because I think they're expecting you downstairs. We've got Elijah Creem in for questioning right now."

CHAPTER

86

BY THE TIME I GOT DOWN TO THE INTERVIEW SUITE ON FOUR, THEY ALREADY HAD Dr. Creem alone in a room with Detective Valente.

I found Huizenga, D'Auria, and Jacobs sitting at the end of the suite's L-shaped hallway, gathered around a laptop and watching and listening in. Chief Perkins must have said something to Huizenga at the morning briefing, because she just nodded and made room for me at the table.

"Good to have you back," she said.

"Shh," D'Auria said, and tapped the screen in front of us.

I could feel the tension in the group. I wasn't sure how long Creem had been in there, but something told me it wasn't going well.

Creem was seated on an aluminum chair bolted to the interview room floor. His body language was open, with his hands at his sides and his legs wide. If anything, it looked studied to me. Arrogant, even, as if he were enjoying this—or at least, wanted us to think so.

Valente had pulled in a folding chair of his own and sat with his back against the door. The wedge-shaped table in the corner was empty, and the only pop of color in the room was the red panic button on the wall.

"Dr. Creem, do you recognize this signature?" Valente asked. He'd just taken a sheet out of an accordion file on the floor and turned it around to show Creem.

"That would be one of my intake forms," he said.

"Yes. For Darcy Vickers," Valente said.

"I can see that."

Valente took the form back and stowed it. He wanted Creem looking at him, not the page.

"Her most recent procedure with you was a neck lift," he said. "Eleven months before she was murdered."

"A platysmaplasty, yes," Creem said. "It's unfortunate. I did some of my best work on her."

I didn't know what his exact goal was here, but he'd played the same game with me while he took putts in his backyard. The last thing Elijah Creem wanted us to think was that he cared about anything but himself. He was going out of his way to make the point.

Valente sat back and crossed his arms. I could tell his patience was running thin.

"It's a lot of coincidences, don't you think?" he said. "Your former patient. Your neighbors in Palm Beach—"

"Now, you see there?" Creem said, suddenly more animated. "Why would you need to ask that question, unless you were short on information? I'm no detective, detective, but even I know that you don't prosecute on coincidences."

To my mind that sounded a lot like *Yes, I'm guilty, but you can't prove it.* One of the most important aspects of any interview is what isn't said. And Creem seemed to be *not* saying a lot. He *liked* us knowing what he'd done, didn't he? Just as long as he stayed on the right side of that very thin line he was treading. It was a game of thrills for him—the killing itself, but this part, too.

"Okay," Valente said. He got up and folded his chair against the wall. "Let me ask you a different question. Did you kill Darcy Vickers?"

"Let's say I wish I'd gotten to her first," Creem said. "That's not illegal, is it?"

"Did you kill Roger and Annette Wettig in Florida?" Valente asked.

Creem seemed to consider it. "Same answer."

"So, you did kill them," Valente pressed. "That's what I'm hearing."

All at once, Creem jumped onto his feet. The two of them were suddenly inches apart. I jumped up, too, but D'Auria held out a hand for me to wait.

"What do you think you're doing?" Valente said.

"You see this?" Creem held his hands up between them. "No cuffs. Not like the first time you people came after me. That means I haven't been arrested, and *that* means I don't have to be here."

"Sit down!" Valente barked at him.

"No, I don't think I will," Creem said. "I'm ready to

speak to my attorney. So you can either give me your phone, or you can let me out of this ridiculous little closet of yours. Either way, this conversation is over."

The fact of the matter was, Creem knew the score. We were onto him, but every piece of evidence we had was circumstantial. All we could do now was keep peeling the layers away until we found a little more blood on the doctor's hands.

In the meantime, he was about to walk out of here, and there was nothing we could do to stop him.

CHAPTER

87

BY SIX O'CLOCK THAT NIGHT, ELIJAH CREEM WAS HOME AGAIN, AND GETTING ready to go out for the evening. When the doorbell rang, he was tying a godforsaken bow tie around his neck for the first time in months.

From the bedroom window, he saw Josh standing outside, looking as strung out as some kind of junkie. It was tempting to ignore the bell, but probably ill advised.

When he went down to answer, Bergman walked right past him and made his usual beeline for the bar. The pits of his wrinkled linen blazer were stained right through with sweat.

"Josh?" Creem said, following him inside.

Bergman's hands trembled as he dropped a couple of ice cubes into a glass, and a few on the custom Oriental carpet, too. He didn't seem to notice.

"They came to my house, Elijah! Asking all kinds of questions."

"Who did?"

"The police! Who do you think?"

"What did you tell them?" Creem asked.

"Nothing! I told them I wanted to speak to my god-damn attorney."

Bergman threw the first shot down his throat and poured another. He was probably on a Klonopin or two as well. Not that it seemed to be helping.

"First of all, just calm down," Creem said.

"Calm down?" Bergman turned on him, wild-eyed. "I'm lucky to be here at all. If I'd known they were coming... well, it all happened too fast, and my gun was in the safe—"

"Whoa, whoa, whoa," Creem said. He walked over and put both hands on Bergman's quivering shoulders. "Believe me, I know how you feel. I was with the police all morning."

"What? Why didn't you warn me?"

"It was the same," Creem said. "I didn't see it coming, and frankly, I've been afraid to call. I know they're watching me now."

Bergman searched his face, before he turned away to take another swig.

"Can you get us out of the country?" he asked.

"No," Creem admitted. "Not anymore. It's too late for that."

His best friend laughed then, a little maniacally, and completely without humor. "Well that's it then," he said. "Game over. I guess we knew it was coming."

When Josh pulled the small black and silver pistol from the back of his waistband, Creem's eyes went wide. The gun shook in Bergman's hand, but he pulled it out of reach when Creem tried to take it.

"Don't you dare try to talk me out of this!" Bergman said. "Not now!"

"I'm not," Creem said. "I even have my own gun upstairs. And I'm not afraid, Josh."

"So? What are you waiting for?" Bergman looked toward the foyer, where the main staircase wound up to the second floor. He was crying, too. Tears ran down from the corners of his eyes and over the cheekbones he'd always been so proud of.

"I need one more night," Creem told him. "And...I need a favor."

That was worth another few fingers of Scotch, apparently. Josh was back at the bar now, and he set the pistol down to pick up a crystal decanter.

"You are unbelievable," he said. "A favor? What kind of favor?"

"What kind do you think?" Creem told him. "You can do it however you like. Shoot her, cut her up, I don't care. I just want it done. After that, we can call it quits."

"Why can't you do it yourself?"

Creem pointed at the tall front window overlooking the lawn. "Did you see the car parked outside? They're all over me, Josh. If they were on you, too, you'd know it. Please—one last favor. That's all I'm asking."

Bergman got to the bottom of his glass one more time before he finally answered.

"Okay, fine," he said. "But you have to do something for me, too."

"What's that?" Creem asked.

Looking him right in the eye, Bergman said, "I want you to kiss me, Elijah."

Creem laughed before he realized how serious Josh was. Of course he was. It was like the longest-running inside joke they had—the kind that grows around a kernel of truth. Josh had wanted him since college.

And clearly, this was going to be his last chance to do anything about it.

"I'm not going to kiss you, Josh," Creem said.

"Fine, then."

In one fast gesture, Josh dropped his glass to the carpet and raised the pistol to his own wide-open mouth.

"No!"

Creem lunged and knocked his hand away. Josh stumbled, weeping, and came to rest against the back of a slipcovered dining room chair. One of his front teeth was chipped and his lip was bleeding, but he didn't seem to notice.

"You can't stop me, Elijah," he said.

"You're unbelievable, you know that?" Creem said. "Jesus Christ!"

There was obviously only one way around this. He took Bergman by the shoulders again and stood him up. Then he pulled him in close. He even let it last a long time. It was a little disgusting, a little strange, and it smelled strongly of booze.

When they pulled apart, Bergman's eyes were red and

puffy, but he'd stopped crying, anyway. His mouth was smeared with his own blood.

"I know you didn't feel anything," he said. "But that's okay. I also know you love me."

"I do, Josh. But for God's sake, enough with the histrionics. Let's finish this with a little bit of dignity. Like men."

Bergman grinned, looking more tired than anything now. Spent.

"Whatever you say, Elijah. Just tell me what to do."

CHAPTER

88

NOW THAT WE HAD A PRIMARY SUSPECT, ELIJAH CREEM QUICKLY BECAME THE subject of MPD surveillance. Commander D'Auria was making the assignments at this point, and mine was to cover a shift at Creem's house that night, whether he was home or not.

When I showed up to relieve the first shift at eight o'clock, word from command was that Creem had gone out in a tux around seven thirty. Hired car service had dropped him off at a private home on the 3000 block of Q Street, one of Georgetown's highest-dollar neighborhoods. Intel on the event said that it was a juvenile diabetes fundraising dinner.

That made sense. I didn't really see "Dr. Creep" being welcomed into society circles anymore, unless he was buying his way in.

My partner for the night was a thick-necked detective from the Second District warrant squad, Jerry Doyle. According to Sampson, the guy's nickname was The Mouth, and it didn't take long to find out why. He was complaining within the first five minutes.

"What are we even doing?" he said. "Creem's out for the night while we sit here getting kidney stones and he makes nice with the richies, eating caviar or whatever. Yeah, sure, that makes a lot of sense."

"Well—" I said, but that was as far as I got.

"Not to mention, if they're going to do this, they should be doing it right," Doyle went on. "Management's pulling all kinds of extra staff and overtime, and if you ask me, we still don't have this guy covered good enough. I mean, if I were him and I wanted to give us the slip, I'm pretty sure I could do it."

"No argument there," I said. "I don't know if I've ever seen the investigative units stretched so thin before."

"Speaking of which, I thought you were out of commission," Doyle went on. "I mean, no judgment. I'm just a little surprised to see you here, I guess."

I wasn't so keen on discussing my situation with The Mouth, so I mostly listened instead. For hours. Doyle didn't seem to notice the difference.

Finally, around midnight, we got a radio call that Creem was on his way. He'd left the party with an unknown female and seemed to be heading home.

"You've got to be shittin' me," Doyle said. "I mean, he knows we're all over him, right? And he's going to bring a broad back here?"

I nodded. "I think it's all part of the show."

Creem didn't do anything without a reason. He was trying to rub his own freedom in our faces, wasn't he? Never mind that the pornography charges alone were enough to send him to jail. He was clearly milking this for all it was worth in the meantime.

Ten minutes later, a black town car pulled up the block and idled to a stop in Creem's driveway. A uniformed driver got out, but Creem was a step ahead of him. He ducked around and helped his date out of the car himself. A faux gas lamp from the front porch threw just enough light to show me that she was tall, blond, and as far as I could tell, exactly Dr. Creem's type.

That was as much as I could sit still for.

"What are you doing?" Doyle asked when I reached for my door handle.

"Whatever I can," I said, and got out of the car. I headed straight across the lawn to cut the couple off as they came up Creem's brick front walk.

"Excuse me," I called out.

The woman started and clutched Creem's arm.

"It's all right," he said to her. "This is one of the police officers I was telling you about. Sheila Bishop, I'd like you to meet Detective Cross. He's here to make sure I don't cut you up into little pieces."

The woman actually rolled her eyes and kept her arm locked onto his. A pair of high-heeled sandals was dangling off one finger, and she had on a long, shimmery dress that pooled around her bare feet.

"I'm sorry to startle you, Ms. Bishop," I said, "but I'm not at all comfortable with you going inside. I'd like to call you a cab, if that's all right."

"And I'd like you to mind your own damn business," she snapped back at me.

Creem only smiled, as if he were leaving this up to the two of us.

"You should know the reason we're here," I told her. "Dr. Creem is the primary suspect in a series of murders in Georgetown. You've probably heard about them. I'd strongly suggest—"

But Ms. Bishop cut me off.

"Just inside, there's an antique mahogany coatrack," she said, pointing at the front door.

"Excuse me?"

"Upstairs, to the left, is the master bedroom. That's where Elijah and Miranda keep their Rookwood pottery collection. There's also a fantastic Lucien Freud hanging over the bed. Should I go on?"

I'd thought Ms. Bishop was embarrassed by my presence, but I was wrong. As far as I could tell now, Dr. Creem's mistress was just pissed off and anxious to get inside.

He'd laid the bait, and I'd taken it, just like he wanted. Unbelievable.

"Don't worry, detective," Creem said ingratiatingly. "It's an understandable mistake. For what it's worth, I don't imagine Sheila could be any safer, with you and your partner out here. Am I right?"

He didn't wait for an answer, and keyed the door to let

Ms. Bishop in ahead of him. As she led the way, Creem turned back to me and spoke low from the porch.

"If it makes you feel any better, I'll leave the curtains open," he said with a smile.

Then he went inside, closed the door, and turned off the lights behind him.

CHAPTER

89

THE NEXT SEVERAL HOURS WERE THEIR OWN KIND OF TORTURE. I FELT MORE than a little burned by Creem, and I hated the way he was playing this.

To make things worse, Doyle kept his own personal monologue going pretty much the entire time. He knew a thing or two about surveillance and had some valid opinions about how these investigations ought to be structured, but most of that was bookended with one long, pointless story after another.

Around 3 a.m., a yellow cab pulled up in front of the house. A minute later, the porch light came on and Creem walked Ms. Bishop outside. She was carrying a shopping bag now and wearing street clothes that, for all I knew, came straight out of Mrs. Creem's closet.

Neither of them even glanced our way, until Creem had put her into the cab and sent her off. Then he turned, gave us a friendly wave, and went back inside.

"What a tool," Doyle said. "I don't get it. What is it about hot women and rich assholes? Actually, never mind. I just answered my own question. But still—"

Bottom line, I don't like to talk when I'm losing the game. I couldn't stand the idea of five more hours of this.

"Doyle, don't take this the wrong way," I said, "but is there any chance we could finish out this shift with a little less conversation?"

It got him all huffy and cold-shouldered, but if that was the price of silence, I was ready to pay it. With any luck, this would be our first and last detail together.

After that it stayed pretty quiet, both in and outside the car. Creem kept the lights on and puttered around the house, doing whatever he was doing in there. At five, he took the paper off his front porch and went back in— upstairs, I think. I didn't see him after that.

Then, just after sunrise, my cell rang.

It's not so unusual for me to get calls at all hours. I expected to see a departmental number on the ID or maybe Bree. But it wasn't either of those. It was Stephanie Gethmann, Ava's social worker. Right away I knew something had to be wrong.

"Stephanie?" I answered.

"I'm sorry to call so early," she said. "I actually wanted to call last night, but...well, it's complicated, of course."

"Something's happened to Ava," I said. It wasn't a question. My heart was thumping, and I was already running through the possibilities in my head. Overdose? Runaway? Accident?

"She's missing, Alex."

"Missing? What does that mean?"

"She didn't come home from school yesterday, and nobody knows where she is. I hope this isn't inappropriate, but I know you and Bree are police officers. I was thinking maybe—"

I only wished Stephanie had called sooner.

"Of course we will," I said. "We'll get right on it. Tell me everything you know."

Part Four
ALL FALL DOWN

90

BREE AND I SPENT THE MORNING IN OUR CARS, KEEPING IN TOUCH BY PHONE and hitting up every resource we could think of to track Ava down.

I started with the Youth Investigations Bureau contacts I knew in the first, third, and sixth police districts. Those covered Ava's group home, her school, our house, and Seward Square, where she used to hang out. The department has a centralized database of missing kids, but there's no substitute for face time with people who are working the streets every day. For that, you have to go district by district.

As it turned out, the picture Nessa had taken of us at the group home was even more valuable than I'd thought. It wasn't much of a shot, but it was something to show people. I texted it to everyone I could think of.

Bree started at Howard House and interviewed several

of the girls there, as well as Sunita, the braided house manager we'd met the other day. From the sound of it, nobody had seen Ava since breakfast the previous morning. She'd been quiet, but that was nothing new. And it didn't look like anything was missing from her room, either. That meant she hadn't intentionally run away.

After that, Bree headed over to Seward Square, walking the neighborhood and looking for any of Ava's old friends. She told me over the phone that she'd found two of them—Patrice and K-Fly. Supposedly, neither of them had seen Ava in weeks, but you have to take anything street kids tell you with a grain of salt. Bree gave them each a card and promised a hundred bucks for anyone who might help find her. Whatever it took.

I hit up all the area hospitals, and then finally headed over to MPD's main Narcotics Unit on Third Street in Northeast. I was starting to grasp at straws, but I thought if anyone knew of specific dealers who pushed Oxy, or fake Oxy, on the streets Ava had frequented, it might be a way in.

The longer this went on, the worse I felt about it. Especially if drugs were involved, which I all but assumed was the case.

Opiates are probably the least-controlled substances out there these days. The high-grade pharmaceutical stuff is highly desirable on the street, and sellers take advantage of that fact all the time. They pass garbage off as true Oxy, and there's no way to control the dosage, much less the contents of street drugs like that. It wasn't just empty talk when we'd told Ava that kids OD all the time.

This country has an opiate epidemic, and it's largely being driven by people under twenty-five.

By midafternoon, we'd come up completely empty-handed. It was getting hard not to play out some worst-case scenarios in my head, and it drove me crazy to think that Ava was around here *somewhere*, while we ran out of ideas about where to look.

I knew I had to stay positive, for Nana's sake and the kids' sake, if not my own. But the truth was, I had a terrible feeling about this.

CHAPTER

91

"ALEX, WHERE THE HELL ARE YOU?"

It was Sergeant Huizenga on the phone. I was driving from the Sixth District station house back to my own place in Southeast when I took the call.

"I'm sorry, sergeant. Something's come up at home."

"Yeah, well, we need you. Now."

"What is it?" I asked.

"Sheila Bishop, Dr. Creem's date from last night. She's been found dead in her apartment."

It might have hit me harder, but I was practically numb by now. Still, this was one more smack in the face on top of everything else.

"Is Creem in custody?" I asked.

"No," Huizenga said tightly. "That's part of the cluster hump we've got going on. The son of a bitch is missing."

That got me. I actually braked right there on D Street

and pulled over. "Missing? How is that even possible? We've been on him since yesterday."

"Slipped out right through the back of his property, it looks like," she said. "Into the woods and God knows where from there."

The first thing I thought of was Jerry Doyle. He'd gone on and on about how Creem's surveillance detail was insufficient—and he'd been right.

I remembered how the place was bordered by Glover-Archbold Park. It's a piece of land that runs from Cathedral Heights all the way down to the Potomac. We'd covered the front of Creem's house, but there had been no way to completely cover the entire track of open ground at the back. It made for a perfect hole in our net. That much was clear—now.

"We've got a BOLO out on him, but meanwhile, I want you over at Sheila Bishop's apartment."

She gave me an address on Logan Circle. There was no question of yes or no. If I wanted to keep showing up for work, I needed to be there.

Still, once I hung up with Huizenga, I continued on home. Screw protocol. I needed to check in with my family, too.

Bree actually encouraged me to go, when I saw her. She and Nana were parked by the home phone, waiting for any word from Stephanie, while Bree worked her cell to be in touch with the districts, the hospital, and Howard House. The kids were with Aunt Tia, and could spend the night there if necessary.

"Go," she said. "You're just a phone call away if anything comes up. I've got Sampson and Billie driving the neighborhood right now, keeping an eye out. You can spell them later."

"You okay?" I asked.

"No," Bree said. "But so what? Just go."

I looked at Nana, who had her hands clasped under her chin. I wasn't sure if she was praying or just thinking, but she didn't look good, either.

I gave them both a kiss good-bye, and kept on moving, out the back door.

92

SHEILA BISHOP'S APARTMENT WAS HALF OF A TURRETED BRICK AND STONE town house on the north side of Logan Circle. Other than a handful of people watching their dogs run around John Logan's statue, and the usual daytime traffic, it was quiet when I got there. No reporters, anyway. That was a relative blessing.

Most of the investigative team was on-site, along with the Mobile Crime Unit from Forensics. They had techs in blue windbreakers on the front door, up and down the stairs, and all over the master bedroom, where Ms. Bishop's body had been discovered by a housekeeper a few hours earlier.

That's also where I found Valente. He was kneeling by the body, and looking from Ms. Bishop to each of the doors and windows when I came in.

She'd been shot once in the chest, and by all appearances had collapsed in front of the open double doors of her walk-in closet. I couldn't say for sure, but it looked like Ms. Bishop was wearing the same clothes she'd had on when she left Dr. Creem's house.

A Barneys shopping bag was on the bed, with her evening gown and shoes inside. And according to Valente, the tub in the adjoining bathroom was just under half full.

"Looks to me like she came in, left the bag on the bed, and started drawing a bath," he said. "Then she comes back out here to get undressed, and bam. He's waiting for her in the closet. No signs of forced entry, either. Creem could have easily had a key to this place."

Most of what Valente had worked out made sense to me—except for the part about Creem himself.

"I watched him put her in a cab at three in the morning," I said. "He didn't go anywhere after that. At least not before five. There's no way he could have beaten her over here."

"I guess the question then is time of death," Valente said.

"That's one question," I said.

"Detectives?"

Errico and I both turned around to see Manny Lapore, one of the forensic techs, standing in the door to the bathroom. He was holding up a clear acrylic lifter with the dark impression of a handprint on it. Even at a glance, the print was too big to have come from Ms. Bishop.

"I got this off the bathroom tile over the tub," Lapore

said. "There's a couple of matching partials on the hot and cold taps, too. Could be something."

My first thought was that the killer had gone in to turn off the tub, to avoid an attention-drawing flood in the bathroom. My second thought was that it seemed like a pretty sloppy mistake—unless he just didn't care. Or wasn't thinking straight.

We followed Lapore downstairs to see what, if anything, this print turned up. With the mobile automated fingerprint ID scanners we're now using, a process that used to take hours—not to mention a trip to the lab—can happen anywhere, and in a matter of minutes. I didn't even have time to check in with Bree before Lapore had found a match and was printing off the results.

"Here's your guy," he said, handing me the report. "Does the name Joshua Bergman mean anything to you?"

93

I CAUGHT UP WITH BREE ON THE PHONE WHILE VALENTE AND I DROVE FROM Logan Circle over to M Street, where Josh Bergman lived. There was no new word about Ava. It was all eerily quiet on that front.

Meanwhile, I had to focus on this if I could.

It can take an hour or more to pull SWAT together, but that was time we didn't have. Instead we dispatched a quick in-house team for the operation. Within thirty minutes, we had five tactically trained officers with one sergeant all ready to go in a parking lot on Water Street, a block from Bergman's building.

Bergman had a high-dollar loft on the top floor of a converted flour mill, from Georgetown's nineteenth-century industrial days. Word from our spotter, stationed on the roof behind his, was that Bergman seemed to be home alone.

After a fast briefing with Commander D'Auria, we piled into two plain white panel vans and pulled around the block. The drivers stopped in front, the van doors slid open, and we made a beeline for the entrance.

Besides the half dozen tactical personnel, the entry team included me, Valente, and two more D-1 detectives from Major Case Squad, winding our way up the three flights of stairs to the top. We had officers stationed around the block, EMTs on standby, and D'Auria with a small crew in a mobile command center back down on Water Street.

The breach team was armed with AR-15 rifles and SIG P226 sidearms. Tasers and pepper spray were standard issue as well.

I had my Glock out, for the first time since I'd been reinstated. All of us wore Kevlar, too. We had more than enough manpower to take Bergman in, but he was very possibly armed and dangerous. Maybe also a little desperate. He might try to get off a few shots of his own.

When we got to the third-floor landing, the sergeant at the head of the line wagged two fingers at a pair of officers, who came forward with the forty-five pound battering ram they'd carried up. Everyone was wired with headsets, but the protocol was for radio silence once we'd entered the building.

Inside I could hear Bergman talking. It sounded like half of a phone conversation.

"Where the hell are you? You said you'd be here an hour ago," he said. He also sounded agitated, and seemed to be moving around. When he spoke again, his voice faded off toward the back of the apartment. "I don't care," he said. "Just…no, you listen to me. Just get here! Now!"

That was it. I could feel the collective pulse of the group start to go up, as the sergeant gave a visual countdown on his fingers—three, two, one. The two cops at the front pulled back with the ram and swung it at Bergman's steel front door. It sent a resounding boom up and down the stairwell. Any cover we had now was blown.

"Units C and D, standby," the sergeant radioed. "He may try to make a run for it."

It took two more fast swings before the door finally tore away from the frame and blew open. My vision tunneled straight ahead as the sergeant corkscrewed his arm, ushering the team inside, double time.

"Go, go, go, go, go!"

CHAPTER

94

VALENTE AND I DIDN'T WAIT FOR CLEARANCE. WE FOLLOWED RIGHT IN BEHIND the breach team. Normally, investigative staff is meant to hold their position until we get an all clear, but neither of us were feeling that patient right now.

The apartment door opened into a wide-open loft space that looked pristine to the point of sterility. Bergman didn't seem to have any *stuff* at all. There was a set of white modular furniture on a huge gray rug, like an island in the middle of the room, with a single tall rubber tree that reached up to the exposed I-beams in the ceiling. A stainless-steel kitchen off to the side looked like it had never been used.

There was no sign of Bergman anywhere in the front. The team quickly moved through, leapfrogging each other across the loft, and then down a long hallway toward the back of the building.

"MPD! Joshua Bergman?" I shouted. "Stay right where you are! Don't move!"

At the very end of the hall there was an open door, with light streaming in through several iron-framed floor-to-ceiling windows. As soon as the first officer got there, I heard Bergman start to yell.

"Get away from me! Stay back!"

"Sir, put down the gun!" one of the officers shouted. "Keep your hands where we can see them and get down on the floor!"

"Go to hell!"

When I came into the room, Bergman was sitting up, cross-legged on a king-size platform bed. He had his back against the painted concrete block wall, with a white iPhone in one hand and a small Smith & Wesson revolver in the other. It could have easily been the same .32 he'd used to kill all those boys, as well as Sheila Bishop.

"Bergman, put the gun down!" I told him. "You don't want to do this."

"Oh yeah? I don't?" He was clearly agitated, but also relatively focused. He looked me right in the eye when he said it.

"Just try to calm down," I told him. "Let's go one thing at a time."

I lowered my own gun and took a step toward him, but only until he pressed the Smith & Wesson up to his chin.

"You think I'm kidding around here?" he said.

"Josh—don't," I said. "Please."

"Too late," he said. He held the phone up to his ear and

spoke a single word to whoever was there. "Good-bye," he said.

Then he pulled the trigger on that Smith & Wesson and blew himself away.

Whatever horrible things Bergman might have done to other people, it was god-awful to see him go out like that. This was an act of pure, irrational desperation. Maybe even insanity.

Not to mention a truly stomach-churning mess.

Everyone started moving at once. There was no question of survival, but Bergman's death had to be confirmed. The sergeant went straight to the body and felt for a pulse on the wrist, while Valente called it in.

"One round fired, subject is down. Self-inflicted GSW," he said. When the sergeant shook his head, Valente added, "No signs of life."

Bergman's gun had dropped onto the bloodstained comforter, and his phone was on the floor. That's what I focused on. I was pretty sure I knew who he'd been talking to, but I needed to confirm it if I could.

I went straight to the phone, picked it up, and hit redial. On the first ring, it sent me right into voice mail.

"Hello," I heard in a familiar voice. "You've reached Dr. Elijah Creem. I can't take your call right now, but please leave a message. Thank you, and have a pleasant day."

CHAPTER

95

THIS WASN'T THE END OF ANYTHING. WE WERE RIGHT IN THE MIDDLE OF IT ALL.

Up until now, with only circumstantial evidence against Creem, it was all we could do to put a surveillance detail on him. Legally speaking, it's one thing to watch someone at home, from the street. It's another to go inside. The courts are jumpy about that kind of thing.

So it was ironic to get the push we needed, not from Creem but from Bergman, our presumed River Killer. The fact that he'd called Creem's cell and home numbers multiple times in the hours before he killed himself was enough to put us over the top. Within an hour of Bergman's death, we had a warrant number for secreted evidence in Creem's house and a one-sheet for Creem himself, circulating up and down the Eastern Seaboard. The special note on this one was that Creem might have been traveling in disguise. The one-sheet included his

DMV photo alongside the clearest image we had of the old man mask he'd been using, but we weren't cutting off any possibilities. He could have easily switched up his look by now—and probably had.

My guess was that Creem had been planning this exit all along. It would explain the way he'd flaunted himself to the police so brazenly. Not to mention Sheila Bishop's and Josh Bergman's deaths. Was that all just one big, high-stakes smokescreen for him?

If so, it had worked. We'd already lost between five and nine hours on Creem, depending on what time he'd slipped away from us.

To search the house in Wesley Heights, Valente and I brought a team of three other detectives, plus four from mobile crime. It's a slow, methodical process—aggravatingly so when your perp is already on the move. We spread out over the home's three floors when we got there, to cover as much area as we could.

I started on the lower level, where Creem had an office, an examination room, and a waiting area with its own separate entrance. There was also a TV room and a garage down there—plenty of places to look.

As it turned out, there were a few things Creem hadn't even tried to hide. Within the first few minutes, I found a makeup kit in his top desk drawer. There were tinting pigments, a dozen different small brushes, a bottle of spirit gum, and several items I didn't recognize. Maybe he'd even worked on his latest mask right there at the desk, while I'd been sitting outside on the curb, watching his house the night before.

The other thing I did while I searched was to keep dialing Creem's number. I didn't really expect him to pick up, but I figured it was worth trying. He was the type who might like to take a parting shot at the cops, given the opportunity.

For the first hour, I got the same response, over and over—straight to voice mail. He'd probably shut the phone down to keep it from pinging off of cell towers and leaving a trail behind him.

But that doesn't mean I was wrong about Creem. He must have tracked my incoming calls somehow, because the next time my phone rang, it was him, calling me back.

On his terms, of course.

CHAPTER

96

"Detective Cross," I answered.

"It's me," Creem said. "The man of the hour."

I banged my knee on his desk as I jumped up. Valente was just coming into the room, and I snapped my fingers to grab his attention.

"Dr. Creem," I said pointedly. "I'm a little surprised to hear from you."

Right away, Valente took out his own phone and started making a call, presumably to try to run a trace.

"I wanted to ask about Josh," Creem told me.

"What about him?" I asked.

"Is he dead?"

Valente motioned at me to take my time and go slow with him.

355

"I'm not going to discuss that with you over the phone," I said. "Tell me where you are. I'll meet you anywhere you like. No other cops."

Creem paused, maybe even just to smile to himself. He was enjoying this, no doubt.

"Don't bother with this phone, by the way," he said. "I bought it an hour ago and I'm throwing it away after this call."

He was probably using a convenience store burner, or something like it. From a cop's perspective, those are the worst. They can be impossible to track down.

I figured the best way to keep Creem talking would be to feed that oversize ego of his. It was the only language he seemed to speak.

"You know, there's a massive manhunt going on right now," I said. "You've given us quite the slip."

"Any luck so far?" he asked.

"If there were—"

"Of course. We wouldn't be having this conversation," Creem said.

I also knew better than to condescend to him. One thing about Creem—he wasn't stupid. If I lost him now, something told me that would be it.

"I'd love to know how you pulled this off," I said. "It's been a fascinating case. You, Bergman, all of it. I assume you were in it together from the start."

This time Creem sighed, almost nostalgically. "All the way back to college, in fact. We got a bit of a taste for it then, just like old Jack Sprat and his wife."

"Excuse me?"

"He liked the boys, I liked the girls. And between the two of us, we licked the platter clean."

His calm, collected pride in the whole thing gave me the creeps. Wherever he was headed, I didn't think for a second he'd be able to stop himself from killing again.

"So what now?" I said. "You disappear, never to be heard from?"

"That's the idea," he said.

"Are you leaving the country?" I asked, but Creem demurred.

"I called because I wanted to know about Josh," he told me. "If you don't have anything to say about that, I'm hanging up."

When I looked at Valente, he just shook his head and raked his fingers through his hair. It wasn't going well.

"What do you want to know?" I asked.

"Is he dead or not?"

"Yes," I told him. It would all be in the news soon enough anyway.

"Where did he do it?" Creem asked.

"In his loft, on M Street," I said, stalling.

"No. I mean, it sounded to me like he shot himself. Was it in the mouth?"

"Under the chin," I said.

"Lord. Must have been a terrible mess."

"It was," I said. "Is that hard for you? He was your friend, after all."

Creem paused again. I listened hard for any kind of telltale background noise, but there was nothing.

"Are you a doctor, Alex?" he asked then.

"I am. A psychologist," I said.

"Ah. One for the books, then."

"Now, I told you about Josh. Give me something in return," I said. "Are there other victims we should know about? Tell me how many you've killed over the years."

"I'm sorry," Creem said, "but we're out of time for today. Isn't that what you shrinks always say?"

"Hang on. One more question."

"It was fun while it lasted, detective, but I think we both know I'm already well beyond your reach. I wouldn't go to too much trouble if I were you."

"Creem, wait!" I said, but it was too late. He'd already hung up.

When I set down my phone, I could see on Valente's face that he hadn't gotten anywhere. Also that he was good and pissed by now. We'd just had a decent shot at Creem, and once again he'd slipped through our fingers.

Maybe for the last time.

CHAPTER

97

I TRIED CALLING CREEM'S NEW NUMBER BACK, BUT ALL I GOT WAS A GENERIC machine-generated voice mail. He'd probably destroyed the phone as soon as he hung up on me.

Right away, I turned my attention back to his home office. Maybe it would give us some clue about where he'd planned on running.

By all appearances, Creem was fastidiously tidy. Possibly even a little OCD. Everything about his house was well ordered, right down to the matching letter-boxes, pencil cup, and stapler sitting at perfect right angles on the desk. It was easy to see as the outward manifestation of a man who needed to control every aspect of his universe—from the mundane physical details to the repetitive, hyper-precise way he'd cut up each of his victims.

Bergman's murders had been self-similar as well, but

there was a difference. With every kill, Bergman had been less controlled. Each one of those young hustlers had been stabbed and mutilated a little more than the one before. In retrospect, Bergman was the ticking time bomb, waiting to go off. Creem was more like the Swiss clock.

From his desk, I worked my way around the office, opening drawers, checking files, and even lifting up furniture to look underneath. It wasn't until I got to the black lacquered media console by the door that I found anything at all out of place.

There, at the back of the cabinet behind a boxed set of date-ordered AMA journals, I found three matching pewter photo frames. It looked like they'd been thrown back there, rather than placed in any kind of deliberate way.

When I pulled them out, I saw the glass was mostly gone, with several shards sitting on the floor of the cabinet itself. Each photo was of the Creem family. There was a group shot in front of a massive Christmas tree; one picture of Miranda Creem, standing on a beach somewhere; and a hinged double frame, with side-by-side school photos of Creem's two daughters.

All three women—Miranda, Chloe, and Justine Creem— were attractive, tall, and blond, I saw. If anything, the two girls were an even closer match to Creem's slate of victims than their mother was.

And then there was the undeniable kicker. Each photo had been pierced with some kind of sharp object, like someone had driven a pair of scissors right through them. Three times each. Everything in threes.

That's who he was trying to kill, wasn't it? Creem had been methodically—and symbolically—erasing the three women who had left him after his scandal. If he'd gone straight for them, it would have been too suspicious. So he did the next best thing. He went after a theoretically endless supply of surrogates, maybe as a way of keeping himself from actually having to kill his own family.

Or maybe he was just building up to it.

I ran upstairs to find Valente. He was in the second-floor master bedroom, going through Mrs. Creem's desk when I got to him.

"What's up?" he said.

"Where's Creem's family right now?" I said.

"Rhode Island. They've been staying at her parents' house in Newport, last I heard. Why?"

I held up one of the mutilated photos to show him.

"Because I don't think he's done yet," I said.

CHAPTER

98

"BUS 53 LEAVING FOR NEW YORK, BRIDGEPORT, PROVIDENCE, AND BOSTON WILL
be boarding in ten minutes. Ticketed passengers should pro-
ceed to the loading area at this time."

Elijah Creem stood at the bathroom mirror in a downtown Philadelphia bus station, looking at himself and
making sure he was good to go for the next leg.

He touched the back of his neck, where the latex was
invisibly spirit gummed to his skin. He patted the dark
wig and adjusted the undergarment. It was a whole new
appreciation, really, for what women went through. The
makeup was no problem, but the body shaper alone was
an all-day ordeal.

Still, it was incredibly effective. It wasn't himself he
saw looking back from the streaked, dirty mirror. It was
a vaguely unfortunate woman of a certain age, with liver-
spotted skin and a small but pronounced wattle under

her chin. Even the yellow smoker's teeth were individually rendered veneers. If Creem had ever had a masterpiece, this was it.

So far, nobody had even batted an eyelash in his direction. Not the old fatty who sold him his bus ticket at Union Station, and not the numbnut kid who sat next to him all the way from DC. The whole getup had allowed him to sail right out of Washington unnoticed, even if it was on a goddamn Greyhound bus. This wouldn't be the last indignity of his little tour, but hopefully it would all be worth it in the end.

Rhode Island. Florida. South America. That was the idea. He'd already arranged passage on a Trinidadian cargo ship out of Miami. After that, it was just a skip to the mainland. Once he made his way to Buenos Aires, he could start to feel out the surgery community to see who might be safe to approach about some major work.

It wouldn't be too much trouble lying low in the meantime. He had eleven million in gold, held in a numbered account at Banco Macro. Plenty to live on, if he was careful. And with US extradition priorities being what they were, he'd be more than safe. It was all about the drug wars now. Nobody paid attention to someone like him once you reached a certain distance.

Meanwhile, as long as he was stateside, Elijah Creem knew full well how to stay invisible—even standing in the middle of a public ladies' room.

When the bathroom door opened, Creem let his hand fall away from his face. He took a plum-colored lipstick out of the purse he carried—one of Miranda's cast-offs—and busied himself with it at the mirror.

He kept his eyes forward, watching the young woman's reflection as she passed behind him and let herself into one of the toilet stalls. She was blond, and pretty, in a trashy sort of way. The kind of girl you might see riding alone on a Greyhound bus.

Was she perfect? Not by any stretch, but it sent a slight itch through Creem's palm, all the same. As he put the lipstick back in the purse, he let his fingers graze over the handle of a number eighteen scalpel, tucked into one of the side pockets.

As the girl's yellow panties slipped down to gather around her sandals near the floor, he turned slowly to face the row of stalls. He checked the entrance again.

It was tempting. So tempting. It had been too long since he'd been able to use a real instrument.

Still, the bus station was crowded. He had a transfer to make. And there would be plenty of opportunity to use the scalpel, soon enough.

"*Hey!*" The girl's voice cut right through his thoughts. "Someone's in here!"

Creem looked down to realize he'd already put a hand on the stall door. His size twelve canvas espadrilles were no doubt showing under the partition wall.

"Oh!" he said. "Sorry!"

His affected voice was something less than ladylike, but it passed well enough. He could see the girl now, just a sliver of her through the crack, hunched over and reaching to hold the stall door closed between them.

"You can relax, sweetheart," he added. "You're safe."

She didn't offer any response, and really, why would she? There was no way for her to know that, on this particular day, she was the luckiest little piece of trash in Philadelphia.

As Creem reached the bathroom door, he turned back one more time.

"You know, you might think about those bags under your eyes before they get away from you," he said.

"*What?*" the girl called back.

But Creem was already gone.

CHAPTER

99

SEVERAL HOURS LATER, DR. CREEM STEPPED OUT OF A TAXI IN FRONT OF THE house in Newport. The driver took his suitcase from the trunk, called him ma'am, and wished him a good night before he took off.

So far, so good.

The place was dark, but he'd brought one of Miranda's keys from home. He let himself in through the porte cochere entrance and up to the grand hall that ran down the center of the old place. It was one of those eight bedroom, twelve-bathroom deals they called a "cottage" around here. Typical WASP understatement.

It was ridiculous, really. Miranda had been rich as Croesus long before the two of them had ever met. Her parents—in Provence for the season—had some kind of bottomless fortune, tied to half a million acres of sugar-cane in Hawaii and Australia. Miranda's stock options alone were worth a hundred million. She may not have married Creem for his money, but she sure as hell was divorcing him for it. The last six months had turned her into a vindictive, greedy little bitch. Her, and her two little clones. There was no preserving those relationships anymore, and no sense trying.

Just the opposite, in fact.

Creem skipped the nostalgia tour this time and went straight to the so-called blue room on the third floor. It was the one Miranda favored. He'd stayed in it several times himself. Chloe was even conceived in the room's nineteenth-century sleigh bed. That's where he stopped to change.

He peeled off the mask, the dress, and the godforsaken undergear, folding them carefully onto the bed. A duplicate pair of masks were rolled in Bubble Wrap inside his suitcase, for the two-day bus trip to Miami.

In the meantime, he took out a few of his own things and quickly re-dressed. He also took out three pairs of steel handcuffs, a roll of black packing tape, and a small, sealed bottle of chloral hydrate.

From the game table in the corner, Creem took one of the straight-back chairs and moved it to the space under the window by the bed. It was all planned out. Miranda would be the last to go, but she'd get the show of her life before she did.

The only thing he kept on him was the scalpel. He slid it carefully into his back pocket as he crossed to the window again and looked outside.

From here he could see where the white crushed-gravel driveway curved around the back of the house to a parking courtyard. There was no sign of Miranda or the girls yet, but there had been a Newport paper in the front hall, open to the movie section. Chances were, they wouldn't be long.

As he stood there at the window, surveying the back of the house, something suddenly caught Creem's eye. A flicker, or a reflection of movement in the glass.

He turned around fast to see the tall shape of a man, silhouetted in the bedroom door against the light from the hall.

"Elijah Creem?" the man said. "You need to come with me. You're under arrest."

Creem still couldn't make out the face, but he recognized the deep tone of the man's voice right away.

It was his new best friend, Alex Cross.

100

MY GUESS IS THAT CREEM THOUGHT FLYING WOULD BE TOO RISKY. IT HAD taken him the better part of the day to reach the house in Newport over land.

Not me. With the favor of a Bell helicopter from the Bureau—and specifically from Ned Mahoney, who was now on the list of people I owed, big-time—Valente and I had gotten to Rhode Island in two and a half hours. We'd also contacted an investigative unit with the Newport County sheriff's office. The house where Miranda Creem and her daughters were staying had been vacated long before Dr. Creem ever got there.

Given my previous contact with Creem, my psych background, and the disaster of Josh Bergman's suicide, it was agreed I'd approach Creem first. I had a two-way radio clipped to my belt, with a backup mike on my cuff. A full team of local police and detectives were all now in position, just outside. Help was a word away, if I needed it.

When I flicked on the bedroom light, it looked to me as if Creem had some kind of lacerations around his face. Then I realized I was looking at the remnants of latex and glue from whatever mask had gotten him this far.

"I'll be honest," Creem said. "I'm surprised to see you."

I motioned with the Glock in my hand. "Get down on your knees and lace your fingers behind your head," I said.

Creem didn't move. I could see him regrouping, and taking in the room around us. He was looking for a way out, even now.

"I have every right to be here," he said, settling back into his usual superiority. "I let myself in with a key. You're the one who's trespassing. I'm here to see my wife."

"I'll bet you are," I said. "Were you going to kill your daughters, too, Creem?"

He grinned at that, in a way I'd seen before. It was pure Elijah Creem, treading that fine line between confident and sociopathic.

"This is a bit of déjà vu, isn't it?" he said. "That night we met in Georgetown, I offered you twenty thousand, or maybe it was thirty, for a little head start out the bedroom window."

"I remember it didn't get you anywhere," I said.

"No. It didn't, did it?" he said. He nodded several times, as if he were finally coming to the logical conclusion here.

But instead, Creem made a break for it. He put his hands on the back of a tall wooden chair and swung it all at once, right through the bedroom's picture window. It brought down a shower of glass, even as he was climbing onto the sill to jump out.

I was right behind, nearly too late to grab him—but not quite. My hand closed around the back of his shirt just as he dropped. It pulled and ripped, but then he snapped back. His body bounced hard off the side of the house. For a brief moment, I lost my footing and nearly went out the window with him. If there had been any broken glass on the sill right there, it would have gone right into my gut.

"Give me your hand!" I shouted, even as he struggled, dangling at the end of my reach. A stream of cops was coming around the house now, and I could hear several others coming into the room behind me.

"Get off me!" Creem said. When he tried to slip out of his shirt, I leaned over and got a grip on his arm, to drag him back in.

That's when he pulled the scalpel I didn't even realize he had. He brought it up all at once and drove the tip right into the back of my hand.

A nauseating bolt of pain ran up my arm. I yelled out and let go before I could stop myself. It was a reflex as much as anything. Drops of blood from my hand followed him down to the ground, three stories below.

Creem pinwheeled his arms as he fell. The motion of it twisted his body around in the air, and there was no time to get himself upright. His legs would have broken anyway, but instead, he landed flat on his back, hitting the patio beneath us with a sickening thud.

Several officers, including Valente, closed in around him with weapons drawn.

"Don't move!" one of them shouted. "Stay right where you are!"

It was a nonissue. At first I thought Creem was dead. Then I heard a slight moan. He turned his head a few inches to the side, and moaned again, but that was it.

Dr. Creem's career was over.

Finally.

CHAPTER

101

ONCE I GOT MY HAND WRAPPED BY THE EMTS ON THE SCENE, I LEFT VALENTE in Rhode Island and flew back to DC in the middle of the night.

I didn't hear anything en route, but Errico called me just as I was disembarking in Quantico. It turned out that Elijah Creem had snapped his spine in the fall, breaking two vertebrae. He'd also given a full confession before they even got him to Newport Hospital. The way Valente put it, Creem had been broken in more ways than one by that fall. Not only was he headed to jail for the rest of his life, but he was going to be spending that time in a wheelchair. I can't say I was too sorry.

I'd see Creem again at his trial, but for now I had other things on my mind.

Actually, just one. Ava.

I went straight to the office without going home. The best way to get back to my family was to get my report done in the quiet of the night, before the office started filling up.

The amount of administrative paperwork on something like this is staggering. The primary burden would fall to Valente, and also to Jacobs for the River Killer case. Each file would have to go through no fewer than seven levels of review at the department before it got its final sign-off. I've seen the process take upwards of six months. It's a big part of what keeps me from trying to go any higher at MPD than I already am. At a certain level, you wind up spending all your time on paperwork and politics instead of in the field, where the real police work gets done.

By seven that morning, I'd written up a full account of the last twenty-four hours, and handed it off to Sergeant Huizenga when she came in for the day. She'd already been in touch with Valente, and her mood was as good as I'd seen it in weeks.

Just as well, since I had to give her my paperwork and ask for a few days off in the same breath.

"I know I just got back on," I said, "but Ava's been missing for three days now—"

Huizenga was blessedly cool about it. She waved me out of her office with the file I'd just handed her.

"Go, before I change my mind," she said. "Find your girl, and get back here as soon as you can. And leave your phone on!"

There would be a dozen or more calls that day, with

half a million questions about Creem and Bergman, but this at least gave me the space I needed to get my priorities back in order.

First stop—home.

CHAPTER

102

I LEFT HEADQUARTERS AND SWUNG THROUGH THE HOUSE LONG ENOUGH TO see the kids before school. Exhausted wasn't really the word. At a certain point, it pushes past that and back into adrenaline. I'd figure out the whole sleep thing when I could.

"Who are you again?" Jannie asked, grinning over her eggs at me as I came down from a quick shower.

"I'm the Invisible Man," I said. "You can call me Ralph E."

"Hi, Ralphie!" Ali said. "Nice to meet you."

"Not funny," Nana said. "You're going to burn yourself out, right down to the nub. And if you hadn't noticed, we've still got a family emergency on our hands."

"That's what I'm doing home, Nana," I said. I gave her a sideways hug at the stove and stole a piece of her amazingly flat bacon off the paper towel where it was draining.

"I'll drop the kids at school, and then I'm heading out to look for her again. All day if I have to."

There was no talk of Elijah Creem or Josh Bergman. Bree already knew, and nobody else in the family needed to be worrying themselves about all that. We made sure to leave the TV off that morning, too.

"I want you to make an appointment with Dr. Finaly," Nana told me, once the kids were in the hall, putting on their jackets. "You need to tend your own garden as well, mister."

"Funny you should say that," I told her. "I had the same thought."

Adele Finaly is the shrink I see from time to time— sometimes more than others. She's always there when I need a smart, objective opinion about my life, my work, my family—and most of all, about the habit those three things have of crashing into each other. First chance I got, I was going to put my figurative feet up on Adele's couch. Just not today.

As soon as I dropped Ali and Jannie off for school, I circled back around to touch base with each of the street cops and Vice Unit detectives I'd been working with since Ava disappeared.

Mostly it was an exercise in frustration. There was no new word anywhere. Things were starting to look worse, and I knew it. I told everyone the same thing. If they so much as spotted someone who looked like Ava, they were to put the grab on her and call me immediately. I'd come and take it from there.

The toughest calls were the ones I'd started making on

the Prostitution Unit and their outreach teams. Like it or not, there was one very nasty and unavoidable possibility in all of this. With a drug habit, no money, and Ava's family history, she might very well have started turning tricks by now—for cash, or for the drugs themselves, if she was desperate enough.

It ground me down every time I thought about it. The girl was fourteen years old! Was that unheard of? Not at all. Nobody knows better than me that life on the streets of DC can get pretty damn bleak.

But this was Ava. *Our* Ava. And nothing I did seemed to get me any closer to finding her.

I was starting to wonder if anything would.

103

IT WAS A FULL TWO DAYS MORE BEFORE WE FINALLY GOT WORD ON AVA.

I was home for a few hours that Wednesday, just grabbing some time with the family before I headed back out. I'd been alternating day and night, trawling the long list of streets where I thought Ava might turn up.

When the doorbell rang, I got up from the couch with the kids and went to answer. Every ring of the bell those days brought a combined sense of hope and dread—maybe this would be the one that gave us some kind of answer.

And in fact, it was.

When I opened the front door, Sampson was standing there on the stoop. It didn't take long to read him. Between the fact that he hadn't come in the back, as usual, and the tears in his eyes, I knew right away why he was there.

It felt like a crater opened up in my chest. My jaw went tight, and some part of me started trying to come up with a different conclusion. Maybe I was misreading Sampson, I thought—even though I knew it wasn't the case.

He didn't have to say a word. I stepped outside and pulled the door closed behind me.

"Jesus, John," I said, choking up.

He pulled me in tight, with his hand on the back of my head.

"I'm so sorry, Alex. I'm so goddamn sorry."

I've been here before. I've lost loved ones, and I've had to give other people the worst news they could possibly get. Nothing—but nothing—ever makes that easier.

Ava was gone. I knew it for sure now. But even so, it didn't feel real.

I stood back from John on the stoop. "Where?" I said.

"An abandoned apartment building on the waterfront, across the river. Junkies flop there all the time. It was a... Jesus, Alex, it was a terrible scene. They took samples, but..."

The tears were streaming down my face, even as the anger started flooding in. Sampson was having a hard time getting through this himself.

"Just tell me everything," I said. "What else do you know?"

John took a long, slow breath. "The body was burned. Beyond recognition. I don't know why. Maybe she'd scored a hit and someone wanted it. Maybe someone killed her on accident and tried to cover up."

"But it was her?" I said. "For sure?"

"It was a young woman. African American. Ava's height and build. And Alex? They found this on the body."

He opened an envelope and poured the blackened pieces of Nana's locket into my hand. The two hinged halves had come apart from the chain, and the photos were either burned up, or missing. But it was most definitely the necklace that Nana Mama had given Ava on the day she'd moved out. I could just make out the engraved R. C. on the back—for Regina Cross.

Suddenly, the front door opened and Nana was there with Bree.

"What is going on out here?" Nana said. She stopped short the second I turned to look at her. It was the same way I'd seen the truth on John's face.

As her eyes traveled down to the pieces of the locket in my hand, I reached over and pulled her close.

"No," she said, stiffening up at first, but then buckling at the knees just as fast. "No, no, no. Not our Miss Ava. Oh, Lord. Please, no!"

"She's gone, Nana," I said. "I'm so sorry."

Bree was crying now, too, and I could see the kids standing behind her, moon-eyed and watching. It was like waves of heartbreak, just seeing their faces and knowing what I had to tell them.

My mind went somewhere else, in a way. Without a word, we all moved back inside as a family. Sampson didn't even come in. There was no good-bye. He left us to grieve, and to try to explain to Jannie and Ali how something like this could possibly happen.

How it could possibly be true.

CHAPTER

104

I DON'T BELIEVE IN A VENGEFUL GOD, BUT I WILL SAY THAT I FELT CONFUSED as much as anything in those first few hours. How could something like this happen? And why? Most of all—*why?*

Had I done something to bring all of this down on my head? On my family's heads?

And Ava's?

It's not the kind of question I ask too frequently—or lightly. But I had to confront the fact that whatever choices I'd made had brought me to this point, in some small or large way. I'd never know now if I could have done something else to stop it.

Jannie and Ali took the news very differently from each other. After we all sat and talked, and cried together, Jannie withdrew. She said she wanted to be alone and think it all over in her room, which we let her do.

Ali stuck close. I think he was just old enough to understand what had happened, but too young to have ever felt anything like this before. I read to him in bed for a long time that night, and held his hand after I turned out the light, like he asked me to.

"All the way to asleep," he said. "Okay, Dad?"

"You got it, bud," I said, and I stayed right there while he slowly drifted off.

I wasn't sure which of my kids my heart was breaking for more. All of them, I suppose. Ava, too.

When we spoke to Damon on the phone, he asked to come home the next morning, on the first bus. I told him he didn't have to if he didn't want to, but I was glad when he insisted. It felt like the right thing, having all of us together now.

Nana went to bed early, but Bree and I sat up late in the attic, talking for hours. Part of me would like to say that I wasn't already thinking about the investigation on this, but I was. Bree, too. We'd been so engaged in looking for Ava, it felt like we already had a blueprint for where to start asking questions.

"Whoever sold to her, or whoever did this...we're going to find them," Bree said. "And they're going to pay, Alex. You can be sure about that."

Bree was the strongest one of all of us that night. In a way, she'd become this linchpin in our family that we didn't even know had been missing until she was there. I love her more every time I think about it.

"Thank you," I told her. "Thank you for being my wife. And for coming into my life exactly when I needed you most. I don't know if I could have—"

"Of course you could," Bree said. "You already did, for years. But I'm glad I'm here now, too. I love you, Alex. And I love this family. That's never going to change."

When we finally went to bed, we made love, and even cried some more in each other's arms before we finally drifted off ourselves, holding each other close.

All the way to asleep, just like Ali.

CHAPTER

105

BREE AND I TOOK SHIFTS THE NEXT DAY. I STAYED HOME WITH NANA AND THE kids through the morning while she went out and spoke with as many people at Ava's school as she could.

When she got back, we all had lunch together, though nobody was too hungry. Then I went out for the afternoon. Technically I was on bereavement, and off duty. I left my gun at home but took my badge.

One of my first stops was Howard House. I'd been in touch with Sunita, the manager, and she'd agreed to call a full house meeting, first thing after school that day. By the time I got there, all eleven girls were already waiting with the staff in the living room.

They knew Ava had died, and I could see there had been some tears, but it was all reined in by the time I was standing in front of them. It actually reminded me of

Ava, the way they seemed so intent on showing as little emotion as possible.

"I know you've already answered some of these questions," I told the group. "But I want you all to think hard. Has anyone remembered anything else about the day Ava disappeared? Anything you hadn't thought about before, or since then?"

What I got back was a room full of silence. Part of it had to do with the fact that we'd been over this before, but that wasn't all. There's an unwritten rule out there on the streets, where a lot of these girls came from. The line between helping and snitching is gray, at best. The safest bet is to just keep your mouth shut, especially if anyone else is listening. It can come off as apathy, but I knew it was more complicated than that.

I asked a few more open-ended questions, but didn't really get anywhere until I moved on to individual interviews. Sunita let me use her office for privacy, and she brought the girls in, one by one.

Ava's roommate, Nessa, was the fifth girl I saw. I could tell she'd been crying again, although she tried to hide it.

I could also tell she was sitting on something the second she walked in the door.

We sat on the same side of Sunita's desk, in two folding chairs. Nessa kept her feet pushed out in the space between us and looked at her phone more than at me, while she flipped it around and around in her hand.

"You seem nervous," I said.

She didn't look up when she started talking. "Just so you know, I wasn't trying to hide nothin' before, okay?"

she said. "I even kind of asked you about it, when you was here the first time."

I tried pulling up whatever memory I had of the day we'd met, outside on the porch. She'd taken our picture—I remembered that much.

"Asked me about what?" I said.

"Well, not asked you, exactly," Nessa said.

"Come on, Nessa. Spit it out. What are we talking about here?"

"Ava's boyfriend, okay? She always sayin' how he wasn't nothing to her, but if you ask me, I think she was just embarrassed. This boy was *old*."

"Who is he?" I said. "How did she know him?"

Nessa gave a shrug and pushed her lips out. "She just said his name was Russell. That's where she gettin' her junk."

That name, Russell, hit me like an electric shock all at once. Could this be *the* Russell? The same phantom boyfriend we were looking for in the Elizabeth Reilly case? Rebecca Reilly's kidnapper?

Or was this just some horrible coincidence?

I tried to stay cool as I pushed on, but it wasn't easy. My mind was racing.

"Nessa, what can you tell me about him?" I asked. "Do you know what he looked like? Or maybe what kind of car he drove?"

"It was a jeep," she said right away. "He was white, too, but Ava didn't care. I think she liked that jeep—and whatever else he was givin' her, if you know what I mean. No disrespect."

I felt sick to my stomach. I still couldn't know if this was the same man, but the similarities were there—to Elizabeth Reilly, and to Amanda Simms as well. All these girls were disconnected from their families in some way.

Young. Vulnerable. Alone.

The idea of this monster plying Ava with drugs, promises, sex—whatever it had been—made me want to excuse myself and puke my guts out in the bathroom.

"You said he was white," I went on. "What else?"

She sat up a little straighter then and started thumbing at her phone. "I got a picture, yo," she said. I think she was just relieved that I wasn't giving her a hard time for holding back this long.

She swiped past several dozen images before she came to the one she was looking for, and then held it up to show me.

"Here," she said. "I used to see her over on Eastern, talkin' to him in that jeep, see? Ava didn't even know I took it, but once I showed it to her, she stopped talkin' shit about not havin' no boyfriend."

The picture had been snapped from maybe half a block away. Ava had her back to the camera, but I easily recognized her long, thin frame, and the suede boots she'd worn almost constantly since Bree bought them for her.

That wasn't all. I also recognized the gray-green jeep in the photo, and the tall, bearded man behind the wheel.

It was Ron Guidice.

106

I DON'T KNOW IF I CAN EXPLAIN WHAT HAPPENED TO ME NEXT. OR IF I EVEN fully understand it myself.

When I left Howard House, it was as if there were no words for anything I was feeling. There was nothing inside me at all but pure, white-hot anger. That, and the image from Nessa's phone, burning into my brain, as clear as anything else.

I barely remember driving home. When I came in, Bree was there, with Sampson and Billie at the kitchen table. I must have looked like hell, because they all stopped what they were doing and stared at me.

"Alex?" Bree said. "What is it?"

I stood at the head of the table, holding myself up with both hands on the back of a kitchen chair.

"Where are the kids?" I said.

"On a walk with Nana. Billie wanted some cornstarch from the store. Why? What's going on?"

"It was Guidice," I said. Already, I was walking out of the room. I headed up the hall toward the stairs at the front.

"Wait—what?" Bree said, catching up behind me. "*What* was Guidice?"

I took the stairs two at a time, even as I tried to explain to Bree what Nessa had shown me. The words practically stuck in my throat. It was hard focusing on anything except what I'd come here to do.

"Did you call it in?" Bree asked as we came into the bedroom.

"No. I'm going out to find him myself."

I opened the closet door and started working the combination on the safe. No electric keypad here—it was twenty-three right, thirty-nine left, nine right.

I took out my Glock and a magazine, slapped it home, and stuck the gun in my jacket pocket. I didn't bother with a holster.

"Hold on," Bree said. She grabbed her own gun out of the safe before I closed the door. "If you're arresting him, I'm coming, too."

"I'm not arresting him," I said.

She grabbed my arm then and looked me deep in the eyes. If I'd been anywhere near myself, I might have seen enough right there to stop what I was doing and pick up the phone. Or even to send Sampson out instead of me. But I didn't.

The only thing I knew for sure in that moment was

that nobody had ever deserved to die as much as Ron Guidice did.

Before Bree could stop me, I was already out of the bedroom, down the stairs, and heading for the back door. Maybe I'd find some sense, or a reason not to do this, by the time I tracked Guidice down. And maybe I wouldn't.

I truly didn't know.

CHAPTER

107

RON GUIDICE TORE HIS HEADPHONES OFF, PULLED THE BERETTA 9MM OUT FROM under the driver's seat, and got out of the jeep.

It was like a starter pistol had gone off. This was all fast-twitch muscle stuff coming back to him, the way his body had been trained to respond without the interference of the mind. The moment he'd heard Alex mention his name, Guidice knew. This operation was about to come to a sudden end.

Looking up Fifth Street from where he'd parked, he could see the front door of Alex's house. There was no sign of him yet, but it wouldn't be long now. His car was right there at the curb. He'd left it wide open when he went inside just moments earlier.

Guidice kept the Beretta pulled up inside the sleeve of his jacket, out of sight. There were several people on the street. A man clipping his hedges. A woman with two small kids riding their trikes up the sidewalk. There was no sense drawing any attention to himself yet. When this happened, it was going to be out in the open, and he needed a certain element of surprise.

It wasn't the time, place, or method Guidice might have chosen, but that was irrelevant now. He'd gotten greedy. He'd let himself watch Alex suffer for one day too many, just long enough to connect the last few dots.

But maybe that was okay. In fact, maybe it was perfect, Guidice thought, as he stood watching the door. Alex was going to take a bullet to the brain, right there on the street where he'd tried so hard—and so much in vain—to keep his little family safe.

And when he did, Detective Alex Cross, paragon of the Metropolitan Police Department, was going to single-handedly prove his own incompetence to the world, in the most definitive possible terms.

So then fine, Guidice thought. Alex wanted to come looking for him? He wouldn't have to look very far.

108

"DON'T DO THIS, ALEX!"

It was only when Bree followed me off the back porch that I remembered I'd come in through the front of the house. Usually I drove around and parked in our garage— but there was nothing usual about today.

When I turned around, she was right there.

"Just give me thirty seconds," she said. "I'm going to tell Sampson to call this in. And then I'm coming with you. At least do that for me."

I think she was grasping at straws. Maybe she thought she could talk me down in the car.

"Yeah, okay," I said. "I'll wait for you out front."

"Good." She looked at me one more time before she ran back into the house. "I'll be right there."

In fact, I had no intention of waiting for Bree. Whatever was going to happen with Guidice, it was going to be just him and me when it did. There was no sense getting her involved. Or anyone else, for that matter.

I walked up the narrow passage between our house and the neighbors', through the locked gate, and out onto Fifth Street, where I'd parked. I didn't look back once. I just got into the car, started it up, and pulled away from the curb. In fact, if I hadn't taken a quick glance in the rearview mirror for oncoming traffic, I never would have seen Guidice at all. He was standing right in the middle of the street, and he raised his arm in my direction just as I spotted him. I didn't actually see the gun, but I recognized the posture right away.

Even as I swerved, and cut the car hard to the left, my back windshield exploded in a shower of glass gravel. When I looked again, Guidice was on the move. He was coming right for me, his gun still raised.

Heart thumping, I rolled onto the seat, threw open the passenger door, and fell out onto the street. My Glock was out now, and I looked over the edge of the door to see him closing the gap between us. I could tell he was trained. He didn't just pepper the car with bullets as he came. He was waiting for a clean shot.

So was I. There were people screaming up and down the block, and running for cover in any number of directions. At this distance, I couldn't afford the possibility of a stray bullet. If I missed him, I might hit someone else.

Guidice didn't have the same problem. As soon as he spotted me over the passenger door, he tried again, with a quick double tap this time. I ducked down and heard the shots hit the side of the car with two dull thuds.

I could still hear a few people running up the sidewalk behind me, too. The situation was only going to get worse if I didn't do something.

Working mostly on instinct, I stayed close to the ground and made my way around the front of the car. Maybe—just maybe—I could catch Guidice off guard as he came within range, too close to miss.

When I got to the front, I tried another quick look. He was right there, less than ten yards away now, and moving at a run. This was it. One of us was going down.

I stood up fast, with a two-hand grip on the Glock, ready to fire—but I never got that far. At the moment I came eye to eye with Guidice, another shot sounded from farther off.

Guidice stumbled hard and fell, face-first onto the street with his arms splayed out in front of him. He didn't even try to catch himself.

"Alex!"

I looked over and saw Bree coming down the front steps of our house. Her own Glock 19 was up, still pointed in Guidice's direction where he lay.

"Are you all right?" she shouted.

"I'm fine," I said.

She'd gotten him in the neck, I saw. Probably hit the carotid artery, too, from the way his blood was pumping. A pool of it had started to spread on the pavement around him.

Sampson was outside now, too, close behind Bree. "EMTs are on the way," he said, and stopped short when he saw Guidice.

I tore my shirt off and pressed it to the wound at his neck, but there was no way to stop the bleeding. Not with a shirt. I think Guidice knew it, too. He struggled to roll over and looked me in the eye, where I was kneeling next to him.

"Congratulations," he slurred out. "Didn't think you had it in you—"

"Yeah, well think again," Bree said, her own voice shaking.

"Listen to me," I said. "Where's Rebecca Reilly? Did you take her, Guidice? Was it you? Are you Russell?"

I was still putting the pieces all together, but if I was right about this, I also knew I didn't have much time here. He was nearly gone already.

Guidice grabbed my arm then, and pulled himself a few inches off the pavement. He tried to swallow back whatever was clogging his throat, and his jaw went slack.

"Tell my girls . . . tell them—"

"Answer my question first!" I said. Even then I was fighting my own feelings. It was everything I could do to keep from stepping back and letting him bleed all the way out.

Before I could say anything else, Guidice convulsed. He spit up a large amount of blood all over himself, shuddered one more time, and then went still. When his head fell back on the street, his eyes were open—still on me. At least, it seemed that way.

I could hear a siren somewhere, coming closer.

"That's it," Sampson said. "He's gone."

"He can rot in hell," Bree said.

When I looked at her, she had an expression on her face I'd never seen before. She's the most caring person I know. In a way, it was as if everything I'd been feeling had shifted to her.

She was crying again, too. Thinking about poor Ava, no doubt. Whatever else Guidice may have done, he'd used her as nothing more than a pawn, just to get back at me.

The most we could say now was that no more lives would be wasted in Ron Guidice's name. I suppose if this were any other case, it might feel good to know that.

But not this time. Rebecca Reilly was still out there somewhere. And Ava was dead. Nothing was going to make us feel better about how all of this had gone down. Certainly not right away. We'd have to get there on our own, and in our own time.

Still, somehow, I knew we would.

Epilogue
CIRCLE OF LIFE

109

NOT LONG AFTER RON GUIDICE DIED, HIS FULL SITUATION CAME TO LIGHT. It was his mother who called the authorities, when her son's name became a national headline.

It took another five days after that and two independent DNA tests to confirm that the baby in Lydia Guidice's care was in fact Rebecca Reilly. Also, that her sister, Emma Lee Guidice, was the biological daughter of both Ron Guidice and Amanda Simms, the first pregnant girl in our pregnant girl cases.

It brought up all kinds of reverberating speculation about Ava, and what Guidice might have had planned for her before she died. But Ava's cremation was already behind us now. A small, intimate memorial service had been held. She had no dental records at all, and her remains had been identified to the extent that they could.

But that was it. None of us were prepared to confront

the possibility that she'd been pregnant at the end. That question was just going to have to fade off into the great unknown, which was probably for the best.

But I'll always wonder, of course. I'll wonder about a lot of things from this case.

When Child and Family Services took custody of Guidice's two daughters, Bree and I worked with the agency to make sure Mrs. Guidice could see the girls from time to time. She may not have been competent to raise them, but she also wasn't criminally negligent here. I felt sorry for her more than anything.

Stephanie agreed to shepherd their case, and she also promised not to give up until she found a home where both girls could live together. In the meantime, they were placed into emergency foster care at a small, well-run facility in Foggy Bottom.

Taking in Rebecca and Emma Lee ourselves wasn't something we could even contemplate, starting with the fact that we'd just lost Ava. But Bree and I did make several visits to the home in those early months.

"Look at you," I said, the first time Bree actually met Rebecca. She was cradling the baby in a rocking chair, going slowly back and forth like she'd done it a million times. "You're good at that."

Bree just shrugged and kept her eyes on Rebecca in the way that—yes, I'm going to say it—only a woman can look at a baby.

The subject of having our own kids wasn't really on the table anymore. We'd talked about it before we got married, and had already put it behind us. But life's a circle sometimes, isn't it? The thing you thought you left behind can come back around, until it's sitting right there in front of you, all over again.

I'm not saying Bree and I made any kind of new plans that day, or even that there were going to *be* any new plans. But if I had to guess, I'd say that we were probably feeling some of the same things as she sat there, rocking Rebecca back to sleep.

After a while, Bree looked up and caught me staring at her.

"What is it?" she said.

"Nothing," I said.

She smiled like she could read my mind. "Nothing, huh?"

Now it was my turn to shrug. "You just look really beautiful right now," I told her. "That's all."

"It's this little girl," she said. "She looks good on me."

And I couldn't argue with that.

110

"ALEX, COME ON IN. HAVE A SEAT. IT'S GOOD TO SEE YOU."

I admire Adele Finaly quite a bit. I think she's one of the finest psychotherapists I've ever seen in action.

I guess that's why I put up with her No Shoes rule during sessions. I didn't even think about it anymore. I just left my trainers on the mat by the door of her plant-filled office, and went to sit in my usual spot on the couch.

"It's been a while," she said, settling into her own flowered armchair. "Was there anything specific that precipitated this call?"

She reminds me of Audrey Hepburn, or Lena Horne. Adele has a way of being incredibly smart and accessible at the same time.

"Just the oldest question in the book," I said. "My book, anyway."

"Ah." She smiled sympathetically. "That one."

I spent a good chunk of the session with her just explaining everything that had happened in the last month. She knew who Ava was, but not how badly it had all turned out.

I told her about Ron Guidice, too. Not just what he'd done, but what had happened to me on that last day—and also what *might* have happened if things had turned out differently. I don't know that I've ever been so consumed by my own hatred of someone before, and it scared me.

"I tell myself it was different this time," I said. "It was *personal*. Having Ava involved changed everything, and I got in over my head. That's not even accounting for the two other major cases I had going."

"Well, yes," Adele said. "It *was* different. You had this girl living in your home, and very possibly lining up to become a legal part of your family. She would have been your daughter."

I nodded, not really sure I could talk about that part without breaking up.

"But Alex," Adele said. She leaned over and put a hand on my wrist. "It's *always* different with you. There's always a reason why you end up pushing yourself—and why you land back in those very dark places."

It was true. In fact, I didn't even know what to say to that. So Adele went on. I can always count on her to show me both sides of any coin.

"You know what else is true?" she said. "There are evil people out there in the world. Someone has to do the work that you do, and we're all very lucky that you do it so well.

"But that doesn't mean you can't care too much sometimes, Alex. I think you do. And that's when I worry about you—about what this might be doing to...well, to your soul."

"You worry about me?" I said, grinning. "Adele, I'm touched."

She knew I was trying to sidestep something and didn't take the bait. Instead, she kept pushing.

"Maybe we should stop asking why you are this way, and start focusing on what, if anything, you want to do about it," she said.

I looked at her, a little sheepish. "I want to keep showing up here until I'm so sick of hearing myself talk that I finally make a change. A real one."

Adele sat back and looked at me like I'd just won the spelling bee.

"That's a pretty good answer. For a start."

"What about you?" I said. "If you were a betting woman, would you say I was going to be seeing you for the rest of my life? Coming in here, and asking the same damn questions, over and over?"

"My God, I hope not. You're twenty years younger than me."

Adele's always good for a well-timed laugh. She gets me, in that way.

"You know what I mean," I said. "When are we going to figure this one out, Adele?"

"If you keep coming in to see me?" she said. "Then... eventually."

"Eventually? That's your answer?"

"And I'm sticking to it," she said.

In fact, she was probably right. We *would* get there one of these days. We'd figure it out.

Unless, of course, we didn't. Nobody knows better than me that *eventually* is an idea, not a given. There's no guarantee I'm going to *eventually* make it to anything, including breakfast tomorrow. But by the same token, I have to allow for the possibility.

Otherwise, I've got nothing. And that's not me.

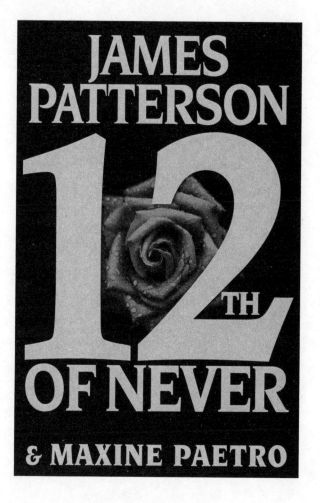

JAMES
PATTERSON
12TH
OF NEVER
& MAXINE PAETRO

FOR AN EXCERPT,
TURN THE PAGE

MERCIFULLY, JOE AND the baby were both sleeping. In the same room. In the same bed. At the same time. It was unbelievable, but true.

I filled Martha's bowl with yummy kibble and brought in the morning paper from the hall.

The headline read, FAYE FARMER DEAD AT 27.

I didn't stop to make coffee, just spread the paper out over the kitchen counter. The shocking story had been written by my great friend Cindy Thomas, charter member of the Women's Murder Club, engaged to marry my partner, Rich Conklin, and a bulldog of a reporter.

Unrelenting tenacity can be an annoying trait in a friend, but it had made Cindy a successful crime reporter with a huge future. Her story on Faye Farmer had shot past the second section of the paper and was on the front page above the fold.

Cindy had written, "Designer Faye Farmer, 27, known for her red carpet styling and must-have wear for the young and famous, was found dead in her car last night on Twenty-Ninth Street and Noe.

"Captain Warren Jacobi has told the *Chronicle* that Ms. Farmer had been the victim of a gunshot wound to the head. An autopsy has been scheduled for Tuesday."

It was almost impossible to believe that such a bright, vivacious young woman was dead, her promising life just…over. Had someone taken her life? Or had she killed herself?

I kept reading.

The article went on to say that Faye Farmer lived with football great Jeffrey Kennedy, who was not a suspect and was cooperating fully with the police.

I'd watched Jeff Kennedy many times from the stands at Candlestick Park. At twenty-five, he was already the NFL's best outside linebacker. His defensive skills and film-star looks had made him an immediate fan favorite, and with a guaranteed ten million dollars a year he was the league's fifth-highest earner.

Faye Farmer had been photographed with Kennedy frequently over the last couple of years and had been quoted as saying that she was going to be married—"to someone." The way it sounded, she wanted to get married to Kennedy, but he wasn't at the until-death-do-us-part stage.

I was dying for more information. This was what's termed a "suspicious death," and my mind just cannot rest until a puzzle is solved.

CLAIRE WASHBURN DIDN'T mind putting on a dog-and-pony show as long as nobody sneezed or puked on the body. A high-profile case like this one would be scrutinized for mistakes, and the last thing she wanted was to have to explain to the court how random DNA got on the victim.

There was a bark of laughter outside the frosted glass of her office door. Claire sighed once, forwarded her phone calls to the front desk, and then went to the conference room.

The twelve people who were waiting for her turned as one.

Claire couldn't stop herself from laughing. To a man, and to a woman, her visitors were dressed in baby-yellow paper scrubs and Tyvek gowns. Most hilarious of all was Rich Conklin, former Mr. September in the Law Enforcement Officer Beefsteak Calendar for 2011.

Great big handsome man, outfitted like a hospital kitchen worker.

Claire said, "Good morning, Easter chicks," and she laughed again, this time joined by the group of cops, junior techs from CSU, and the law school grads from the DA's office who were getting on-the-job education this morning.

She caught her breath and said, "If we've never met, I'm Dr. Washburn, Chief Medical Examiner, and before I begin this morning's autopsy, please introduce yourselves."

Claire had everyone's attention, and when the introductions were concluded she began a condensed lecture on the purpose of an autopsy: to discover the cause and manner of death.

"You'll see that the victim will be wearing what she had on when she was recovered from the scene. She'll have bags on her hands to preserve any DNA she may have scraped from a possible attacker. She will have a complete external exam, including total body X-rays, before we ever do an internal exam. And then, I'm going to do that.

"If Ms. Farmer's death is determined to be a homicide—not saying it *was* a homicide, but if she was killed and the evidence leads to an indictment, the defense may try to prove that our evidence was contaminated. That we're a bunch of fumble-fingered idiots. *Remember O.J.* Protecting the integrity of this postmortem is critical to catching and holding a bad guy. Because of lousy forensics, there are innocent people in jail for crimes they never committed and murderers walking the streets free.

"To the dead, we owe respect. To the living, we owe the truth. Nothing less, nothing more, no matter where the evidence leads us.

"House rules. Keep your prophylactic outerwear in place. Masks must be worn in the surgery and kept on. Understand? If you forgot to turn off your cell phone, do it now. Save your questions until I ask for them. When I'm done, I'll memorialize my findings for the record. Everything you see or hear from now on is highly confidential and leaks will not be tolerated.

"Are there any questions now?

"All right then. If we're all clear on the house rules..." Claire turned to her assistant, the fetching Bunny Ellis, her hair done up like mouse ears, reverent eyes turned toward her boss.

"Bunny, will you please wheel Ms. Farmer into the autopsy suite? Everyone else, follow me."

CLAIRE HIP-BUTTED THE swinging door and entered the autopsy suite. The cops and the junior-grade assistants behind her were excited, speaking in whispers that seemed to cut loose, rise in volume, loop around her, and then die down to a hush again.

Conklin had the summer intern under his wing. Mackie Morales seemed bright and eager and maybe a little bit too much into Richie. The way she looked at him, the way he was a little puffed up, explaining things to her. Cindy would not be happy if she saw this.

And not too much escaped Cindy.

Claire laughed quietly, but she didn't say anything to Conklin, just went to the far corner of the room and pushed the button that turned on the video camera. The light on the camera didn't go on. She punched it a couple of times, and still the little red eye was dark.

That was weird. The camera had been fine yesterday.

She pressed the intercom button, said, "Ryan, check the video setup, please."

"Yes, ma'am. It was unplugged. It's on, now."

"Why was it unplugged?"

"I don't know. I just found it this way."

Bunny entered the room from the door leading to the morgue. She signaled to Claire, like, *I need to talk to you.*

"What's the holdup, Bunny?"

"I need to see you for a second, doctor."

Claire sighed again, crossed the room, and followed Bunny to the morgue, a refrigerated room lined with stacks of stainless-steel drawers, each designed to hold a body. Some of Claire's patients had recently checked in. Some had been waiting for months for someone to ID them before they were buried as J. Does.

"What is it, Bunny?"

The girl's blue eyes were shifting and her lips were trembling. Claire didn't get it. What the hell?

"I can't find her," Bunny said.

"What are you talking about?"

"Faye Farmer," Bunny said. "She's gone."

"What's her drawer number?" Claire asked, exasperated. She went to the whiteboard, ran her finger down the list.

"Twelve," said Bunny Ellis.

Claire turned away from the whiteboard, crossed to the wall of drawers, and pulled the handle of number twelve. The drawer slid out smoothly, bringing the corpse into view, tag tied to the big toe. Claire saw instantly that there had been a screwup. Faye Farmer was not and had never been a seventy-year-old black man.

She said, "Who mixed up the bodies? What drawer is this man supposed to be in?"

"Seventeen," said Bunny. "Dr. Washburn, I already checked."

Claire reached down, opened the drawer marked seventeen. It was empty. She started pulling out drawers, slamming them closed, each body in its assigned box except for the black John Doe in Faye Farmer's drawer.

Bunny was crying now. She was a competent young woman and liked to do a good job.

"Stop that," Claire snapped. "Think. Did you see Ms. Farmer's body after she was checked in yesterday?"

"Not after I logged her in. She's supposed to be in twelve."

"Who moved John Doe one thirty-two out of box seventeen?"

Bunny shrugged miserably. "Not me."

The body couldn't have left the premises.

That was impossible.

ABOUT THE AUTHOR

JAMES PATTERSON has created more enduring fictional characters than any other novelist writing today. He is the author of the Alex Cross novels, the most popular detective series of the past twenty-five years, including *Kiss the Girls* and *Along Came a Spider.* Mr. Patterson also writes the bestselling Women's Murder Club novels, set in San Francisco, and the top-selling New York detective series of all time, featuring Detective Michael Bennett. James Patterson has had more *New York Times* bestsellers than any other writer, ever, according to *Guinness World Records.* Since his first novel won the Edgar Award in 1977, James Patterson's books have sold more than 275 million copies.

James Patterson has also written numerous #1 best-sellers for young readers, including the Maximum Ride, Witch & Wizard, and Middle School series. In total, these books have spent more than 220 weeks on national bestseller lists. In 2010, James Patterson was named Author of the Year at the Children's Choice Book Awards.

His lifelong passion for books and reading led James Patterson to create the innovative website ReadKiddoRead.com, giving adults an invaluable tool to find the books that get kids reading for life. He writes full-time and lives in Florida with his family.

BOOKS BY JAMES PATTERSON

FEATURING ALEX CROSS

Alex Cross, Run • *Merry Christmas, Alex Cross* • *Kill Alex Cross* • *Cross Fire* • *I, Alex Cross* • *Alex Cross's* Trial (with Richard DiLallo) • *Cross Country* • *Double Cross* • *Cross* (also published as *Alex Cross*) • *Mary, Mary* • *London Bridges* • *The Big Bad Wolf* • *Four Blind Mice* • *Violets Are Blue* • *Roses Are Red* • *Pop Goes the Weasel* • *Cat & Mouse* • *Jack & Jill* • *Kiss the Girls* • *Along Came a Spider*

THE WOMEN'S MURDER CLUB

12th of Never (with Maxine Paetro) • *11th Hour* (with Maxine Paetro) • *10th Anniversary* (with Maxine Paetro) • *The 9th Judgment* (with Maxine Paetro) • *The 8th Confession* (with Maxine Paetro) • *7th Heaven* (with Maxine Paetro) • *The 6th Target* (with Maxine Paetro) • *The 5th Horseman* (with Maxine Paetro) • *4th of July* (with Maxine Paetro) • *3rd Degree* (with Andrew Gross) • *2nd Chance* (with Andrew Gross) • *1st to Die*

FEATURING MICHAEL BENNETT

I, Michael Bennett (with Michael Ledwidge) • *Tick Tock* (with Michael Ledwidge) • *Worst Case* (with Michael Ledwidge) • *Run for Your Life* (with Michael Ledwidge) • *Step on a Crack* (with Michael Ledwidge)

THE PRIVATE NOVELS

Private Berlin (with Mark Sullivan) • *Private London* (with Mark Pearson) • *Private Games* (with Mark Sullivan) • *Private: #1 Suspect* (with Maxine Paetro) • *Private* (with Maxine Paetro)

STAND-ALONE BOOKS

NYPD Red (with Marshall Karp) • *Zoo* (with Michael Ledwidge) • *Guilty Wives* (with David Ellis) • *The Christmas Wedding* (with Richard DiLallo) • *Kill Me If You Can* (with Marshall Karp) • *Now You See Her* (with Michael Ledwidge) • *Toys* (with Neil McMahon) • *Don't Blink* (with Howard Roughan) • *The Postcard Killers* (with Liza Marklund) • *The Murder of King Tut* (with Martin Dugard) • *Swimsuit* (with Maxine Paetro) • *Against Medical Advice* (with Hal Friedman) • *Sail* (with Howard Roughan) • *Sundays at Tiffany's* (with Gabrielle Charbonnet) • *You've Been Warned* (with Howard Roughan) • *The Quickie* (with Michael Ledwidge) • *Judge & Jury* (with Andrew Gross) • *Beach Road* (with Peter de Jonge) • *Lifeguard* (with Andrew Gross) • *Honeymoon* (with Howard Roughan) • *Sam's Letters to Jennifer* • *The Lake House* • *The Jester* (with Andrew Gross) • *The Beach House* (with Peter de Jonge) • *Suzanne's Diary for Nicholas* • *Cradle and All* • *When the Wind Blows* • *Miracle on the 17th Green* (with Peter de Jonge) • *Hide & Seek* • *The Midnight Club* • *Black Friday* (originally published as *Black Market*) • *See How They Run* • *Season of the Machete* • *The Thomas Berryman Number*

FOR READERS OF ALL AGES

Maximum Ride

Nevermore: The Final Maximum Ride Adventure • Angel: A Maximum Ride Novel • Fang: A Maximum Ride Novel • Max: A Maximum Ride Novel • Final Warning: A Maximum Ride Novel • Saving the World and Other Extreme Sports: A Maximum Ride Novel • School's Out—Forever: A Maximum Ride Novel • The Angel Experiment: A Maximum Ride Novel

Daniel X

Daniel X: Armageddon (with Chris Grabenstein) • Daniel X: Game Over (with Ned Rust) • Daniel X: Demons and Druids (with Adam Sadler) • Daniel X: Watch the Skies (with Ned Rust) • The Dangerous Days of Daniel X (with Michael Ledwidge)

Witch & Wizard

Witch & Wizard: The Kiss (with Jill Dembowski) • Witch & Wizard: The Fire (with Jill Dembowski) • Witch & Wizard: The Gift (with Ned Rust) • Witch & Wizard (with Gabrielle Charbonnet)

Middle School

Middle School: Get Me Out of Here (with Chris Tebbetts, illustrated by Laura Park) • Middle School: The Worst Years of My Life (with Chris Tebbetts, illustrated by Laura Park)

Other Books for Readers of All Ages

I Funny: A Middle School Story (with Chris Grabenstein, illustrated by Laura Park) • *Confessions of a Murder Suspect* (with Maxine Paetro) • *santaKid* (illustrated by Michael Gorland)

For previews and information about the author, visit JamesPatterson.com or find him on Facebook or at your app store.